‘An interesting exposition of the psychology and the insidious methods that govern cults’
Daily Mail

‘I loved it – tense and atmospheric, slowly drawing the reader in to a reality that is utterly terrifying’
Lisa Hall, bestselling author of *Have You Seen Her* and *The Perfect Couple*

‘An intense, terrifying, and utterly believable journey into the shadowy world of cult leaders and cult members. A just-one-more-page thriller that will have you reading late into the night and holding your breath until the very end. I loved it!’
Karen Dionne, No. 1 international bestselling author of *Home*

‘This intense thriller completely grips you from the off’
Heat

‘A vivid crime novel’
Express

Mariette Lindstein was born and raised in Halmstad on the west coast of Sweden. At the age of 20, she joined the Church of Scientology and worked for the next 25 years at all levels of the organization, including at its international headquarters outside Los Angeles. Mariette left the Church in 2004 and is now married to Dan Koon, an author and artist. They live in a forest outside Halmstad with their three dogs. *Fog Island,* her debut novel, was first published in Sweden where it won the Best Crime Debut at the Specsavers CrimeTime Awards. Mariette now dedicates her life to writing and lecturing to warn others about the dangers of cults and cult mentality. *Shadow of Fog Island* is the second book in the *Fog Island* Trilogy.

Also by Mariette Lindstein:

Fog Island

Shadow of Fog Island

Mariette Lindstein

Translation by Rachel Willson-Broyles

ONE PLACE. MANY STORIES

This novel is entirely a work of fiction. The names, characters and incidents portrayed in it are the work of the author's imagination. Any resemblance to actual persons, living or dead, events or localities is entirely coincidental.

HQ
An imprint of HarperCollins*Publishers* Ltd
1 London Bridge Street
London SE1 9GF

HarperCollins*Publishers*
1st Floor, Watermarque Building, Ringsend Road
Dublin 4, Ireland

This paperback edition 2021
1
First published in Great Britain by
HQ, an imprint of HarperCollins*Publishers* Ltd 2021

Mariette Lindstein asserts the moral right to be identified as the author of this work.
A catalogue record for this book is available from the British Library.

Rachel Willson-Broyles asserts the moral right to be identified as the author of the Translation.

ISBN: 978-0-00-824538-2

MIX
Paper from responsible sources
FSC™ C007454

This book is produced from independently certified FSC™ paper to ensure responsible forest management.

For more information visit: www.harpercollins.co.uk/green

This book is set in 11.4/15.5 pt. Bembo

Printed and bound in Great Britain by
CPI Group (UK) Ltd, Croydon, CR0 4YY

Shadow of Fog Island

Prologue

The nightmare is back again. Her heart races and her skin is covered in a sheen of sweat. Her body is heavy and sluggish and she has trouble emerging from the stifling haze of sleep. But at last she yanks herself out and wakes with a gasp.

Immediately she is lost. Something is missing, that relief when the light hits your eye, the objects in her room. Total darkness. Not a single contour or shadow. It smells like earth and mould, and there's a draught from an open window.

There's something wrong with her body. A heaviness in her head and eyelids. Dizziness and nausea. Her brain is on strike; it can't seem to get into gear. Her breath carries a dull fear, but it doesn't quite take hold. Her mouth is itchy and her eyes sting. Her memory seems empty. She battles the void for a moment before the images return. The bed in the apartment. The wine, the drowsiness. A hand on her forehead. *Relax!* One word before the room seemed to dilute and vanish. A flash of sharpness much later. The shuddering and the sound of screeching gulls. A quick glance upward, and she saw fog, fog everywhere. A sting in her thigh before darkness returned.

Her stomach sinks. Now she knows. She doesn't want to let any more images in. Doesn't want to understand what happened. Yet she knows. Somewhere inside, she has always feared that this is what awaited her.

The light that streams in when the door opens gives her a spark of hope – until she hears the familiar footsteps. The scent of his aftershave floats on the air. His proximity is like a maddening itch that spreads all over her body. Then comes the impulse to get up and run, so strong that it sucks the air out of her. But she is pressed back down, a burning force against her chest. She can't breathe. The energy drains from her muscles. Her heart pounds unevenly. Tiny black dots dance before her eyes.

His voice is calm and friendly.

'Welcome back.'

The door closes with a hard thud.

A bestial whine comes from her mouth. Her scream begins as a tickle on her palate, rising from her lungs, pouring from her throat like a wave, and its crescendo is so loud it is deafening.

Then: silence, and it's just the two of them in the dark.

Notes
Jail, the Prison Service, Gothenburg

From ash you have risen; to ash you will return.

The phoenix burns himself on a pyre from which a new bird, younger and stronger, rises. He lives for five hundred years and then destroys himself in a magnificent ritual. He resurrects to become an even more majestic form.

Floating high in the sky.

His sharp eyes searching the barren landscape of Earth.

His dazzling beauty arousing intense desire and infinite inspiration.

Just like the phoenix, I, and everything I stand for, will rise again.

Everything that Man seeks is here, within me.

These thick concrete walls, the odour of detergents, the filth on the walls, and the flies in the light fixtures.

None of this concerns me.

It only allows me to see the possibilities I never would have imagined in my darkest dreams.

I can move through space and time, outside this shithole, and see everything from above.

This brief moment in captivity is only a heartbeat in the infinite pulse of eternity.

A few months, and then I'll be back. Stronger. More powerful.

I already long for her.

The faintest whiff of perfume from her skin. The strands of hair that slipped from her braid and curled down her white nape.

Her soft jawline.

The way the corners of her lips twitched when she was flustered. The thunderclouds that gathered in her eyes sometimes.

The tiny yawns she couldn't manage to suppress. And the amusing way she said 'Yes, sir!' without meaning it.

All that sass I never had time to extinguish.

I've always been a master at sussing out details, and the details that formed the entirety of her were irresistible. She was so delightfully artless.

I feel my heart beating faster when I think about her.

There is also a nagging rage, something I haven't come to terms with. But when I do, I will project that pent-up energy onto her. I sink into that thought, and for a moment I find myself in a very dark place.

As if I have fallen into the shadow of something ominous. But then I think of the future that spreads out before me like a dewy, shimmering spider's web in the morning sun.

Now I hear footsteps. High heels drumming against the concrete floor, coming closer.

I know at once who it is.

Another mortal being who will pass through my eternal life.

Anna-Maria Callini.

Oh, Anna-Maria, you haven't the foggiest idea about my plans for you.

Soon you will be standing there in the doorway. And I will put on my very best smile.

Let the show begin!

1

Anna-Maria Callini laid out her clothes on the ottoman. Straight and neat. Blouse on top and skirt beneath. Bra on the blouse and panties on the skirt, stay-ups stretched out full-length. She set out her shoes and hung her jacket on the rack, then placed her handbag on the table. She inspected her creation for a moment, with a critical eye. A tight, steel-grey A-line skirt by Armani, a white blouse, a grey Prada jacket, and a red handbag from Louis Vuitton. Manolo Blahnik shoes with metal heels. All purchased on her most recent trip to New York, for a sum of around fifty thousand kronor. But now, in some strange way, the sight of the garments made her feel cheap. As if he would see right through this expensive façade. But at least she was prepared for the next day. She felt the stress evaporate from her body.

She pulled down the bedspread and crawled under the covers, settling on her back with a sigh. If only she could sleep – she needed her beauty rest. As she set the alarm clock she double-checked to make sure it would go off at the right time, then turned out the light. She wanted to get the night over with and see him again. It took some battling against impatience before she managed to relax, and she let her mind wander to the first time they'd met. It lingered there. As usual.

Her skin began to tingle restlessly as a throbbing rose between her legs. She slipped a finger into her panties and tried getting herself off, but not even that helped.

*

She had made a fool of herself the first time they met, had gone weak in the knees and trembly, but she would see to it that this didn't happen again. That was before she'd had the chance to ground herself ahead of the storm Franz Oswald blew into her life. Yet once again she had the aching sense that she was in the process of a change. It was a voice nagging in the back of her mind. The powerful woman who never backed down in a courtroom chiding the bimbo she transformed into in the presence of Oswald.

It all started when she was reading the case file and caught sight of his picture among the documents. Those eyes. Sure, she had seen him in the newspapers; his image had been on almost every newsagent's billboard. But now that she was supposed to represent him, it had become more personal.

Even before their first meeting, she had been drawn to him like a magnet. It had continued in the car on the way to the jail: a tension headache that wouldn't let up, a warning whisper that lingered somewhere on the periphery.

The air was sucked from her lungs when she opened the door to the room at the jail. He was sitting there with his long legs stretched out before him. His dark hair was loose over his shoulders, lending him an Adonic look. The scent of his aftershave wafted by, overpowering the odour of cleaning agents that rose from the floor.

She took a few steps forward, but suddenly felt weak and had to grab a visitor's chair. Then came the moment she would later replay again and again in her mind: how the fabric of his T-shirt stretched over his broad shoulders as he stood. Her eyes fastened on his body and wouldn't come loose. She felt awkward even as an unpleasant thought struck her like lightning. Something about maintaining a professional distance with clients.

Once she sat down, he laid it all out: how they would take this journey together. The trial, prison time if he got any, and then they would meet on a more private level. He had promised. And then, of course, there was the mind-boggling fee he had mentioned in passing, so nonchalantly. An amount that had nearly stopped her heart. She hadn't been able to focus as her ears buzzed, sweat broke out under her arms, and her mouth turned to cotton.

'Everything okay?' he asked, concerned.

'Of course, it's just… I think I'm coming down with a cold.'

'I don't think so.'

'Excuse me?'

'Something else just happened.'

'I don't understand.'

'I think you do. What you're feeling now is something you'll never experience with another person.'

He gazed at the dusty jail wall. She could see the gears turning in his brain. She loved it when he looked like that. So intense. As if he was about to have a brilliant idea and solve all the world's problems.

'Right, well, if we put our heads together I'm sure we can win this case,' she managed.

'Or else we'll short-circuit it.' He grabbed her hand. 'Aw, I'm just kidding. We'll do just fine, obviously.'

It was a warm, dry hand. Long fingers. His thumb fluttered against her palm like a butterfly.

With great effort, she pulled herself together. Babbled on about how they would present the case, run that Sofia Bauman through the wringer and prove that she was an extremely unreliable witness.

But Oswald smiled indulgently.

'We're not going to do that.'

'Why not?'

'Have you ever seen how a spider uses its web, Anna-Maria?'

She shook her head, puzzled.

'Well, it has flies and other insects all wrapped up in its silk. At first you think they're dead, but you see, they're only stunned. Then one moves. Pulls on a thread. And the spider, sitting at the very top of the web, rushes over. You think it's going to eat the fly, but no. He stuns the fly again. Paralyses it. Because it's the spider who decides when and whom to eat. Everything in the web happens on his terms. Understand?'

She nodded, not wanting to seem dense in front of him.

'Some female spiders let their offspring eat them up to improve the odds of their line's survival. Talk about devotion. Not like the dimwits in ViaTerra,' he added with a chuckle.

What he suggested then made her legs shake uncontrollably under the ugly metal table.

It had been several years since she'd devoted any energy to a relationship. Men in smart suits were usually losers, pathetic idiots who could hardly get it up. But Franz Oswald was different. He was a man with a plan.

A diabolical plan.

2

Franz Oswald was already sitting in the courtroom with his attorney when Sofia walked in. This was the moment she had been dreading. It felt like the floor had vanished from beneath her feet. Her stomach was turning, but she managed to swallow down her queasiness.

Take a deep breath.

The fear came less frequently these days, but when it did come it felt like a punch to the gut. She lifted her head and met his gaze. The memories hit her so hard that she had trouble taking them in. She discovered that her hatred for him was still just as strong, as she'd expected, but that the absence of hate in his eyes was disarming. He was the one to look away first, giving her the space she needed to get her legs moving so she could sit down.

Relief washed over her in waves as she sat there, and then came the rage. *God damn him. I've got the upper hand now.*

Elvira and Sofia were the plaintiffs in this trial. They were an odd couple. Throughout their pre-trial preparations, Elvira had had a constant stream of tears running down her face. Sofia, repressing all her emotions, gritting her teeth with bitter stubbornness, only yearned for the moment when it would all be over.

The gallery was full. The media ate up the proceedings, favouring this tale over all sorts of other news – politics, war, and disasters alike. Each article included images of Oswald's sober face and intense gaze. There were blogs, forum discussions, and sites for and against him. Not a day went by that the case wasn't mentioned in the news. In the beginning, a gang of reporters had encircled her parents' house like hyenas, in the hope that she would reveal some salacious detail about Oswald. Although she had avoided the media, they had referred to her using terms like 'cult fanatic' and 'Oswald's woman'. But she'd also been called 'brave' – probably a hundred times; it was an adjective beloved by journalists. Even though she had refused to give any interviews. It was too early to speak out so frankly.

She cast a glance at Oswald as he sat whispering with his defence attorney, Anna-Maria Callini. That woman wasn't classically beautiful; she had sharp features and her nose was too big. But she had put on makeup and dressed in a manner that emphasized her slim figure and large, dark eyes. Sexy and sassy as hell. When she wasn't speaking, her eyes roved the courtroom, fixating on various individuals at random; she reminded Sofia of a bird of prey. The voice that came out of that tiny being was deep and scratchy, and once she had the floor there was no stopping her. There was nothing you could do to shut out her penetrating tones.

They were sitting close together, Anna-Maria and Oswald. His hand rested casually on the back of her chair. He leaned toward her and whispered into her ear, and she flashed a pasted-on, fake smile.

When it was Sofia's turn to speak, she focused on prosecutor Gunhild Strömberg's face. She forced herself to ignore her surroundings. It worked – her voice didn't fail her, even during Anna-Maria Callini's pointed cross-examination.

But the moments when Elvira was speaking were the worst. She was the focus of the trial: the fourteen-year-old Oswald had kept locked in the attic and forced into asphyxiation sex. Everything Sofia had talked about, like the way Oswald had treated the staff, was immediately overshadowed when Elvira began to speak in her trembling voice. She looked like a little kid in her floral sundress and she could hardly produce words. And when Callini attacked her, claiming that Elvira had tempted Oswald into their games in the attic, she began to sob in such despair that all you wanted to do was sweep her into your arms and comfort her. The judge had sent the onlookers out while Elvira was questioned, but Sofia noticed a single tear making its way down the cheek of one of the lay judges. The plaintiffs' counsel, a gentle woman in her sixties, placed a steady arm around Elvira's shoulders during the better part of her tale. She stroked the girl's back now and again. Still, Elvira's tears flowed like a waterfall.

When it was Gunhild Strömberg's turn to cross-examine Oswald, she went straight for the jugular.

'I want to shed light upon the defendant's background; in my opinion it is relevant to this case,' she said, turning to Oswald. 'Tell us about the confession you recorded about your life prior to ViaTerra.'

Everyone knew what she was referring to. The recording Oswald had made in which he confessed to the most repulsive crimes. How he had strangled a young girl as a teenager. How he later ran away from Fog Island to track down and murder his whole family in France, with the goal of inheriting their money. And how he later returned to the manor house on Fog Island to start the ViaTerra cult. A recording he'd been careful to call 'a rough draft of a novel'. There was no way to prove any of it.

Callini objected.

'Irrelevant. This has nothing to do with the case.'

But Oswald nailed her with a glance that would not brook any contradiction, so the judge allowed him to respond.

'It's a draft of a novel, not a confession. My life philosophy, and the entire basis for ViaTerra, is grounded in drawing strength from the past. It's a process that can take a long time and demand a certain amount of exaggeration before you are able to drain the detrimental energy. No one has come so far in this research as I—'

Sofia caught Elvira's gaze and rolled her eyes, which caused Elvira to break into a smile behind her tears. Impatient, Gunhild Strömberg cut Oswald off.

'But is it true that you killed your family in France?'

Callini exploded, but once again Oswald gave her a sharp glance. He had an audience now. He was in his element.

'What is wrong with people in this country? Can't a person write a novel if he wants to? My family has a tragic history. It's been hard for me to get over their loss. Surely you don't seriously think I could hurt someone? My work is to give people life, not kill them. I would never harm a fly.'

Sofia glanced at one of the lay judges, who was nodding along rapidly and unconsciously. You could have heard a pin drop. Everyone's eyes were on Oswald. His voice was so clear and calm that it spread a hypnotic tranquillity throughout the room.

Gunhild Strömberg cleared her throat and fixed her gaze on Oswald once more.

'So, forcing strangulation sex on a minor, does that count as "giving people life"? The rest of us call that rape.'

'I'm not a rapist; I perform healing rituals. Elvira told me she was sixteen. And she had a huge crush on me, she was head over heels, so it can hardly be considered rape. But now to your question, *Gunhild*. That's your name, right?'

The way he said her name made it sound silly and old-fashioned.

'As I understand it, it's perfectly legal to experiment with sex games in Sweden, as long as both parties give their consent. Sex with a limited element of asphyxiation can result in a fantastic, freeing sensation. Perhaps you'd like to try it, Gunhild?'

Laughter broke out in the gallery and a faint blush spread across Gunhild Strömberg's cheeks. Chaos reigned until the judge demanded order in the court.

★

Then it was time for the witnesses. Only Benjamin, Sofia's boyfriend, and Simon, who had been the head gardener at ViaTerra, dared to testify against Oswald. Some other members of the staff decided not to give evidence, perhaps because there were bloggers who threatened all kinds of hell if anyone attacked Oswald. It didn't matter how much bad press Oswald received; he still had a devoted group of followers, and it only kept growing. In addition, there were still celebrities who worshipped him.

Other members of the staff testified on Oswald's behalf.

Sofia had once called some of them friends. Madeleine, who had been Oswald's secretary, and Bosse, who had been his right-hand man. Benny and Sten, the dumb but obstinate security guards. And the worst betrayal of all: Mona and Anders, Elvira's parents. Sofia stared at them, her eyes full of spite, but their blank gazes just went straight through her.

One by one, they came in to testify. To swear that Oswald was the kindest leader in the world. That he took care of them. Guided them in their work. Toiled day and night to keep the wheels turning, always with a smile on his face. Yes, they had noticed that Elvira had been in the midst of some teenage crisis and had become fixated on Oswald.

Sofia dug her nails into her palms. She wanted to scream out loud that those bastards were lying. She noticed Simon and Benjamin, who had taken seats in the gallery. She trained her gaze on Simon's expressionless profile. He felt her looking and turned, shaking his head slowly. Then he smiled, perfectly at ease, as if the hypocrisy in this courtroom didn't exist. That was so Simon. But it did make her a smidgen more relaxed.

Everything had seemed so obvious on the day Oswald was apprehended by the police. It was as if she were playing a role in an action film and had fired the final, deadly shot. Oswald had gone to jail. She had gone home. Adrenaline still pumping through her veins. Dazed with an intoxicating sense of freedom that lasted for weeks.

But then the memories that had lain dormant, bubbling under the surface, began to burst through and overwhelm her. The nights were the worst. Those memories were at their most powerful in the dark, at their clearest in the hour before the pale light of dawn. And when she wasn't brooding on them, her sleep was restless and full of nightmares. Different versions of the same dream. Oswald, accosting her in the office. She might wake up screeching like a hyena, her heart pounding, wondering if that had even been her screaming. She couldn't stand to think of Oswald; it made her heart stop. Sometimes she convinced herself he was standing in the shadows behind the door in her bedroom; she could see his face slipping in and out of the dark. Two black holes where his eyes should be. Just as he had been standing in wait on that night when he assaulted her in the office.

The dream was so sharp and clear that she had to get out of bed and pace back and forth until her pulse went back to normal. She made herself conjure up comforting thoughts: he hadn't gone all the way, there are people who are much worse off, stop being such a wuss. Yet a grim sense of foreboding lingered with her. That was where she was heading, to that wall in the office.

She had even tried sleep aids, but they had no effect on the ever-recurring dream that ripped her nights to shreds.

At the same time, the entire judicial system started up its moaning and groaning, and suddenly it was as if Oswald was breathing down her neck again.

Sofia thought this trial was spitting in the face of justice. The way Oswald was allowed to carry on and spread his lies. The way Callini was permitted to harass Elvira until she nearly broke down. But during the closing arguments, the prosecutor threw up her hands in frustration and cried, 'She was only fourteen, for God's sake, and that bastard locked her in the attic and raped her!'

And despite protests from both attorney and judge, it must have made an impression.

*

They waited for four hours as the lead judge and lay judges deliberated in private. The sun sank behind the rain-heavy clouds beyond the courthouse windows as they waited, full of both expectation and nervousness.

By the time they were summoned back to the courtroom, Elvira was about to gnaw off her very last fingernail. Sofia had sunk into Benjamin's embrace, thinking terrible thoughts about what life would be like if Oswald was acquitted.

But in the end, he was sentenced to prison. For two measly years. After everything he'd done to them out there on Fog Island. The list was long, but 'rape of a child', which had somehow been diminished to 'sexual exploitation', was the only one they had been able to prove.

When the verdict was announced and it was all over, Sofia took one last look at Oswald. He had stood up and was nodding at Callini in satisfaction. Her head was spinning. Was this a good outcome for him? After all, he would be doing time. Then it struck her that he'd planned it this way. He would never get off scot-free, so he accepted his two years; he would likely be placed in a single cell, spend some time resting, write his stupid novel. And, with certainty, retain control over what was left of ViaTerra.

But I don't give a shit about that, she thought. Never again. Never in my life will I have to be close to you, to smell your nasty aftershave, type up your hogwash, or listen to your nagging voice. Never again will you be able to touch me. I hope you get what you deserve in prison. That you end up alone in a shower with three guys and a broomstick and… But then she decided that sort of thing only ever happens on TV or in American prisons.

He turned around and caught her gaze as he passed. A shiver went through her body and she gasped. She recognized that spark in his eye. A faint smile, mirrored in his eyes even as his lips remained still.

And that expression, which she remembered so well, made her wonder.

How could it have gone so wrong? How did he become the person he was?

And where did that evil really come from?

3

Simon glanced at Sofia, in profile. She was tense. Her jaw was clenched and he could hear a faint, strident sound coming from her. She was unconsciously grinding her teeth. He thought she looked pale and exhausted. Even more exhausted than when they'd been slave labour at ViaTerra and had only slept five or six hours each night.

Simon was in two minds. On the one hand, he was relatively uninterested in everything that had happened in the courtroom. Oswald had too much on his conscience, and it had caught up with him. It could only have ended in prison time. On the other hand, Simon was full of an indefinable, unpleasant feeling that was very unlike him. It was something about Oswald's attitude. If you hadn't known he was the defendant, you would have thought he was in charge of the courtroom. He seemed unconcerned and indifferent, and occasionally amused. And now Simon didn't know whether his misgivings were warranted, or had something to do with the paranoia he was experiencing more and more frequently.

What he wanted more than anything was to return to the pension on Fog Island, where he worked these days. He hoped they were taking good care of his greenhouses while he was away. He liked his new job. Autumn was almost upon them, and there was a lot to do ensure they could continue to grow produce over the winter. But he had all the time in the world – never again would life be like it had been at ViaTerra. No one at the pension shouted at him to work faster, it was disaster-free, and he was never lent out to work on other projects like a damn pawn. No, the new job was good. It would be nice to get back to the island.

But Simon didn't like how serious Sofia looked. Pale, with dark shadows under her eyes. It was clear she wasn't doing well, despite the fancy suit she had on. Still, there was something special about Sofia that drew glances. It wasn't every man who saw the beauty shimmering beneath her surface. She seldom put on makeup, and she usually wore her long, wavy hair in a braid. But those who felt her magnetism were caught. Simon thought it was lucky he didn't like her that way. He wanted her to be happy again, the way she had been when they worked together in the cult: feeding the pigs and talking about books, plodding through the snow and making faces behind their guard Benny's back, laughing at everything and everyone. The slave labour hadn't made them crack, no way. They had both been aware that Oswald had lost his mind, but they had kept fighting. Simon wanted that Sofia back again.

But not even when they met outside the courtroom, after the verdict had been handed down, did she seem happy.

So Simon took her by the arm.

'Lunch is on me. Who's coming?'

Sofia, Benjamin, and Elvira took him up on his offer.

'Don't be upset,' Benjamin told Sofia once they'd taken their seats at the restaurant. 'He's going to prison, and that's what we were hoping for, isn't it?'

'Two measly years,' Sofia said. 'For everything he did to the staff. It's not going to change him a bit. He'll use it as a vacation. Rest up and come back, more evil than ever. And think of all the love letters he'll get in prison. Nothing can touch a man like him.'

'But ViaTerra's done for, at least,' said Elvira. Simon scratched his head. He hadn't wanted to say anything, but he was bad at keeping things to himself. So he told them about everything that had happened on the island. From the day the police raided the cult's property to the day the staff were sent home on the ferry.

Simon had been putting up a trellis for the grapevines in the greenhouse when the police arrived. The air inside those glass walls was so warm and humid that it was hard to breathe. It was sunny, and the greenhouse felt like a sauna. The plants fought for oxygen, and he was sweating masses. Then he saw the gate open and the police storm in, an entire army with weapons drawn. They took over the manor, turning everything upside down. At first Simon just stood there gaping, staring at the windows of the building, trying to figure out what was going on inside. He caught sight of Elvira, who came out wrapped in a blanket, in the company of a female officer. And then he understood. His heart skipped a beat. This was serious; the walls had crumbled. He stood there staring until an officer came to fetch him.

'You have to come with us,' she said, her eyes on his dirty coverall. 'Perhaps you'd like to wash up first. We're going to question the entire staff.'

The interrogations lasted for three days, and Simon told them everything. About the punishments, the forced lack of sleep, the way they'd been kept prisoner behind those walls. The words flowed from his mouth like a gurgling stream. Never had he talked so much.

After the three days of questioning, they were sent home, even those who had no place to go but ViaTerra. When they arrived there, they found that the property was a crime scene and was cordoned off.

And this is how they came to be sitting together on the five o'clock ferry back over the sound. Forty-eight individuals, without Oswald who had been their guiding star for so many years. Without jobs or plans for the future. Despondent and ashamed. Some of them confused and upset. Some secretly excited and relieved.

Madeleine was the first to open her mouth, that woman with her colourless eyes that gave Simon the shivers.

'This is just wrong, I will never betray Franz,' she said. 'Sofia is bloody insane.'

Anna, who had always had a crush on Oswald, agreed.

'Did you see Elvira? She was bawling like a baby when they led her out. So fake.'

'They'll let Franz go soon,' Madeleine said. 'He'll be back, you know that, right? We have to stick together until everything goes back to normal.'

But Mira, who had spent most of her time in the cult on punishment detail, looked uncertain as she sat there on her bench.

'I guess I'll probably go home and think it over,' she murmured.

'What is there to think about?' said Bosse, Oswald's right-hand man. 'ViaTerra is the only truth, so of course they're trying to silence Franz. Of course we have to stick together.'

And on and on, like this. You were either wholeheartedly with the group, or you were against it.

But Simon was a little distracted. He couldn't bring himself to take part in this remarkable conversation. He hadn't left the island in three years. When they first boarded the ferry to leave, he was so certain: he would go home to his parents on their farm in Småland. Get his hands in the earth, because there was nothing left for him on Fog Island. And not a soul knew what he was thinking and feeling, or that he had helped Sofia escape, and he wanted it to stay that way. But when the mainland began to take form, a thin streak on the horizon, doubt stole in. His mother's shrill voice echoed in his mind. Daniel's sad eyes on that fateful night. He had promised himself never to return. Never to forgive his mother. To stuff that whole goddamn farm into a mental filing cabinet. And now here he was, on the way from one sort of evil right into the embrace of another. He didn't know which way was up; he couldn't bring himself to decide.

He pulled himself out of his ruminations and took a look at the group, which had divided into two teams: those who were in, and those who were out.

The 'in' group was considerably larger. Anders and Mona, Elvira's parents, sat in silence, leaning against the railing. Madeleine, too, had realized they hadn't made a peep.

'How about you two? What are you going to do?'

Mona pressed her lips into a narrow line and turned her head away. But Anders stood and put a hand on Mona's shoulder.

'We're with you, Madeleine. It's Elvira's own fault it ended up like this. She was always going on about wanting to be with Franz. We won't betray ViaTerra for her sake. Right, Mona? We're going to disown Elvira.'

Madeleine gave a delighted cry. 'That's what I like to hear!'

Rage began to throb in Simon's veins. He stood up and took a few steps toward Anders, overcome by the urge to give him a sound walloping and toss him overboard. But just then, the ferryman, Edwin Björk, called Simon's name from the bridge.

'Someone wants to talk to you on my mobile. Please come and take this call.'

Simon was startled; he went over to Björk and took the phone from his outstretched hand.

The woman's voice was unfamiliar, but she introduced herself as Inga Hermansson, owner of the village pension. After a series of apologies and laments about the terrible situation with the cult, she got to the point: she had heard about Simon's gardens. She wanted to hire him, because the pension was going to move to using only locally-grown and organic resources. She laid it on thick, all the good things she'd heard about Simon from the guests at ViaTerra. His heart swelled in his chest and his thoughts were drawn to the greenhouse and fields at ViaTerra. The grapevines and tomato plants that would wither and die away. The crops that would turn into an overgrown wasteland. He pictured everything he'd created over the last few years neglected, ruined, and abandoned. His mother's voice quickly returned, only to fade out and become part of the sound of the water hitting the sides of the ferry. The tension in his chest let go.

'When would I start?' he asked.

'As soon as you can.'

'I'll take the next ferry back,' he told Inga Hermansson, hanging up without waiting for a response.

He returned to the island that same day and got started

on his job at the pension. His memories of the cult faded as soon as he got his hands in the earth. But now he wondered if ViaTerra had come back to life after all, a living being, moving and breathing. Somewhere. Somehow.

No one said anything for a moment once he'd finished speaking.

'But surely you don't think they'll come back to the island?' Elvira said in horror.

'Who knows?' Simon said. 'It feels like something's up.'

'Aw, it'll just be a huge mess if Madde's in charge,' Benjamin said. 'And why should we even care? What could they do to us? Not a damn thing.'

'I don't even want to think about it,' said Sofia. 'But Simon, you'll keep an eye on the place, won't you?'

Simon nodded. He felt like they were brushing off his concerns. But it was best to keep his mouth shut until he had something concrete.

'What are you going to do now, Elvira?' Sofia asked. 'Do you have anyone to take care of you?'

'I'm going to live with my aunt in Lund. And finish school. After that, we'll see.'

A shadow passed over Elvira's face and a wrinkle appeared between her pale eyebrows. She was brooding over something, and Simon wasn't sure it had to do with the trial.

The black circles under eyes looked permanent. And her eyes had already been bloodshot this morning. Something wasn't quite right with Elvira.

'Are you sure you don't need any help? Are you upset about how Anders and Mona are treating you?' he asked.

'No, it's fine. We've never been all that tight anyway. Sure,

I like them and stuff, but we've always been part of religious groups and I've had enough. It's Dad, he'll never give up. He says we have to forget about the material world. You know? And when you do that, it doesn't matter where you live or whether you go to school.'

'Or whether a sadistic pig rapes your daughter,' Sofia added. As soon as the words left her mouth, she sucked in air as if to pull them back inside. But Elvira didn't seem to take offence; she just nodded and rolled her eyes so hard her long eyelashes brushed her eyebrows.

'But there's one thing I don't get,' Benjamin said. 'How come Anders and Mona let you testify against Oswald? You're not of legal age yet.'

'They said I should do what I wanted. They disowned me. In their eyes, I no longer exist.'

'That's so messed up!' Sofia said.

'It's better this way. I just want to be normal, and stop being a cult kid. Make some friends. Finish school.'

Simon looked at Sofia, who was sitting across from him. Her cheeks had taken on some colour and her eyes had regained their lustre. He expected she would be just fine, now that the trial was over.

'How about you, what will you do now?' he asked her. 'Do you have a job?'

'I'm looking,' she said, and suddenly she seemed to be gazing inwards. Simon realized at once he had hit a nerve.

4

There it was again. The question she had been dreading, waiting for; the question she knew would come. She had rattled off the answer silently in her head, practising on her way. This time, she told herself, it would go just fine. All she had to do was seem unconcerned, bordering on nonchalant.

The woman with the round face and grey eyes squinted at her over her glasses.

'So what have you been doing for the last two years?'

Sofia prepared herself to respond. Dammit, she was stumbling over her words again; her voice sounded rough and guilty, full of that stupid confusion, as if this lady had caught her red-handed somehow.

'Well, I sort of got side-tracked. I joined a cult.'

The woman was startled.

'Which I have left now,' Sofia hurried to add. 'I mean, I am definitely no longer a member.'

'I see. Which cult was it, if I may ask?'

'You might not have heard of it. ViaTerra.'

But it seemed the woman had heard of ViaTerra. She raised her eyebrows and pursed her lips, then gazed out at the lawn. It was an overcast morning; heavy clouds drifted by and cool air was drawn through the cracked window, bringing the smell of rain. Sofia shivered. She tried to catch the woman's eye, but now she was gazing down at the desk. There was a strained, anxious tension between them that hadn't been there before. The mood was suddenly awkward.

'Well, I have your CV, so I'll be in touch if we're interested.'

The hell you will.

There was that sinking feeling in her stomach. Several job interviews had ended this way. And no one had contacted her. *ViaTerra.* The very act of uttering the words automatically disqualified her for employment. Surely anyone so stupid as to join that crazy cult couldn't be a good fit for a job. Sofia had applied to several positions since returning to Lund. She wanted to work in a library. But finding a job was easier said than done. Especially with a background as a cult member.

The woman looked up, mildly annoyed now. 'You're all set, then.'

This was the moment when you were supposed to stand up, say thanks, and never apply for another job there ever again. But Sofia wasn't feeling quite normal today. She was desperate for this job as an assistant librarian at the university library. She loved the library. The smell of old dust and leather. The light when the sun shined in on the great room. The blazing colours of the trees beyond the windows in the autumn.

The lump in her throat grew until she felt like she might cry – this whole situation was so unfair.

She rose to leave, but she couldn't get her legs to move. Should she say what she was thinking? Vent about the injustice? A series of roadblocks towered before her. It wasn't a good idea to be pushy. She risked getting a bad reputation if she made a fuss; she might destroy any chance she had of landing a job at another library.

Don't act like a victim!

She caught the woman's eye again.

'I know you think I'm crazy for having joined that cult, but the thing is, I am extremely qualified for this job. I have a bachelor's degree in literature and have built an entire library on my own. I can rattle off the alphabet forwards and backwards, if you want to hear. Really fast. I'm good with computers. And I promise that not a single book will end up mis-shelved.'

The woman's lips twitched with amusement.

'I'll be in touch this afternoon. Just have to check on a few things.'

★

The bus home was crowded and Sofia had to stand. When soft jazz began to stream from her phone, she thought at first it was coming from the guy next to her. She'd changed her ringtone a number of times. Blaring ones made her jump, because she always thought it would be the police calling to say Oswald had escaped and was coming after her. But this ringtone only sounded like a gentle thought, and the music was already dying away when she got her phone out of her pocket. She recognized the voice immediately; it was matter-of-fact and a bit formal, but now with a hint of warmth.

'When can you start, Sofia?'

'Immediately. Tomorrow, if you want me to.'

'Tomorrow is Saturday.'

'That doesn't matter.'

★

Her dad met her in the entryway. She wanted to share her news right away, but she couldn't get a word in edgeways.

'Sofia, there's a very nice studio available downtown. I was there and had a look. I know you don't have a job yet, but your mom and I can help you until you get back on your feet...'

'I *do* have a job!'

And at that moment, her life turned around.

Everything that had been crushed to pieces became whole again. Details she hadn't noticed before took on an almost eerie sharpness: how the sun laid a glittering net over the city in the evenings, the heavenly scents that poured from bakeries and cafés each morning, and the monotonous, soothing sound of the highway in the distance before she fell asleep.

Things she used to take for granted took on new meaning. Having weekends off, eating whatever she wanted, spending time with her parents and friends. Sleeping in was especially significant after the forced sleeplessness of the cult. One Sunday she set her alarm for six, got up for a while, and then crawled back into bed and fell asleep again. Just because she could. Writing emails and sending texts without having them censored was freeing, not to mention surfing the internet however she liked.

All of these little things made her happy.

★

The apartment was small, with a corner for sleeping, a corner for the kitchen, and a living room that hardly fit a sofa set, a stereo, and a few shelves. But she decorated in bright colours and kept it neat and tidy, with a zealous devotion that was really quite unlike her. She wrapped herself in blankets and sat on the balcony in the mornings, watching Lund appear as a mirage before the rising sun, soaking in the feeling of freedom that had returned now that she had a stable place on earth.

Her job mostly involved shelving books, but she immediately found a rhythm, fell into a comfortable routine. She thought often of her time in ViaTerra and always tried to figure out why she had stayed so long, but she always came to the same conclusion: that it didn't really matter why. It wasn't the sort of mistake you make twice, and that was what counted.

She got back in touch with Wilma, who had been her best friend before she joined the cult. Wilma had changed since she began to work in the fashion industry, dressing in natural-coloured, faded, half-wrinkly clothes that still looked surprisingly expensive. Her hair was bobbed and dyed black. Her soft, lovely curves had been dieted out of existence, and whenever they went out to eat she mostly poked at her salads. Sofia wondered if they had grown apart, but Wilma was determined that they should see each other once a week. The first few times they met, she made Sofia tell her everything that had happened on the island, down to the tiniest detail. Wilma was especially fascinated by Oswald.

'In some ways, I understand why you were drawn to him,' she said one day. 'He's super hot, there's no denying that. Do you know where he buys his clothes? I mean, everything he wears is the latest fashion.'

'He thinks he's above things like fashion, Wilma. Everything is tailor-made. He's the only person I've ever heard of who has his jeans made to order.'

'Jesus.'

'Whatever you think of him, he treated the staff like shit.'

'I can't believe he turned out to be such a monster. It's hard to wrap my head around.'

'You're wrong about that,' Sofia said. 'People like Oswald are far too easy to understand. He seems like a perfectly normal guy – that's the problem.'

'I wonder if he could be converted…'

'Believe me, Wilma. He's impossible to change, you would never manage it.'

'I can't believe he was so obsessed with you. I mean, no offence, but…'

'Wilma, can you just shut up?'

'Fine, I'll stop. But just one more thing. After having a super-hot guy like Oswald be into you, I don't get why you have to hang around with a boring, spineless guy like Benjamin.'

'You don't know him, Wilma. Benjamin is good for me. He's everything I need.'

Wilma made a face and went back to poking at her salad.

*

Sofia remained faithful to Benjamin. The mere sight of him set her heart aflutter. He had stayed in Gothenburg, where he could live with his sister and work at a carrier company, but he visited Sofia in Lund on weekends. Every Friday evening at eight, there he was, outside her door. She always prepared herself before his visits; she would start fantasizing about sex sometime on Wednesday night, and by the time she got home from work on Friday she was so horny that she spent the half hour before he showed up pacing her apartment. As if his train might have suddenly arrived early. She put on sexy underwear. As soon as he came through the door they clung to one another, giddy with excitement. Most times they were too impatient to make it to the bed and ended up having sex on the floor in the hall. Their relationship had never been simple, but the sex had always been good. Better than good.

★

It was a cold, snowy winter. But the days grew longer and brighter in January. Only the nights were dark and difficult. She still dreamed about Oswald, and it only got worse when Benjamin was there. Maybe he reminded her of her time on the island. Sometimes he couldn't deal with her screams and woke her up gently.

'You were having a nightmare again.'

Typically, she was drenched with sweat and all in a daze.

'You were shouting, really loud.'

'Shit!'

'I can't handle you suffering like this.'

'I'm sure it will get better. There must be something I haven't figured out yet.'

'What is there to figure out? You have to let it go sometime, Sofia.'

'Let what go?'

'All the trauma.'

She clung to him until her heartbeat slowed. 'Don't you ever have nightmares, Benjamin?'

'Sure, sometimes. But they're just annoying. Not like yours.'

'What do you dream about?'

'It's always the same dream. I'm in a city. It's Gothenburg, but not Gothenburg at the same time, because there are hills and a cliff over the sea.'

'Like on Fog Island?'

'Right. I feel anxious and confused. I walk around looking for something, but I'm not sure what. Then I come to a tunnel and my skin starts to crawl. Someone is standing there. Different people from ViaTerra. Sometimes it's Madeleine, sometimes Bosse or Benny. And then I remember I'm looking for you and ask where you are. It's always the same answer: "Don't you know? She came back. She's working with Franz again." And then I get so desperate. I know I have to get you out, but I don't know how. And when I wake up, it takes me a minute to realize I'm at home. And that you're fine.'

'I wonder why we can't stop dreaming about that place. Why are we so stuck?'

'Oh, my dreams will probably go away eventually. They're nothing compared to yours. Can't you please go see a psychologist? Oswald almost raped you. You need professional help.'

'They'll just say I've got Stockholm Syndrome because I can't get him out of my head. I don't feel like listening to all that nonsense.'

'You don't know that.'

'Yeah, I do. Why doesn't anyone ever say, "It's great that you managed to get out of there, that you put him away?" No, they just want to know how many times he molested me in the office.'

'He didn't do that, did he?' Benjamin asked, horrified.

'No, you know that already.'

'Call a psychologist, please. At least give it a try.'

So she promised she would, but she never got around to it.

5

Anna-Maria was having a hard time focusing on the road ahead of her. The knowledge that she would soon see him again was dizzying, and this meeting was crucial. They would be laying the groundwork for their collaboration, now that he was an inmate. In some ways, she would become his lifeline out to the real world, and the thought that he would be dependent on her was a little bit intoxicating.

The loops of razor wire were visible from a long way off, and then Skogome Prison itself appeared down in its valley. Nestled cosily in amber-coloured forest, but bleak thanks to its concrete walls. Grey, drab, and ugly. She'd been there before; sex offenders were her speciality. She understood them. Could follow along in their reasoning.

The parking lot was surprisingly empty, even though it was visiting hours. She parked her car, approached the outer gate, and identified herself. The gate unlocked with a dull buzz. When she got to the main guard post, she left her ID and placed her phone in a locked cabinet, exchanging pleasantries with the female guard in the booth. She recognized the woman immediately: her name was Helga McLean. She had worked there for years. Tough as nails.

'He's really been waiting for you,' she said.

'But I'm here on time.'

'You know how he is,' McLean said with a small smile. Callini regarded her and realized with a cold stab in her chest that the woman had lovely eyes. But that sort of thing would never happen here. Although you never knew with Franz; you could never really be sure. She took a deep breath in an attempt to get away from this annoying train of thought.

A male guard met her in the corridor where the visiting rooms were located. He showed her to a room somewhere in the middle. When the guard opened the door, the sight of Oswald took her breath away. He appeared to have shrunk. He was slumped in a low yellow chair and wearing shapeless grey clothing. Franz Oswald in ugly sweatpants – it was unthinkable. The harsh lighting washed out his skin. But then he stood up and quickly regained his authority. She felt awkward; she wanted to embrace him but knew that Franz Oswald was a man who preferred to avoid displays of affection.

'Can you believe this?' he said, pointing at the easy chairs. 'That we have to sit on this goddamn dwarf furniture. But by all means, please have a seat.'

She placed her handbag on a side table and sank down in a chair. He remained standing, watching her with a caustic smile on his lips.

'So, how is it going, Franz? How are you feeling?' she tried.

'What do you think? I told you I would be a model prisoner. I've signed up for every single goddamn study group and educational program. I slave away in the heat from the monster of a washing machine they purchased for six million kronor. Oh yes, everything is great. Can we dispense with the pleasantries now and get to the goddamn point?'

She noticed the neat stack of paper on a table that stood between the chairs.

'This is the plan I was talking about,' he said. 'Down to the last detail. You can take it with you. I've printed out a copy. We can discuss the details on your next visit. There's also a list of items I need. The plan is divided up into three separate parts. First, the idiots at ViaTerra who have sunk straight through the mud to their lowest level of intelligence thus far. Someone needs to keep an eye on them. Then there's the book. You'll have to take care of all the contacts with the editors and so forth. And then there's Sofia Bauman, of course. Time to deal with her.'

As always, Anna-Maria took Oswald's mention of Sofia Bauman like a punch to the gut. Something in his eyes changed; their clarity was broken and replaced by an eerie, dreamy glow. Obviously, she wanted bad things to happen to that bitch. The worse, the better. But first Oswald's almost manic fixation on her had to be broken. *How*, she didn't yet know.

'That part about Sofia. Is it really necessary? After all, she hasn't made any trouble since the trial. Why would we even care about someone so pathetic—'

'Have you begun to study the theses?' he interrupted.

'Sorry?'

'I asked if you'd started studying the theses, as I told you to.'

'No, I mean… it's only been a week, and I thought—'

'That explains your naïve attitude towards Sofia Bauman. You don't even understand what ViaTerra stands for, do you?'

'No, I mean, yes I do. I'll get informed about all of it, I promise. But if you want to, we can sue Bauman.'

'Sue her? Why on earth would we do that? That wouldn't be any fun.'

'For slander, I was thinking.'

He laughed out loud. The peal of laughter bounced around the room, echoing coldly in the small room.

'Are you really that dumb? People like Sofia Bauman must be dealt with slowly, Annie. Just a hint at first, but enough to raise the hair on the back of her neck. I thought I'd explained all this to you. Start by reading the theses. And reread *The Art of War* by Sun Tzu. You have read that before, haven't you?'

Anna-Maria shook her head, baffled.

'What? You're a failure of a lawyer, did you know that?'

She nodded eagerly, although she didn't really understand what this had to do with Sofia Bauman.

'I just want to clarify a few things before you go,' he said. 'No one here is allowed to read, listen to, or otherwise take part in what we discuss, since you are my attorney, correct?'

'That's right.'

'And you must abide by complete confidentiality, and will sign all the necessary papers to that effect.'

'Naturally.'

'Okay then, we have a deal.'

He bent down, placed his hands under her forearms, and pulled her to her feet. He was standing so close she could smell the faintly burned odour of the newly washed prison clothes, so different from the fresh aroma of his usual aftershave. She suddenly remembered the little bottle she'd brought and reached for her handbag.

'I have your aftershave.'

He pulled her arm close and shook his head.

'Forget it. I can't use it in here anyway. Maybe when I get furlough, but that could be awhile. And they force you to strip after every visit. But you should already know that sort of thing.'

'Yes, I'm sorry, I forgot.'

'Stark naked. The female guards too,' he added with a grin.

He had both her arms in an iron grip and shuffled her backwards until her back was pressed to the wall; he got so close to her that she almost couldn't breathe. That familiar excitement made the blood rush to her groin. When he finally pressed his body to hers, she whined with desire. He quickly put one hand over her mouth while the other grasped her throat.

'It's too early to break the rules here. You'll have to hold out for a while longer,' he whispered in her ear.

'I like…' she managed to say.

'Shh,' he whispered, squeezing her throat. 'I know what you like.'

6

There was one thing Simon hadn't mentioned when they were eating lunch on the last day of the trial. It was really just a feeling he'd had when he walked by the manor one morning: something was going on in there.

A few weeks after the trial, he walked there again. It was late October. A raw, chilly wind found its way under his clothes. The sky was iron-grey and the leaves glowed yellow and orange. There were two ways to get from the village to ViaTerra – the tarmac road, which followed the island's eastern coast and led to a gravel drive up to the manor, and the shortcut: narrow paths through the woods that were often overgrown during the warm months.

Dusk was falling, so Simon took the road. He walked slowly, his hands stuffed in his pockets, whistling to himself. There wasn't a car in sight; the island felt deserted now that the summer tourists had left for the season. The darkness was oppressive; no moon, no stars, only a thick blanket settling across the road. There was a fresh breeze, and the sea hissed and frothed to his right. A couple of gulls sailed on the wind, apparently keeping pace with him for some peculiar reason. As he turned onto the gravel path that led to ViaTerra, he could see the façade of the manor house towering up against the sky.

Stately and gleaming white in the dim light. All the windows were dark. Everything was quiet and still. Good – it had only been his imagination.

The manor house was enclosed by a three-metre wall topped with an electric fence. A massive iron gate formed the main entrance, and next to it stood a sentry box. When he reached the gate, Simon discovered a motorcycle standing next to the booth where the guard typically sat. Strange. He was almost positive it hadn't been there last time he walked by. It was chained into place. It must have been Benny's bike, the one he used to patrol the property. Simon was curious; he tried to open the gate, but found it locked. He followed the wall around to the smaller gate that led from the grounds into the forest. It, too, was locked. Franz Oswald had used it on occasion, and was the only one who'd had the key. On the day the police had stormed the manor, he had snuck out through the gate and run down to the sea, where he had hidden in a cave.

Simon looked up at the manor house again and noticed the flag fluttering in the breeze. It was the flag of ViaTerra, green and white, symbolizing the power of nature over humanity. Now Simon felt wary; there had been no flag on the pole last time.

The wall was too high for him to peer over. The first autumn storm had already felled some trees, and by putting his back into it, he dragged over a small birch and leaned it against the wall. He climbed up, slipping a few times, but at last he could grab the edge of the wall. Gazing down at the open yard on the other side, he saw something huge: a large removal truck parked at the main entrance. It was full of furniture and suitcases. A couple of guys he didn't recognize were carrying a chest of drawers through the door.

Someone was moving in.

Simon climbed back down, then lifted the tree away from the wall and placed it on the ground. He tried the handle of the gate again, just to make sure. It was definitely locked.

As he turned homeward, it was so dark he could hardly see where the gravel drive ended and the ditch began. He walked slowly, tentatively, and was suddenly blinded by the headlights of an oncoming car. Though he had to shield his eyes with one hand, he was able to see the figure in the driver's seat: a woman. Sharp features and a familiar, pale face. It was Anna-Maria Callini, Oswald's defence attorney. He was so curious that he considered going back to spy on her. But he decided to take one thing at a time. For now, he had to figure out how to gain access to the place.

*

That evening, Simon spent a long time online. When he was done, he knew all there was to know about changing a lock. The next day was a Saturday. After seeing to the greenhouses, he took the ferry to the mainland and purchased everything he would need.

When darkness fell, he set off for the manor house. This time he was sure no one was there; the windows were dark and it was quiet, aside from an owl hooting now and then from the forest. He walked to the far side, where the smaller gate was, fastened his flashlight to a tree, aimed it at the gate, and got started. Simon first picked the lock, a skill he had learned as a boy. He then preceded to remove the lock itself. Now he would have access to the manor whenever he pleased. But there was one more thing he had to do.

He hummed as he walked home in the dark, sweeping the treetops with his flashlight and blinding an owl and laughing at the way it stared down at him. The bird took off with a screech; it flew so low and so fast that its talons brushed his hair and he could feel the whorls of air coming off its wings. Simon cried out, dropped his flashlight, and suddenly found himself in total darkness. He crawled around on the gravel path, fumbling until he found the flashlight.

An unpleasant lump of fear lingered in his belly all the rest of the way home. Perhaps the owl was a bad omen, a warning that he would do best to keep away from ViaTerra. But he knew that what he planned to do was important.

Back home in his cottage, which was on the pension's property, he sat down at the computer and sent an email to Sofia. They wrote to each other now and then – that is, when Simon managed to drag himself to the computer and log in. But Sofia always responded right away.

Do you have Ellis's email address? I need some expert advice about my computer, he wrote.

Ellis was Sofia's ex-boyfriend, from the time before she had joined the cult; he was a computer genius who had harassed her and hung her out to dry online. But he wasn't all bad: when Sofia fled ViaTerra, Ellis had come to her aid by hacking Oswald's computer and digging up evidence.

Sofia sent Simon Ellis's email address that same evening, and wrote that she had just found a job and an apartment. Simon felt warm inside; he wrote back to congratulate her on the job but said nothing about his discoveries at the manor house. He didn't want to upset her when she was so happy.

He emailed Ellis to explain what he wanted and received

a reply the next morning. Sure, Ellis could help Simon, for a small fee. The kind of falsification he was talking about was illegal, but by all means, if it could help Sofia…

★

The envelope from Ellis arrived a few days later. Inside was a letter on police letterhead, addressed to the owners of ViaTerra. Without mincing words, it said that they had been forced to break the lock during the raid but had now replaced it, and were sending along the new keys to the gate. Simon took out an envelope he'd addressed to the manor. The lock he'd just installed had three keys. He put two into the envelope and kept one, then sealed the envelope, which he would drop in the mailbox next time he went to the mainland. The extent of his own daring made him dizzy.

★

From then on, Simon visited the manor once a week, typically on the weekends. He sneaked through the forest to the gate and opened it with his key. Within the gate was a stretch of woods that bordered the huge lawn. If he stood perfectly still and kept quiet, no one could see him from there.

Sometimes he went to the sea first, and sat on the cliff rocks to spend some time with his thoughts. The fog had begun to move in at night and the air was damp and raw. He found the coastal landscape was most beautiful when it was swept in fog. No shadows, no sharp reflections. Gentle silence. It made him so calm he nearly dozed off, but his thoughts were always drawn back to the manor.

After their ferry trip, once Madeleine had cobbled together that new group, he'd figured they would all meet up on the mainland. Talk about old memories, write loving letters to Oswald in prison. It hadn't occurred to him that they would return to the island. And he didn't like the fact that they had. Not at all.

*

One morning in early November, he heard voices on the other side of the wall. Followed by sounds that reminded him of his time in ViaTerra: feet scraping on the gravel, chatter, those rare moments before roll call, before everything began in earnest.

So they had begun to hold assembly again.

Christ, this is nuts, he thought. How was it even possible? It had to be against the law for them to come back and start up all their shit again.

Curious, he hurried to the far side of the property and slipped through the gate. Now that the trees had lost their leaves, he had to hide behind the trunk of a big oak.

They were all lined up in rows. Twenty-five or thirty individuals – half the former group. Madeleine and Bosse in front of the staff. Katarina, Anna, Benny, and Sten were in the first row.

Bosse was preaching about priorities. His voice made Simon nervous, like an annoying itch under his skin.

They'd managed to scrape together uniforms; everyone was dressed in grey, but he spotted jackets that hung like sacks and trouser legs that left ankles exposed. And they all looked worn out and tired. Far from the cocksure group he was used to. But how fun was it, really, to stand there listening to Bosse? There was something contradictory about the heavy, grey bodies and ViaTerra's flag, waving so freely in the wind. But indeed, the cult had returned.

★

The accident happened on Christmas Day. Simon was drowsy after a big Christmas dinner at the pension and decided to take a walk to perk himself up. When he turned onto the gravel drive that led to the manor, he saw an ambulance and two police cars outside the gate and a group of people gathered on the road. He didn't want to be recognized, so he slipped into the forest. Two men came out of the gate carrying a stretcher covered in a big grey blanket. They hopped into the ambulance, which raced past him, sirens blaring. Clearly something serious had happened.

The group of people began to scatter, and he saw Edwin Björk, the ferry captain, come walking down the road. Simon emerged from the forest and fell into step beside Björk.

'Hi, Simon!' he said. 'They're up to all that devilry again. Can you believe those idiots came back?'

'No, I really can't. What happened?'

'Not sure. They carried someone out under that blanket. A suicide, I heard.'

Simon didn't learn any more that day. He couldn't concentrate on anything as he tried to figure out who had been on the stretcher. He *had* to know, so he returned the next day, to sneak through the gate and hide behind the oak. And there stood the staff, their shoulders slumped, a sad, grey mass. Bosse stood before them, holding a bundle of papers in one arm. He spoke loudly, so loudly that Simon could make out a few words: 'don't panic' and 'keep working just like normal' were two phrases that reached Simon's hiding spot.

As Bosse was about to hand out the papers, a gust of wind blew several sheets from his grip. They fluttered across the lawn like butterflies, landing here and there on the wilting grass. Simon's eye caught a sheet that seemed to be heading his way, but Anna came running and picked it up. Once all the papers had been gathered up and handed out, the staff dispersed.

Jacob, the caretaker of animals who had been one of Simon's few friends, plodded toward the farm area. Simon felt a stab of pity; Jacob looked sad.

Simon was just about to sneak back out through the gate when he noticed something white lying on a pile of pine needles. He got down on his belly and crawled his way to the pile to retrieve the white thing. It was a piece of paper; he stuck it under his jacket.

Not until he was back home did he read what it said; it was a list of bullet points that together formed a plan. Things that needed doing around the property. Renovations, purchases, cleaning. He sneered as he read *Find someone to take care of cultivation.* So they were fixing up the manor again, preparing it for something. Oswald's return? Hardly. He would be behind bars for a good while longer. But it occurred to Simon that perhaps such an operation could be managed from prison.

His eye was drawn to the very last point on the list; it was slightly separate from the others. Almost like an afterthought.

Sofia Bauman? It said. Just her name, followed by a question mark.

7

Sofia was just about to go to bed. She placed her phone and keys on the coffee table, turned off the TV, and headed to the bathroom to brush her teeth. She was wearing a nightgown and had wrapped herself in a robe; the January cold had seeped through the window frames. When the doorbell rang, she thought at first that Benjamin must have missed his train. But he always rang three times. This was a brief, hesitant ring. And following it she could hear feet scraping anxiously against the stone floor in the hallway.

She went to the door, peered through the peephole, and found it was Elvira. In a split second, her mood took a serious nosedive. All she and Elvira had in common was ViaTerra, and she suspected Elvira wasn't there for a cheerful chat about old times. What was more, she looked awful: her hair was tangled, there were black mascara tracks down her cheeks; she was dressed all in black and was so pale her skin took on a greenish hue in the stairwell lighting.

A number of alternatives popped up in Sofia's head. She could stand perfectly still, quiet, not even breathing, until Elvira left. She could call through the mail slot that she was sick with something contagious like the stomach flu. Or she could open the door, just a crack, and explain that she simply couldn't deal with this right now. *It's nothing personal, but I've cut all ties with ViaTerra.*

This brief moment at the door, which by now felt like a whole eternity, gave her a sense of déjà vu. She had made important decisions at the drop of a hat like this before. And it had always gone awry.

The air was motionless in her tiny apartment. The faint rumble of traffic outside fell away, as if it had been turned off with a button. The ceiling light faded. *I'm going to regret this,* she thought, and opened the door.

As she let Elvira into the entryway, she wondered how she could make this visit as short as possible: ask if Elvira needed clothing or money. Help her, as long as it had nothing to do with ViaTerra.

Elvira burst into tears as she took off her coat. 'Those bastards won't let me go to Mom's funeral,' she sobbed.

But Sofia hardly registered the words, because as Elvira removed her coat everything went strange and wrong. Sofia stared in shock at Elvira's belly, which was huge and swollen – in stark contrast to her skinny body.

Elvira shrugged in a gesture of hopelessness.

'Is the baby his?' Sofia asked, still in a state of mild shock.

'What the fuck do you think?' Elvira snapped. 'It's not like I had that many options when it came to guys seven months ago. How can everything be so wrong? It's just so fucking unbelievable.'

She was wearing black maternity pants and a sleeveless black shirt and had pierced her nose and gotten a tattoo on her neck – a bee. Although it was below freezing out, she didn't have a hat or mittens, just a huge black coat over her light clothing, and boots on her feet.

'Come in and sit down,' Sofia said. 'What happened?'

Elvira stepped into the living room and tossed her coat on the sofa.

'Dad says I can't go to the funeral.'

'What funeral?'

'Mom's. You didn't know? Mom hanged herself.'

'What? For real?'

'People don't fucking hang themselves for pretend, do they?' This was a whole new Elvira. Angry as the bee on her neck.

'Sit down and tell me about it. Start from the beginning.'

Elvira sank onto the sofa and let out a heavy sigh. She glanced around the apartment.

'Nice place.'

As Sofia went to the kitchenette and put on coffee, she was flooded with a feeling of hopeless melancholy. Mona was dead. Her memories of Mona's first suicide attempt crowded their way into her brain. That time, Oswald had bullied her so severely that Mona had gone to her room and tried to hang herself from the ceiling fixture. If Sofia hadn't noticed she was missing, she would have died. She and Sofia had never been close, but now she was ashamed at how Mona had been mistreated in the cult. Elvira's mother had become the constant scapegoat, picked on by everyone.

When she came back to the living room, Elvira was staring out the window, her gaze empty and indifferent. Sofia put down the mugs of coffee and took a seat next to her on the sofa.

'Tell me everything.'

So Elvira did. She had started school and was living with her aunt in Lund. She hadn't heard from her parents since the trial, but that was only to be expected. But then, on the day after Christmas, Anders had called their home phone and asked to speak to Elvira's aunt. Elvira had recognized his voice right away and said her aunt wasn't home, so he had shared the news with her. Mona had hanged herself in her room on Christmas Day. She had died almost immediately and couldn't be resuscitated.

'You mean they're back at the manor? At ViaTerra?' Sofia asked.

'You seriously don't have a clue, do you? They've been there for months. I know because they sent me all my things. And Dad told my aunt – that they were back on the island, I mean. Although nowadays Dad has broken off contact with my aunt too. Just because I'm living with her.'

Sofia suddenly got a bitter and metallic taste in her mouth, that sick feeling that was linked to all the injustices at ViaTerra.

'But then what happened? What did Anders say?'

'At first I couldn't even talk, I was so upset. But then I asked about the funeral and all that. And Dad said that my presence was not requested. My own fucking dad. Can you believe it? He said Mom's funeral would be held at the manor and the guard wouldn't let me in.'

'Jesus, Elvira, that's terrible. I don't know what to say.'

'Help me get back at them, that's all I want.'

'But they can't bury her there, on the property, can they?'

'They're going to have some sort of gross ceremony and then send the body to the mainland to be cremated.'

'Is that all?'

'Isn't that enough?'

Sofia aimed a meaningful gaze at Elvira's stomach.

'Oh, that. Yeah, that's another little problem. I don't know how I'm supposed to finish school and become a mum at the same time.' Her eyes brimmed with tears, but she was biting her lip firmly to keep them from falling.

Sofia drew in what felt like an endless breath. She really didn't want to get involved in this mess, but the injustice of it all was whining in her head like a chainsaw. Was it even legal? Can you forbid a child from attending their mother's funeral?

'Does he even know about this? The baby, I mean,' she wondered.

And then something remarkable happened. Elvira began to laugh. It started as a tiny chuckle but grew into a shrill peal of laughter that forced her double over her huge belly. The tears began to flow. She made several attempts to form words, but just cracked up again. And then Sofia began to laugh as well.

'So, *does* he know anything about the baby?' she finally managed to say.

'It's two. Two kids!'

'What? Twins?'

'Yeah. Boys.'

'Jesus Christ. What are you going to do, Elvira?'

'Give them up for adoption, I think. I'm not even fifteen. I don't have my own place. My life is going to go to shit if I keep them.'

'What does your aunt say?'

'She says I can do whatever I want. But she did say she won't be taking care of any babies, that's for sure. So what else can I do?'

'But couldn't you have… when did you find out?'

'I couldn't. It seemed wrong. I suppose it's my religious upbringing, I've probably been brainwashed or something.

I went to a clinic, but when they were about to start… I started screaming like an idiot.'

'So, does he know?'

Elvira shook her head.

'I think you have to tell him.'

'Not before I've made his life into its own little hell. Right now he's in prison, and I'm sure he's got it made there. I want to do something. That's why I came to you.'

'What do you want to do?'

'I don't know, Sofia. I just don't get how this can be my fault. He ruined my whole life, and no one cares.'

'I care.'

Sofia stood up, the gears in her mind turning full-speed. Warning bells were going off, but it didn't matter. There was no justice to be found for a defector like Elvira. The only way to deal with this sort of thing was by taking matters into your own hands.

'I know what we can do. It's an idea I had before I escaped, actually. We'll start a blog. We'll call it "At the Mercy of the Cult" or something along those lines. No, even better: "Cult Kid", because you were just a kid when everything happened. And we'll write your story and spread it everywhere. We'll get a Facebook page, and contact the media, and…'

Elvira laughed.

'That sounds awesome. I knew you would help me.'

'I know someone who might be of use. I'll get in touch with him tonight and call you tomorrow.'

Elvira left the apartment soon thereafter. Some colour had returned to her cheeks and her eyes were clearer. It had started to snow, and Sofia watched from the window as she wandered down the street. Snowflakes hung about her head like a halo. Her figure slowly receded into the darkness beyond the reach of the streetlights.

Sofia took her phone from her pocket and sent a text to Ellis. Then she called Benjamin to tell him everything: about Elvira, the babies, and Monica's suicide. The resurrection of the cult. They spoke until Benjamin's voice grew sleepy, and she realized he wanted to go to bed. Then she thought of Simon, out there on the island. It was eleven p.m., too late to call. At first she thought she would send an email, but he always took forever to respond to those, so she sent a text instead, although she wondered if he even knew how to text. Hers was short: *Elvira's pregnant. Oswald's. Mona hanged herself. VT is back at the manor. Call when you wake up.*

The response was almost immediate.

There are some things I need to tell you. Can we meet up?

Her curiosity was piqued.

Can't you send an email?

This time the response *was* immediate. Apparently Simon did know how to text, and fast.

Better to tell you in person.

Her heart leapt; she really did want to see him again.

I'd love to, but I'm not setting foot on that %€#& island ever again.

This time it took a moment, but at last her phone dinged.

Then I'll come visit you.

And that's how Simon popped back up in her life again.

8

Simon awoke to the sun streaming through the window. He tried to hold onto the slippery fragments of a pleasant dream where everything in the garden was growing and thriving, but he saw the ring of frost around the windowpane and realized with a heavy heart that it was still winter.

His phone dinged and he knew immediately that he'd received an email from Sofia, but decided to get through the workday before reading it. He always enjoyed hearing from Sofia, but she was unpredictable: her messages demanded his undivided attention, and right now he just wanted to get to work.

But after a few hours he found he was too curious, so he opened his phone and found the email, which contained only a link. Once he'd opened it he gasped; the image was so shocking. There was Elvira, totally nude, her arms crossed to hide her breasts. Her belly was exposed, and it was enormous. A long tendril of her loose hair coiled down to her navel. The rest was a golden wave down her back. Her eyes were made up to look huge; her lips were parted and her front teeth rested on her lower lip. *Cult Kid,* read the title.

Simon typically didn't surf the internet during his working hours, but now he sat down on an overturned bucket to read the blog. It was Elvira's story in grisly detail. It was especially unpleasant to read the description of what Oswald had done to her in the attic, forcing her to have sex while choking her; he had nearly strangled her.

There was a childish tone to the text and it had obviously been written by Elvira herself – there were a number of spelling errors and curse words. But that only made it better. More real. There were already several comments on the entry.

An anxious, crawling sensation filled his belly, and he realized he was sweating even though it was rather chilly in the greenhouse. *This is going to be big,* he thought, with a hunch that the blog was a bomb soon to explode. He didn't know if this was a good or bad thing, but he knew one thing for sure: the truth was out, and Franz Oswald would certainly not give it his stamp of approval. He fervently hoped that Sofia and Elvira knew what they were getting into.

★

The trip to Lund went more smoothly than he'd expected, even though he disliked travel. Strangers, unpleasant odours and sounds. His parents had never taken him on trips; they couldn't leave the animals alone on the farm. But he wanted to see Sofia, and of course there were things he needed to tell her. When he reached Central Station in Gothenburg he stopped at Pressbyrån to buy a newspaper, and right away he noticed the headlines on the posted billboards.

STRANGLED AND RAPED BY THE CULT LEADER

Fourteen-year-old Tells All

SHE WAS FRANZ OSWALD'S SEX SLAVE
Now Forced to Bear His Children

MARKED FOR LIFE BY THE CULT
Fourteen-year-old Speaks Out

Only the more sensational evening papers had the story on the front page, but Simon even found an article about Elvira in *Göteborgs-Posten*. The papers had used the image from the blog, with those huge, innocent eyes gazing into the camera.

Simon sat on a bench at the station and tore at his hair. Good or bad? He couldn't decide. But he was glad Oswald would have something to worry about in prison. And in some ways he was relieved, because what he was going to tell Sofia was nothing compared to this.

She met him at the station. She had grown out her hair; it reached her waist. There was no makeup on her face and she was wearing an anorak with a huge fur collar and jeans with big holes at the knees. In the middle of winter. Her cheeks were rosy red and he wondered if it was from the cold or because she was glad to see him again.

'Come on, let's go eat, you must be hungry.' He always was. She knew that.

'Quite the commotion you two have caused,' he said once they were seated at the restaurant.

'About time, wasn't it?'

He let her speak first. Her mouth moved nonstop. They'd already had over one hundred thousand hits on their site; others had written to them to tell their own stories. Elvira had already been booked on a talk show on TV, and there would be more offers down the line.

It'll go on like this for a few months, while she's got that big belly, Simon thought. *And then I'm sure there'll be a heck of a fuss when the babies come. But what will she do after that?* He wondered how long a person could live that way.

Sofia realized she'd lost him in the middle of a sentence.

'Are you listening?'

'Of course. It's just a lot to take in. Is she going to give the babies up for adoption?'

'She still hasn't decided. But how could she keep them? Don't you imagine they'd just be a constant reminder of him?'

'I don't think that's how kids work. I guess they're just themselves when they come out.'

Sofia nodded. She took Simon's hand on top of the table. 'It's so great to see you again.'

'Same to you. I'm glad you two did this. And I hope Oswald reads the blog.'

'There was something you wanted to tell me?'

'Yes, is Benjamin coming? Because if he is, I'll tell you both.'

'No, not this weekend. It's just you and me.'

So he couldn't put it off any longer. He told her everything he knew about the cult's return to the manor: who was there, when they gathered, all about the gate and the lock. Her expression didn't change as he spoke. She just nodded now and then, squinting as if she were trying to transform his words into images.

'Well, that's terrific!' she said when she was done. 'Well done, changing the lock. You should have emailed me. That's the kind of news I like to hear. And Elvira told me they're back on the island, so I knew that part already.'

'And then there's this.'

He pulled a piece of paper from his pocket, unfolded it, and placed it on the table in front of her. As she read it, he watched her face; he noticed that she was startled when she read the very last line. She rested her finger on it and looked up at him.

'What do you think this means?'

'Not sure. It could mean anything from that they're going to send you your stuff, to that they're planning to kill you.'

He immediately regretted those last words.

'Someone from the police sent my stuff. Ages ago. I asked them to, because I didn't want to go there again.'

'Oh, so that's not it then.'

Simon thought she looked lovely as she sat there trying to figure out what the bullet point meant. She stared at nothing as if in a trance, her features soft and smooth. Sofia had always been apt to zone out while they were talking. One second she was there; the next she was swept away in her thoughts. He understood why men were drawn to her, why Oswald had become fixated on her. There was so much life in Sofia, in her eyes, her body, and even out to the ends of her unruly hair. Yet she was capable of looking so calm when she was pondering something. She was like the fog out on the island. Encircling everything with her attention, then setting it free in a split second when she was done thinking.

'Simon, what the heck do they mean by this?'

'Maybe it doesn't mean anything,' he said. 'You know how it was there. One disaster after the next. They've had more than six months to come after you. But nothing has happened, right?'

'No, but now we've got the blog...' Her gaze turned inward again.

'Simon, you were always so good at ferreting things out. "Think like him," you used to say about Oswald. What do you think he's really up to these days?'

Simon thought about the blog and then about Oswald, and it made him shudder.

'To be honest, I think he's royally pissed off. He's already being hung out to dry by the media, and then that's how he finds out he's going to be a father. You know what, I bet his mind is elsewhere for the moment, not on you. Although if you two keep blogging, of course, you'll have to be prepared to accept the consequences.'

*

The day ended up even better than Simon had imagined. The skies had begun to clear, and all of Gothenburg glowed with the fantastic sharpness a ray of sunlight brings on an overcast day. They strolled around the city for hours. Sofia took him to the cathedral, which was so majestic it gave Simon the shivers. At last she had to drag him away, because he'd found himself captivated by the medieval astronomical clock near the entrance and couldn't tear himself away. He read and reread the sign that explained how the clock worked, drinking in the details: how you could see the phases of the moon, the position of the sun relative to the horizon, the knight that showed the time, and the calendar that extended all the way to the year 2123.

'What will happen then, after 2123?' he asked Sofia.

'How should I know? We'll be dead by then anyway. Come on, let's go.'

They wandered around the campus of the university, where

Sofia showed him the library where she worked and told him that they lent out over half a million books per year. They sat on a park bench in Lundagård as the sun set and Sofia got him to tell her everything he'd seen at the manor. She made him repeat some parts of his tale several times. In the end they agreed that the new group was nothing but a big joke. A bunch of failures who couldn't even come close to posing any sort of threat.

Sofia made dinner for him back at her little place. He slept on her sofa that night and took the train home the next morning. Before he left, he promised Sofia he would keep an eye on ViaTerra and be in contact with her at least once a week.

As he sank into his seat on the train and gazed out at the bare winter landscape, he decided it really wasn't so terrible to take a little trip now and then.

9

It was sheer coincidence that Anna-Maria noticed the article in the paper. A client had left a copy of *Expressen* in her waiting room. She immediately recognized Elvira's face on the front page.

A shiver ran down her spine as she slowly picked up the paper from the coffee table and unfolded it. The headline made her feel so sick that she had to grab the wall for support.

SHE WAS FRANZ OSWALD'S SEX SLAVE
Now Forced to Bear His Children

As she read, the rest of the world was made fuzzy by her increasing dizziness. It wasn't so much the fact that that vapid little girl was knocked up, it was the blog. That there was a blog Anna-Maria didn't know about, even though it had been live for days. One of her agreements with Oswald was that she would keep track of what the media was saying about him. She'd made a huge blunder, and could only hope he hadn't read the paper. But she was all too familiar with his routines – there was no way he didn't know. The vibes of his rage made it all the way from Skogome to her office.

All at once she knew this couldn't wait. Anything could

happen. He must be absolutely furious – what if he fired her and decided to find another attorney? Her fears attacked her like tiny demons, until she was so worked up that she was pacing the floor in desperation. It was just her luck that this would happen! Everything had been going so well. Oswald's plan was proceeding smoothly and she had started to bring about some order with the dummies at ViaTerra.

Franz had even hinted at a more intimate relationship in the future. Several times. And now this…

She looked at her watch; it was seven-thirty, so visiting hours were long over. She told herself it couldn't be helped, and dialled the number of Skogome. Helga McLean picked up. Anna-Maria steeled herself for the confrontation it would take to make an exception to visiting time, but it turned out to be unnecessary.

'I think it would be best if you came in,' McLean said as soon as Anna-Maria had introduced herself. 'Your client isn't doing very well right now. He's in observation.'

'What? He's not a suicide risk, is he?'

'No, not at all. Just furious. Truly furious. He was shouting and threatening us and disrupting everything, so we had to isolate him. And I'm sure you already know what the issue is.'

'Elvira Asplund.'

'Exactly. He's demanding to see her. Immediately. And you know our rules – it's out of the question.'

'I'll be there right away. How long will you be keeping him under observation?'

'Until you get here.'

★

All the way to Skogome, she heard a voice in her head. It was her own voice of reason, speaking to her, just as it had sounded in the courtroom. Now it was laying out a plan: *Just stand there and take it until his rage ebbs out. It always does eventually. Then you can present your arguments without his talking back.* But then the voice began to mock her and she decided she was not about to accept any more of his relentless criticism. She sure as heck wasn't the one behind bars. Time to smarten up and take control of the situation.

Once she'd made it through all the gates and doors and spotted him behind the glass wall that surrounded the observation unit, it struck her that he looked far too calm. He was bent forward, his elbows on his knees and his head resting in clasped hands. Only his slightly mussed hair let on that there had been some sort of turmoil. She caught a glimpse of her own face in the glass and thought she looked tired and grumpy, but imagined that couldn't be true.

'Go to visiting room seven, and I'll bring him in,' said the guard.

She tried to slow her breathing as she waited, and she cast her eyes downward as Oswald was led in. The guard closed the door and left them alone. Oswald didn't take a seat, electing instead to lean against the wall.

'I want to see Elvira,' he said right away.

'Franz, you know that's not possible. Of course I can try, but…'

'Then I want to see her dad,' he cut her off. 'Anders.'

His lack of resistance was surprising and gave her a moment of respite.

'I can probably make that happen. He's still at ViaTerra, isn't he?'

'Right.'

'If you're worried about the babies, I can…'

He barked a short, hoarse laugh.

'The babies? Are you really that stupid? Do you think this is about them? How would it look if the greatest spiritual leader in Sweden abandoned his children? It's a matter of PR. Come on. I thought we had the same end goal in sight here.'

'Yes, we do,' she hurried to say. 'Of course I will straighten this out.'

'And I want sole custody of the babies. It's my own business why.'

'Okay, I understand. I can help with all of that, I promise.' She hadn't quite dropped the placating tone in her voice. He still hadn't mentioned the blog.

He reached out a hand and pulled over her notepad, then took the pen from her hand. After scribbling a few digits on the paper, he handed it back.

'Call this number. Tell him hello from me. He'll deal with that blog and a few other things. All you will do is thank him and accept his help, understood? I'm depending on you, Annie. You know that.'

He was the only one who called her Annie. It was a miracle. He wasn't angry with her anymore.

His words swirled in her mind and set off a rush of joy. *I'm depending on you, Annie.*

'Thank you, Franz. Is there anything else you need?'

'No, you go take care of all this and I'll put on my very best smile and convince the guard I've calmed down.' He waved his hand dismissively.

She was afraid the magic spell would break. That this tiny,

intimate moment would transform into a fresh burst of rage. She hurried away, and when she closed the door she took a big, greedy breath of relief. The cruel little devil did a backflip in her heart.

It was going to be okay. Everything would work itself out.

10

The first sign of a problem was when the blog disappeared. It was the second week of February. As Sofia was walking home from work, through the park, she realized it was brighter out. The air felt milder. Contrails from jets drew lines across the pale sky. A few big clouds had parked themselves in the distance, their undersides painted deep pink.

Her life was moving forward; she was kept very busy at the library and had her hands full with the blog once she got home each evening. They'd had over three million visitors and received so many comments each day that they couldn't read them all. Elvira had been a guest on nearly every talk show, visiting each program with her big belly, looking divinely beautiful. No one could doubt that she was telling the truth. Now and then the thought entered Sofia's mind that it was strange Oswald hadn't responded. He'd had a whole month by now. But nothing had happened.

*

Elvira was waiting for her in the stairwell. Panting, she trudged up the stairs to the apartment.

'I don't know if I can manage another month,' she said. 'I can hardly breathe, and these little jerks are kicking me to pieces. All I want to do is sleep, and I've been eating like a horse.'

'Well, it will be over soon. Have you decided what to do yet?'

Elvira didn't respond.

'Shall we work on the blog for a bit, and then you can go home and sleep?'

'Yes, but you'll have to write the entries, my spelling's not so good.'

Sofia sat down at the computer and logged in. She searched for the blog among her favourites, but when she clicked on it, it was gone. *That's weird,* she thought, wondering if Ellis might have taken it down for maintenance, or whether it had become such a big hit it exceeded its allotted gigabytes. She decided to check in with him.

'What's wrong?' Elvira asked from the sofa.

'The blog's gone. Bizarre. But I'm sure Ellis is just up to something. Don't worry. I'll call him.'

Elvira stretched out on the sofa. Her eyelids fluttered; she was dozing off. Sofia went to the kitchenette and made a cup of strong coffee, but by the time she got back Elvira was asleep. Sofia called Ellis from her mobile. He hadn't touched the blog and was as baffled as she was.

'Someone must have hacked into it and taken it down. Those bastards!' he said.

'Can you find out who did it?'

'I'll try. Call you back soon.'

As Sofia waited, she searched YouTube for clips from Elvira's interviews. But she found only messages from YouTube stating that they had been forced to remove them.

All at once she knew something was wrong. It was just a feeling, but it was so strong she felt her dinner turning in her stomach.

Ellis called not long after.

'Someone hacked into the blog and erased it. I can probably get it back up today.'

'Can you tell who did it?'

'That might be a tall order, but I'm sure I can figure out where they were.'

Sofia told him about the YouTube clips.

'Then someone pressured them to take them down. We can find out who it was if we contact YouTube. And listen, there's something else you should see. I sent you a link.'

The link led to another blog. It seemed to imitate their blog, but in this case downturned lips had been drawn over Elvira's mouth and there were horns on her head. The name *Cult Kid* remained, but it had a subtitle: *The Truth About Elvira*. Probably so that anyone who googled Elvira's blog would encounter this one instead. The text was a lengthy rant that described Elvira as a gold-digger who had done her utmost to ensnare Franz Oswald. The language was so vulgar that the text was entirely repellent. There were tabs, too, showing every non-disclosure agreement Elvira had signed as well as short entries from the staff at ViaTerra about how awful she was. Sofia imagined that no one in their right mind would ever believe this. Yet her eyes stung as she scanned the words. People would read this. Maybe they wouldn't believe everything, but it would change the way they looked at Elvira in one way or another.

She went over and gazed at Elvira, who was asleep on the sofa with her mouth agape. She was snoring gently and having a dream; her eyes flicked back and forth under their lids. All of a sudden, Sofia was flooded with an immense wave of affection. Elvira was in no shape to fight a battle against Franz Oswald. She had to take care of herself and the babies. Maybe it would be best to shelve the blog, turn their backs on the whole mess, and devote themselves to real life.

Her phone rang; it was Ellis.

'Okay, so whoever demanded the clips be taken down was on West Fog Island. I think that's all we need to know.'

Sofia realized she had no reply. All of her attention had gotten stuck somewhere between her brain and her phone. An increasing dizziness was pressing at the back of her head.

'Hello? Are you there? Do you still want me to publish the blog again?'

She forced her attention back to their conversation. 'Yeah, but I want you to do me a favour.'

'Anything.'

'Write a comment under the picture of Elvira. Say that she's taking a break from blogging right now – I guess we can call it maternity leave. And then write that her friend Sofia Bauman will take over the blog for a while. That I'll respond to questions and all that, as time allows.'

'Are you sure you want your name on it?'

'Absolutely.'

'Okay. One more thing, Sofia.'

'What?'

'Do you remember the night I went out to Fog Island and stood outside the wall to demand they let you go?'

'How could I forget?'

It had happened when Sofia had started working on the staff

at ViaTerra. Ellis had taken the boat to the island one night, drunk as a skunk, to stand there shouting from the other side of the wall, ordering them to let Sofia out. It had been beyond embarrassing.

'Well, I was right.'

'Oh, lay off. And those blog entries with my face photoshopped onto naked bodies were so nice. No, you're not getting off that easy. You'll be indebted to me for the rest of your life.'

Ellis laughed. Sofia thought it was strange how life could change people and mould them into new creations. One day, your worst enemy could become your lifeline.

Elvira had woken up and was moaning from the sofa. 'What's going on?'

Sofia walked over to sit beside her. Elvira's forehead was sweaty; her legs were swollen and the veins on her calves had burst here and there. Only fifteen, and looking like that. When she should be going to school, meeting boys, and thinking about her future.

'They've taken down your blog and put up another one, and it's disgusting – I really don't think you should read it. Ellis is fixing it right now.'

'I figured as much. That they would attack me, I mean. I don't want to read that crap. I just want to be left alone, get these babies out of me, and have some sort of life.'

'I know.'

'I have to go home and get ready for that TV interview tomorrow. It's the last one. I can't take any more.'

'Okay, do you want me to walk you home?'

'Why? Do you think they're going to come after me? Attack a pregnant woman? Yeah, actually, that wouldn't surprise me.'

'No, that's not what I meant. I just thought I could keep you company. It's dark out.'

'Nah, I'll be fine. Although there's something I have to tell you before I go.'

Elvira flushed and her eyes darted away from Sofia's.

'Dad called me yesterday.'

'What? Are you joking?'

'No. He said Franz wants me to come to Fog Island with the babies. That they'll build me a little house on the property, and give me half a million kronor a year. A nanny and everything. Private tutoring so I can finish school. I don't have to have anything to do with Franz if I don't want to. He just wants custody of the babies. Dad said Franz isn't interested in anything sexual, since pregnancy changes your body so much. Perfect little girl bodies, you know. That's what Franz gets off on.'

Sofia felt like the floor was dissolving beneath her feet. Her mouth went dry and her heart shrank in her chest. Elvira began to cry; the silent tears ran down her cheeks in a steady stream.

'For Christ's sake, Elvira. You cannot accept this!'

'No, you can say that again. Dad said there are certain conditions. The most important one being that I have to break off all contact with you and Benjamin.'

Elvira backed up against the entryway wall and slid down until she was sitting on the floor. She clapped her hands to her belly and swayed back and forth as if she were rocking her unborn children. In a split second she had grown so pale that the dark circles under her eyes stood out. Tears dripped onto her stomach.

Sofia leaned against the wall to steady her body, still overwhelmed by what Elvira had told her. She stared at the girl's belly with an increasing sense of hopelessness. What was the point of all this?

'Elvira, you absolutely cannot go back there.'

'You think everything's so simple,' Elvira sobbed. 'But I have no life. No fucking future. Everything is ruined.'

'He raped you!'

'That's not exactly what happened. At first I was into it, but then it all went to hell.'

'You were only fourteen!' Sofia felt her desperation growing. The buzz in her ears that meant she was about to lose control. 'You can stay here. I'll help you take care of the babies. Just as long as you don't go back.'

Elvira stood up, leaned over her belly, and hugged Sofia so hard she almost couldn't breathe.

'You're so nice. ViaTerra is the last place on earth I want to go. As I'm sure you understand. But maybe I can come back here once the babies are born. That way he'll have his kids and I'll get my life back.'

'He would never let you.'

'You don't know that. Please, I have to think about this for a while, on my own.'

'Of course. You have to make up your own mind.'

Sofia helped her put on her jacket and boots, then watched her go as she half-staggered, half-trudged back toward downtown. She looked like a perfectly normal girl. There wasn't a soul on the street besides Elvira, who weaved in and out of the shadows of trees along the way. The streetlights turned her long hair blue.

It was the last Sofia would see of Elvira for a very long time.

11

That night, Sofia dreamed about Franz Oswald again, but in this dream he touched her tenderly, as he had done at first. Massaging her shoulders and back.

She woke up feeling slightly horny and very ashamed. She had never forgiven herself for being drawn to him, and it disgusted her to think of how susceptible to his flirting she'd been at first. But then she decided that Oswald must be hanging around in her mind because she'd never understood how he turned out the way he did. A family history had been written about his relatives, and she'd searched for it while she worked for the cult. But it was in Oswald's hands now, so she would probably never find out.

With a deep sigh, she got out of bed. It struck her that she hadn't seen Elvira in three days, and just then she caught sight of a note on the doormat. A small, crumpled piece of paper that had been tossed through the mail slot. She picked it up and recognized Elvira's sprawling penmanship right away. It seemed she'd scribbled down the message as fast as she could.

Sorry, have to think of the babies.

That was all. Not even a signature. But Sofia knew exactly what those words meant. She had guessed as much while she watched Elvira walk down the road in the dark.

All at once, she felt bitter and betrayed. Her thoughts wandered to Simon; she wanted to talk to someone about this right away. He was probably out working, but maybe she could send a quick email before she left her apartment.

It took a lot of effort to focus on her job that day. Elvira's betrayal still stung, making tears burn her eyes. Then there was the thought that Oswald had gotten his claws into the innocent children, and the irritating knowledge that he'd won some sort of victory.

*

When she returned home that night, a plastic bag was hanging from the handle of her apartment door. She peered into it, but at first she couldn't tell what was inside. Resisting the urge to stick her hand inside, she instead dumped its contents onto the hallway floor. Her scream echoed off the walls. It was a toad. Flattened, dead as a doornail. She used the plastic bag as a glove to pick it up, then went out the building's front door and tossed it into the bushes, thoroughly disgusted. Assuming one of the neighbourhood kids must have been behind it, she went back to her apartment to wash her hands.

She sat down at the computer and logged in to see if she'd received a response from Simon. An email from an unnamed sender popped up – an order confirmation, five hundred kronor spent on something she'd never ordered. The items weren't listed; it just said 'adult contents'. She figured it was spam and opened the next email. This one was from Simon. He had written 'Is this you?' in response to an email from her account that was nothing but foul language. The fact that he could even think she would write that was offensive. Someone had hacked her account.

She opened the folder of sent messages and her suspicions were confirmed. Several obscene emails had been sent to her friends and acquaintances. She quickly logged into her bank account and found that five hundred kronor had been debited, the money that had been used to order those 'adult contents', apparently from a company in Great Britain.

The urgency of the situation made her hands tremble. She dialled the wrong number more than once before she managed to get hold of the bank and ask them to freeze her account. Then she sent an apology to everyone who had received the obscene message, including her parents and Edith Bergman, her boss at the library. She shuddered to think of what her boss would think when she read those terrible words. That done, she opened a new email account with a different password and sent the address to all her contacts. At last she sank onto the sofa, feeling absolutely drained and almost faint.

Something wasn't right. If someone had gone to the trouble of hacking her bank account to steal her money, they never would have settled for just five hundred kronor. And that toad on the door. This was about something else. And she had only one enemy in the whole world.

The certainty that a living hell was about to engulf her found her guts and squeezed. Her eyes went to the window; she thought she saw a figure there. She lived on the ground floor, which was nice in a building with no elevator, but now she realized that anyone could watch her from outside.

She went over to the window, but there was no one there. What was going on? Why did they want to come after her now, after more than six months? They'd got Elvira back, so what more did they want? But then, Sofia herself was primarily responsible for the blog.

The emails left a bitter aftertaste. They had been written for the sole purpose of causing offence. Whoever had written them wasn't smart; in fact, they were probably so dense they would stop at nothing. Her mind went to Benny and Sten, the guards at ViaTerra.

Just when she'd managed to get her heart rate back down, the jangle of her doorbell startled her. She peered through the peephole and saw her neighbour, a woman in her eighties who always gave her a friendly smile when they passed each other on the stairs. But now she didn't look friendly at all. She looked furious.

Sofia opened the door.

'This isn't funny,' Alma said, holding a box up right before Sofia's nose.

'I'm sorry, I don't understand…'

'Don't play dumb.'

Sofia looked into the box and saw a large, realistic dildo resting on a bed of tissue paper. The woman took a card from the box and handed it to Sofia.

From Sofia in number one, for those lonely nights.

Her stomach knotted and bile rose into her mouth like the prelude to a sudden case of stomach flu.

'Oh my god! This is all a misunderstanding, my bank account was hacked…'

But the woman didn't seem to understand what a hacked bank account meant. She threw the box at Sofia's feet, did an about-face, and limped back to her apartment. Sofia felt so ashamed her cheeks burned. She barely managed to run over and stick a foot into the doorway; she couldn't stand the thought that the woman might think she had done something so heinous. The tears began to flow and she felt stupid and humiliated. Sobbing, she explained to Alma that she was being harassed by a cult. That she would never send such terrible items to someone. She begged for forgiveness again and again.

In the end Alma invited her in for coffee, fascinated by Sofia's story, and promised to keep an eye out for shady types in the area. And as they shared coffee in the cosy kitchen, Sofia began to feel a little bit better.

But her anguish returned when she got back to her own apartment. The sky outside the window had lost its colour and plunged the room into a gloomy half-darkness. It was so quiet that the fridge sounded like a highway cutting through the apartment. She called Benjamin, who became furious, cursing Oswald and saying he would jump in the car and come down right away. But Sofia assured him she would be okay until he got there on Friday, as usual.

All I can do is find the silver lining, she thought. *Now I'm friends with my neighbour and I have a new email account, so I won't get spam. They'll never break me.*

Yet the apartment felt lonely and too quiet.

She tried to call Wilma, who'd been hired by a fashion magazine in Stockholm, but she only got her voicemail. This was the first time since leaving the cult that she'd felt so alone. She hadn't had a choice about spending most of her time with other people at ViaTerra, so these days she usually enjoyed being by herself. But now the solitude made her consider moving in with Benjamin. Although she didn't feel prepared to allow his aimless ways back in her life again. She imagined what it would be like to have his clothes scattered all over the floor, the doors to every cabinet left wide open, and his snores accompanying her sleep at night.

She decided to email Simon, write the fear away, relieve the pressure. She wrote about the harassment and suggested they talk the next day, then realized it was past midnight; she put on her pyjamas and brushed her teeth as she stared into her own frightened eyes in the mirror above the sink. Feeling how exhausted she was, she went to the apartment door and made sure it was locked, then turned out all the lights but one lamp in the living room.

Not until she was under the covers did it all sink it. It had happened so fast. A typical day at work. Life had felt perfectly normal until she saw that plastic bag on the door. *This is insane,* she thought. *Who sends a dildo to an eighty-year-old woman? What kind of people am I dealing with?* An icy chill spread through her nerves. The certainty that this sort of individual had no limits was the worst part of all. The dildo in its box flashed into her mind. Shit! It was still outside her door. What if someone else in the building saw it? She threw on her robe and went out to pick up the box, which she carried to the trash receptacle behind the building. It was painfully cold out, and even though it was still winter, there was a rumble of thunder in the distance. The hair rose on the back of her neck and she turned around, but there was no one there.

As soon as she opened the trash receptacle, she saw the garbage bag she'd tossed in on her way to work that morning. There was a large slit in the bag, as if had been given a C-section. Someone had gone through her trash. The remains of yesterday's noodles had slithered through the hole, along with an empty tampon box. A sudden wave of nausea welled up inside her and she doubled over. The sight was so repulsive and private that she was forced to grab the receptacle and throw up into the flowerbed.

12

Anna-Maria disliked their intermediary from the start: the way he looked at her, as if she were an object; the way he made her wait in the stairwell and never invited her into his apartment; the arrogant tilt of his head. *She* was Oswald's right-hand man, but this guy was treating her like a messenger.

His attitude rekindled the jealousy that was always smouldering inside her. It made her wonder whether Franz had been talking about her behind her back and why this idiot hadn't introduced himself. He must have a name, damn it! No, he just stood there in his flip-flops and ratty jeans, yawning hugely and looking as if he'd just dragged himself out of bed, all mussed hair and blank gaze. Her rage at Franz's choice of this loser as their intermediary was eating Anna-Maria up from the inside.

And then there were the envelopes Oswald sent him. So carefully sealed, every time. Not even a name on the front, just the address of the apartment. Once she had taken a detour to her own apartment to hold the envelope under a bright light, but she still couldn't make out any letters. She could only tell it was Franz's handwriting on the page.

Now she was sitting on the balcony and trying to figure out how to make Franz get rid of this loser. Now and then, a thought niggled at her: *What is happening to me? What is the point of falling in love if it's going to hurt this much?*

The day's last bit of pale glow was dissolving on the horizon. It smelled like rain. She took a deep breath and soaked up the fresh air until her ruminations swallowed her up again. She was so caught up in her spiralling thoughts that she lost track of time.

She realized too late that she should already be on her way to Skogome. She made it through the car ride there in a fog of anguish, fully aware that Oswald would be furious that she was late. She convinced herself that everything would get better eventually. When he got out of prison. After all, prison would be stressful for anyone. She began to imagine the future, picturing herself hanging casually on his arm at gatherings and parties in the limelight. Wedding photos in women's magazines, their noses nudging each other all lovingly.

But her fantasies were no cure for her anxiety, so she tried to come up with a believable lie to explain her tardiness. There had been a lot of Google activity surrounding Sofia Bauman in the past week. Nothing concrete, but still.

*

Her heart in her throat, she arrived at the central security station. A male guard was on duty – young, a little absent-minded – and Anna-Maria felt a rush of relief. More and more often, it seemed McLean's eyes saw right through her. The guard raised his hand towards her while he finished a phone call.

'Franz Oswald is no longer in the visitors' room,' he said then. 'He asked to return to his studies after waiting for you for fifteen minutes.'

'Damn, I really have to talk to him today.'

'We can ask, but it's not as if we can force him to see you.'

'No, I understand. But tell him I had to take care of something regarding his case,' she lied. 'And that I have some information he'll find interesting.'

The guard sighed in resignation.

'Okay, but it would be best if you're on time next visit. Visiting hours are almost over by now.'

He turned around to make a call.

'He'll be there in a minute.'

Oswald made her wait fifteen minutes. When the guard escorted her into the visitors' room, he was sitting there with a cruel gleam in his eye.

'What did you want?'

'I'm sorry to make you wait, but Sofia Bauman's name popped up in my Google alerts. I thought it would be best to read it all before I came.'

'I see. Anything concrete?'

'No, not yet. Just posts on Facebook and that sort of thing. She was writing about Elvira. How it sucks that she's back at ViaTerra.'

'Did she mention me by name?'

'Excuse me?'

'You heard me. Did she mention me? My name, Franz-Fucking-Oswald?'

'I mean, I don't recall exactly. But I think so. Or, maybe not directly, but she implied…'

'Shut up.'

'Excuse me?'

'Stop waffling. Do you think I can't tell you're lying?'

He ran his fingers through his hair in the unconscious, recurring gesture she knew so well. But now she realized, for the first time, that this particular gesture meant he was ramping up to a burst of rage. His jaw clenched. His eyes went dark and that wrinkle appeared between his eyebrows.

'You don't have this under control in the least. What kind of hourly fee am I paying you, again? For you to sit there and lie to me? This is fucking absurd.'

His voice was vicious and shrill. When he got this way, he would twist everything she said and turn it against her. Best to keep quiet until he calmed down.

'I want to know every move she makes. Everything. Understood? Every comment. Every silly little picture she posts. Every goddamn smiley she uses. The whole fucking nine yards.'

For a brief moment, Anna-Maria's mind went fully quiet. Oswald's mouth was moving, but it turned into a silent hole. It felt like someone was squeezing her ribcage hard. She heard herself breathing through her nose; she could feel her heart beating, softly, steadily. The pressure around her chest let go, but it left a mild dizziness behind. She had to lean against the wall when her legs could no longer bear her weight. She was only vaguely aware of the room around her. Oswald's voice had begun to hum again, in the distance. As she stood there she was filled with a horrible sensation, a mixture of clarity and fear. This was something she'd suspected all along, but the thought had never come to complete fruition in her brain. Now she understood Oswald's relationship with Sofia Bauman in a whole new light. This wasn't about revenge. Or PR. Or even the good name of ViaTerra. This was personal. A frantic obsession that could not be swayed, much less stopped.

'Did you hear what I said?' he shouted.

'Yes, every word. I understand. You'll get all the information, I promise.'

'Good, because I'm tired of your lies and your incompetence. Now I'm going to show you what I have to tolerate while you don't give a single shit about how things are going for me.'

She was about to protest, but he put up one hand to stop her. He stuck the other hand into his trouser pocket and took out an object wrapped in toilet paper. He held the small bundle in one palm and unwrapped the paper before her eyes. She recoiled and the dizziness returned; for an instant she thought she was staring at an amputated finger. She tried to make out the details of the object – it was like a bloody tendon with white specks.

'What is that?'

'*Isterband*. Lard sausage, this is the kind of thing I'm forced to eat while you wreck my life and fritter away my money. I think you should take it home and eat it up. Then maybe you'll understand how serious this is.'

Anna-Maria swallowed hard as crushing hopelessness washed over her.

13

Despite his promise to Sofia, Simon didn't go to ViaTerra every week. He didn't like the feeling of sneaking around the manor like a common thief or a spy. It made him feel silly. But he did take daily walks and always gazed up at the façade of the manor house when he walked by on the road.

Life at the pension was busy. They had three greenhouses now, and he was preparing the spring outdoor plantings. A well-known gourmet magazine had learned about the pension's organic food and had done a feature. 'Organic Farming at its Best,' read the headline, and under it was a picture of Simon leaning on a shovel. Simon had no desire to become famous or receive such praise for his work. The article did, however, make him feel an almost intoxicating schadenfreude towards Oswald. *Look at this, you bastard,* he thought. *And you said no one cared about my plants.*

Inga Hermansson was so happy about the article that she suggested a raise for Simon, but he declined.

'What I really want is for us to enter the Ekogrupp competition this summer,' he said. 'And for me to keep some of the money if we win.'

Ekogrupp was an organization that held an annual competition for the best organic farm in the country. Simon had read about it online. The prize money was substantial. He actually had no idea what he would do with so much money, but he knew a win would annoy Oswald to no end. Oswald had always preached to the staff that they were of little worth 'out in the real world'. That only he, Oswald, was capable of dealing with the media and the VIPs of Sweden. He had also repeatedly said that if they left ViaTerra the would end up unemployed. At best, they might be able to flip burgers at McDonald's. These days Simon found it amusing to see that they were apparently having a hard time finding a replacement for him at ViaTerra.

Inga Hermansson was over the moon at Simon's suggestion. 'But you can keep all the money if we win, Simon.'

'Half would be plenty. But now that we're on the topic, I need to plough up more of the fields. I want to start doing permaculture this spring. And I was thinking we could put a few benches in the herb garden so our guests can sit there. It smells so good in the summer, you know? They can bring herbs home with them too, since we never use anywhere near everything that grows there.'

Inga Hermansson seemed bowled over to hear so many words come out of Simon's mouth all at once.

'How was I lucky enough to find you?'

Later that day, Simon's mother called after reading the article. At first Simon didn't recognize her voice. He hadn't spoken to her once since moving out. He'd only sent a few Christmas cards, the kind with *tomtar* and sleds, never anything religious. His mother's voice sounded weak and gentle, not shrill as it had often been.

'I just wanted to congratulate you on the article, Simon.'

'Thanks. Was that all?'

'I want you to come home to the farm for a visit.'

'Are you still members of God's Way?'

'Of course, Simon honey. It's not as if you can abandon God, is it? He is eternal, and life itself.'

'I've heard enough. Thanks for calling. I have to get back to work.'

'I promise not to nag you if you come.'

'Do you still pray at the table?'

'We have to, Simon, you know that. Can't you accept us as we are?'

'Not after what happened to Daniel.'

'Daniel is in heaven, Simon. Despite what he did, I believe God has embraced him.'

Simon hung up. His breathing had grown heavy. How could she still have such an effect on him? Images from that terrible night rushed to meet him, the night when the Devil was to be driven out of his little brother Daniel, whose only crime had been loving another boy. The images of the naked screams from the barn, where the pastor and the so-called counsellors flogged him, invoking God and shouting at the Devil to leave his body. The sorrow in Daniel's eyes when he left the farm the next day.

Only a few hours later, Daniel had called Simon's mobile phone, his voice thick with tears. He'd asked Simon not to judge him – Simon had misunderstood, and each time he thought of this horrific misunderstanding, he wanted to pound his own head bloody. Simon had replied that he wished Daniel all the good in the world. A strange thing to say to someone his mother now claimed was in Heaven.

But somewhere in the very deepest part of his gut, Simon

knew how it would end. And when the police car pulled up outside, he screamed until he thought his eardrums would burst. Until an officer came in, grabbed him, and sat him down on the kitchen bench. He held him in a vice-like grip when Simon tried to break loose and attack his parents. He screamed until his voice was hoarse and turned into a bestial howl.

Everyone said it would get better eventually. But it never did. He knew exactly where Daniel had stood on the tracks. They had snuck down there without permission as kids to sit on the embankment, enjoying the rush of wind when the trains raced past and counting the cars on the freight trains. But Simon had never gone back there. He never would go back. Not to that spot, and not to the farm. Never.

★

Simon was still distracted by melancholy thoughts when he got Sofia's email. He suspected she hadn't written it but sent a response anyway. Immediately he regretted it and cursed himself now that he couldn't take it back. When he received an explanation later that evening, and understood what she had been subjected to, he got so mad that it took some effort to keep from hitting the computer monitor.

He knew at once that it was time for another visit to ViaTerra.

★

There was a hint of spring in the air, even though it was only the beginning of March. It had nothing to do with the sun nor the temperature, because it was cloudy and the hoarfrost lay thick and unyielding on forest and field. No, it was something in the air itself, a warmer humidity, a hint that the cold barrenness was would soon break up. Frost covered the heather like a heavy blanket. The frozen twigs crunched under Simon's boots.

He walked to the slope where the cliffs plunged into the sea, climbed down to Devil's Rock and planted himself on the very edge. The sea was calm, a darker shade of grey than the sky, which met the horizon like a curtain of smoke.

Simon thought of the people Oswald had forced to jump off the cliff. It had been their punishment for breaking the rules. They had jumped into big waves, strong winds, and ice-cold water. He'd never had to do it, thank God, but he'd come close a few times.

He sat down on the edge of the rock, his legs dangling over the sea, and listened to the water breathing – lapping and sighing. A few gulls hung motionless in the sky. Mallards lay on the rocks, resting with their beaks under their wings. A cormorant stood on a boulder, its wings extended like a glider. Everything was quiet, except for a dog barking somewhere inland.

He thought about climbing down the rocks to the sea, to see if he could find any mussels, but he knew he was only putting off his visit to the manor. And he had to have something to tell Sofia when he responded to her email.

Simon barely made it through the gate in time for assembly. He took up position behind the oak, sucking in his gut and trying to blend in with the trees.

The group gathering before the manor house seemed to have grown since the last time he was there. Their uniforms appeared to fit better, and the staff stood in line, backs straight – even their formation seemed neater. He noticed a few individuals he hadn't seen before: a thin guy with medium-length hair who stood behind Benny and Sten, and a girl who hadn't received a uniform yet. Her red anorak stood out like a lure, the only spot of colour in the otherwise grey surroundings. Simon wondered how they could recruit new members to an organization as infamous as ViaTerra. But he supposed some people must be curious. And Oswald's charisma was always a draw. Some girls were so blindly infatuated that they accepted a position there in the hope that he would notice them.

Simon glanced around at the property and discovered that the big shed where he'd kept his tools had been renovated into living quarters. It had a fresh coat of paint, more windows, and a new roof. A fence surrounded the building, and some sort of climbing structure rose up in front of it.

That was when he spotted Elvira. She was standing in front of the building in a huge, shapeless, black coat, observing the assembly. Her hair was loose and flowed over her shoulders, down to the sides of the coat – it looked like a black triangle with golden edges glowing against the wall of the building. For a moment, Simon was fully aware of her feelings. It was the closest to telepathy he'd ever come: the weight on her chest, the lump in her throat, the anguish brought on by the walls and barbed wire. Everyone who had worked there had felt it at one time or another. And now he could feel it coming from Elvira. *I can't hear her or see it, but I know she's crying,* he thought.

He backed out of the gate and carefully locked it behind him. His thoughts were still with Elvira when he turned around; he wasn't watching where he was going and tripped over the birch log he'd put there himself. He fell to the ground with

14

For two weeks, nothing happened. No emails, packages, or other unpleasant surprises.

It was as if the whole world was taking a deep breath, and she was enveloped in a remarkable peacefulness. But nothing felt normal – time seemed to fray at the edges and she found herself constantly interrupting her own routine to look around, spy out the window, check to see if she had gotten any sketchy emails. A faint sense of unease snuck up on her when she went out for a walk. Shadows that had once been invisible grew and shrank behind the bushes. And in some ways, the fact that nothing was happening frightened her even more. It was like they were keeping an eye on her from a distance; she felt watched. Sometimes she went to the dumpster to double-check that no one had gone through her trash. She imagined she must look completely ridiculous, standing there poking through refuse. But the trash bags remained untouched.

The people who'd received the fake emails took it better than she'd expected. Her boss, Edith Bergman, had merely laughed awkwardly, and said she'd realized right away that the email hadn't come from Sofia. Her parents hadn't even read their email. They mostly kept in touch over the phone these days. Wilma called to ask if Sofia missed her so much she'd gone crazy.

She spent more time at her parents' house, but whenever she tried to bring up her time in the cult, everything went off the rails. Her mother brushed her off immediately: 'Don't think about that anymore. You have your whole life ahead of you!'

Mom's voice went brisk and shrill. Like an actress in the theatre.

'I think you should have a party here at our place,' she went on cheerfully. 'Invite all your childhood friends. Reconnect with people.'

This suggestion seemed so idiotic that at first Sofia couldn't make a sound.

'Thanks, but right now I just want peace and quiet,' she said at last.

She never brought up ViaTerra with her mother again.

Sometimes she chastised herself for having started the blog. Why had she been so pig-headed? Why couldn't she just do as everyone told her and forget Oswald and ViaTerra? But that line of reasoning didn't work; she couldn't keep her inner voice from talking back, bringing up every possible argument.

Benjamin had been by to secure her apartment. An extra lock with a chain on the door, and black blinds – which Sofia truly hated, but Benjamin pointed out that they would stop anyone from spying in. When he wanted to call a security company and order an alarm system, though, she put her foot down. After all, the harassment seemed to have stopped.

Yet she was still having trouble sleeping. She was afraid of having more nightmares, which had only gotten worse. Oftentimes she woke up thrashing, startled, drenched in sweat. Sometimes, before she even opened her eyes, she lay there petrified, scared she might find herself back in the dorms at ViaTerra.

One morning, when the dream seemed particularly clear in her mind, she tried to hold onto it and sink back into her body, where it had been pressed to the wall under Oswald's weight. She purposely relived the fear tingling up and down her spine and tried to make herself turn around and kick him in the crotch. But his body had dissolved as she rose to consciousness, and the way back into her dream was blocked.

She got out of bed and went to the window. The streetlights had gone out and the room was full of a pale dawn light. A strange, surreal feeling washed over her. The morning outside was so quiet, aside from a faint breeze that was shaking the leaves of the aspens. Someone walked across the lawn in front of her building, then turned around and looked at her. For an instant she went stiff, but the man looked away and resumed his walk towards the city centre. She noticed his backpack and decided it must just be someone on his way to work. Even so, a warning buzzed in her bones, like the background music of a horror film.

★

Late one night, she received an unexpected call from Ellis. 'What do you want to do about the blog?'

'Shit, I almost forgot about it.'

Sofia hadn't told Ellis about her hacked email account, but as they spoke she realized that had been a mistake. If anyone could help her, it was Ellis. So she did something she'd promised herself she would never do: she invited Ellis to come over to her apartment. It turned out to be a good idea in the end, because he installed extra security on her computer. Firewalls, encryption, and other safeguards she didn't even understand.

Then there was the blog. Interest in it had cooled; after all, Elvira was gone and probably wouldn't turn up again. There were still several people leaving comments, mostly with questions about Elvira: *Where did she go? Did she have the babies?*

Ellis and Sofia sat down to chat over a glass of red wine. She still couldn't look him in the eyes without a certain amount of hesitation. He had been such a jerk in the past, and it was hard to trust him. She even wondered if his almost overwhelming helpfulness was him trying to wiggle his way back into her life. It seemed he had read her mind, because he laughed suddenly.

'Are you stewing about the good old days? Listen, I really have changed. You don't owe me a damn thing for helping you. And look, I can have a glass of wine with you without getting drunk. But you do have to decide what you want to do about the blog.'

It was tempting to tell him to delete it. Everything had calmed down. Benjamin and Ellis had transformed her apartment into some sort of armoured submarine. No one could enter her home, and her accounts would be difficult to hack. It seemed like a good time to get out of the fight.

But the injustice of it all was still pounding stubbornly at her temples.

I'm not going to let any of those bastards keep me from speaking out.

'What do you say, Sofia, should we take down the blog?'

'Nope, I don't want to.'

'Are you kidding me?'

'No, we'll turn it into my own blog instead. I'm sure I won't get as many followers as Elvira, but that doesn't matter. I'll just describe what it was like for me. If I can scare a single person out of joining a cult, it will be worth it.'

'That's a big risk you're taking...'

'That's the point, isn't it?'

They were up all night. They changed the name to *After the Cult* and took down the photo of Elvira, replacing it with a gloomy picture of the manor house swept in fog, barbed wire in the foreground. It was the same image that the journalist Magnus Strid had used in an article about ViaTerra. They kept Elvira's story and added Sofia's. Ellis took care of the design and layout. Sofia took out the secret diary she'd kept on the island. The last entries had been written on the train from Lund to Haparanda when she was escaping ViaTerra, and what she had written was useful – she had been upset and angry when she'd written it. There were detailed descriptions of the way Oswald had treated the staff – the punishments, the violence, everything that had happened before her escape. She wrote a lengthy entry based on the diary and Ellis published it on the blog.

'We have to include what happened to Elvira,' he said.

'Yeah, we'll say that Oswald bought her back, offered her so much money she couldn't refuse. People will be furious. Maybe it will even lead to a demonstration out on the island. A mob with signs protesting outside the gates. That would be amazing.'

'Sure. Just like the time I stood there shouting at them to free you, Sofia.'

*

By the early hours, the blog was live.

'Damn, it looks good,' she said. 'Seriously creepy. You're awesome.'

'What do you suppose Benjamin will think of this?'

'That's my problem. Either I keep living in denial, or I do something about it. I'll just have to deal with the consequences.'

By the time Ellis left, it was too late to go to bed; she had to work in a few hours. She sat down on the balcony and watched the moon shining through broken bits of thin clouds. It was nearly dawn, and there was a faint light on the horizon. She walked to the bathroom and let her clothes drop to the floor.

The tile was cold beneath her feet. She turned on the shower, hot water – so hot the whole bathroom filled with steam and her face vanished from the mirror. She stood there for a long time, letting the water lash at her body and rinse away the exhaustion that was starting to creep up on her. Then she dried off, got dressed, and made a cup of strong coffee.

She went back to the balcony to watch the sun rise over Lund, enjoying the fighting spirit that had been reborn inside her.

15

Simon lay breathless and still, just where he'd fallen. He cursed himself inwardly for his clumsiness. The alarm was blaring and he was just about to get up and run away, but then he realized that the guard might spot him from the booth at the main gate. Suddenly he heard a motorcycle roar to life and come his way. His heart was pounding so hard that it had to be audible on this quiet, still morning. The chill of the ground penetrated his clothing and spread through his body. The motorcycle had stopped. Now he could hear the kickstand flipping down, followed by boots on the ground. A beep, a crackling sound, and a voice on the walkie-talkie.

'Can you see anyone there? The alarm was tripped right next to the gate.'

'Nope, no one here.' It was Benny's drawling voice. 'Must have been a squirrel or a bird.'

'Can't you go check?'

'Nope, don't have the key.'

'It's here in the booth. Come get it. And bring the dog, too.'

The dog? Simon remembered the barking he'd heard from up at Devil's Rock. He'd assumed it had come from one of the farms inland. But now that he was lying there, sprawled on the ice-cold ground, his mind forced him to imagine an enormous

Rottweiler with mean eyes, huge jaws, bared teeth, and drool dripping from its mouth.

'Okay, I'll come get it.'

The motorcycle started, skidded on the gravel, and zoomed off. Simon realized he had forgotten to breathe and that his body had, for the moment, frozen to the frosty ground. But his legs got him up of their own accord, and he hurtled off.

He ran helter-skelter straight into the forest, ignoring his heavy winter boots, no idea where he was going. His lungs burned and his heart pounded. He had no idea how long he ran, because there was no time, only an image of the dog etched into his brain, pushing him to run faster.

Past trees, up hills, across clearings, and into the woods he ran. All he could hear was his own panting gasps and the crunching sounds as his boots trampled the frostbitten moss and brambles.

Behind him, the alarm had stopped. Nature held its breath. It was as if he were running through a vacuum. He didn't stop until his chest was burning and he couldn't go on. All he could see were trees, bushes, and the sparkling white ground. Wreaths of steam rose from his body, which was drenched in sweat.

His breathing slowed as his gaze swept the terrain, and at once he realized he was lost. His mind returned to the dog. Why a dog? Had they noticed he was using the gate? But if they had, surely they would have changed the lock. What were they so afraid of?

He took a deep breath and guided his thoughts towards the problem at hand: finding his way home. He knew he had to find a rise high enough to give him a view of the island. Otherwise he would only go around in circles. Luckily the trees were bare, and if he could get a few metres higher he would have an unobstructed view. He wandered around for a bit until he found a slope made of moss-covered boulders. The melting frost had made the rock surface wet and he couldn't get a toehold; he kept sliding down and landing on his ass with a thump. He swore inwardly, cursing his own stupidity. Why did he even care about this stupid cult? Then he managed to get his hands into a crack between the rocks and heaved himself onto the pile.

Certain landmarks became visible through the windswept trees. The church in the village, the manor, and the sea, grey and still in the far distance. He slid back down the boulders and set course for the village, mumbling to himself in irritation. He used his forehead as a compass to guide him along his path. He was no longer running, but his strides were long and quick.

Once he calmed down, he realized how lovely it was. The air was delicate and damp, and the sun had found a crack in the clouds, to glitter in the frost that still coated the pine needles. Now and then the sun vanished behind a cloud and a fresh gust of wind passed over the land.

It struck him that he had never run like that before. So frantically. He noticed how good he felt now that it was all over, and he began to whistle as he trampled along. After some time, the trees thinned out and the road to the village popped up like a winding snake. Part of him was still exhilarated, but another, more characteristic part of him kept muttering inwardly that he was an idiot.

By the time he got back to the pension, it was lunchtime. He decided to skip the meal and visit the greenhouses instead. He hoped no one had missed him. He pulled a carrot out of the earth and munched on it as he set about his tasks for the day. It didn't take long to settle into his usual routine.

That evening, he wrote an email to Sofia and told her about the day's events. He spiced it up with a few details and when he reread what he'd written, he chuckled to himself. He ended with the question, *A dog?*

Sofia responded almost immediately and said it was the funniest email she'd ever read. The dog must be an outlet for Oswald's paranoia, she suggested, now that Elvira was back at ViaTerra. Then she sent him the link to her new blog. He felt a sinking feeling in his stomach as he read it, although he wasn't surprised. What else could one expect from Sofia? Anyway, he thought it was well-written. He decided to answer later. After the day's drama, he was exhausted. The last thing he thought about before he dropped off was the dog. He wondered if it really was a Rottweiler.

⋆

Simon had a morning routine. He considered it holy and wouldn't dream of changing it. He went for breakfast an hour before he was expected to be on the job. This way he got to eat the pension's breakfast at its best, when it was fresh and steaming hot. As he ate, he read the local paper and *Göteborgs-Posten*. The newspapers were his lifeline to the outside world, his way of taking part in what happened beyond the little island. They were his only source of information, aside from sporadic conversations with guests and his contact with Sofia.

By the time he was done eating and had drunk at least three cups of coffee, and had finished the papers, he felt satisfied

– both physically and mentally – and had absolutely no interest in anything but his plants.

The news turned up a week after the episode at the manor. He had reached the family section of the local paper, the obituaries and wedding and baby announcements. He typically skipped them, but sometimes he skimmed through to see if anyone he knew had died. Today, though, his eye caught an item under the *BIRTHS* heading.

Twins
Thor Oswald and Invictus Oswald
von Bärensten
Elvira Asplund & Franz Oswald von Bärensten

Simon read through the item carefully – something was missing. There was no picture of the children, as was otherwise typical. There was none of the usual 'Welcome to the world!' or 'Welcome, our beloved Invictus and Thor!' Instead there was just a green and white flag and the ViaTerra logo: three Ws surrounded by what looked like a mouth, the shorthand for Oswald's motto: 'We walk the way of the earth.' Those who worked at ViaTerra knew there was hidden meaning behind the three letters: *win, win, win*. Because Oswald was certain he would one day conquer the world.

Simon thought about Elvira, and then Oswald. Of the babies, who had come into the world unaware of what awaited them. Then he put the paper on the table and shuddered.

When he called Sofia that night, she didn't think it was all that strange to find the flag and Oswald's logo on the birth announcement.

'That's just who he is. Everything has to be all mysterious and weird. You know why the logo looks like a mouth, right?'

'Nope, not really.'

Sofia chuckled.

'He told me once. The kiss of death, would you believe it? That's how sick he is.'

Simon felt a tiny moment of clarity. He had never understood the odd symbol on Oswald's letterhead, which he had used even to send simple directives to the staff.

'Well, now you know,' Sofia went on. 'But those names! Who names a baby Invictus? All I can do is laugh, it's so sick. Just setting them up to be bullied at school. Poor kids.'

'Yeah, although I'm sure they'll go to some stuck-up private school, where all the kids have names that go back to Swedish nobility. Benedictus von Krusenstjerna and stuff like that.'

Sofia laughed again, but he sensed a hint of gravity in her voice. Just a tiny bit, but it was there.

'Is something wrong?'

'Not exactly... or, well, maybe, but it's just a gut feeling. Nothing concrete. I'll let you know if anything happens.'

He let it go, but an uneasy feeling lingered after they hung up.

16

She didn't feel nervous until they had entered the apartment. That voice of reason droned on and on in the back of her mind: *What the hell are you doing? What is wrong with you? What is going on?* But she had learned to turn it off. A deep breath through her nose – she made her mind focus on that. As she blew the air out through her mouth, she found herself back in the moment. That voice was really just a little coward that had been holding her back all these years.

'Well, that was pretty damn easy,' said Damian Dwight, her partner in crime. Damian hadn't been Anna-Maria's first choice – she didn't know whether he could keep his mouth shut. But he was the only person she knew who could do this sort of job without breaking the bank. He was an Englishman but had lived in Sweden his entire adult life. They had met at university and had had a brief relationship that went nowhere fast, after she got tired of his lies and unhealthy habits. He was one of those suit-clad guys with a polished façade who seemed very impressive until you scratched the surface. He had quit school, and these days he kept busy doing sketchy odd jobs. He could essentially be hired for anything, if the price was right. Even though they didn't have much in common anymore, she kept in touch.

He was good to have around when you needed something stronger than alcohol at a party.

And now he had broken into the apartment in under a minute – it was so astonishing, so phenomenal that she got gooseflesh.

Damian looked around.

'They've secured the front door, but they completely ignored the balcony door. Idiots.'

Anna-Maria's gaze swept the studio. Neat, not a thing out of place. The air was nearly vibrating with sterile emptiness. As if someone were using this place for a hideout, but didn't live there permanently. Just as she liked it herself. She felt a burning irritation at Sofia Bauman's meticulousness. Then again, the apartment was so full of cheap IKEA crap that it smelled like plastic. This chick had no style.

'How illegal is this, really?' she asked Damian.

'You're the lawyer.'

'I have, like, no experience with this sort of thing.'

'Illegal enough to ruin your career forever. And unorthodox, pretty fucking unorthodox.'

'It's not like this is anything new,' Anna-Maria grinned. 'Franz had cameras all over ViaTerra. This is only the beginning. It seems like Franz has a number of things up his sleeve. But what the hell. None of them are as bold as this.'

Damian raised an eyebrow. 'Does he know about this?'

'Of course not. Not yet, anyway.'

'What did this poor girl do to deserve all this?'

'You don't want to know. You'll keep this quiet, right?'

'I already promised I would. How long do we have?'

'She's at work – she'll be home late afternoon.'

'This won't take more than an hour.'

Anna-Maria sat down on the sofa and watched Damian in silence as he installed a camera near the ceiling. A tiny eye that fit behind a vent high up on the wall.

'It will let you see the whole apartment,' he said. 'You'll have a bird's eye view of her. You can keep her under constant watch.'

'Except in the bathroom,' Anna-Maria grinned. 'Should we put one in the shower too?'

'What the hell? I didn't know you were into that.'

'I'm not, but I know someone who likes girls in the shower.' She let out a hoarse little laugh that caught in her throat as an unpleasant thought came to her. 'What happens if she finds the camera? Can it be traced? I don't want anyone to be able to trace it to my apartment, as I'm sure you understand.'

'Of course it can be traced.'

She flew off the sofa as if someone had stabbed her in the ass with a fork.

'Chill out,' he said. 'There's an alarm – you'll know if someone touches the camera. If that happens, you just have to break the connection and no one can trace it.'

When they were done, Anna-Maria cleaned up fastidiously, until the real-life image of the apartment was an exact match to the one in her head, of the way it had looked when they first walked through the door.

'Now we'll go to your place,' Damian said. 'I'll install the equipment and hook it up and show you how to use it.'

'Are you sure it'll work? From so far away?'

'Totally sure. Come on, let's get out of here before this chick gets home.'

*

She let Damian drive. Meanwhile she sank down in the passenger seat and smiled inwardly. It had been so ridiculously easy. Rain was starting to fall, whipping violently at the windshield and making it hard to see, so they travelled along the highway at a snail's pace. But that only made everything feel cosy; she was purring like a cat and letting her gaze melt into the fat raindrops on the wet glass.

Franz had been so grumpy ever since the kids were born. It hadn't helped that Anna-Maria had brought Elvira and the babies to the manor, and that they were living so well. Now he'd got it into his head that the kids wouldn't be raised properly, and he wanted out of prison. For 'good behaviour'. As if she could wave a magic wand and set him free. When she tried to explain that it didn't work that way, he threatened her, saying that maybe he didn't have any use for her after all. So cruel. But everything would be different soon, because now she had something Franz wouldn't be able to resist: a glimpse into Sofia Bauman's daily life.

Anna-Maria wondered how she would smuggle in the recordings. Franz would enjoy watching the videos in his cell. She was amazed to find she didn't feel jealous, but wasn't that the point? If Franz could see how that IKEA slut lived her life, he would be disgusted and get tired of her. Nothing that went on in that claustrophobic little place could possibly be stimulating for a man like Franz Oswald. And then he would definitely realize how much Anna-Maria had to offer. It was clearly a win-win situation for her.

She turned to Damian.

'Hey, could you show me how to edit the recordings together and make a DVD of them?'

'Sure, that shouldn't be hard. I can do that. For a small sum, that is.'

Anna-Maria's phone vibrated in her pocket. A call from Skogome – so timely. It was Helga McLean.

'When do you plan to visit next?'

'Tomorrow, during visiting hours. Why?'

'Just wanted to check. We'll talk then.'

'Is something wrong?'

'No, not exactly. Except your client has convinced all the inmates in his unit to get saved. They're studying the ViaTerra theses at night. We'd really like to put an end to this mess, if you get my drift. Maybe you can help us out. Change his mind.'

Anna-Maria muffled a guffaw. She pictured Franz, surrounded by the inmates he'd turned into his underlings. The thought was so hilarious that she had to bite her lip to keep from laughing out loud. There was a lengthy silence before she heard McLean's voice once more.

'Are you still there?'

'Yes, I was just thinking. Listen, you know what might distract him at night, and maybe put a stop to his preaching? I'm sure you know he likes watching old movies?'

'No, I didn't.'

'Well, he does. But they have to be particular movies, made by directors he likes. May I bring some DVDs when I visit? He has a TV with a DVD player, doesn't he?'

'He doesn't, but we can discuss it while you're here. Maybe we can make an exception,' said McLean. 'And another thing, before I forget. It's almost time for his first supervised furlough. Just so you know. And it will definitely be supervised, no matter his opinion on the matter. I have to go now. See you tomorrow.'

Anna-Maria's sense of satisfaction had turned into a feeling that approached ecstasy. Everything was going to be just fine. Really, really fine. She flipped down the mirror to fix her makeup and got caught up in her own gaze for a moment. She saw something there, something new. *Am I an evil person?* she wondered. *But who can really define evil? Well, now it's my turn to have some fun.*

17

Sofia's boss, Edith Bergman, had a stiff smile on her face when Sofia arrived at work that morning. It seemed out of place to Sofia right away, because she was sure her performance at work was excellent so far.

A week ago, Edith had asked if she wanted to be in charge of certain inquiries and helping the patrons find books. A new substitute would help shelve books. So now Sofia got to meet interesting, eager readers every day. Edith had also specifically mentioned how pleased she was with Sofia's work, so seeing her smile so strangely caught Sofia unawares. Suddenly there was an uncomfortable tension between her and her boss, and those vibes weren't coming from Sofia's end. Just as she was about to go to lunch, Edith popped up.

'Can you come by my office after lunch, Sofia?'

'Sure, what's going on?'

'I'd prefer to discuss it in private.'

*

She ate at her usual lunch spot, but the food seemed to expand in her mouth. Was she going to be fired? Was the university cutting staff? Or was it something else? Edith had approached

Sofia hesitantly, fumblingly, as if there was something left unsaid between the two of them. She couldn't imagine what it might be. She'd been honest during her interview, had made it clear she used to be part of ViaTerra. Had someone sent more emails to Edith? It seemed unlikely, because Sofia was almost positive her new email account was unhackable.

When Sofia stepped into Edith's office, her boss was already behind her desk, looking at a folder. She closed it when she caught sight of Sofia.

'Please, Sofia, have a seat.'

She waited an unbearable length of time before opening her mouth again. An ice-cold hand squeezed Sofia's heart. What had happened? What could be so serious?

'First off I'd like to say that we are happy with your work here – you've really exceeded our expectations.'

'Thanks, I'm glad to hear it.'

'But the fact is, the university library is held in high regard, a respectable place, and, well, we have certain ethical demands of our staff.'

'What is this all about?'

Edith slowly slid the folder across the desk to Sofia and allowed her to open it herself. The suspense was a rising wave of static between them. The first thing Sofia saw when she opened the folder was a picture of her face pasted onto a nude body. As disgust rose inside her, she began to read the text and realized it was a printout of Ellis's old blog, the one he'd put up years ago as revenge. Her panic receded. This was old; she could explain.

'Oh my God! I didn't know this was still around. It's ancient. My ex put it up. I had nothing to do with it. It was taken down ages ago, or at least I thought it was.'

'Yes, I noticed that, actually,' said Edith, taking the folder back. She paged through its contents and set another document before Sofia. This time, as she began to read, it was as if a violent undertow sucked the floor out from under her feet. She felt the colour drain from her face. This was something else that had been printed off the internet. *Sofia's Cosy Corner,* it said. The image was one of Ellis's old ones, but the words were new, and this blog had been uploaded only a few days previously.

Call me if you feel lonely.

Satisfaction guaranteed, and a little more besides. I'm up for anything, and I mean anything.

Her phone number.

Her address.

An open invitation for 'drop-in sex' at night.

But Edith wasn't done. With the sure movements of someone who pages through books every day, she spread a series of other documents before Sofia.

'Here you are on a site called *Sex4You,* and here's an entry on something called *My own Venus*. Some of these are only a few weeks old. Surely you understand that we can't employ people who offer themselves up online. That wouldn't be a good look for us.'

Sofia rested her elbows on Edith's massive desk, buried her face in her hands, and began to cry. The tears poured out, unstoppable – this was all so horrible and unfair. Not only the fact that Edith had *seen* all of this, but that she actually believed it was Sofia's doing. As if Sofia lived some sort of double life that had now come to light. Once a cult member, always a crazy person.

'Sofia, dear, what is it? You're not short of money, are you?'

Her voice thick, she managed to tell Edith about the harassment, the hacked email account, and the dildo that had been sent to her neighbour Alma. She looked up at Edith and saw that the suspicion in her eyes had been replaced by pity.

'Good heavens, this is madness! I had no idea. But how come you didn't realize it was going on? I mean, haven't you received propositions or anything?'

'I've changed emails like a dozen times in the last month. I got a little paranoid after my account was hacked the first time.'

'And you haven't had any… um… home visits?'

'No, but that last blog is only a few days old. This is really starting to freak me out… it's just sick!'

'Oh Sofia, don't worry. I'm sure this can be fixed.'

'Who sent you all this stuff?' Sofia asked.

'I don't know. An anonymous sender. No letter. Just an envelope with the folder inside.'

She picked up an envelope from the desk. 'Postmarked in Lund.'

'Please, I'll fix this. I have a friend who knows all about computers, he can take down the blogs and track down whoever was behind it, I promise.'

'He couldn't be the one behind all this?'

A streak of doubt ran through her mind. Ellis? No, it couldn't be – but now she wasn't sure. He had been sort of overly helpful recently. Was he doing this to get closer to her? It seemed extremely unlikely, but she knew from experience that people you knew and trusted could suddenly transform into an unrecognizable version of themselves.

Edith's voice drew her back to the room.

'We thought you had broken off contact with that cult, and now this. It doesn't look good, but if what you say is true, if the cult is behind this, we'll support you. This sort of harassment is indefensible. You have to go to the police right away.'

It hadn't even occurred to her to turn to the police, since her previous contact with them had been fruitless, but now it seemed like the obvious thing to do. She wondered if Wilgot Östling, the police chief who had been a member of ViaTerra and worshipped Oswald, had gotten his job back. If so, things didn't look so good for her.

Edith pulled a tissue from a box and handed it to Sofia.

'Like I said, I'm very happy with your work here. Take the rest of the day off. Go to the police and file a report. With any luck we can put this behind us. And take this with you, because it's polluting my office.' She handed the folder to Sofia.

'But don't I have to work today?'

'I'll cover for you the rest of the day. It's more important for you to get this cleared up, or soon enough we won't be able to keep you on here.'

This sounded like a threat to Sofia, and definitely discrimination, but she didn't want to say anything. She just stood up, thanked Edith, and said she would take care of everything and be back to work the next day.

*

She took her time and walked to the police station. The air smelled like spring. She thought of how lovely springtime had been on Fog Island, and found herself missing the place – not the cult, but the untamed, barren scenery. Each memory brought a flood of emotions, and she tasked her brain with picking them out one by one, distracting herself from what had just happened. She didn't want to start crying again – she was sick to death of being turned into a sobbing martyr.

'Is Wilgot Östling still the county police commissioner?' she asked the receptionist at the station.

'No, he's retired. Why?'

Hope rose inside her.

'Just curious. I'd like to file a report about online harassment.'

The receptionist, a young woman with enormous, round glasses that made her look like an insect, shrugged helplessly. A sort of 'good luck', hinting that Sofia's report would never go anywhere. Sofia asked if there was a copy machine, because she wanted to attach the blog entries to her report. The receptionist's sigh suggested that this was a great burden, but she took the document, disappeared into a room behind the reception area, and returned with a copy, which she handed to Sofia. An amused smile full of schadenfreude played on her lips.

Sofia filled in the complicated form, gave it to the receptionist, and hurried home – it was time to deal with Ellis. She wondered if she should have demanded to speak to a police officer and decided to go back the next day and do so.

Ellis was insulted and angry when she suggested he might have been involved.

'What's wrong with you? I almost ended up in jail last time. Why would I do something like that?'

'I just wanted to be sure. It would have been awfully easy for you, if you wanted to do it.'

'Get out! I can't believe the thought even crossed your mind.'

'Well, then, who could it be? The staff on Fog Island are all technophobes. Every last one. Even Oswald, for that matter – he always had to ask me for help with the simplest stuff. They must have hired someone. You know all about the inner circle of computer geniuses and secret societies. Can't you ferret out who's behind this? Maybe someone who has a connection to ViaTerra, a guest or one of Oswald's contacts?'

'Okay, I'll make some discreet inquiries.'

'Good, and then you have to take this shit down, because I just almost got fired. And I don't want any visits from sex-crazed men tonight.'

After they hung up, she lay on her bed staring at the ceiling. The fear hadn't reached her yet, because her brain was working overtime trying to come up with solutions and had shut out all emotions. She knew two things for certain. Ellis wasn't the one who sent the letter to Edith, and she wasn't going to get any help from the police. She had seen it in the eyes of the woman who took her report. A condescending attitude that said 'you have no idea how busy we are, and how unimportant your problem is.'

She hesitated for a moment, but then she brought up Magnus Strid's number on her phone. The voicemail picked up, so she left a message.

Strid called back almost immediately.

'Hey there, Sofia Bauman, what have you done now?'

'Yeah, that's the million-dollar question.'

Strid seemed to have the ability to read Sofia's mind, even from a distance. It had started on Fog Island when he'd asked if she truly liked working for ViaTerra. His eyes had bored into her soul even back then, and ever since, they seemed able to communicate without words.

Sofia began to tell him what was going on.

'I have an idea,' Strid interrupted her in the middle of a sentence. 'I can write an article about you. A follow-up. "After the Cult", we'll call it, or maybe "Aftermath". We'll start with Oswald's trial and move forward from there. It will be an exposé of what life is like for a defector. What do you say?'

'Sure, but I don't have any way to prove that they're behind all this.'

'Are you kidding? Who else would it be? Come on, Sofia, I thought you were a smart woman.'

'It's like, I promised myself to put everything behind me, and yet I'm still pursuing this.'

'Know what? One time, several years ago, when I had just returned home and was about to open the door to my apartment, someone came up behind me and put a gun to my head. Some bastard who told me I had to drop an investigation, something I was poking around in back then. It only took a split second, standing there with the mouth of a pistol against my skull, to swear to myself that I would give up investigative journalism if only I survived. It was a serious promise, to myself and to God, who I've never even believed in.'

'What happened?'

'He ran. Just turned tail and dashed off. Just an hour later I broke the promise to myself and God. I kept on reporting. I dug even deeper. And nothing happened. Not a damn thing.'

'But weren't you scared?'

'Hell yes, but that's part of the job. So what do you say?'

'Let's do it. Do you want to come down here, or should I come up to Stockholm?'

'I'll come down. We'll get pictures in your apartment and

at the library. I can probably get a whole spread. That should shut up that old bag at the library. And we'll send the paper to Oswald: suggested reading.'

Nothing else happened that night. No one came to her door. When she googled the blog the cult had posted, it was gone. Her apartment was perfectly quiet. It wasn't an entirely comfortable silence, but it was enough to let her fall asleep.

She didn't dream about Oswald that night.

18

Simon couldn't stop thinking about the dog. For once he had trouble concentrating on his tasks in the greenhouses. He was awfully curious – if it was one of those game dogs, he wouldn't be able to spy on the cult members anymore. It would be too dangerous.

In the moments he wasn't dwelling on the dog, his thoughts turned to Sofia. He hadn't heard from her for a few days, which was par for the course. But this time, for no real reason, he suspected something was wrong. It was just a gut feeling, but it was the same as when Daniel had disappeared. He had been worried about Sofia ever since the trial – how hastily she and Benjamin had brushed off Oswald. As if it were all over. Simon had known people like Oswald before. They weren't apt to allow themselves to be humiliated without consequences. Something was up. The staff, back on the property. The dog. Elvira, looking so sad. But how could he warn Sofia without scaring the daylights out of her? Typically, Simon's troubles receded as soon as he got his hands into the dirt. But today not even that was enough.

★

After dinner he went to his little cottage and took the shotgun from the wardrobe. He'd used it to hunt hares and pheasants on the farm in Småland. There it had been so natural to go out and shoot your supper, but these days he didn't even have any ammunition. The shotgun had stood there unused, but now it would be of help. If someone discovered him sneaking around the manor, he could say he was out hunting. It wasn't hunting season, but the dummies at ViaTerra were clueless about that sort of thing. He was sure of it.

He changed into his warmest winter overalls and thickest coat, then went to the greenhouse for a knife to carry in his pocket. He'd seen a movie once where a guy slit the throat of a German shepherd that was attacking him. In self-defence. Then he headed for the manor. It took just over half an hour of brisk walking to get there. The village was on the southern end of the island; the manor on the northern point. He took the car road along the coast this evening; the air was chilly and bracing. The view from the road was dazzlingly beautiful all year round. The cliffs at the side of the road plunged straight into the sea. It was a little breezy, but it wasn't enough to whip up waves, so the water just seethed and hissed with white foam. The sun was setting, but all you could see from the road was the red glow of the sky.

Simon walked fast. He stuffed his hands into his roomy coat pockets. The road was deserted; no cars, not a soul in sight. He turned off at the gravel road to the manor and slipped into the forest when he was almost at the gate. It was almost pitch black now, but he had walked this path so many times that his legs moved of their own accord. He had timed his trip well – he could hear the murmur of voices within the walls, almost time for assembly. So it was seven o'clock. If he was lucky, they would have brought the dog along.

He didn't dare enter the gate as he didn't want to be discovered on the property. If they found him here in the woods, he could say he was out hunting, but that lie wouldn't hold up if they caught him on ViaTerra property. Instead he lifted the birch that was still resting against the wall, thrust his knife into its trunk, and used it as a handle. He climbed up and grabbed the edge of the wall. It occurred to him that it would look ridiculous if his head suddenly popped up behind the barbed wire, but no one noticed him. The yard was bathed in the glow of the floodlights. The staff were lined up, backs straight and tense, almost as it had looked back when Oswald was there. His eyes swept the group. He saw a few faces he recognized, but no Elvira.

Madeleine and Bosse were standing in front of the staff, but neither had begun to speak. He searched in vain for the dog and wondered if they kept it in a doghouse – and at that moment, he saw it. It was lying down, head on its paws, on the lawn nearby. And it was huge. Simon had to stifle a laugh. This whole situation was absurd – the fact that he was there spying; the fact that the staff thought they were so clever, getting a guard dog. It was a giant, shaggy Saint Bernard, and it looked old, tired, and fat. Simon grinned to himself. Those idiots couldn't do anything right.

His courage returned. He decided to sneak through the gate after all, so he opened it up with his key, quietly, gently, and went to stand behind the big oak.

The assembly had begun by now. Madeleine was speaking, and Simon could hear most of what she said. It was as if she were burning with fresh passion. Her voice was strong and piercing and her gestures sweeping but firm. The tiny, delicate girl Simon remembered her to be was gone. Now she had a force-field, an aura, that seemed to envelop the entire staff. The lighting even created a halo around her head, and her breath rose in an impressive column of condensation as she proclaimed directives at the group.

Simon knew at once that she was Oswald's mouthpiece. In some peculiar way, Oswald was there in Madeleine's body, telling off the staff, just like usual. *This is the moment she's been waiting for,* he thought, *the chance to become Oswald's stand-in.* He didn't even want to think about what life was like for the poor bastards all lined up in rows.

Simon's suspicions were confirmed as he listened to her words. They were all 'Franz says…' and 'Franz wants this and that done.' Franz, Franz, Franz.

Then she spoke about new rules, and punishments for bad behaviour that would soon take effect. They sounded even worse than the punishments Oswald had come up with in the past. Rice and beans, hard labour as a penalty, and compensatory projects. And from now on the staff would have to jump in the icy waters of the sea after certain transgressions.

This is unbelievable, Simon thought. This was what almost did them in last time. What Oswald had to defend in court. The scandals that made a whole year's worth of fodder for the media. Yet they were acting as if nothing had happened.

At that moment, it dawned on Simon that ViaTerra really had been resurrected. That the poor bastards lined up on the lawn would go through the same hell he had been through not so long ago. And that some who had already gone through that hell were still standing there in line, nodding eagerly.

Simon mused that it took a lot more than a media scandal and a trial to eradicate a cult, and that Oswald was still very much a presence there. His physical absence made no difference whatsoever.

Madeleine's sermon had turned into a droning hum in his mind, but then she said something that made his ears prick up. She was picking on Benny, who had apparently looked bored while she was speaking.

'You have no right to stand here and slack off,' she said. 'Franz said the Sofia Bauman project is our highest priority right now.'

Benny was startled.

'We've got it under control,' he said.

'You'd better. Franz wants a report. You aren't to go to bed until it's on my desk.'

With these words, she ended the assembly. The staff scattered. Simon lingered.

Then he did something he'd never done before. He sent a text to Sofia while he was still within the walls of the manor.

19

Sofia didn't see Simon's text until a few days after he sent it. She typically read texts right away, but these past few days had been chaotic. She had basically crashed each night as soon as she got home.

First there were the preparations for Magnus Strid's visit. He wanted her to retrieve a few documents from Oswald's trial, and to arrange for permission to photograph Sofia at the library. This in and of itself had a positive effect, because Edith Bergman was absolutely ecstatic to hear that *Dagens Nyheter* would be doing a feature on Sofia. She even looked a little ashamed; she must have been truly thankful she hadn't fired Sofia the other day.

Then there was the police; Sofia had become extremely annoyed with them and visited daily. The first time, she had been brushed off by the girl at the reception desk, who had said no officers had time to talk to her right then. The next day, Sofia refused to leave before speaking with someone. She waited for two hours; she and the receptionist had glared at each other the whole time. The officer who finally interviewed her was in his twenties and had shifty eyes. His Adam's apple bobbed when he spoke, to the extent that Sofia had trouble taking her eyes from it. But he didn't notice her gaze, because he spent most of his time staring out the window. Once she had finished telling him her story, and had shown him the printouts of the blog, he didn't say anything for a moment.

'Okay, so what do you want us to do?' he said at last.

'Well, that's up to you to figure out. I came here looking for help.'

The officer scratched his head. By now it was clear to Sofia that he had never dealt with an online hate crime before.

'Okay, well, we've got an IT expert, obviously…'

'Great. Then that person can trace the site and figure out who put it up, right?'

'Yes, we can certainly hope so,' the officer said with a sigh.

Sofia was boiling inside. She took her phone from her pocket and slammed it onto the officer's desk. Not even that got a reaction.

'Have you ever been a victim of online bullying?' she asked.

'Huh? No, definitely not.'

Sofia brought up her phone camera and held it towards him.

'Then I'll take a picture of you right now, and I'll go home and put up a truly disgusting porn site about you. Cut and paste your face onto naked bodies. Maybe that will help you take this seriously.'

The indifferent look on his face disappeared, and his eyes took on a malicious glimmer. He snorted and assured her that he *was* taking the situation seriously and would handle it. Then he sent Sofia home, more furious now than she had been when she arrived.

*

And then there was Benjamin. He couldn't visit that weekend because his sister was throwing a party with a bunch of people who wanted to meet him and Sofia. Benjamin said they wanted to hear about their escape from the cult, but the last thing she wanted to do was answer people's cult-related questions. Those sorts of people always had a sympathetic smile on their faces, but you could see what they were really thinking in their eyes: *You are stupid and gullible.* They only pretended to be compassionate.

Benjamin hadn't been upset by the online harassment. He just said Ellis would surely take care of it, and that there was so much shit on the internet that no one would even notice the entries about her. He wasn't even on Facebook and only used the internet to order materials for his company. When Sofia declined the invitation to the party, Benjamin was grumpy. And when she told him about Magnus Strid and the newspaper article, he was truly annoyed.

'Why do you keep making yourself a target for those idiots? Let Oswald have his nasty cult out there on the island. When are we going to start acting like normal people?'

'He won't fucking leave me alone!'

'That's because you're always provoking him with your blogging. What he wants to do with ViaTerra is his own business. Ignore him, and it will all go away.'

Now it definitely sounded like Benjamin was defending Oswald, and Sofia completely lost her temper and called him cruel names – they just fell out of her mouth.

'Go ahead and ruin your own life if you want, but leave mine out of it!' he snapped, then hung up on her.

A whole day passed before they made up. Temporarily, anyway. Benjamin was starting to seem distant. He didn't really want much out of life, aside from his job and the chance to see Sofia on weekends. That was enough for him. If someone spread lies about him all over the internet, he would only shrug and move on. He had left ViaTerra behind with such ease and nonchalance that Sofia was jealous.

And then there was the letter incident. A piece of mail thumped through her mail slot one day, a white envelope with no return address. She picked it up and felt something firm, narrow, and oblong inside. After slitting the envelope with her finger, she stuck in her hand and took out a pencil. There were obviously bite marks on the shaft, and a rubber band was wound around the end. Her head spun. She forced herself to sit down on the sofa. It was *her* pencil, one of the ones she'd used in Oswald's office. Its plainness was so familiar that the stress she'd felt when holding it at ViaTerra returned. There was no letter in the envelope. Why had someone gone to the trouble of sending something so silly?

Just as she set the pencil on the coffee table, her phone dinged with an incoming text. A brief message from an unknown number.

Write 'I'm sorry' a thousand times for all the lies you've spread about us.

She darted up and went to look out the window, but there was no one there. She opened the apartment door, but the hallway was empty, full of a gentle, sunny haze that streamed through the windows. The silence that surrounded her had become so palpable that it felt like she was in a vacuum. She pulled herself together and hurried off to work. But she couldn't stop thinking about the pencil all day, and her workday was ruined.

All of this was going on in her life as a pile of unanswered texts grew on her phone. Now she was sitting in the park outside the library after a long day at work. She took her phone from her pocket and saw that there were thirty unread messages.

Spring had come early. April had only just begun, but the grass in the park was lush and daffodils brightened up the flowerbeds. The light was pale and fell across the park like a veil. An airplane passed slowly, high in the sky. She was alone in the park, and the silence felt unnatural. As her eyes swept across the ethereal spring sky, she was flooded with relief. Soon it would be summer. The one-year anniversary of her escape from the cult was approaching. And she was still free.

She tackled the thirty texts as she sat there, but she saved Simon's for last. The others were less important, although one had arrived from Strid to let her know what time he would be arriving on the train the next day. Her chest constricted when she read what Simon had sent. It was concise, as usual, but it was perfectly clear.

Oswald is controlling ViaTerra again, through Madde. Like Nazi rules and punishment, worse than before. Benny has a project that will make life tough for you. Call when you have a chance. But not right away. Sending this from within ViaTerra's walls. The dog is a fat old Saint Bernard, not a guard dog.

The fear she felt wasn't unmanageable. Not yet. Before her years in the cult, fear had been something diffuse and difficult to deal with. It had sometimes paralysed her. These days, it prompted her to search for a way out, no hesitation. Life at ViaTerra, towards the end, had been about finding ways out. She had gotten good at it: sneaking a bit of extra sleep while sitting on the lid of the toilet. Swiping some extra food from the kitchen when the thought of rice and beans again made her feel nauseated. Coming up with a believable lie in a split second when Oswald caught her snooping. Experience had taught her that there was always a way out. And then came the next step: turning her fear to her own advantage. She had gotten really good at that too.

That was what she needed to do now. She wondered if she could find out more information on the project Simon had written about. Use it against them. Or at least stay a step ahead of them.

She decided to call Simon, who picked up right away.

'How did you find all this out?' she asked.

'Hello to you too. And I'm fine, by the way, thanks for asking.'

'Oh, don't be so formal, Simon. Obviously you're fine. But I'm not, because those bastards won't leave me alone. So tell me.'

She stood up and set off for home as he spoke. By the time he was done, her knees were so trembly that she had to find another bench to sit on. It wasn't so much the project, as that the whole hellish machine had been set in motion again. It had been quiet for too long.

Simon discreetly cleared his throat. 'Are you still there?'

'Yes, I was just thinking. You don't suppose you could get hold of that memo, do you?'

'Well, I could go visit Benny in the guard booth and ask him for a copy.'

'Very funny. But wait, I know how we can get it. Ellis can hack their computers. After all, they hacked mine, right? Then we'll be, like, even.'

'How will you explain how you got access to it later on?'

'Oh, we could always say you were on a walk and found a copy that blew away in the wind, just like that first piece of paper you found. We could even dirty it up a little to make it seem believable.'

'You're too funny, you know that?'

'I'll check with Ellis and get back to you later. And before I forget, everything okay with you?'

'Couldn't be better. Spring is here. I'm in my element.'

In some ways she had known this would be coming. They had terrible plans for her – it was only to be expected. Now, if she could just find out what those plans were...

She saw the mess the second she arrived at her building. Someone had opened the dumpster and emptied the bags of garbage, which were strewn over the grass, tossed every which way. On one side of the dumpster, someone had written:

A WHORE LIVES HERE

A sudden wave of nausea welled up inside her and she had to steady herself against the dumpster as she threw up. It was the very same spot as when she'd found the slit-open garbage bag. Traces of dried food were even still there, in the flowerbeds. She squatted down, pressed her hands to her stomach, and swallowed again and again. Then she forced herself to stand up again and take pictures of the dumpster on her phone. She gathered up the bags and tossed them back inside. All the milk cartons, aluminium cans, and soda bottles had leaked a little, and her fingers were disgustingly sticky once she had gathered them up.

She noticed the writing on her apartment door as soon as she stepped into the stairwell.

SLUT

The word was painted in thick, black, scrawling letters, and it covered half the door. And something had been written in even bigger letters right over Alma's door:

OLD BITCH

20

The police said they would get there as fast as they could. Sofia took pictures of the doors, then went outside to wait. She called Benjamin as she sat there. It felt good to hear his horrified gasp when she told him what had happened. Now he would understand that some things were more important than his sister's boring party. But when he offered to come straight to Lund and stay the night, she said no. It would be so late by the time he got there, and she was still upset with him. She suspected they would just start fighting about that party, and she was exhausted after the day's incidents – she felt hot and sick and wondered if she was coming down with something.

Her building was two storeys high and contained four apartments. She and Alma lived on the ground floor. She had never talked to the upstairs neighbours, having only run into them and said hello on the stairs a time or two. An older man with a dachshund and a younger couple lived up there. The couple seemed to hardly ever be home. But now the man with the dachshund popped up in the park in front of the building. The dog was tugging at its leash, making him stagger forward, his back bent. He stopped short when he saw her on the steps.

'Everything okay?'

'Yes. Or, well, no, someone came here and made a mess.

Opened up the trash bags and spray-painted horrible words on my door and Alma's. I called the police.'

The man's forehead wrinkled in concern.

'I saw the mess when I went by. I have sciatica, so I couldn't bend down and pick up the trash. I thought someone else…' he looked mildly ashamed.

'It doesn't matter. I took care of it,' she said.

'But there was nothing there when I went out shopping a few hours ago,' he said, shaking his head.

It struck her that whoever had done this must have stood there in broad daylight, heaving the rubbish bags out of the dumpster and spraying those words on their doors despite the risk of being caught red-handed. It was frighteningly bold, almost desperate.

'You haven't seen anyone prowling around here?' she asked the man.

He considered her question for a moment.

'Actually, I did see someone. But he didn't look suspicious. A young man, on his way down the stairs. I only saw his back. But he was wearing nice clothes, and it wasn't Jonas from number four, I know what he looks like. Always wearing a hoodie and jeans and so forth. This man was wearing a suit.'

'Please, can you stay and talk to the police?'

The man nodded, and just then the patrol car arrived.

The officer who stepped out gave Sofia an apologetic look and shook her head when he saw the words on the dumpster. She was short and muscular with black hair in a tight ponytail. Her eyes were light brown and her eyebrows formed two perfect arches over them. She had a ring in one nostril. An unusual sense of calm emanated from her. She put out her hand and introduced herself as Andrea Claesson.

'I picked up the trash,' Sofia said. 'Maybe I shouldn't have…'

'It's fine,' said Andrea. She spoke first to the man with the dog, who now recalled that the stranger in the stairwell had had a backpack, and that it didn't seem to match his fancy clothing. Otherwise, his description wasn't much to go on. Short hair, average height, medium blond – it could have been anyone.

They headed into the stairwell. Andrea grimaced when she saw the words on the doors. Alma stuck her head out and they spoke to her for a while. She hadn't heard or seen anything because the TV had been on, but she didn't seem upset in the least about her door – if anything, she was exhilarated over the drama Sofia had brought to the otherwise quiet neighbourhood.

'I hope you get them,' she told the officer. 'Sofia, you have to tell the officer all about that horrible cult. They must be behind this.'

Andrea and Sofia went to Sofia's apartment and sat down at the kitchen table. Sofia bared it all, from the moment she had fled ViaTerra to the current day's events. It was like pouring water from a bucket, because by the time she was finished she felt empty inside. She watched Andrea's face transform as she listened. First there was a flicker of recognition in her eyes – she must have heard of ViaTerra – but then her expression became determined. When Sofia was done talking, Andrea stood up so quickly that her chair fell to the floor with a bang.

'This is just awful. I am so sorry you haven't been taken seriously. I promise we will help you deal with this.'

She handed Sofia her card.

'Call me right away if anything else happens. Day or night.'

★

Sofia stood in the window, watching the patrol car turn onto the street and drive off. Loneliness crept in. She thought she saw something behind the dumpster. A long shadow reached across the parking lot. She opened the window and leaned out to see better. A loud noise made her recoil, and an empty can rolled across the asphalt, propelled by the breeze. The shadow was gone. She closed the window and double-checked that the apartment door was locked. Suddenly she was freezing. Her heart was pounding so hard that she could feel it in her jugular. She turned on the TV and pulled down the blinds, but she was so restless. To take the edge off her anxiety. She had a beer along with the sandwich she ate at the kitchen counter.

It was hard to fall asleep that night. She kept thinking she heard sounds outside, and she wished Benjamin were there. Why had she refused his offer to come?

*

Magnus Strid was supposed to arrive on the noon train the next day, so Sofia had taken the day off. She spent the morning buying paint and covering up the graffiti. Luckily, both the doors and the dumpster were grey, and it only took a few coats to make the insults disappear. She had just enough time to wash up and change clothes before it was time to meet Magnus's train. She biked to the station at top speed.

Sofia saw him as soon as she stepped onto the platform. He was trudging towards her like a bear, loaded with bags and camera equipment, and he laughed when he spotted her.

'Time to have some fun with that perfect ass Oswald!'

They gathered material for his article that afternoon: he

photographed her at the library and at home and took notes as she told him everything that had happened. They went through all the material she'd gathered from Oswald's trial, as well as copies of the hate mail and the pictures she'd taken of the doors and the dumpster. He gathered it all in a folder and helped her transfer the pictures to his laptop.

When they were done, they had dinner in downtown Lund. 'Let's go somewhere where we can talk undisturbed,' he said.

They went to a nearly empty Thai place on Stortorget; she knew the food there was good.

'Listen, you might want to think about going away for a while,' Magnus said when they were done eating. 'Get away from everything for a good long time.'

'What? That would be like giving up!'

'Not at all. You would have room to breathe. It doesn't mean you can't keep blogging and making Oswald miserable.'

She considered it for a moment. But the thought of leaving everything she had so recently built for herself in Lund was overwhelming. Her job, her proximity to her parents, her apartment.

'Maybe. I have to think about it.'

'You know that none of what they're doing to you is new, right? They harass everyone who criticizes them.'

'What do you mean?'

'When I wrote that article about ViaTerra, they did everything they could to ruin my life. They hired a private detective to follow me around the clock. They went through my trash, hacked my email, and sent horrible letters to the newspapers I write for. Don't tell me you didn't know? You worked with Oswald for almost two years.'

Her mind brought her back to Oswald's office. The meetings with Bosse, leader of the ethics unit. The extensive archive of folders where they stored personal information about anyone who'd ever been to ViaTerra. And sure, she'd known someone had tailed Strid. But it had felt different back then. It had been understood that ViaTerra would wage a merciless battle against all enemies, because anyone who wanted to stop ViaTerra was in opposition to all of humanity.

'Sure, but it seemed right back then. Although they never shared details with me,' she rushed to add.

'You should know that Oswald has unlimited financial resources. I've been snooping in his affairs. He inherited billions from his family in France. What's more, ViaTerra has been running in the black. People paid a small fortune for his so-called programs. I actually believe he's one of the richest men in Sweden. Which means that he can essentially buy whatever abominable services he likes. He sees you as an annoying little mosquito he can squash easy as anything.' He paused, squinting at her under his unruly hair. 'But that's what makes this so exciting. It's a challenge, you know? To be that little mosquito who pops up time and again, buzzing around and being irritating. Biting him when he least expects it. One he never manages to kill.'

The jovial atmosphere they had enjoyed together earlier that day had cooled a bit. He was poking at a sensitive spot that Sofia couldn't quite understand. He'd touched on something that troubled her, something she didn't want to admit to.

'Yeah, but almost everyone says I should put this behind me.'

'Of course they do. "Just move on." I've heard it a thousand times. But this world is full of way too much crap. Some of us can't just sit by and watch as the big guys attack those who are weak. That's just the way it is. I think you're that sort of person, too. All you can do is accept it.'

They didn't say anything for a moment. She thought back to the first time she'd met Magnus Strid. Oswald had thought he was coming to ViaTerra to write some positive coverage of them. The place had been almost paralysed when the article came out. Oswald had gone all paranoid and had taken it out on the staff.

'But it always seemed to me that you were sailing in under a false flag when you came to ViaTerra and pretended to be interested,' she said.

'I *was* interested, Sofia. I walked through that gate with a completely open mind. And what I saw made me sick. Know what I thought was worst?'

'No?'

'It was the girls. The guys who worked there were idiots. Robots. They thought Oswald was so cool and tried to ape him. But it was like the girls didn't have a chance. They were drawn to him like flies to honey. I was absolutely shocked at the way he treated them.'

Sofia felt herself turning red; it spread from her cheeks and up to her forehead. Magnus noticed.

'Oh, you saw through him in the end, right? Think of the ones who are still there, worshipping him like a god.'

'So what do you think I should do?'

'Don't take down the blog. Keep writing. Write about all the shit they give you. You might even consider penning a book, since you enjoy writing.'

'I've thought about it. I wanted to write a thriller about the manor on the island. They were so prone to misfortune, the family that lived there. Oswald was the son of the last count, you know. I suspect something happened there when he was little. There's a family history that supposedly contains all the answers, but it's in Oswald's hands.'

'There you go! There's something to sink your teeth into. Start by doing some research. It's incredible, all the stuff you can find out online. But do get out of town for a while if it gets to be too much. One day it will all be over, I'm sure, but my article will have consequences. Be prepared. Call me if you need someone to talk to.'

*

As she watched Magnus's train vanish down the tracks the next morning, she felt different, as if she were part of an undefeated team.

She went straight from the station to her job. It was Friday, and the library was relatively quiet, which gave her time to think about everything Magnus had said. She was beginning to understand the inner struggle she'd been grappling with since leaving the cult. Everyone dealt with traumatic experiences in different ways, and she wasn't one of the fortunate ones who could simply shrug and it put it all behind them.

On her way home from work she sank into thoughts of how to spend the weekend. Benjamin wasn't coming, and she had borrowed a few good books from the library.

She imagined a weekend of taking warm baths and reading on the sofa with a cup of coffee. She thought of everyone she'd neglected over the past week, whom she could turn to now – her parents, Wilma, Simon. And maybe even Benjamin, if he'd calmed down.

A car was parked outside the building's front door. Benjamin was leaning against the car door and his face lit up when he saw her.

'You're here! What about your sister's party?'

'It's not as important as seeing you.'

She was just about to throw her arms around his neck, but he held up one hand to stop her.

'Hold on, I brought you a present.'

'What?'

'Stand perfectly still, right there.'

He slowly opened the car door.

A dog came flying out of the car and bounced around like a ball before it threw its body at Sofia out of pure enthusiasm. It was brown and white, and small, with short legs. One ear stood straight up, while the other flopped down. It was ugly in a funny sort of way.

'Tell me this is a joke, Benjamin. I'm pretty sure I can't have a dog.'

He looked hurt.

'No, you have to take him. He can guard the apartment.'

'What? Are you kidding?'

She looked at the dog; it was staring at her, its tail wagging frantically.

'No, it's a terrier-farmdog mix. It can keep watch; it's in its genes.'

'You mean it will bark nonstop every time someone comes up the stairs or walks by the house?'

'No, the lady I bought it from said it will learn to recognize sounds. Eventually it will only warn you when it hears something unusual.'

'And how long will that take?'

'Sofia, look at him. He likes you already. I don't want you to be alone.'

The dog hadn't taken its eyes off her, and now it was whining softly. She squatted down to pet it. Its coat was soft and smooth. The nose that nudged her cheek was cool and wet.

'I can't, Benjamin. I can't have a dog. I work full-time.'

'I already talked to your neighbour, Alma. She goes on two walks every day and is happy to bring him along.'

'You can't just talk to my neighbours like that.'

'She thought it was fun. She invited me in for coffee. And then she made me tell her about when I escaped from ViaTerra. I had to tell her the whole story twice.'

'Benjamin, this is a terrible idea.'

'Actually, it's a great idea.'

'What's his name?'

'Dilbert.'

The dog looked up and pricked its floppy ear. Then it attacked her in a fit of genuine love.

21

It was cold and draughty at Central Station. Anna-Maria decided to go into the café and sit far away from the small group.

Originally she had only planned to peek in and see who Oswald was meeting there. But now her curiosity was getting the better of her. If he spotted her, she could pretend she was just having coffee on her way to Stockholm. She had a client there, after all. *As if Oswald wouldn't see right through that lie.* The persistent thought popped up in her mind again. This was bananas, what she was doing. Sunglasses on such a cloudy day, the collar turned up on her jacket. Like some sort of spy. But it was impossible to stay away. She had paced back and forth in the apartment. Biting her nails to the quick. She hated herself for what she had become – a fucking twit who couldn't keep her own emotions under control. But the moment she was longing for was so close. She had seen it in his eyes. She could tell the question was on the tip of his tongue. She couldn't let anything threaten what they had now.

Things had been better between them since she'd given him the videos. Little clips from Bauman's super-boring nights. Most of the time, she just sat around reading. Once in a while the camera caught her and her boyfriend getting busy on the sofa. They went at it like bunnies. Once she had danced around naked in the living room, all skinny, tiny tits bobbing. If *that* didn't disgust Franz, Anna-Maria didn't know what would.

When she first brought in the videos and told him about the camera, he was furious.

'What the hell have you done? Are you out of your mind?'

But soon the corners of his mouth were twitching and a sly gleam appeared in his eyes. He eagerly snatched the DVD from her hands. That day, before she left, he hugged her and nipped playfully at her earlobe.

'You're naughty, Anna-Maria. I like naughty girls.'

When she turned around to leave, he slapped her ass and she shuddered with delight.

It had seemed obvious that she should join him on his first furlough. When she realized he was planning to go alone, she was absolutely beside herself. But he made it sound so reasonable.

'There are people I have to meet. You and I already see each other almost every day. We belong together – when will you get that through your head? You're not going to act all jealous, are you, when I get out? Because I can't deal with that.'

'Of course not,' she assured him as image after image of women flashed through her mind. Beautiful women, hanging out with Oswald on his furlough.

'Okay then. Read Thesis Two again. The one about how you are your past. And chill out. It's distasteful when you chew on your lips like that. Jesus Christ, relax.'

So she gave in, as usual, and looked on the bright side: he had said they belonged together. *You and me against the whole world.* He had told her that more than once.

*

She slowly turned around and looked at the small group. Everything was dark through the sunglasses, but she recognized the people at the table. Bosse, the bag of bones from ViaTerra who always smelled like sweat. Madeleine, the dumb girl with white eyebrows. And the intermediary loser, although this time he wasn't wearing flip-flops and jeans but a shirt and tie, of *course.* The guard was leaning against a wall, a respectable distance from the group. Franz's voice was thundering through the whole restaurant. He kept the group engaged with his authority and passion, telling them something that made them howl with laughter. Nearby patrons had turned around; they couldn't help but listen. Some of them must have recognized him, because she saw a pair of girls staring at him and whispering to each other.

She became aware of how tense she had been, but now she could feel herself relax. This was work talk, not a date with another woman. All she had to do was get out of the café without being seen.

After sneaking out the door, she lingered outside. She went stiff as she heard Franz's voice behind her, and she turned around to see him walking out with the others in tow. She only just had time to turn her face away. He was making a joke about something and the others laughed, a little too shrilly. So it had gone well. She couldn't resist the temptation to trail behind them at a distance and set her sights on Oswald's broad back. After giving them a head start, she followed them until they were out of the station. She stood just inside the glass doors and observed them. Oswald stepped into a car with the guard. He was going to do some shopping, he had said. Bosse and Madeleine stood around for a moment, staring after him, unsure of what to do, and then they vanished in the throng of people. The loser raised a hand towards Oswald's car and then jumped into another, particularly shiny, car. She waited until they were gone.

For some strange reason, her thoughts were drawn to Oswald's analogy about the spider's web, and then she understood. Those pathetic individuals were all stuck in his net. Just like Sofia Bauman. He pulled the strings, and they obeyed his every whim. But he and she sat in the centre, together, directing everything. That was why he didn't need her during his furlough. To think she hadn't understood this earlier! What was she even doing here, in this ridiculous disguise?

*

As soon as she got back to her apartment she felt restless. She wanted to see him again, but it would be several days. And there was something else hanging over her, chafing at her. She decided to take her motorcycle for a spin; that always helped clear her thoughts.

She'd purchased the Harley in London. It had cost a fortune, but it was worth it. She'd taken a year off after finishing school to live in London. When she arrived at girls' nights on her hog, in full leather gear, her girlfriends had called her 'the bitch lawyer from hell.' She liked that nickname. There was only one person she knew who had a nicer Harley, and that was Franz. He'd asked her to keep an eye on it at ViaTerra. She'd almost had a heart attack when she saw it gleaming in the garage. A specially-built custom machine, scaled back, with a personal finish: ViaTerra's logo on either side of the gas tank.

She knew he only used it on special occasions. For long trips he had a Honda Shadow 1100, which wasn't too bad itself. But the Harley was a masterpiece.

He had been delighted when she told him she had one too.

'Look at that,' he'd said. 'I told you we were meant for each other.'

She changed clothes, feeling sexy as soon as she put on her leather jacket and boots. It was a cool, sunny spring day and it hadn't rained in a while, so the ground was dry and the gravel crunched pleasantly under her hard heels. It took some time to get out of the city, but there was one road where she could get up to almost 130. A tendril of hair had slipped out of her helmet and was whipping at her face, but she didn't mind. Her mind cleared almost immediately, and all at once she realized what she had missed. She had seen that car before, the one the loser had driven off in. It was Oswald's Mercedes. The one he'd had since he was twenty – he'd taken such good care of it that it looked brand new. Why on earth would he let someone else drive it? Or was it just being taken in to be serviced?

The clarity in her head was replaced by a dull buzz. She slowed down, and suddenly her ride was no longer quite so much fun. She had a sneaking suspicion that she was missing part of the Franz Oswald puzzle. There was a piece she didn't have access to.

22

Simon went out to buy *Dagens Nyheter* on the morning when the article about Sofia was published. Once he got home, he sank into his easy chair and read the piece through twice. *AFTERSHOCKS: Life after the Cult*, read the headline.

In the first picture, Sofia was leaning against the railing of her balcony. Her profile was etched against a hazy sky. In the second picture, she was standing on a ladder that was leaning against a bookshelf in the library. She was about to place a book on the shelf. The photographer had gotten her to turn towards the camera. Her mouth was half open and she looked surprised.

There was also a picture of a slur someone had spray-painted on a door. He knew what that was all about, of course; Sofia had told him. Simon thought it was a good article, especially the end, where Magnus Strid seriously cracked down on Oswald. Strid claimed Oswald was running a criminal organization from prison, under the very nose of the justice system. At the end of the article was a link to Sofia's blog.

When Simon was done reading, he placed the paper on the coffee table, closed his eyes, and sat silently for a moment. It was so quiet in his little cabin. The only sound was that of a fly battling against the windowpane. The feeling of being part of something huge, incomprehensible, grew inside him and he wasn't sure he disliked it. For some reason, his thoughts turned to Jacob, the animal caretaker at the manor. He liked Jacob – besides Sofia, the man had been his only friend at ViaTerra. He had never understood why Jacob elected to go back to the cult after the raid. Maybe it was for the animals' sake. Maybe he suffered the same feelings of guilt as Simon did when he abandoned his plants.

But now his mind was stuck on Jacob, who must have to stand there listening to Madeleine's nagging every day, struggling on just for the sake of the livestock. The thought made him restless. He wanted to reach Jacob, get him a message. Tell him there was life outside the walls for anyone who wasn't scared off by the prospect of a little hard work. Simon went to the kitchen and dug around under the sink until he found what he was looking for: a box from online superstore AdLibris. Simon read a lot – one, sometimes two, books per week. Since there was no library on the island, and he didn't travel to the mainland often, he ordered books online. It was a convenience he'd learned from Sofia, and it had been a great help to him. And he didn't know what else he would spend his salary on. He ate meals for free at the pension, his rent was included in his salary, and the only clothes he wore were work clothes. He always felt the same joy when a book arrived in the mail. When he opened a box to see a book, it was like a friend had come to keep him company for a while.

He went to his desk and set the box down. Looking through the bookshelf, he found the volume that this box had brought him. It was about permaculture, and he'd already finished it. He grabbed *Dagens Nyheter* from the coffee table and sat down at the desk to cut out the article about Sofia. Back at the coffee table, he found the newspaper with the article about himself and clipped that out too. He folded both articles and popped them into the book, which was large and full of colour pictures. The articles weren't visible from the outside, but they did make the pages a little fatter. He went back to the kitchen counter and found the bubble wrap the original book had come in. He wound it around the book and taped up the ends. It looked a little sloppy, but it would have to do. He stuck it in the box and sealed it up, then set to the difficult task of scraping off the address label with his name. Pulling up a new document on his computer, he typed *Jacob Runesson* and the address of the manor. He printed it out, cut it to size, and stuck it to the box where his own name had stood. The AdLibris return address was still there, so it really looked believable. Simon wondered if the guards at ViaTerra would think it was fishy that their animal caretaker was ordering books about permaculture. He laughed – no, they were way too stupid. But Jacob would certainly realize who'd sent the package once he caught sight of the articles.

*

The girl at the register at the grocery store in the village said they didn't accept packages on Saturdays. Simon looked around the empty store and asked if she could make an exception. Then the cashier smiled and said 'Sure.' Anything for Simon. He thought he could see a blush on her cheeks – she was really cute.

'Don't you want a return address on here?' she asked.

'No, it's fine as is. It's a book I'm forwarding on to a friend.'

When he left the store, he felt exhilarated. It was exciting, spying on the cult. Trying to make contact so boldly – personal contact, so strictly forbidden – was truly monumental.

He spoke to Sofia that night and congratulated her on the article.

'I have so many readers and comments on my blog that I'm scared to look at it anymore,' she said.

He heard a dog barking in the background. 'Are you outside?'

'Nope, I'm at home.'

'Did you get a dog?'

'No, Benjamin got the dog. He thinks it's going to protect me. This pup is ugly as sin, but there's something about him… he seems to have decided to take care of me.'

'Well, there you go. It's nice to know you have a dog now.'

Simon told her about the package and she laughed.

'Soon you'll be able to get a job as one of those snooping private eyes.'

Simon would remember this conversation, because it would be the last time he heard Sofia sound so bubbly and happy for a long time.

*

Since spring had come for real, Simon's workdays were long and he often worked seven days a week. Now he had the outdoor garden plots to take care of, in addition to the three greenhouses. What was more, everything had to be in perfect order for the organic farming competition he had entered.

One night in late April, Simon didn't return to his cottage until nine. It was already getting dark, and he couldn't wait to rest his head on his pillow. He knew he would fall asleep in no time. After a long, hot shower he put on his robe and sank onto the sofa to glance through the paper before bed.

There was a knock at the door. At first he thought it was Inga Hermansson, but the knock was too brusque and impatient. He hesitated for a moment. There was no one at the pension who would bother him at such a late hour, and he had no desire to put down the paper to answer the door. But he did so anyway, with a heavy sigh.

Outside was Benny from ViaTerra.

23

Sofia felt like she was being followed every time she went out for a walk. It started with a shiver on the back of her neck that spread down her spine. The feeling was so strong that she had to stop and look around. But everything seemed normal. People going about their business, not a single set of eyes on her. At first she thought she was just being paranoid. But then, one day, she saw the car.

She got home late that evening – it was already dusk. Dilbert had been alone for too long and she hurried to get inside. Yet something made her stop in the parking lot. There was that feeling again. A chill on the back of her neck.

The car was parked outside her building. A black Volvo, nothing out of the ordinary at all, but for some reason her eye was drawn to it. The roof light was on inside and she could make out the vague contours of a man. The vibes he was giving off made her shudder.

She went up to her apartment and as she put the key in the lock she noticed her hand trembling. Dilbert jumped on her with his usual enthusiasm. She didn't stop him. The dog baffled her – it was like he had adopted her and not the other way around. He followed her like a skilled dance partner, always by her side, never in her way, yet so close. After just a few days he had learned to recognize the footsteps of the other tenants and the sound of the mail carrier, so he didn't bark when they arrived. It was like the pup was programmed to react to unfamiliar noises, like he had a built-in sensor that could sense danger. If she knew him, he would bark now.

She left her shoes and clothes on and took a notepad and pen from the coffee table. Grabbing the bag of trash from its bin under the sink, she went out with Dilbert tripping at her heels. As soon as they walked out the front door, the dog pricked its floppy ear and headed for the car. He threw himself at the passenger-side door and started barking furiously. Sofia went over to grab his collar. The man had turned out the roof light, but light from outside lit up his face: he was thick-lipped and fat, and bald aside from a ring of hair around the crown of his head.

He aimed an empty, sunken gaze at her. Dilbert kept barking, and she told him to be quiet. The man turned his face away so all she could see was his bald pate and the fat rolls on the back of his neck.

Sofia knocked gently at the car window. 'Excuse me, can I help you?'

The man shook his head slowly, his face still turned away.

'This is a private parking lot.'

Not a sound. Not a movement. He just sat there, mute and still.

'If it's my trash you want, here it is,' she said, holding up the bag, but he didn't move a muscle.

She walked around the car and took down the licence plate number as Dilbert peed on one tyre. Then she went to the dumpster, tossed the bag in, and slammed the lid. When she got back to her apartment, she dialled the number to Andrea Claesson, the police officer, who answered immediately.

'There's a man in a parked car outside my apartment. Looks shady. He refused to talk to me.'

'Is he still there?'

Sofia went to the kitchen window and looked down at the parking lot. The car was gone.

'No, ugh, he drove off. But I have a description and the licence plate number.'

'Good. Text them to me.'

Once Sofia had sent the text, she lowered all the blinds and locked the front door and the one to the balcony. She went to the kitchen and gave Dilbert some food, but he didn't want to eat. Instead he followed her around and hopped onto the sofa when she sat down. He lay on his back in an attempt to get her to scratch his belly. He was starting to look a little round; Sofia suspected that Alma liked to give him a treat or two during the day. She kicked off her shoes, lay down on the sofa, and closed her eyes. Tried to ignore the unease that was crowding in on her. She had felt safe in her apartment, until now. The sensation of being watched no longer dissipated when she got home. Now she felt the same unpleasant feeling she had felt back in the cult. Eyes watching. Eyes monitoring her every move.

She figured she should try to eat something, but she had lost her appetite, just like Dilbert, and lay there for a long time, Dilbert's body stretched out alongside hers. He was warm and reassuring, and she fell asleep almost immediately – but then her phone rang. It was Andrea Claesson.

'The owner of the car is named Gunnar Wahlin. I know who he is. A private detective. He's a real pig, if I may say so. Any number of reports from people he's harassed. He's not violent, though, just awfully aggravating. I can't arrest him for sitting in a car in front of your building, of course, but at least now we know someone hired a private eye. Do you think it's the cult?'

'Definitely. But what can he do?'

'Hopefully nothing. I'm sure they're just trying to put pressure on you. But I've talked to your landlord, and he's promised to put up a security camera.'

Sofia wondered why the police were suddenly being so helpful, and whether it had anything to do with the article in *Dagens Nyheter.* But it didn't matter; she was grateful for any help she could get. And there was something in Andrea's voice to suggest she actually cared.

She decided to ignore Wahlin, but it didn't work – he popped up again and again. The car would roll slowly past her on the street, or it would be parked outside when she came out of the library. It appeared out of nowhere time after time, plaguing her no end. She had never been followed like this before, and now she understood why it was so unpleasant. The feeling that there were always eyes on her; the foreboding sense that it would lead to something more, something much worse. And when nothing else happened, the tension was unbearable. She was able to vent a little by making faces in his direction, giving him the finger, or taking a picture of him on her phone. But his expressionless face didn't change, no matter what she did.

At the end of the week, when Benjamin arrived, Wahlin vanished. It must have been his weekend off. It was annoying, though, because she could only show Benjamin the blurry pictures she'd taken on her phone. Gunnar Wahlin didn't show up again until Monday.

And so it went for a few weeks. Nothing else happened,

just this constant shadow that drove her insane. She felt more and more paranoid when she was alone in her apartment. She lowered the blinds and locked the front door, even using the chain Benjamin had installed, but it didn't help. When she slept, she left a small piece of her consciousness awake. Sometimes she dreamed that someone was sitting on her bed and watching her, which made her wake with a start.

The blog had grown into a project that kept her busy a few hours each night. She used it as a diary where she recorded the harassment, but she also wrote about memories from the island. She had a lot of followers, and some felt almost like friends. But then there were the trolls, the ones who were obviously sitting in the guard booth on Fog Island and writing negative comments. Although they were easy to spot thanks to their nearly illiterate responses. And no one seemed to care about them.

★

One weekend in early May, she went up to Gothenburg to visit Liseberg with Benjamin. She tried nearly every attraction at the amusement park – Helix, Balder, the Ferris wheel, and Atmosfear – and got dizzy and giggly and almost felt free. But her joy clouded when they ran into a tanned, rail-thin blonde woman who Benjamin introduced as 'Sienna, a friend from work.' She couldn't have been more than eighteen and was wearing denim shorts that started a centimetre below her navel, sandals with four-inch stiletto heels, and a dove-blue leather jacket. Her hair was short and her blue eyes were huge. She was gorgeous! Sofia was immediately annoyed with her.

Even her name, Sienna. It was like being named Turquoise or Maroon, and it seemed somehow to confirm how naïve and incurably dumb this individual must be. Sienna gazed adoringly at Benjamin and shot disdainful looks at Sofia. Benjamin swore she was only a colleague, but it seemed to Sofia that he spent far too much time staring at her bare stomach. Benjamin was way too rash and irresponsible to withstand a whirlwind like Sienna. And Sofia wasn't stupid. It was only a matter of time.

She felt despondent and melancholy when she said goodbye to Benjamin. She loved him deeply and tenderly. But Benjamin was so straightforward and uncomplicated. Sometimes she wondered if an entire life with him would be boring. If they would one day realize that they didn't have much in common.

He followed her to the train station and they shared a long kiss on the platform. Benjamin's hand slipped under her blouse and she pressed herself hard against his crotch until he let out a quiet groan. Suddenly she didn't want to go home. She thought about going back to Benjamin's little room in his sister's apartment. But she was still a little grumpy about that Sienna girl. And, of course, she had her job.

On the train on the way home she mulled and mulled. Dilbert, who she had managed to sneak into the park in her bag, could sense her gloomy mood. He grew restless and wanted to jump into her lap, even though Sofia kept setting him down on the floor.

*

The air in Lund was chilly and raw and crept under her thin blouse. She walked faster, tugging at Dilbert, who wanted to stop and smell every patch of grass. Once they were through the door of her building, the dog seemed to transform. He tugged at the leash and sniffed as though he'd caught the scent of an animal in the stairwell. In the end she had to pick him up and carry him into the apartment.

She picked up Friday's mail from the doormat and placed it on the coffee table. There was a small, hand-addressed envelope among the advertisements, but she decided to open it later. Now Dilbert was sniffing intently at the crack under the door. She couldn't even distract him from his odd behaviour by pouring food into his bowl.

'What's with all this damn sniffing?' she said to the dog. But he paid no attention to her; he was too fixated on whatever new smell he had discovered.

She heated noodles and ate them at the counter, then showered and put on her robe – but she still felt sticky and dirty. When she called Benjamin, she only got his voicemail. An image of Sienna's bare stomach flickered through her mind. She left a message to say she already missed him. Exhausted, she lay down on the sofa and dozed off.

She didn't know how long she'd been asleep, but she woke to the sound of Dilbert growling and barking. The hair on his back was standing up. She knew something must be outside her door. Then there was a heavy thud and a terrified whine from the dog, followed by a crackling sound. Smoke spread so quickly through the entryway that she didn't even have time to see whatever had been tossed through the mail slot.

Her body moved on autopilot – she rushed up and grabbed the dog, then darted through the smoke and out the door. She didn't stop until she was outside the building. She was barefoot, wearing nothing but a robe, holding the still-barking dog under her arm.

Once she reached the lawn, the shivers overtook her. Her body wouldn't stop shaking. All she could think about was the moment the smoke spread through the apartment, and it made her head spin. She wobbled and fell forward, her knees striking the asphalt. Sitting on the ground, she wrapped her arms around her knees. The cold air nipped at her cheeks and burned her lungs. Suddenly her teeth were chattering. Her muscles wouldn't obey; her whole body was out of order.

Her cheeks felt wet. She was crying. Why was she crying?

Through her window she could tell that the smoke had spread through her whole apartment. A painful sob escaped her, and she fumbled for her phone in the pocket of her robe. She let go of the dog and called the emergency number. Her voice was raspy – it was as if flames were licking at her lungs – but she managed to make herself heard above the blaring alarm and report that her apartment was on fire. What had happened? She was still stuck in the instant when she woke up to that thud. When she thought about all her belongings, the fear got a stranglehold on her. Her computer and purse – would they burn up? It seemed strange that there had been no fire, only smoke.

She had to stop shaking.

The police arrived quickly, and then a fire truck. Curious faces appeared in the neighbours' windows. Eventually it became clear that someone had tossed a small smoke bomb through her mail slot. Andrea Claesson had responded as well, and suggested that she sleep at a friend's place, or at her parents', while the apartment aired out. They would have an officer keep watch overnight. Andrea tried to understand what had happened.

'Did you see anyone when you got home?'

Sofia shook her head.

'Try to recall when you walked across the lawn here. Did you see or hear anything unusual? Something out of the ordinary?'

Sofia shook her head more firmly, and then she caught sight of the smoke trailing out of her kitchen window like a poison cloud and began to sob uncontrollably.

Andrea embraced her for a moment.

'What the hell am I going to do?'

'The landlord said they've just installed a security camera. I'll take a look at it tonight. We'll get whoever did this.'

Sofia called her parents. Her father answered and promised to come pick her up right away.

She went up to her apartment to pack a few things for overnight. A firefighter was squatting in the entryway, analysing a small object that was still smoking unpleasantly. Some of the smoke had cleared, but a haze still hung in the air. Dilbert, who was at her heels, began to sneeze as he stepped into the apartment.

'Please be quick,' said the firefighter. 'It's not healthy to be in here right now.'

She went to the bedroom and put on underwear, jeans, and a sweater, and tossed her robe on the floor, then grabbed her purse, computer, toothbrush, nightgown, and a set of clothes for the next day. Just as she was leaving she caught sight of the little envelope on the coffee table, so she brought it too. All at once, it seemed important. That sprawling cursive. No address or stamp, just her name. Her thoughts were still all over the place, but now it was sinking in: someone had done this to her on purpose.

As she stood waiting inside the building's front door, she slit the envelope with her finger and took out its contents. There was no letter. Only a single photograph.

A picture of her parents.

24

'No thank you!' he said, slamming the door in Benny's face, as you might do to a pushy door-to-door salesperson.

But Benny kept pounding at the door.

'Open up, Simon! I just want to ask you for some help.'

So this wasn't about the package he'd sent Jacob. Simon's curiosity was piqued, so he opened the door.

'What with?'

'I just want to talk, Simon. We think there's something you can help us with.'

'I am done with ViaTerra, completely and forever.'

'We know. It's not about that. Can I come in for a minute?'

Simon was in two minds. On the one hand, he wanted to tell Benny to go to hell, but on the other, something made him want to let him in. It would be a chance to pry a little, to find out what they were up to at the manor. He wasn't afraid of Benny; Simon was bigger and stronger.

'Hold on while I clean up a little.'

He shut the door without waiting for a response. Then he straightened the shoes on the floor and hung up a sweater that had fallen off its hanger. He looked around. The cottage was as neat as usual. Really, he had just wanted to give himself a moment to breathe.

Benny's impatient 'ahem' came from outside. Simon opened the door. As Benny stepped in, his gaze roamed about the place as if he were looking for something. He was carrying a fat binder under one arm and didn't remove his jacket or his shoes, just stepped onto the living room rug. When Simon saw the wet leaves and smudges of dirt, he regretted letting Benny in. But now all he could do was try to make the visit as brief as possible.

'Have a seat, but I don't have anything to offer.'

'That's okay.'

Benny sat down in Simon's favourite chair, and Simon was immediately annoyed. He selected a chair across from Benny, who looked tired and worn out. His eyes were wandering more than usual. His hair was greasy and uncombed; his skin was pale. He obviously hadn't been able to spend much time on his motorcycle in the spring sunshine. And angry pimples had erupted from his face.

'So, what do you want?'

'Look, we get that you don't want to come back, that you have a job here. But we know you still support ViaTerra, right? At least, Franz said he thinks you do. That you only testified against him because Sofia Bauman pressured you to.'

All at once, Simon was on the alert. Benny seemed to know something about what Oswald was up to.

'Tell me what you really want from me.'

'Well, you know, everything Elvira and Sofia said about Franz during the trial was a lie. Just so you know. I have documents here that prove…'

He began to flip through the binder. Simon held up one hand.

'No, put that crap down and get to the point.'

'We were wondering if you have any contact with Sofia.'

'Why?'

'Well, there ended up being a lot of misunderstandings between her and Franz. Things he wants to get to the bottom of sooner or later. To clear the air.'

Simon sighed. They thought he was so damn stupid. A big, dumb farmer they could dupe as easy as pie.

'We know she liked you.'

'What is it you want me to do?'

Benny squirmed, wringing his hands nervously. His forehead was beaded with sweat, which Simon hoped would not drip onto his chair. Furthermore, an acrid stench emanated from Benny, probably a result of stress. Simon saw in his mind what must have happened: Oswald had a meeting with Madeleine, furious that the Sofia Bauman project wasn't going as he wished. Madeleine chewed Benny out. *Go see that dolt Simon right away! Before you go to bed!*

He supposed Benny didn't exactly have it easy.

'Do you have any contact with Sofia?' he asked again.

'Of course not. You know me. I keep to myself.'

'I mean, we were thinking maybe you could contact her. Do some prying. Surely you use email?'

Simon ignored Benny's vaguely condescending tone of voice.

'Do some spying, you mean?'

'No, not exactly, just get in touch. Give us some information.'

'Isn't that called being an informant?'

Benny responded with a nervous yelp of laughter that sounded fake.

'Call it whatever you want. Look, we know it's hard to manage on a gardener's salary. This is your chance to earn a nice chunk of change. Consider it an extra gig.'

'I still don't understand what you want me to do.'

'Get back in touch with Sofia. Find out what she's up to these days. And next year, when Franz gets back, maybe you can invite her to visit. I'm sure she'll want to see your plants. You've been in the paper, for Christ's sake. While she's here, Franz can take the opportunity to contact her, see?'

'Why doesn't he just call her? Surely he has access to a phone in prison.'

'He believes in direct confrontation, if you know what I mean.'

Simon didn't want to ask any more. He didn't want to hear another word. All he wanted to do was stand up and punch the sweaty, stinky individual that was sitting in his good chair. But he kept it together. He stood up so quickly that Benny, too, rose automatically.

'Listen, I have to think about this. Is there a number I can reach you at?'

Simon gave him a notepad and a pen, and Benny wrote down a number.

'And this will stay between us, right?'

'Who would I tell?'

'Yeah, that's a good question.'

*

Simon heard the motorcycle roar to life outside. He watched from the window to reassure himself that Benny really was gone, then sat down in his easy chair and exhaled. He realized that his cheeks were burning. *This is bananas, this is absolutely fucking bananas!* Once he had pulled himself together, he called Sofia.

She started to cry the second she heard his voice.

'What is it, Sofia? Is something wrong?'

'Those bastards threw a smoke bomb through my mail slot.'

She told him the story in one very long sentence, then drew in a breath and started crying again.

'Maybe you don't want to talk right this minute, I mean…' Simon said.

'There's no one I would rather talk to. I'm at my parents' place. I can't even deal with going back to my apartment. I haven't been to work in two days.'

'Shit! What are the police doing?'

'They got the landlord to put up a security camera, but whoever threw in the bomb hung something over it. From the side. You can't tell who it is.'

'This is just nuts!'

'I know, right? But that's not the worst of it. They took a picture of my parents and sent it to me. What does that mean? Is it some sort of fucking threat, do you think?'

'I don't know. But I think you should quit blogging. It's not healthy for you – you can't keep going like this.'

'I have no intention of doing that.' She was already gathering up her courage again; her voice had regained some of its steadiness. 'But what do you suppose they want from me?'

'I think they mostly want to mess with you, in every way they can.'

'Yeah, but a smoke bomb? That's the sort of thing you expect from hooligans.'

'Exactly. Speaking of bombs, are you ready for another one?'

He told her about Benny's visit. For some strange reason, Sofia burst out laughing. This was always the way with her. She was full of unpredictable reactions. Her sense of humour was variable, like the swinging of a metronome. It was one of the traits Simon found so irresistible in her, this constant emotional turmoil. But right now, it almost sounded creepy.

'Well, damn! We can use this to our advantage.'

'But how?'

'Don't you see? You can trick them, pretend that you're spying on me, and give them false information.'

He considered this for a moment, unsure whether he liked this new role she was trying to foist on him. Life was busy now; he had the whole summer ahead of him, and he hadn't thought to focus on anything but trying to win that competition. Yet there was something to her idea. He wouldn't have to put a lot of effort into it. Just play dumb and pretend to misunderstand what was going on.

'Are you still there, Simon?'

'Sure am. Just thinking.'

'Listen, it sort of sounds like Oswald is planning to kidnap me.'

'Is that even possible these days? In Sweden?'

'He already tried once. Don't you remember? He sent Benny and Sten to pick me up when I was hiding out in the cottage in Norrland.'

'Yeah, but I don't think he'll try that again. No way he'll take that kind of risk after he's been in prison.'

'Oswald will try anything. He thinks he's God. Omnipotent.'

'Why do you sound so excited? You were so sad just a few minutes ago.'

'It's only when I don't know what's going to happen that I get so upset. Look, we have to turn this to our advantage!'

Just a little bit ago, she had been overwrought. Now she was all keyed up. For Simon, this would have felt like going from dead to alive in a matter of seconds. He had an unpleasant feeling that he was about to be dragged into something he wouldn't like. A speck of dust being sucked into a maelstrom.

'Listen, can I think this over and call you back?'

'Of course.'

He sat in his chair to reflect on everything. A crescent moon glowed beyond the pine trees outside his window. Everything was calm; the air was no longer trembling as it had in Benny's presence. Simon closed his eyes and let his mind wander. He replayed the conversation with Benny several times and found that it made him angry. The way Benny had treated him. Like a village idiot they could trick into anything.

His thoughts were drawn to the time Oswald had beaten him in front of the whole staff. Now he wished he had hit back. Crushed Oswald. Done away with that monster on the spot. Everything that had happened recently seemed too random. Hacked email accounts, threatening words spray-painted on doors, smoke bombs. Oswald was more systematic than that. He had to be the one behind it all, but it must be part of some overarching plan. Now Simon wondered what Oswald wanted from Sofia. Why she was so important to him. He suspected there was a reason he couldn't comprehend.

The thought of this inexplicable thing made him shudder.

25

June began with a heatwave. The temperature rose steadily until it was over thirty degrees. There was no breeze, and the heat settled like a quivering blanket over streets and parks. The scents of early summer competed with fumes from traffic; the air was stifling. Even in the shade it was stuffy and hot. The elderly suffered from heatstroke. The grass, so recently turned lush and green, dried out and turned yellow, burnishing the city in a strange, pale glow. People were driven to extremes in their attempts to cool off. They waded into fountains, walked around with umbrellas, and bought so much ice cream that shops ran out and the phrase 'ice cream crisis' was coined by the media. On the beaches out at Lomma, people fried like bacon in the sunshine. Those who lacked the energy to drag themselves to the coast sought shelter indoors. The number of library patrons doubled, because it was still relatively cool within the thick stone walls of the old building.

Sofia had so much to do that she hardly had time to worry. Even Wahlin seemed to have capitulated to the heat – the black car had disappeared. Most days, when she got home after work, she was beyond tired and spent her evenings drinking iced tea and blogging.

But she wasn't sleeping well. It was hot in the apartment, and she didn't dare leave the windows open. She bought a fan, but all it did was blow the air around and keep her awake with its humming. She found herself waking and gasping for air during the long, sticky nights.

The heat turned into fuel for her nightmares, which had returned with renewed intensity. It was always the same dream: Oswald was pinning her to the wall. Only the details varied. Sometimes he was panting; sometimes his breathing rattled and rasped. In this dream, her senses were always painfully sharp. The pain when he bit her neck. The sound of the buttons striking the marble floor when he tore her blouse open. She felt exhausted by the time she woke up. She tried to convince herself that the nightmares would end someday, that she would stop replaying the scene in her mind.

She had never written about that night. Only Benjamin and Simon knew what had happened. Yet she suspected that the key to Oswald's deranged pursuit of her lay in his panting breaths that time. Maybe she *had* to write about it.

She hesitated at first, because she sensed a pattern. It was when she spoke out that the attacks came, with ever-increasing intensity. There was something to what Benjamin and Simon were always nagging her about. All she had to do was shut her mouth, and Oswald would leave her alone. But the same wasn't true of the nightmares, nor the feelings of guilt. She still had friends in ViaTerra. Friends who were forced to jump off cliffs into freezing cold water and eat rice and beans every day. She thought of Elvira and just knew that she wasn't doing well. Magnus Strid's words came back to her: *Some of us can't just sit by and watch as the big guys attack those who are weak.*

One particularly hot and steamy afternoon, she composed

the entry. Writing and deleting, rewriting and editing. She turned a critical eye towards her words until she could find nothing else to change, and by then Dilbert had been snoring on her bed for hours.

When she checked the blog the next morning, there were lots of comments. Most of them said things like *Poor you* and *So brave of you to share your story.* But one comment made her burn inside. *You should have kicked that bastard in the nuts. It's your own fault, you never said no.*

The commenter's handle was Ultrafemina. Sofia was immediately annoyed, mostly because she thought there was a kernel of truth to the comment. But then she decided that Ultrafemina could go to hell – she had no idea what it had been like out on the island. Or what the consequences would have been if Sofia had defied Oswald. She made up her mind that Ultrafemina was an old hag who had never had sex, and was taking out her frustrations by leaving mean comments on the internet.

What Sofia hadn't expected was for the evening papers to jump all over her disclosure a few days later, blaring twisted, sensational headlines.

OSWALD'S BRUTAL RAPE OF SOFIA

SOFIA BAUMAN SPEAKS OUT ABOUT RAPE

They had essentially copied the blog entry, and added sordid headlines and a picture of her. Benjamin called her at work, even though he knew it was strictly forbidden.

'What's all this?' His voice sounded weak and anxious.

'Ask the newspapers who published it. They just copied my

blog. For Chrissake, I can write whatever I want on my blog, can't I?'

'But he never raped you, did he?'

'No, and I never said he did.'

There was a sigh of relief on the other end of the line.

'But listen, he could sue you for this.'

'No, he can sue the papers. Will you quit picking on me? It's not my fault the media got it all wrong. I have to work. See you this weekend.'

'Hey wait, something came up…'

'What's that?'

'Work party on Saturday. You're welcome to come, but it's mostly for the staff.'

An image of Sienna flashed through her mind even as she noticed Edith Bergman shooting her a look of warning. Several people were lined up in front of her counter.

'I have to go. Have fun at the party.'

She hung up on Benjamin before he could respond.

It's only a matter of time…

She gave the first man in line an apologetic smile. 'How can I help you?'

'Well, there's this book I can't find, but tell me – weren't you on the front page of *Expressen* today?'

And so it went. All goddamn day.

★

At last the heat gave way to cooler air that streamed into the city, bringing relief and comfort. Then the air turned heavy and humid, and the rain came. Small, stubborn drops in the evening, and a serious downpour the next morning. By lunch the sky had cleared and the air was clean, fresh, and bright.

It was Friday. She'd managed to swallow her anger over her conversation with Benjamin, but now that the weekend was upon her she couldn't hold it in. He hadn't called again, and she wasn't about to go crawling back. The animosity between them was so strong it ran like an electric wire between Gothenburg and Lund. As she walked through the park toward her building, she kicked pebbles on the gravel path so hard they bounced across the lawn. She looked up at the building and caught sight of Alma. She couldn't see her face, but she could sense the worry pouring from her. Sofia jogged to the front door.

'What's wrong?'

'It's Dilbert – someone has taken him.'

'What?'

'It's my fault, please forgive me. I needed to buy milk and I tied him up outside the store. It was only supposed to take a few minutes, but there was a long line and the credit card machine was acting up. When I came back, he was gone.' By now she was crying. 'I never thought… his leash was gone too. He just vanished into thin air.'

Sofia figured Alma had just forgotten where she had left the dog. Dilbert was probably sitting outside the convenience store, looking silly, waiting.

'Come on, Alma. Let's go have another look. Maybe he got loose and by now he's back.'

But there was no dog outside the store. Alma showed Sofia where she had tied Dilbert's leash to a bike rack. Sofia was worried, but she tried not to let the panic overtake her. She was convinced that Alma simply hadn't made a secure knot.

The dog must have gotten loose, found the scent of something exciting, and gotten lost.

*

The panic didn't come until later. Once she'd helped Alma home she walked around calling for Dilbert and realized how much she loved that little beast. A void formed inside her, and she filled it with horrible images: Dilbert, run over on the highway. Dilbert, his leash caught on a tree or stump. Dilbert, lured away with poisoned meat, now in agony. Dilbert, stoned to death by a gang of thugs.

She called her dad, who brought the car. They drove in endless circles searching for the dog. Her eyes were riveted to the edge of the road, where she feared Dilbert's lifeless body would turn up at any second. In the end, they drove to the police station and reported the dog missing. When her dad dropped her off at her apartment again, he tried to reassure her.

'Don't worry. I'm sure he'll turn up soon. Dogs have an incredible ability to find their way home. And after all, Dilbert seems to have a keen sense of smell.'

Back at home, she posted to her blog, plus Instagram and Facebook. *Has anyone seen my little dog?*

Darkness had already begun to fall, but she headed out with a blurry picture of Dilbert, which she posted at the convenience store and on trees and buildings nearby. She realized she didn't even have a good picture of Dilbert to remember him by, and her throat constricted.

She couldn't sleep, and lay there staring at the wall late into the night. Imagining that she heard barking, she went to the window and gazed out at the dark, deserted neighbourhood. She hadn't called Benjamin – she was still angry at him and his stupid work party that was more important than she was.

The next day, she kept looking. Biking around, talking to people. Everyone was friendly and helpful, but no one had seen Dilbert. She forgot to eat lunch and made a silent vow to God that she would do anything, if only Dilbert came back.

The day was overcast and the slate-grey sky hung over the city and made everything seem even more dismal. When tiny droplets of rain began to speckle the ground, everything felt so miserable that she sat down on a park bench and cried for a while. She pulled up her hood and gritted her teeth and decided to stop at the park by the store where Dilbert had vanished.

She whistled and called his name. Her phone dinged. At first she thought she would ignore it, because she was exhausted – she had drained every reserve of energy. But then she sank onto a bench, took her phone from her pocket, and brought up the text. It was an image. Dilbert, sitting on a set of stone stairs. Her heart did a cartwheel. Had someone found him? Was there a message? But no, it was just a picture, and it had been sent from a hidden number. Her hope plummeted like a bird shot from the sky. Was it a threat? Her phone dinged again – another image. She opened it, trying to figure out what she was looking at. And then she dropped her phone on the grass. But the image was burned into her mind. A face covered in a black hood, only its eyes visible. A message in capital letters: *ONE MAIMED DOG FOR EVERY TIME YOU TELL LIES ABOUT US.*

She picked up her phone and set off across the lawn, running full-speed through the park, towards home, because now she knew where that picture had been taken. She recognized the surroundings: the front door of her building. And now, certain she would find Dilbert's lifeless body there, she howled in despair as she ran.

As she approached the door, she caught sight of something white. Squinting, she saw the brown spots. That familiar shape. She saw movement, a head turning as the dog heard her coming. She dashed to him and scooped him up, crying tears of joy. But something wasn't right. He hadn't jumped up to greet her. His constantly wagging tail lay slack on the concrete. The dog was shaking like a leaf; his whole body trembling. Then she felt something warm and sticky on her hand. Blood spread across her palm and dripped onto her jeans. A tiny chunk had been clipped or cut from his always-pricked ear. Most of the blood had congealed, but in one spot it was dripping onto her hands. The images that came to her were gruesome. Someone must have held him down. He must have been so scared. It must have hurt so much. He must have been thinking about her, wondering why she wasn't there to rescue him.

At last Dilbert seemed to realize he was home, because he licked her face and his shaking began to subside. She carried him inside and held him tightly under one arm as she dug through her bag for the key.

She sank onto the sofa with the dog, stroking his fur again and again. Then she called the veterinarian, who told her how to care for the wound until she could bring him in the next day. As she washed the injured ear she began to cry loudly, but that made Dilbert wriggle anxiously in her arms, so she forced herself to stop.

Another ding came from her phone. She didn't want to look but thought it might be a clue, so she extracted one hand from around the dog and looked at the message.

It was a picture of her. Half-naked, about to pull on a pair of jeans. Her gaze wandered to the background: the sofa, the black blinds, and then the words. *WE SEE YOU. ALWAYS.* But she hardly had time to digest the meaning before she was on her feet. It was something about the image. It had been taken from above. The blinds in the background. Suddenly she knew without a doubt that this picture had been taken from inside the apartment.

She tossed a blanket over Dilbert, who was dozing but trying to follow her movements through one cracked eye. Her eyes searched the walls for a vent near the ceiling – after all, she knew how everything worked at ViaTerra, knew where the tiny watching eyes had been placed. Discovering the vent way up high, she dragged a kitchen chair over and stood on it. It wasn't hard to find, the little eye staring boldly at her. Enraged, she yanked the camera out of the vent so hard it fell from her hand and landed on the parquet. As she climbed down and bent over to pick up the camera, she wobbled and almost lost her balance. Black spots danced in her vision; her legs began to tremble and a wave of dizziness forced her to sink to the floor. But that didn't stop the spinning. She heard herself utter a laugh, creepily shrill, and then she flat-out screamed. Dilbert jumped off the sofa in terror and tried to crawl into her embrace, but she couldn't put her arms around him. Nothing seemed to work. Her arms were locked around her body in a spasmodic grip. Her legs felt like jelly. Her blood felt too hot as it throbbed through her veins. She tried to pull herself together. Tried to reach down to that inner strength, the last reserves she had always been able to count on.

But it didn't work.

Everything had burst inside her, a silent, painful crash.

26

Oswald was in a good mood, feeling friendly and loving. Today he preferred to discuss their future together rather than talking shop. He pulled something from his pocket. Anna-Maria recoiled at first – she thought it was some sort of leftover food, like the lard sausage – but it was a clothespin.

'I've kept it in my pocket since I arrived here,' he said. 'The old bitch dropped them all over the house. It reminds me of how disappointing life can be if you don't look out for number one. We couldn't even afford a washing machine.'

'What old bitch?'

'My mother. Now there was a person the world would have been better off without.'

'Is she dead?'

He had never spoken of his family before, and now she wanted to know more.

'No, but she's as good as. Dead to me, in any case. You're not about to start interrogating me, are you?'

'Of course not,' she said, lowering her gaze.

'Besides, it's good to have around in case I need to make one of the imbecilic inmates here zip their lips.'

He laughed and moved closer, pretending to trap her lips in the clothespin.

'But seriously. There were good days too.'

And then he told her about his childhood on Fog Island. The beautiful nature there. Places he wanted to show her. How even as a child, he'd known that life had grand plans for him. He went deeper into his spider analogy. One time he had pulled the wings off a bumblebee, and sure, it seemed horrifying, but didn't all little boys do that sort of thing? In any case, it prompted him to realize that there were two types of insects. Some were cunning and dangerous like a scorpion. Did she know that scorpions killed up to five thousand people each year? Or like the lethal Japanese giant hornet – a swarm of those could eat up an animal in a matter of minutes. And the spider, absolute ruler of its web. But the clumsy little bumblebee was so unsuspecting, so easy to outwit. He had realized that the same went for people. You had to choose how you wanted to live your life or else, one day, your wings would be plucked off.

'It feels like yesterday, all that,' he said with a melancholy smile. The sad thing about life isn't all the horrible stuff that happens but the fact that your life has passed you by before you even have time to think. Your time on earth is only a short breath in all of eternity. That's why it's so important that we spread the message of ViaTerra. Make it part of that very eternity.'

Anna-Maria found this so moving that her throat ached with tears. That he would open up to her like this. She was almost certain he'd never done so with anyone else.

They sat there chatting for an hour.

He held her hand for a while. Drew her to her feet and embraced her. He began to unbutton her blouse, but when she tilted her head back for a kiss, he turned away.

'Best not to take any risks. After all, we have our whole lives ahead of us once I get out.' He grinned and buttoned her blouse again, with a suggestive wink.

At last he said he had to get back to his biography. That writing was going well. She already had several publishing houses drooling over the rights, and when she told him that he seemed genuinely touched.

'You're a gem, Annie. How did I get so lucky?'

When she returned home to her apartment, she was so excited that she didn't notice the beeping. She didn't hear the faint, persistent tone – like a whistle that was stuck on – until she'd taken off her jacket and shoes. She searched the apartment frantically until she remembered the recording device. The warning tone. And sure enough, a red light was blinking on it. Her brain froze until she realized what the sound meant.

Goddamn fucking shit!

Her hands trembling, she picked up the gadget, went back to the entryway, and deposited it in her handbag. She put her shoes back on and tossed on her coat – as she went down the stairs she realized she was wearing mismatched pumps, but time was of the essence.

She got in the car, unsure, at first, of where to go. She drove around aimlessly until she happened to think of the small lake she sometimes rode to. The voice in her head was distracting; it almost made her drive off the road.

This is your punishment. Your entire life will be ruined.

There was no one by the lake. The water was smooth as a mirror, shining blue beyond the small dock. She took the gadget from her bag and threw it on the ground, then stomped on it until she had flattened it into a shapeless hunk of metal.

Out on the end of the dock, she hurled it into the water. She watched it sink slowly and vanish into the muck on the bottom. Standing still for a few minutes, she breathed heavily and gazed around. Still no one there.

Nothing happened that night. The next day was Saturday. As she stared out at the city, watching the sun glitter on the rooftops, she exhaled. Detectives didn't work on Saturdays. If they hadn't come the day before, it must mean that they hadn't traced the receiver. Now she had to figure out how to break this to Franz. Make him get rid of the recordings. She decided to call Skogome and ask for an early visit. Helga McLean was getting suspicious. She tossed out comments like 'Does he really need to see a lawyer so often?' But she couldn't put off this visit. She had to warn Franz.

As she reached for her phone, the doorbell rang. All at once, she knew. Before she even opened the door, she had played out the better part of the conversation that would take place. She had to be convincing.

At the door were two police officers. One of them showed her ID and introduced herself and her colleague.

'Are you Anna-Maria Callini?'

'Yes, that's me.'

'May we come in?'

She opened the door and assumed an expression of surprise.

'Has something happened? Oh my God, did someone die?'

'No, it's nothing like that,' said one officer, taking a seat on the white sofa set. The other leaned against the wall.

'Could you have a seat? We need to show you something,' said the first officer, gesturing at the easy chair across from the sofa. Anna-Maria quickly sat down, pressing her knees together and pulling her skirt over her legs so their trembling wouldn't be noticeable.

'Do you know a Sofia Bauman?'

Anna-Maria acted puzzled, frowning and pretending to wrack her brains.

'Do you mean the girl who testified against one of my clients?'

'Exactly. Someone installed a spy camera in her apartment – a truly troubling situation – and sent her images taken from it.'

He held out a phone showing an image of Bauman putting on jeans. She stared at the picture until she recognized the details of Bauman's apartment. The blinds. The cheap furniture.

It was in that exact moment that Anna-Maria almost fell into the trap. She lost her footing as different scenarios buzzed around in her mind. Lying about the camera was one thing. The realization that the images had, in some unimaginable way, ended up on someone's phone was so overwhelming that she choked and ended up in a coughing fit that ended with a squeak. She couldn't breathe. The officer who had been leaning against the wall came over to thump her on the back.

'Are you okay?'

'This is certainly creepy,' she wheezed. 'But why are you here?'

'Because the camera was traced here, to your apartment, by our computer experts.'

'That's impossible. This is absurd! Surely you don't think I had anything to do with it. That would be ridiculous. You're welcome to search the apartment.'

'We plan to,' said the officer, handing her a warrant.

*

They spent over an hour searching the apartment, stomping around with their shoes on, tracking dirt onto her floors and rugs. They opened and shut every damn drawer and every cabinet as she sat there holding back tears. Each time she tried to speak, to defend herself, an officer held up a hand.

'We'll deal with that when we're done here.'

Now her thoughts were running away with her. She wondered if she had been sloppy somehow. Left some part of the equipment behind. Or was there a DVD she'd forgotten to take with her? The officers turned her lovely apartment upside down. At last one of them came to sit on the sofa.

'We didn't find anything. I don't suppose you hid it somewhere, or got rid of it?'

By now she had gathered her courage; some of her attorney spirit had returned.

'This is especially serious, what you've come here to accuse me of. Why on earth would I hide a camera in the apartment of someone I don't even know? My God. I'm an attorney. Don't you get it?'

'Sure, but it's not as if your client is a big fan of Bauman.'

'Don't you realize that this is a setup? Some IT guy did this to drag me through the mud. They know I defended Franz. You should look into what types of contacts Bauman has instead.'

'She's had to deal with an awful lot of harassment, were you aware of that?'

'No, I certainly wasn't. But it doesn't surprise me, the way she's spread lies about my client. Franz is a popular man, and he has contacts in many important circles.'

The officer gave a protracted sigh.

'Well, anyway, we didn't find anything. We had to check,

perhaps you understand. Would you like us to clean up after ourselves?'

'No, I'll take care of it.'

★

She stood at the window, watching the patrol car leave the parking lot and turn onto the street. She felt empty and both ears were full of a persistent ringing. That had been a hell of a close call; her life had almost ended up in the trash. In the midst of her misery, one thought stuck with her: only Franz had had access to the recordings. There was no other explanation. She grabbed her phone and dialled the number to Skogome.

McLean picked up.

'You're visiting again? You were just here yesterday.'

'As if it's any of your business,' Anna-Maria snapped. 'I have an important matter to take care of, and I want to see him this morning. That is the only time that will work for me.'

McLean sighed.

'Fine, come on over then.'

★

She began to shout at him the instant she closed the door to the visitors' room behind her. But Oswald was neither surprised nor angry. He just started laughing.

'You want to drag the guard in here before we've even had a chance to talk?'

'Jesus Christ, God damn it, this is terrible, how could you do this?'

She threw herself at him and pounded his chest with her fists, shocked to find that she really was capable of attacking him. But it only made him laugh harder.

'Quit that. What's going on?'

'How did you get the recordings out of here? I've felt every envelope you've sent, and there has never been any sort of hard object.'

'No, that's true. Why would I do something so stupid?'

'Someone copied the contents from one of them and emailed a picture to Bauman. The police came sniffing around my apartment today. They wrecked everything. If I hadn't gotten rid of the receiver, my life would have become pure hell. Can you explain yourself?'

A few flecks of spit flew from her lips and hit his cheek, which made her feel ashamed and even more miserable.

'Maybe you should check with your buddy. Damian, wasn't that his name? He'll do just about anything if the price is right. And he sure is awfully good at breaking into apartments. Or perhaps you gave him a key?'

'What? How did you end up in touch with him?'

'I'm sure you can work that out for yourself, Little Miss Smartypants. You're my messenger, after all.'

Anna-Maria sank into the small yellow easy chair, buried her head in her hands, and began to cry. There was nothing else she could do. Her powerlessness had completely destroyed her.

'You can always ask him, but it seems likely he'll deny everything,' Oswald's voice reached her, now dry and cynical.

'I trusted you,' she managed to say. Her voice came out as squeaky as a little kid's, but she couldn't help it.

Oswald came over to her and pulled her to her feet. He

threw his arms around her, rocking her in his embrace. That warm, firm, safe embrace she had longed for so much.

'There, there, calm down. I'll explain why it was necessary. Surely you know I would never deliberately hurt you?'

'But this can't continue,' she sobbed, burying her face in the soft prison sweater, which smelled like burned fibres and cheap detergent. She took a deep breath, trying to get a whiff of his real scent, which was always so clean and fresh.

He placed one finger under her chin, lifting her face.

'No, my dear Annie. Everything has only just begun. Now comes the fun part!'

27

The first thing Sofia saw was the low, green mountains along the coast, which gave way to gentle rolling hills further inland. A wide, deep valley stretched as far as the eye could see into the distance. The Golden Gate Bridge appeared, and then the contours of San Francisco took shape. Skyscrapers towering at the edge of the sea, swept in a light haze – or maybe it was just that her eyes weren't used to this new light and couldn't quite focus. There were several islands in the ocean, one with what looked like a fortress – that must be Alcatraz.

The day was sunny, but a curtain of fog rested at sea, past the Golden Gate Bridge, as if it were waiting to sneak under the bridge and swallow the whole city. As the plane descended over the peninsula, the city seemed enormous – but she'd read somewhere that the cities around the bay all melted into one another, so you never knew where one stopped and the next began. Really, only the skyscrapers separated San Francisco from this jumble of buildings. Both sides of the bay were edged with houses, high-rises, streets, and highways, in a chaotic scene that seemed to have been erected according to no plan whatsoever.

They flew over another bridge, this one so tall that a ship was sailing under it. The water shimmered green. The rippling waves seemed so close that she felt dizzy, but at that moment there was a thud as the plane landed. She'd been in the air for over ten hours and hadn't gotten a wink of sleep, but she wasn't tired at all.

Here we go, she thought. *My new life can begin.*

*

It had all happened so fast. She'd decided to move the night they cut Dilbert's ear. The walls she had built, the constant denial that she wasn't in top shape mentally, that the harassment had even affected her – it had all come crumbling down that evening. As soon as she regained control of her body – whether it took ten minutes or an hour, she didn't know – she had lain down on the sofa and sobbed into Dilbert's fur until she was hoarse. Croaking like a frog, she called her parents and asked them to pick her up. She didn't even want to wait for the police to arrive; she couldn't stand to spend another moment in the apartment.

It didn't help when the police first traced the camera to Anna-Maria Callini and then returned to say that it must have been a mistake, that someone had likely wanted to frame the lawyer. But when she tried to work through what Oswald might do next, she decided to move. If not for her own sake, then for that of her family and the dog.

She had called Magnus Strid late that night out of sheer desperation. He'd told her he had recently done a story on San Francisco, and that it was a fantastic city. He said the Bay Area was so large and multi-cultural that she would be able to blend in among the millions who lived there and feel both anonymous and safe.

That night, she made up with Benjamin. He didn't want her to go but realized she had to, so they made a promise to each other: no trouble, no slip-ups while she was away.

She had found a job posting on Craigslist, of all places: *Wanted: Library assistant in Palo Alto*, it had said. She'd sent an email, along with references from the university library and her résumé, and received a response the next day. A woman named Melissa Arbor had replied to say that the library would be happy to hire someone with as much experience as Sofia had. The email read like it was from a friend, not an employer. Sofia was suspicious, but when she googled the library and its staff, sure enough, Melissa Arbor was the human resources manager. And with this woman's help, Sofia had both a residence permit and a work permit within a few weeks.

Once Sofia had made it through customs and passport control and had gathered her luggage, she made her way to arrivals and there she was, Melissa, holding a sign that said *Welcome to San Francisco, Sofia Bauman!*

Melissa was African-American, tall and curvy, and had kind eyes. She was wearing black tights and a green skirt, a white blouse, and stiletto boots. She walked up and hugged Sofia as soon as she spotted her.

'You must be hungry and tired,' Melissa said. 'We'll grab a bite to eat on the way, and then I'll drive you to the apartment.'

Melissa had helped her find the apartment as well, and Sofia had rented it after seeing only a picture of the living room – she didn't have much time to look around. The position would begin immediately, and the apartment was within walking distance of the library.

Sofia explained that she hadn't had time to get furniture and had been planning to check into a motel for a few days.

Melissa laughed.

'We took the liberty of getting a bed and a few other things. Nothing expensive, just enough for you to manage for the time being. I'd be happy to take you to IKEA this weekend.'

As they drove, Melissa talked almost nonstop. Sofia listened, but she kept her eyes on the view passing by outside.

Her first impressions were that the light was brighter, the sun was warmer, and that she had never seen so many cars. Each time they passed a shopping centre, she noticed signs for the same stores. This happened again and again and made her feel like they were standing still, not getting anywhere on their car ride. But then they took an exit, the green hills returned, and the landscape was open and free.

They had been driving for half an hour when Melissa stopped at a restaurant that served excellent Japanese food: bowls of rice, pork, and vegetables. They ate outdoors. The sun was setting and the sky turned deep orange and pink. Sofia was still overwhelmed by all the new impressions. She didn't feel homesick yet, there was still no lump in her throat, because everything was so fresh and exciting.

They finished their meal and got back in the car, driving over a bridge that crossed some railroad tracks, before they arrived at her new home. The building was four storeys high, with a white façade and a row of long, narrow balconies. Melissa drove down and parked the car in the garage. It was full of an unfamiliar smell: the faint odour of garbage combined with exotic scents, mimosa and eucalyptus. Melissa showed her a pool area with lounge chairs and a sauna.

'The pool is open around the clock,' she said, 'and sometimes that's a blessing, because the apartments aren't air-conditioned. Yours is on the top floor, and when the sun has been beating down on the roof all day it gets really hot.'

The elevator up to the apartment was creaky – it reminded her of a freight elevator. The whole area was a little run down, but not in complete decline. At first, when they entered the apartment, Sofia thought they were in the wrong place. Melissa had told her it was a one-bedroom. In Sweden this would have meant one room and nothing more, but here it seemed that you got a living room into the bargain. That explained the scandalous rent, which Sofia had brushed off, figuring that was just the way it was in San Francisco. The empty apartment seemed enormous. Everything had a fresh coat of white paint, and there was beige wall-to-wall carpet. The kitchen, done in brown wood, looked well-used. And she caught a glimpse of a balcony outside the living room.

Melissa said goodbye but turned around in the doorway.

'Oh, one more thing… well, it's a little embarrassing, but sometimes there are cockroaches in apartments around here. They don't bite, but they're nasty, to say the least. The key is to keep everything clean, because they're drawn to food, crumbs and so on, and you have to complain to the landlord if any do show up.'

Cockroaches. Sofia had never seen a cockroach. She wondered what made them so unpleasant. Were they like silverfish, dashing away when you found them in cabinets or drawers? Or would they actually attack you?

Melissa left an echoing silence when she departed. Sofia began to unpack her suitcases. In some unsettling way, it reminded of her of when she'd arrived as staff to ViaTerra three years ago – the feeling of being alone in a strange world.

Once everything was in its place, she went out on the balcony. A tree grew just on the other side of the railing. Later she would learn that it was an olive tree, but at the moment its only purpose seemed to be to hide the view of the street below. This was a quiet neighbourhood, despite its proximity to the highway and the railroad tracks. All she could hear was the hum of traffic in the distance, and the eager voices of a couple walking by on the street.

Only now did she realize how tired she was, as a numbness spread through her mind and kept her from really focusing on the present moment. She thought of everyone back home. Of Benjamin, who had cried when they said goodbye. Of Simon, who was probably awake and poking around in his greenhouses. She thought of Dilbert, wondering how fat he would get in Alma's care. She imagined them all as tiny dots, hardly visible, almost nine thousand kilometres away.

Then she thought of Franz Oswald and realized that he too felt distant. She wondered if she was finally rid of the evil eye that had watched over her for so long.

★

She had two days off before her new job would start, and she used them to settle into her apartment. On the first day she got internet and a landline with an unlisted number. A man came to install everything in the morning, and afterwards she took a walk to a nearby shopping centre, where she bought a mobile phone that wasn't linked to her name or new address.

She bought a cheap bike, which she locked to a pole in the garage. Then she took a dip in the pool before going back up to her apartment, because the cool morning air had given way to ruthless heat. Up in the apartment, she created two email accounts on her new computer: one from Hushmail, to keep in touch with friends and family in Sweden, and one regular one for new contacts in the US. She used a street sign she'd noticed as the username: woodsideroad99@gmail.com. Impossible to trace.

She biked around the neighbourhood for a while, looking for something to eat, and found a deli where she could buy a takeout sandwich. She ate it at the counter as she considered the empty apartment. Then she decided to call Melissa and ask if the IKEA offer still stood.

Melissa showed up almost immediately, wearing denim shorts, flip-flops, and a red tank top, car keys dangling from one hand. On the way to IKEA, Sofia asked if it would be possible to keep her name off the library's website. When Melissa didn't say anything for a long time, Sofia realized she would have to tell her about ViaTerra. She poured it all out as they sat with hundreds of other cars in a traffic jam that didn't seem to bother Melissa in the least. When Sofia had finished the tale, Melissa cocked her head and thought for a while. The sun shone in on her brown hands, which were adorned with a couple of flashy rings. Her mouth was half open.

'That won't be a problem,' she said at last. 'We'll just call you Sofia Andersson – isn't that what just about everyone in Sweden is called? And we won't put up a photo.'

They found everything she needed at IKEA: a small kitchen

table with two stools, a few lamps, a sofa, a bookcase, and kitchen implements. It would all be delivered the next day.

As they got back in the car, she wondered when payday came in the US, because although she had received a loan from her parents, with no obligation to pay it back anytime soon, she didn't want to be broke after a few months. Everything seemed at least as expensive here as in Sweden, and her salary would be lower than it had been in Lund.

'There's a lot you can do to live on the cheap here,' said Melissa, who appeared to have read Sofia's mind. 'There's a market just past your neighbourhood where they sell cheap fruit and vegetables. I'll show you another day. And coupons show up in the mail every day.'

*

The next day, she took her bike to a grocery store and caught a glimpse of the little market Melissa had mentioned. It looked like a big tent, but people there sold fruits and vegetables in colours and sizes Sofia had never seen. She rode home with two bags hanging from the handlebars. Just as she turned onto her street, the IKEA delivery truck arrived and the driver helped her carry all the furniture up to her apartment.

It was five o'clock by the time she was finished. She had been so eager to get everything set up that she'd forgotten to eat lunch, and she was dripping with sweat. She went to the balcony to fetch her swimsuit, which was hung to dry outside. Until it got cooler in the apartment, she would hang out in a lounger by the pool.

The sharp ring of her landline startled her. Only her parents had the number. Some quick math in her head told her it was two in the morning in Sweden, and images of accidents and death flashed through her mind before she could pick up the phone.

'Hi!' She recognized Wilma's voice right away. 'You're harder to get hold of than some major mafia boss in the underworld. You really went underground. I had to get awfully pushy with your parents before they would give me your number. Hope it's okay that I have it now?'

'As long as you don't give it out to anyone. What are you doing up at two in the morning?'

'I'm sitting here gazing at the Stockholm archipelago after a crayfish party that went off the rails when ninety per cent of the partygoers got drunk off their asses. You can guess what happened after that.'

'Damn, Wilma, it's good to hear your voice. You have no idea – everything is so different and exciting here.'

She was just about to launch into a description, but Wilma interrupted her.

'You can tell me everything later, but there's something I have to tell you first. It's kind of unpleasant, the sort of thing you might not want to hear during your first few days over there, but it can't wait.'

'What, did something happen?'

'Not exactly… or, well, yeah, someone called me today. He said his name was Åke Svensson, and he was one of your old classmates, but I saw through that lie right away. He wanted your contact info.'

For a brief moment, Sofia found herself deep in her own mind – Wilma's voice suddenly sounded like a vacuum droning in the background. She was yanked back to reality when Wilma's cough crackled over the line.

'Shit! What did you say?'

'I told him to get fucked, but in a slightly more polite way, and then he offered me a massive amount of money if I'd give him your number. Ten thousand kronor, to be exact.'

'Christ, that's nuts!'

'When I told him I didn't have your number, and would never give it out even if I did, he bumped it up to twenty thousand.'

'What else?'

'Well, it was kind of weird, because when I told him you'd moved to some secret location outside Sweden it was like he was happy with that. He stopped pressuring me.'

'This is just insane. Why are they so desperate?'

'I'm sure you know better than I do. But hey – tell me about San Francisco.'

'Wilma, I want you to report this to the police. There's an officer named Andrea Claesson in Lund, she's a decent person – I'll give you her number.'

She heard her own voice thinning out as she spoke and she grew hyperaware of her body: the heat in her cheeks, the annoying fact that she was sweating even as her mouth felt like it was full of cotton. The chills running down her spine felt like ice water as they blended with her sweat. She felt Oswald's existence thousands of miles away, and was suddenly aware that he had been there all along, like an underground current. A faint buzz in her consciousness that had never faded away completely.

She forced herself to sound cheerful and told Wilma about

her first few days in San Francisco, but in reality, by the time she ended the call and stepped out on the balcony, her mind was somewhere far away. Now she could see all the tiny olives on the tree, and smell the faint, musty scent the blazing sun drew out of the leaves. She stood there for a long time, just thinking, until her thoughts turned to Simon. All at once she knew she had to talk to him.

28

Simon had made one of his rare journeys to the mainland that morning, mostly to take care of some work-related shopping. Since the off-season had begun, most of the stores in the village were closed. He spoke with Edwin Björk on the trip over.

'Jeez, I think the visitors to the island must have doubled since you started working at the pension,' Björk said. 'They come year-round now. Last winter I had to run an extra ferry over the Christmas holidays. How's Sofia?'

'I don't know,' Simon replied. 'She moved abroad, although she only left a few days ago. Haven't heard from her yet.'

'So it all got to be too much for her, the pressure from those pigs in the cult?'

'Yes, she'd had enough. It's so revolting, what they've done to her. They put a spy camera in her apartment and cut her dog's ear off.'

This made Björk, a dog-owner himself, particularly furious, and he spent the whole trip getting himself worked up and cursing the name of ViaTerra. He threatened awful things, including burning down the manor. Simon placed a hand on his shoulder and remarked that justice would probably be served in the end. In fact, he thought this was a ridiculous thing to say, but it seemed to appease Björk.

Simon still had an hour before the ferry back by the time he was done with his shopping, so he stopped by a bookstore. Right away he spotted something on the shelf of new books, in the very centre of the store.

How I Walk the Way of the Earth, by Franz Oswald von Bärensten.

The image on the cover looked recent. Oswald was wearing a pale grey suit, his hair was down, and that blinding smile was pasted on his face. It must have been taken in prison, since Oswald wasn't his usual shade of tan. He even looked a bit pasty. Simon was pleased to know that at least Oswald didn't have access to a tanning booth there. He didn't want to buy the book – the thought of paying a single krona for it made him feel ill – but he couldn't stop himself.

On the ferry back, he avoided Björk and sat on a bench at the stern, reading. A strong breeze had blown up. When they docked on the island, a gust caught the book and it almost slipped from Simon's grasp.

He aimed for the pension and walked slowly as he absorbed the fresh air. On his way, he gazed up at the pines on the hills. Wisps of clouds dashed above the treetops as if they were in a hurry to get somewhere. Each time he returned to the island it was like a fissure opened up in his life and he found himself in a strange world – even though he had lived there for four years. He didn't feel at home until he saw the pointed roofs of the greenhouses against the sky.

Once home, he sat down in his easy chair to keep reading, stopping only to eat dinner. By nine o'clock he had finished the book. It was an autobiography, but it was also sprinkled with plucky tips for living a better life. The most troublesome parts were the lies – among other things, the book claimed that Elvira had seduced Oswald and lied about her age. And that he lived in a state of constant grief for his family.

But the very worst part was what he wrote about Sofia. It was only a few lines, but it was enough.

Sofia Bauman was my secretary for two years. She was efficient, competent, and clear-sighted. Anyhow, Sofia often made sexual advances when we worked together. I never responded to these, for reasons of professional decorum. Perhaps that's why she turned on me in the end. I have no feelings of ill will towards Sofia, and I'm sure we will see each other again someday, under different, better circumstances.

Simon's immediate thought was that, whatever it took, he must make sure Sofia never saw the book. She would hit the roof. Then he thought about the injustice of the whole situation. Oswald, sitting in prison and penning lies. He logged onto his computer and googled the book, which had already been covered by every media outlet imaginable. The promotional material blared phrases like *page-turner of the year* and *explosive glimpses into Franz Oswald's private life.*

Simon stared at the picture of Oswald, unable to curb his irritation at the way this man sucked people in. Even from his prison cell. He decided to call Magnus Strid. He'd never done so before, but now had an idea.

The journalist sounded as affable as ever.

'Simon! It's been ages, what's on your mind?'

'Well, I'm wondering if you've read Oswald's book.'

'Yes, it's the worst drivel I've read in my life.'

'I think so too. It makes me so furious that so many people will read his lies. But then I heard you're writing a book about ViaTerra too. When is that coming out?'

'Sometime in the spring.'

Simon considered this. The spring would work well. That way he could serve as Sofia's spy for a few months before the book came out.

'In that case, I'd like to be interviewed for it.'

'Wonderful! That will be a big help. Not everyone is so forthright, you know.'

Simon felt better after their conversation and was able to tackle his evening chores.

Just as he was about to go to bed, he caught sight of the morning paper on the coffee table – he hadn't had time to read it yet. This ran so contrary to his principles that he sat down on the sofa and opened it. The article showed up in the arts and culture section: Oswald's book was expected to break all Swedish sales records for an autobiography. There was also a review. It wasn't exactly glowing, but what did that matter?

He couldn't imagine a greater injustice. A killer and rapist, leading a cult from prison as he wrote books and got his picture taken in a suit.

★

The call from Sofia came at six in the morning, just as he was dragging himself out of bed. It was from an unfamiliar number, but he suspected she was on the other end.

Not a word about how things were going, how the flight had been, work, or anything like that. She just got straight to the point, as always.

'I need your help with something, Simon, please!'

'You haven't told me what you need help with, or how you're feeling.'

'I'm fine, as I'm sure you can hear, but Oswald is already reaching out his tentacles for me and it's starting to creep me out.'

'He wrote a book.'

'What the hell?'

'It's true. It's terrible. I don't want you to read it. It will make you so angry, I don't even want to think about it. Suddenly I'm glad you're on the other side of the Atlantic. It's full of praise from celebrities, too, even though that pig is in prison.'

'Send it to me!'

'Not on your life!'

'Come on, I want it.'

'Fine, if you really do I'll dig it out of the trash and mail it over. But it's going to smell like garbage.'

She laughed.

'Simon, some jerk called Wilma and offered her money in exchange for my contact info.'

'Jesus. But it doesn't surprise me. You've got to be careful, Sofia. Something isn't right. My gut is telling me that things are only going to get worse.'

'What do you think they want? Why won't they leave me alone?'

'I'm not sure, but it's a good thing you're in the US. I miss you, but you'll be better off there.'

'What do you think I should do?'

'Lay low, like you're doing now. They can't get you there,' Simon said, as he wondered whether, in fact, they could. He told her about Magnus Strid's book and how he was going to be interviewed for it. He felt proud when she expressed genuine happiness.

'Anyway, why were you calling?' he asked.

'I want you to talk to Benny again.'

'Why? I called him the other day to say I decided not to have any contact with you.'

'You'll have to tell him you changed your mind, that you're hurting for cash.'

'Then what?'

'Then he'll ask you where I am.'

'What will I say?'

'Tell him I wrote you from Italy. That's all, to start. You don't know more than that. Call me after you talk to him.'

'Fine, I'll do it, but I'm not taking any of their money.'

'Burn the money!'

'Not even that. I guess I'll have to say I'm tired of your whining and I can't stand you anymore.'

They talked for a long time. She suggested he come visit, and he laughed and said the farthest he'd ever travelled was to Stockholm, where the sight of all the tall buildings made him dizzy. Yet to his surprise, he felt a flash of curiosity when he thought about travelling to the other end of the earth. After their conversation, he sank down in his chair but was soon interrupted by a gentle knock at the door. It was Inga Hermansson, who said he would have to dress up the next day – the Ekogrupp jury would be coming by to look at his crops. Simon was already aware of their planned visit, but he had only set out his usual work clothes that evening. Surely the jury members would prefer everything to seem natural – gardening gloves covered in dirt, muddy boots. Still, he nodded in response to

Inga Hermansson's request, because he was still distracted by a lingering thought: how much horsepower was there in the engines of a plane that flew all the way across the Atlantic?

29

Wilma's call gave Sofia a proper fright. She called her parents, Benjamin, Alma, and even Edith Bergman at the university library, but no one had been asking after her. Then she wondered if all her phone calls could give the cult fresh clues, and decided to lay low instead. They were probably looking for her somewhere in Italy.

Life in Palo Alto soon settled into a comfortable routine. She biked to work in the morning, always towards the rising sun. She finally asked someone if it was always sunny there, and how anything could ever grow if so, and was told that almost all the rain fell between December and March. And when she asked if it was always so hot, she learned that the heat often lasted well into October.

She spent most evenings by the pool, reading books in a lounger and taking dips every so often, so her wet suit could cool her body. On a few nights, it was so hot in her apartment that she hauled a mattress onto the balcony and slept there. She woke up at dawn to chirping birds in the olive tree. It seemed the birds only sang in the morning; during the day even they were struck dumb by the heat.

The library where she worked was new and modern; the staff were friendly and she quickly felt at home. Melissa kick-started her social life with the same enthusiasm as she tackled everything else. She invited Sofia to dinners with her friends and brought her to parties, outdoor concerts, and music clubs.

Sofia went all over Palo Alto on her bike. Sometimes she devoted whole days to riding, circling residential neighbourhoods full of fancy houses that were shaded by enormous oaks, maples, and elms, with flowers climbing over fences and exteriors. Almost all the houses were enclosed behind high walls, like little oases, which made her wonder why you would want to hide away in such a beautiful city.

She roamed around parks, embracing the immense trunks of redwoods and staring up at their crowns, so high in the eternally blue sky; she couldn't get enough of the scent of pine and eucalyptus that hung over the city like a veil. She often strolled down University Avenue in downtown Palo Alto, which really consisted of nothing more than a long street full of shops, cafés, and restaurants. She was surprised at how many people smiled at her. The men seemed more forward than in Sweden, but usually in a pleasant way. A few times she let herself be hit on by Stanford students, and enjoyed the attention even if she did eventually reject their propositioning.

I fit in here, she thought. *This is a place I could spend my life.*

She often sat at Starbucks or Peet's, sipping a cup of coffee and surfing the internet. She chatted with other patrons. It was so easy to start a conversation. *You're from Sweden? Oh, wow! What's it like there? Does it snow all the time?*

During her café visits she worked on the blog, because she was afraid her entries might be traceable to her apartment otherwise. One day as she was sitting there surfing after work, she decided to download Oswald's autobiography as an e-book.

It stung her to pay money for it, but what the hell – Simon had never sent the book, and she was curious. At first she was surprised to find that the text didn't upset her. His lies about his childhood and family, the nonsense about how he invented the theses. When she got to a chapter where he described ground-breaking insights he'd had in prison, which would lead to new theses, she laughed – it was so transparent.

But this was before she got to the part about her. She read it several times as a restless, nagging feeling spread through her body. It was the last sentence, the one about how they would meet again. How could he even suggest such a thing? She tried to write an angry entry about him for the blog, but it all came out wrong. And then came the dark, gnawing rage that he could still affect her like this.

She was so restless that night that she paced back and forth in her apartment and didn't even notice the blazing sunset until the last few rays of light were licking at the night sky. Despite the late hour, she called Melissa to ask if she had any tips for sightseeing in San Francisco. Melissa didn't hesitate to say she wanted to come along and show Sofia around.

They took the train up the next day. In under an hour they were in San Francisco, doing all the typical tourist stuff: walking across the Golden Gate bridge and crowding with other tourists at Fisherman's Wharf. They walked out on the piers, looked at the sea lions, ate creamy mussel soup in bread bowls, and listened to street musicians. Then they did some shopping and had dinner in Chinatown.

Sofia was so exhausted by all the new impressions that she declined Melissa's offer to see a baseball game the next day.

For her next trip, she went to San Francisco alone. She

brought her bike on the train and rode it around with no destination in mind. She walked it up the steep hills and sped down them at ridiculous speeds, until she finally found herself at the coast. The ocean seemed deeper and wilder here. She sat down on the shore and enjoyed the fresh breeze, then rolled up her jeans and waded into the water. It was freezing cold, and the undertow almost pulled her down, so she went back to sit in the sand. A dog was throwing itself into the waves again and again, fetching a stick, and she watched it as she hugged her knees to her chest. The horizon wasn't visible – only a haze that grew fainter and fainter until it turned into white sky.

She realized that someone had sat down next to her in the sand. It was a man in his forties, with shoulder-length sun-bleached hair. He was tanned, with deep creases around his eyes and mouth.

'What a shame that we have this beautiful place, and we can't even swim! I tried to take a dip too, but it's hella cold.'

'Is the water always this chilly?'

'Yeah, pretty much. Although it's warmer now, in the fall, than it is in the summer.'

'Why's that?'

'In the summer there's fog at night, and it comes in and covers the whole city. It drives the temperature way down. It will be five or ten degrees cooler than it is inland. You're from Sweden, aren't you?'

'Is my accent that obvious?'

'Yes, but it sounds nice. How come you Swedes speak such good English?'

'TV and music, and we visit American websites and stuff like that.'

The man, who introduced himself as Orson King, was easy to talk to and suddenly, before she could stop herself, she had told him why she was there.

'I already know who you are,' he cut her off. 'I misled you a little there at first.'

Her heart jumped into her throat. *They found me. It's all over.*

'Don't worry,' King said when he saw her frightened expression. 'I read everything there is to read about cults, and there was an article about you and that asshole Oswald in an American paper. I work at a shelter for defectors a little inland. When I saw you, I recognized you right away from the picture in the paper. Weird coincidence, right?'

'Jeez, you scared me! I thought you were a private eye they'd sent after me.'

'No, definitely not. I'm as anti-cult as they come. Listen, it would be great if you would come to see us. Talk to the teenagers there, tell them about your experience. I bet they'd like that.'

'It would only scare them if I told them what happened to me.'

'I don't think so. I think it would help their problems seem more manageable. Make them want to keep fighting.'

'Well, in that case, I want to remain anonymous. No one can know that I was there.'

'We can make that happen.'

★

And that's how Sofia ended up spending a Saturday talking to teenagers who had escaped from cults. The shelter was out in a valley in the desert. The little hollow itself was green, but all around it was an expanse of endless sand with cactus-like plants and tumbleweeds. The building was painted red, like a Swedish cottage, and looked out of place in the barren landscape. A couple of horses walked around a paddock, nibbling at the almost non-existent grass. It was quiet as she and Orson King stepped out of the car. Way too quiet.

'Lots of the kids here have it tough,' said King. 'They're struggling with religious convictions they've had drummed into them all their lives, things they've never dared to question.'

He showed her around the stables and the main building. Everyone inside was so young. Mostly teenagers. They gazed at Sofia, full of curiosity; some of them gave her hesitant smiles, and some looked away. She asked King about their parents, and he said they were all still in the various cults. These kids had been shunned; their families had rejected them.

They gathered in the mess hall: about twenty teenagers, King, a female counsellor, and Sofia herself. She was going to tell her story – that was all they expected from her. As she began to speak, the images that she created with her story seemed foreign, as if they belonged to someone else. But everyone listened breathlessly. Her monologue turned into a Q&A session. A red-headed, freckle-faced boy, who reminded Sofia of a younger version of Benjamin, raised his hand.

'Is it true that Elvira wasn't allowed to go to her mother's funeral?'

Sofia was caught so off-guard that at first she couldn't say a word.

'How do you know about Elvira?' she asked at last.

A skinny girl of around fifteen with big eyes and thin lips stood up.

'I'm half Swedish, or whatever. My mom's from Sweden, and my dad's from the US. I translated part of Elvira's blog so everyone could read it. We liked it so much. What happened to her?'

A silent battle played out in Sofia's mind: tell the truth and kill these kids' last shred of hope, or think up a decently believable lie? But she didn't have to rack her brains, because the freckled kid shook his head.

'She went back to the cult, didn't she? She gave up. What the hell else could she do, when she was pregnant and all? She didn't really have a choice.'

'You always have a choice,' Sofia said. 'But still, Elvira did win one battle. She's being taken care of now, but doesn't have to actually be part of the cult itself. The babies are fine.'

'Yeah, except they'll probably be raised as ViaTerra kids,' said the girl. 'And that's not exactly awesome.'

'No, it's not,' Sofia agreed. She wanted to squeeze in that it was lucky that none of them were pregnant with the child of a perverted cult leader, but then she changed her mind. Because how could she be sure of that?

Another girl, slightly older, who had been sitting silently in the back row, stood up.

'Listen, we know you have a blog too. I don't suppose you could translate some of the entries, could you?'

'I'd be happy to. I didn't know you were reading it… or that you even existed.'

It struck her, now that she was standing there, that perhaps she had been careless. That the teenagers might leak the news that she'd been there.

'I hope you understand that I don't want anyone to find out I was here,' she said tentatively.

The guy who looked like Benjamin laughed.

'Who do you think we are? I can assure you there are no Oswald fans around here. And anyway, Orson would kill us if we said a word.'

A wave of laughter broke out, relieving the tension. It was the perfect moment to end her address.

*

It was already dark by the time Orson would drive her home. They sat on a bench in the garden for a while, looking up at the starry sky and listening to the crickets serenade them. Shooting stars seemed to fall one after the next. The air was dry and cool – soon it would be cold. She thought of the kids she'd spoken with, of their parents' betrayal. Knowing that they'd found Elvira's blog and had tried to follow it moved her so much that she felt a lump in her throat.

'How can this happen?' she said out loud. 'Why do parents abandon their children? I felt a little powerless when I was talking to them.'

King considered this for a moment.

'The last little shred of respect I had for religion disappeared when I got this job,' he said at last. She couldn't see his face in the dark; she could only smell his tobacco scent. It wasn't disagreeable, but it stood in sharp contrast to the scent of mimosa that wafted by on the air.

'Ugh, I'm sorry for being a downer,' he said. 'It's a good thing you came here to talk to them. You can be sure they enjoyed it.'

'It was fun to visit. Although sometimes I wonder how you explain to someone that their parents don't want them. And if there's really all that much you can do for them.'

'Sure there is,' he said. 'You can help them find their way back to real life.'

Before Orson dropped Sofia off outside her apartment, he gave her a few booklets full of information on the shelter, and phone numbers she could call at any time.

'If anything does happen to you here, against all expectations, if you need help, just let me know,' he said before they went their separate ways.

Just as she walked through the door, Benjamin called.

'I love you, Sofia,' he breathed.

'I love you too. Nothing has changed.'

30

Winter went by so quickly and peacefully that Simon began to think Oswald truly had given up on his deranged hunt for Sofia. The pension had been full of Christmas cheer all December. Lights on the trees and lanterns in the snow. After one cold spell, the snow had fallen so heavily that Simon had to shovel every day.

He didn't have any visitors from ViaTerra. When Sofia called she was always in a good mood; she said that Oswald must have found someone else to harass, and didn't even want to talk about it. She went on and on about how much she liked San Francisco until Simon almost wished he were there with her.

It was only when he walked by the manor that he felt that unpleasant sensation in his belly. So he kept a watchful eye on them. He had ignored that feeling once before and would never make the same mistake again.

But in late February, he received an email, the strangest one he'd ever gotten. At first he thought it was spam, it was such gibberish, but the sender's address caught him off-guard: info@viaterra.se. Simon knew the cult's ethics unit used this address to respond to email from anxious relatives of disgraced members. Since these members were not allowed to have contact with the outside world, the ethics unit would write that the person in question was in good health but unavailable for the time being. It was a standard measure. But now he had received an email from this account. He wondered if Benny might have sent it, but why on earth would he send a bunch of random letters and numbers?

T15G K150B
T14AW T21O
Don't respond

It was the 'don't respond' part that Simon was hung up on. Why send an email if you didn't want a response? If anyone but Benny had sent this is, it meant they had taken a great risk. They must have sneaked into the guards' booth or the staff office to use the computer there. But why send this nonsense to Simon?

Then he realized that the second letter in each word had been replaced by a number. He took out a notebook and a pen and copied down the message, trying to replace the numbers with their corresponding letters of the alphabet. 15 was O, 14 was N, and so on. But the message was still illegible. Now Simon was sure it was a code, a message for him. He turned the paper upside down, feeling hopeless, and then he saw the word 'book' written backwards. All at once, he could read the message.

GOT BOOK
WANT OUT
Don't respond

He had made contact with Jacob. Simon had almost forgotten he'd sent the book. He had the sudden urge to go straight to the ViaTerra gate and demand that they free Jacob. But he knew it wasn't that simple. The certainty that Jacob wanted out made Simon's heart beat faster. He'd suspected that there were others who were sick of being enslaved but didn't know how to escape. *This is it,* he thought. *I really need to think this through. It's important not to be too rash.*

The next day, after work, he went to the village and bought an invitation card for a baptism, the kind where you fill in the date and write a greeting to the recipient. Back at home he thought for a long time about how to formulate his message. He disguised his handwriting, making it elegant and soft. He put the date for the baptism a week away, at five o'clock in the afternoon. That seemed a little late in the day, but he had no choice. Then he wrote his greeting on the blank, right-hand side of the card.

Hi, Jacob!
Hope you can come to Elin's baptism.
We'll gather by the little gate outside the church.
Warm greetings
Cousin Beata

He inspected the card before inserting it into the envelope, almost certain that the guards would allow Jacob to receive it. Not because it was innocent, but because this sort of invitation was upsetting to the recipient. Another family event to decline – it was a reminder that they could no longer see their relatives. And the guards liked messing with the staff. Also, they were too lazy to find out if Jacob really had a cousin named Beata.

The letter felt warm and alive in his hand as he addressed

and stamped it. The closest mailbox was a few hundred metres away, and as the letter thumped into it he sent up a silent prayer that everything would be as hectic and chaotic as usual over at the manor. That the guards wouldn't notice it had been postmarked on the island. And that the letter would slip right past the censors.

That was the start of a week of impatient waiting. What if they didn't have time to deal with the mail? What would happen if they asked Jacob who Beata was? Maybe the email was a trap – maybe Jacob was working with Benny to figure out whether Simon was a traitor. So much could go wrong. And yet he wouldn't give up hope.

★

One week later, he was standing outside the small gate at quarter to five, breathless and tense. At first he thought he would wait outside the gate, but then he realized that it would be stupid to whisper over the wall. His mind was going a mile a minute: *He's not coming, he didn't get my letter, this is completely nuts, I'm acting like the place is a prison, no, worse, it's like I'm trying to sneak over the border into North Korea.*

He was standing behind his usual oak trunk. The yard was deserted, aside from a duck strutting around on the lawn. The aspens and maples had changed colour and created a red-and-yellow dome over the annexes.

There was a sudden snapping sound from the ground next to him. When he turned, Jacob was standing right there. His eyes were wide, as if he was seeing a ghost.

'You scared me!' Simon said, sizing up Jacob. Beyond the

fear on his face, he hadn't changed a bit: his farmer clothes, his tan, and the faint odour of cow manure were all the same.

Simon wanted to hug him, but it seemed premature.

'How did you get in?'

'I have a key to the gate.'

'What the hell? That's incredible!'

'Great, isn't it? You can leave with me if you want to. All you have to do is step out into freedom.'

'Simon, I can't believe you're standing right here. This is crazy.'

'So are you coming with me?'

'It's a little complicated. I spent all night thinking about it. It's the animals. They'll neglect them if I leave, and maybe even slaughter them. What do I do?'

Jacob's voice had risen; Simon put a finger to his lips.

'What did you think about the card I sent? Was it easy to understand?'

'At first I thought I had lost my mind. That I had some cousin I didn't even know about, but then I figured it out. This is just insane, that you're *here.* That this gate can be opened.'

'Do you think there's anyone else who wants to leave? You can pass through freely, there's no alarm, it doesn't leave any sort of trace, and they can hide at my place to start with.'

Simon wondered what the heck he had just said, but it did actually seem like a good idea.

'I'll ask around. Can you come back in a few days?'

'Of course, but you have to keep this quiet. Not a word about me, or the gate. Is Oswald back yet?'

'He'll be here in early April. Madde's been turning the place upside down, polishing everything, even the damn doorknobs.

I can hardly find time to feed the animals, and the manure is piling up in the barn – as you may be able to smell.'

Simon didn't say anything, although the odour wafting off Jacob was overwhelming when he stood so close.

'Listen, Simon, what's it like out there? Will I be okay?'

'Definitely. You could easily get a job on one of the farms. The pension is doing better than ever, and all the meat and eggs and stuff come from here on the island. I'm sure they need workers.'

'Shit, I want to get out, but what about the animals? The cows are already staring at me with their big, sad eyes. It's like they know I want to take off.'

'There's no rush. Just think about it.'

Suddenly they heard a motorcycle roar to life. 'I have to go. See you the day after tomorrow. Same time. Leave a note at the gate if you get held up. Use your secret code.'

Jacob grinned, gave a thumbs up, and vanished.

*

When Simon returned two days later, he was a little late to arrive. Inga Hermansson had come to find Simon out in the field where he was working; she was all keyed up.

'A member of the jury called. He wondered if you and I would be home this evening. We will be, right?'

'I just have to run an errand in town, but I'll be home by dinnertime.'

'Do you suppose…' she said.

'I guess we'll see.'

When Simon opened the gate to the manor, something

seemed off. Everything was quiet and still. Not a single sound was coming from within the walls. *He got held up,* Simon thought. *Something happened. They caught him out.* But he opened the gate and slipped in anyway.

There they stood before him, as stiff as statues. Jacob with his mouth agape and Anna with a backpack slung over one shoulder, eyes wide. The beginning of a sound, a cry, came from her mouth when she saw Simon, but Jacob shook his head in warning.

'I can't stand it anymore,' Anna whispered.

Simon could see in her eyes that she truly meant it.

31

Everything got better during that winter. Oswald transformed. His fanatical obsession with Sofia Bauman disappeared. He stopped sending letters to the intermediary loser. He seemed absolutely consumed by the new theses he was writing.

He was sometimes euphoric about them when Anna-Maria showed up for a meeting, and he read them out loud to her, his eyes blazing.

'Did you know that most people spend more time in their heads than on Earth?' he said one day. 'That's why we have ViaTerra. To give people their lives back.'

She didn't always understand what he meant, but she supposed he could reach such depths that it was practically inhuman, so she affirmed him with words of praise and delighted cries.

Oswald was so friendly during these months that Anna-Maria was bewildered. Her visits, formerly so hectic and businesslike, now felt like cosy get-togethers for chatting and reading letters from Oswald's fans. The piles of mail had grown considerably since he'd published his book. Women sent half-naked pictures of themselves, and some of them were incredibly attractive. But Oswald just laughed.

'Look at that idiot. It's disgusting how she's whoring herself out like this. Good thing I have a classy lady,' he said, running a finger over her cheek.

He was being so tender that Anna-Maria got suspicious. She almost missed those moments of roughness, when he messed with her, and she wanted to reassure herself that that side of him still existed. So she brought up Sofia Bauman, usually a topic that unleashed his rage, but not even that got him going this time.

'You've got to let go sometime, right? Didn't you see her in those recordings? Just unbelievable. Her guilty conscience about all the lies she spread about me will be the end of her – we don't need to lift a finger. Believe me, she's going to self-destruct.'

One day, Anna-Maria put on a blouse with a neckline so low it barely covered her nipples, and she didn't bother with a bra. She put her hair up to bare her neck and throat, then dabbed on the perfume he said he liked. Standing close to him, she bent her head back, pretending she needed to crack her joints. She knew that, like her, he liked choking sex.

He took the bait right away, squeezing his hand around her throat and shoving her up against the wall. It turned her on – she began to breathe heavily, and he squeezed harder. Just the perfect amount, making her slightly dizzy.

It ended there, but it was enough for her to realize that the spark was in no way gone from him. Still, she wondered sometimes. He'd gone without sex for over a year. It would have been easy to have a quickie against the wall. Not once had a guard entered the room during her visits. But he always stopped himself at the last second, giving some excuse about how he didn't want to put their future at risk. He was a man who liked to drive things to the very edge, test every last boundary.

Despite this troublesome moment, the whole winter passed in a pleasant rush. He sent her to ViaTerra sometimes – *that* sure wasn't an honourable task. Those idiots were a few sandwiches short of a picnic. They mostly looked like zombies, and never got a damn thing done – the place was starting to look neglected. She was glad she wouldn't be in Bosse's or Madeleine's shoes when Oswald was released. He would unleash hell on them.

Christmas and New Year's came and went, and they got to spend one hour together on Christmas Eve. They didn't do anything traditional; Oswald hated Christmas. Despite that, however, he gave her a gentle kiss on the lips and said, 'Merry Christmas, hottie!' at which point she almost levitated off the cold concrete floor out of sheer joy.

*

It wasn't until the end of February, about a month before Oswald's release, that he began to get restless. He made her confirm the date several times, and the exact procedure for how it would all happen. In the end he decided he would spend his first night out at a hotel in Gothenburg, and head to ViaTerra the next day. He had started asking awkward questions about ViaTerra – how it looked, whether the staff understood the importance of the success he'd found with his autobiography. She told him the truth: the staff seemed lost without a leader. The manor looked neglected, and she had pointed this out to Madde, with no results. This unleashed a tirade that was not, thank God, directed at her, but at the incompetence of the staff.

'I want you to do me a favour,' he said one day.

'Anything.'

'Get me a meeting with that Damian. I want to talk to him in private.'

'Not on your life!' The words slipped out of her before she could stop them. 'I mean, I've broken off contact with him since what happened with the camera,' she hurried to add.

'Then you'll have to initiate contact again.'

'But why?'

'Jesus Christ, are you going to pry into my personal business like this when I get out, too?' he snapped.

'No, of course not, but I don't understand. You have that character you were sending letters to. Why do you need to meet with Damian?'

'For one thing, that guy is no longer working for me in that capacity. For another, this isn't the kind of thing I'd want to put in writing.'

'What do you mean? Why can't you tell me?'

'Because it's extremely personal.'

'I don't understand why he gets to know about your personal matters, and I don't.'

'You don't have to understand,' he interrupted her. He had that look on his face. The one that wouldn't brook any contradiction. Soon everything they had built up over the past few months would be destroyed.

'The reason you don't understand is because you still don't trust me. And I take offence at that.'

But now a sly expression appeared on his face; his eyes looked playful. The realization came to her along with a wave of relief. How had she not seen it? He was obviously preparing something for the two of them for when he was released. Some sort of thank you for her help and her friendship, and maybe even something to celebrate their love. Naturally, that was what was going on. She gave him a hesitant smile.

'I can call him. But this is all between the two of you.'

'Exactly. Because I don't want you there.'

'But what should I tell the guards? You're not even related. Or friends.'

'Tell them he's your assistant. Taking over your duties for a day.'

When Anna-Maria thought about what Helga McLean would have to say about this, it felt like there was a snake twisting in her belly.

'Okay, fine,' she sighed, and his mood changed as suddenly as a chameleon changing colours. He was back to being super pleasant again.

Before she left that day, he took her head between his hands and gazed into her eyes for a long moment.

'You're my Annie, my sweet, wonderful Annie,' he said, giving her a light kiss on the lips. 'Tell the trash at ViaTerra that they'd better make sure the place is tip-top when I get home,' he added. 'The water out at Devil's Rock is freezing cold.'

32

There it was again, that gaze. Like a magnet from across the room. Sofia didn't even have to glance up to know he was looking at her. For three days in a row, he had visited the library. He always sat in the reading corner with a periodical, hanging out for a few hours and pretending to read. But in fact, his eyes were following her.

Normally she would have walked over to him and told him to stop staring. But there was nothing threatening about his behaviour, and besides, he was cute. His hair was longish, and a little shaggy. She was sure his eyes were blue. Clean facial features, his nose a little long, his mouth soft and sensual. There was something attractive about his posture; he moved freely and languidly. He seemed at home in his body. And there was something more, too. A feeling that this was an opportunity she shouldn't blow.

The California winter had exceeded her expectations. Her job was going well, she had made new friends, and the sun shone almost constantly from the clear blue sky. Only in the mornings was Palo Alto shrouded in fog, which soon dissolved into a mild heat haze. The rain didn't come until January, and when it did arrive it was as a stubborn cloudburst that lasted for a few weeks.

Then the sun returned. She was happy; full of a joyful delirium she hadn't experienced since before the cult. The days were long and warm; the nights short and mild. Her nightmares had stopped. Now all she needed was the cherry on top: she wanted to experience something special before returning to Sweden. Something exciting, and maybe a little naughty.

And then this super cute guy just walked through the door one day, sat down on a sofa, and checked her out.

She managed to tear her attention away from him and focus on her job. She registered a few new books on the computer. Then she heard an 'ahem' and there he was, standing right in front of her. His eyes were definitely blue. His bold smile brought a blush to her face. There was that little jump in her stomach.

'You're Swedish, aren't you?' he said. In Swedish.

She nodded, trying to be professional, as if he had just asked about a book.

'How can I help you?'

'Well, I've got a problem. I can't stop looking at you.'

She laughed at the line. She felt embarrassed, the way you do when the cheesy banter in a Hollywood film makes you squirm.

'You'll have to go to an eye doctor about that. As you can see, I'm busy here.'

He put out his hand. She took it automatically.

'Mattias Wilander, from Gothenburg.'

He held onto her hand when she tried to take it back. His forwardness was making her uncomfortable. She preferred to move slowly when flirting. Stolen glances, hands brushing, all that. He was too blunt.

But it was exciting that they'd run into each other. He was the first Swede she'd met so far.

She looked at him, her eyes urging him to leave, but he stayed put. She had the vague feeling he was dangerous. Just the type of guy she was drawn to. Like Oswald, and Ellis once upon a time. Men who left her life in a shambles.

'I apologize for being so forward,' he said. 'I noticed you when I came here a few days ago. I felt drawn to you. As if we've met before. Have we? Met?'

'I don't think so.'

'How long have you lived here?'

'Almost eight months.'

'I'm pretty new here. I arrived a few months ago. Still feeling a little lost, and I could use some pointers. Clubs where they play good music. That kind of thing. Could we grab coffee when you're done with work?'

You promised yourself, you promised Benjamin, no relationships, no getting laid while you're here!

But coffee couldn't hurt. There was nothing wrong with meeting new people.

He hung around until she was done for the day. They went to a café nearby. He was easy to talk to; he'd recently finished a degree in psychology and was taking a year off. He would be spending a few months in Palo Alto but had no concrete plans – he said he just wanted to stand on his own two legs for a while.

'Although to be honest, I'm pretty boring. A total bookworm. I just got so tired of all the drinking and fucking, pardon my French.'

A thrill ran through her body.

'It's like I'm either on or off,' he continued. 'Either I'm totally chilled, or else I take things to the very limit. That's how I want my life to be.'

She gave him a few tips, good spots to visit in Palo Alto and San Francisco. But he just wanted to talk about her. She couldn't remember ever having met a guy who was so interested in her life. Not even Benjamin.

When it was time to part ways, he just said thanks and bye. He didn't ask for her number and he didn't ask to see her again, which made her feel duped and disappointed.

★

She couldn't fall asleep that night and didn't want to call Benjamin, so she decided to Skype with Ellis, since she hadn't talked to him for a while. Ellis was happy to hear from her and talked nonstop. He had created a new dating site called FeelYou, or FYou for short. The basic premise was to get to know someone without a lot of chatting and pictures. You created an account and gave your gender and age, then selected a single word to describe your character. Whoever took the bait sent a single word back, and then you tossed words back and forth until good – or bad – vibes appeared. Incredibly enough, many successful relationships had emerged thanks to the service, and Ellis had made a small fortune. He tipped Sofia off about a *Wired* article that mentioned him.

This sounded so fantastic that Sofia felt like she had to tell him something in return, to compensate, so she spilled what had just happened with Mattias at the library.

'Oh, that's nothing,' Ellis said. 'Shit, you're only twenty-four, Sofia. Have some fun. You're hot as hell. Surely you aren't planning to remain faithful to Benjamin forever? It's just that cult, they made you think like a goddamn nun.'

Even though this advice was coming from someone with a dubious sexual past, it was still comforting. What was the point of going abroad if you didn't allow yourself one tiny little slip-up?

Mattias didn't return to the library the next day. She was extremely disappointed and kept staring in the direction of the reading corner. She found herself furious when an overweight man settled into the chair where Mattias liked to sit. But when she walked out the door at the end of the day, he was there waiting for her. He was leaning against a tree, giving her a crooked smile, and she walked toward him. His eyes were so blue she wondered if he used tinted contacts. He was wearing distressed jeans and a leather jacket, and he came over to her and took her hands. Christ, he had such a great smile!

This is the moment when I have to say no, she thought. *If I don't it will all go to hell.* But what she really wanted, in that moment, was to live two parallel lives: one where she was with Benjamin, and another where she followed this stranger and lived out all her secret sexual fantasies. But you could only live one life at a time. And suddenly Benjamin seemed so far away.

'I rented a car,' Mattias said. 'Come with me to Half Moon Bay and we'll take a walk by the ocean.'

'I have to work tomorrow.'

'Just for a few hours. Dinner's on me.'

She had never been to Half Moon Bay but had heard it was beautiful.

'Sorry I was so forward yesterday,' he said as she got in the car. 'We'll take it slow, okay? Until further notice.'

Why have I not mentioned Benjamin? She wondered. *Why can't I just spit it out? I never get tongue-tied – it's not like me.*

'How did you know I was Swedish?' she asked instead.

'It's the accent, I heard you talking. I can even hear the Swedish accent in my own voice. I suppose it will never go away.'

The road to the coast made sharp curves between enormous redwoods that spread their spicy scent through the half-open car window.

Half Moon Bay was covered in a gentle haze that lent a soft, lovely sheen to the scenery. They walked along the shore for a while, then sat down on a bench and gazed out at the ocean, which glittered with sunlight. A pair of pelicans glided down like sailplanes and landed on the water. The waves were crested with white and a couple of surfers were tossed off their boards again and again.

'I surf,' he said. 'That's why I've been here a few times before. Have you heard of mavericks? They're huge waves that form about three kilometres out, in the wintertime. The place is called Pillar Point Harbor – it's a little north of here. The waves can get up to seven metres high. Every year, all the top surfers have a competition there. You have to be invited to participate. I've always dreamed of being part of that. I can teach you to surf, if you want.'

'I'd love to. That would be fun.'

She wondered what on earth she had just said – she'd never been interested in surfing. But his presence basically made it impossible to think clearly. She felt strange when she was with him. A little dizzy, bordering on giggly. As if there were no limits. *Surfing? Sure, why not go skydiving too, while we're at it?*

'So why did you come here?' he asked. 'Just for work, or… ?'

She thought for a moment, wondering why she felt like she

could trust him. Maybe it was because he seemed so uncomplicated. Not judgemental in the least. Yet she felt her cheeks burning before she even managed to finish her first sentence.

'It's kind of complicated. I mean, you can't post this on Facebook or Twitter or anything, but I was trying to get away from a cult.'

He laughed.

'Shit, that's nothing to be ashamed of. Isn't everyone part of some cult these days? Listen, the two of us can start our own cult, you and me.'

They chatted on the bench for a long time. The breeze died down; the waves settled into faint ripples on the water. The sun bled through the airy clouds on the horizon, splashing gold on the surface of the ocean. When the sun sank into the water, she heard him take a deep breath and let it out fast. He moved closer. She felt his warmth against her arm and was going to place her hand over his, but right then he stood up and asked if she wanted to grab a bite to eat.

They had dinner at a restaurant in town. Only once did he touch her – a passing stroke of his hand on her thigh under the table. It was so gentle and quick that she thought she might have imagined it. That she had merely brushed against the tablecloth.

On the way home they were quiet – it was a companionable silence. When he dropped her off at her apartment, they exchanged numbers. He ran a finger down her nose and kissed her lips. It was a quick kiss, fluttering and soft; his lips were cool, and yet it set off fireworks in her body.

There was a weight on her chest when she walked into her apartment; it was so heavy that she had to call Benjamin, even though she knew he was at work.

He sounded annoyed when he picked up.

'I'm in the car, Sofia, I can't talk.'

'It won't take long. Just one fucking minute.'

'Fine, what is it?'

'Look, do you think we could have an open relationship while I'm here?'

'What do you mean?'

'Like, see other people a little bit. Take a short break.'

'What the hell? Did you meet someone?'

'No, nothing has happened! I mean… nothing serious.'

'I can't believe you're just calling me out of the blue.'

'Sorry. But do you think it would work?'

'No way! Go to hell.'

He hung up on her. She started crying right away – she felt so rotten and ashamed at how desperate she was. Maybe she needed some space. Why was she acting so crazy? She sank onto the sofa and sent up a silent prayer to God, asking him to help her make the right decision. And she got an answer right away: the phone rang, and it was Simon.

'We won!'

'Huh?'

'The competition, I mean.'

'Congratulations, Simon, that's awesome!'

'Yeah, except now I have so much dough it just feels wrong. So I'm coming to visit you in San Francisco.'

33

They ran through the woods to Simon's cabin. Anna stubbornly tried to keep pace with Simon; she stumbled a few times but got up and snapped at him peevishly when he asked if he should slow down. When they got to his place, Anna threw herself onto the sofa, panting, as Simon sat down in his chair. He didn't know what to say to her – he basically didn't know her at all. Simon had avoided talking to her while he was in the cult, mostly because she was ridiculously pretty and seemed to be in completely out of his league with those high cheekbones, turned-up nose, dark eyes with even darker eyelashes, and a cascade of dark blonde hair she was always twirling around her fingers. She had seemed inaccessible and a little cold. But as soon as she caught her breath, she began to talk and didn't stop, and Simon realized she was, in fact, perfectly nice.

'Madde has gone crazy, I swear, she's out of her mind. Although everyone knows *he's* controlling her, sort of. She visited him in prison. And Oswald's lawyer, that Anna-Maria Callini, she came out to the manor and acted like she owned the place. It's like straight-up Nazi shit, Simon. Framed photos of Franz everywhere, and we're supposed to stand in front of them and applaud before we go to bed. Some tone-deaf bastard wrote a battle song called 'ViaTerra Victorious' that we have to, like, shout out at morning assembly, in unison. It sounds deranged.'

Simon realized she was talking like she was still there.

'That book he wrote, we had to read it like a hundred times, and then Madde came to check that we understood it, and anyone who didn't understand something had to jump off the Rock. In this cold. They changed the schedule so we only get to sleep for five hours every night. If you oversleep you have to eat rice and beans for a week.'

Simon tried to get her to slow down by placing a hand on her shoulder, but she kept talking.

'And then Franz said something about how we had to learn to march, as some sort of discipline, so we've been marching back and forth across the front drive several times a day. It has to be in rhythm, so we become a team. And all the girls in high heels! It looks demented.'

Simon tried to slip in that he understood exactly, but she went on before he had the chance to speak.

'And now there are going to be new rules once he comes home. We have to salute every time we see him. And it's somehow our fault that the media writes shitty stories about him. So we owe him fifty hours of compensation work, every damn one of us, which means we'll have to iron his shirts, clean his room, and use our salary, which we've barely even gotten lately, to buy him a welcome-home present. A super-expensive camera with a big lens and everything. And we've been working day and night to prepare the property for his return. We've even polished every last fucking doorknob.'

'Jacob told me about that,' Simon said. 'You must be hungry. Let's have something to eat, and then you can tell me more.'

*

Once he'd fetched food from the pension restaurant, Anna was quiet for a while. She must not have eaten for a long time, the way she was bolting her meal. She ended up eating half of Simon's portion as well.

'But I think the worst part is his new policy,' she said once she had finished, muffling a burp behind her hand. 'He wrote it in prison. It's about battling the enemies of ViaTerra. He wrote that any means of silencing the opposition is allowed, because they're "the scum of the earth". Yes, he really did use those words, don't you believe me?'

'Of course, but Anna, how long have you felt this way? How long have you known that what's happening there is wrong?'

Then she began to cry in despair as he sat helplessly by and watched. He always felt awkward around crying girls. He didn't know how to comfort them.

'I don't know,' she said at last. 'I don't know even know what's right or wrong right now. All I know is that I can't take it anymore.'

'Let's deal with one thing at a time,' Simon said, moving to sit on the sofa beside her. 'First you can have a shower and get some sleep. You look tired. Tomorrow I'll give you some stuff to read. A few articles, a couple of websites. Then you can form your own opinion about all this.'

*

Just as Anna got out of the shower, wrapped in Simon's huge robe, Inga Hermansson came through the door. She typically knocked, but right now she was so excited that she forgot.

'Simon, they sent us an email full of questions to respond to. It's obvious that they have us in mind to win the competition.'

She froze when she saw Anna.

'Oops, I'm sorry. I didn't know you had company. Oh, Simon, you got a girlfriend, how lovely!'

'She's not my girlfriend. She escaped from the cult up there.'

This news certainly got Hermansson moving. She embraced Anna – something Simon realized perhaps he should have done as well – and then rushed out the door. She soon returned with soup from the restaurant, some clothes, and a toothbrush.

At last Anna fell asleep on the sofa, and didn't wake up until Simon looked in on her the next morning. By that point, Simon was well aware of the efforts to find her. He could hear shouts and the barking of a dog from the forest, where they were clearly performing a search. Motorcycles went back and forth on the road to the village.

Inga Hermansson came to the greenhouse to report that someone in a guard's uniform had come to the pension to ask about Anna. But no one had come to Simon's cottage, which he thought was strange. He knew why it was so important to get Anna back. She had worked directly under Oswald and knew some of his secrets. Plus, she was beautiful, so the media would jump at the chance to hear her story. Oswald certainly didn't want to be saddled with another Sofia Bauman. And now that Simon had Anna in his cottage, he wasn't sure whether he liked it. He wanted to live in peace and quiet. He would have to find some way to occupy Anna's time, then send her somewhere where she would feel safe. But when he asked about her parents, she shot him down and said she didn't want to contact them yet, that she was ashamed.

'Why are you ashamed?'

'I'm such a failure. They warned me time and time again, but I wouldn't listen. I wrote like a hundred letters to them where I talked about how great ViaTerra was. So to come home with my tail between my legs…'

'Anna, I'm sure they don't care about all that. They'll just be glad that you left ViaTerra.'

'Maybe. Can I stay a few more days?'

Simon couldn't say no. He decided to let her use his computer while he worked, and got her to read everything there was to read about ViaTerra online – including Sofia's blog and the newspaper articles he'd saved. When she was done reading, she seemed livelier. But she still walked around in Inga Hermansson's nightgown and slept twelve hours a day.

'I thought of something you can do,' he said. 'Something that helped Sofia. Write it all down, from beginning to end. From the day you first heard of ViaTerra until the day you escaped.'

When he returned after work, she was still at the computer; she turned around when she heard him coming. For the first time, she gave him a big smile.

'This is crazy!'

'Right? When you're done, you can put it all online. Anonymously, if you want to. You could even write an entry for Sofia's blog. Divide up the story into chapters. One a day.'

★

Simon read Anna's story with great interest. Especially the chapter about the Sofia Bauman project. She wrote that it was a plan Oswald had dictated himself, from prison, and no one had been allowed to read it besides the security guards and the head of ViaTerra's ethics unit. When the project hadn't gone according to Oswald's plan, he'd made Callini kick the security guards off it, so she could take over. Rumour had it that he'd hired private eyes and other outside contacts to get it done. Simon wondered how on earth he was doing this all from prison.

'So Benny and Sten are in Penance?'

'They were for a while, but now they're just sitting in the booth and patrolling the property. Franz has other contacts looking for Sofia, I've heard.'

'Anna, why is he so fixated on Sofia?'

'You know why – after all she's done. She was the one who got him thrown in prison, after all.'

But Simon suspected it was more complicated. He wondered if he ought to report all of this to the police. It sounded unpleasant and illegal, but convincing Anna to go to the authorities seemed rash.

After a week of blogging, surfing, and talking to Simon late into the night, Anna started to look like a normal human again. At that point, he supplied her with books from his collection – books about other cults, written by psychologists and defectors. After a week she called her parents and asked to come home. Just as Simon had expected, they were beside themselves with joy and relief.

But Anna always found a reason to stay just one more day. One morning, as Simon was working, he wondered if Anna was afraid of being stalked like Sofia. Maybe she even thought there was an 'Anna Hedberg project.' She'd found a safe little corner in Simon's cottage, and she wasn't about to let go of it.

'Listen, Anna,' he said when he came home that day. 'They really can't do anything to you. They can't touch you – it's illegal. Understand? I think it's time for you to go home to your parents. They miss you.'

She didn't have a chance to respond. Inga Hermansson hurtled through the door to say that they'd won the competition. She hugged Simon, which he found exceedingly embarrassing.

'I'll stay for a few days in case they want to do interviews,' he said. 'Then I'm taking a week of vacation, and you can take all the credit.'

Once Inga had left the cottage, Simon turned to Anna.

'Tomorrow I'll borrow Inga's car and drive you home to your parents. Then I'm going to take a little trip.'

And he saw in her eyes that she was ready.

⋆

Two days before his flight to San Francisco, Simon took a walk to the manor to meet Jacob. It started snowing as Simon went along the path – a heavy snowfall that limited visibility. It seemed to take ages to reach the manor. Simon ended up so wet and cold that he was shaking. At first he assumed Jacob wouldn't show up. But then there he was, wearing only a coverall.

'Don't you have a coat?'

'It's part of the new program to toughen us up. No outerwear, because then we'll move faster in the cold, and walking is strictly forbidden – we have to run. Not a single one of these bastards thought about those of us who work outside sometimes. Franz will be back next week. There's a list of about a hundred impossible tasks we have to finish before then.'

'I can't believe you haven't left.'

'It's worse for the animals in this cold. I've made up my mind, Simon. As soon as spring is here for real, I'm out.'

Simon realized he had to be brief, so that Jacob wouldn't have to stand around shivering in the snow. Simon himself had worked in the barn one winter, and it was hardly warm in there. It made him furious to think that Jacob was forced to work in there without a coat. Next time he visited, he would simply take Jacob with him when he left.

Jacob seemed to read his mind.

'I promise, Simon. As soon as the ground thaws, I'll escape.'

'If you can stand it that much longer.'

'I can. For the animals.'

Simon thought of Anna, who was with her parents now, and of how happy they had been when she returned home. He wanted Jacob to experience the same thing.

'Listen, I'm going away for a little over a week,' he said. 'And then I'll be ready for the next escapee.'

34

Sofia had taken a week off work and texted Mattias to let him know she would be unavailable. As she waited for Simon in the arrivals hall of the airport, she wondered if the trip would be too much for him – flying for the first time, so many people, all these cars, the language… but Simon didn't look at all overwhelmed as he walked out with a tiny little bag over one shoulder. As they headed out to get a taxi, he went on and on about the plane, its horsepower, its wingspan – all the kind of things that Sofia certainly hadn't registered on her first flight.

They'd promised each other not to talk about ViaTerra, that they would just have a real vacation, but Sofia began to grill Simon about Anna and Jacob while they were still in the taxi.

'Let's get it over with while we're in this car,' she said. 'Then we'll transform into tourists for a week and forget about ViaTerra. So, what will happen now that Anna is back home?'

'I can take in the next defector.'

'Are you serious?'

'Why not? It's fun to watch them vanish under Oswald's very nose. I like messing with him, and besides, it feels good to help them. Anna's feeling better these days. First she read everything online, and then she read some books, and at last she wrote everything down. She's been posting her whole story on Facebook.'

'That's awesome! But Oswald's going to find you out eventually, Simon.'

'I'm not worried.'

'So who's next in line?'

'We'll see when I get back.'

'You know what? Sometimes I miss the island. It probably sounds crazy, but it's so beautiful there. It's a magical place, somehow. The sea and the cliffs, the foghorn that sounds every time something horrible is about to happen – it *does*, I swear. When the windows rattled in storm winds, or when you could hardly see your hand in front of your face in the fog… all that stuff made me feel alive. If I had my way, I would bulldoze the manor house, but not the library, and build a shelter for defectors there. And you would take care of the fields, and Jacob would take care of the animals, and…'

'And there would be framed pictures of Oswald all over, with devil horns and moustaches drawn on them, and everyone would boo when they saw them.'

They kept talking until they got to Sofia's apartment.

'We're tourists, starting now,' she said.

'There's just one more thing I want to say.'

'Out with it.'

'It was something Anna said. It might not mean anything, but apparently Oswald has hired private eyes and other outsiders to track you down. It seems like he hasn't given up.'

'No, I think he has. Anna probably just has old info. I haven't heard a whisper since you told Benny I was in Italy. I think he's lost interest in me.'

'Okay then, that's that.'

*

As they walked around Golden Gate Park the next day, Sofia noticed a few girls casting lingering gazes after Simon. A little while later, she saw another girl turn around to look at him. All at once, it struck her that Simon really fitted in there. His brawny frame, the jeans hanging just so on his hips, his plaid shirt, his messy blond mane of hair.

'Girls are checking you out, Simon.'

'Like I care.'

They leaned over the railing of the Golden Gate bridge. She asked him if it made him dizzy to look down, but he just laughed and shook his head. She herself got lightheaded and a little bit sick to her stomach when she looked over the edge. The buildings looked like toys and the people were smaller than ants. The ocean below pulled and sucked, almost demanding that you jump in.

'I want you to be honest with me now,' she said, and then she told him all about Mattias. 'What am I doing?'

'Has Benjamin been in touch at all since you so tactfully explained what was up?'

'You don't have to be sarcastic.'

A smile tugged at the corners of Simon's lips.

'No,' she said. 'I haven't heard from him. I've called and texted and emailed a hundred times. He's so freaking stubborn. I haven't even *done* anything yet, have I?'

Simon placed a hand over hers. The gesture made her tremble, because he never touched her. But he left his hand where it was.

'Here's the thing, Sofia. It doesn't matter what I say. You're still going to do what you want, aren't you? Do what feels right. It will all work out in the end.'

'You know what? There's this little devil inside me that has to get out. I've never exactly been sexually inhibited, so the forced chastity at ViaTerra almost did me in. All those rules: shirts buttoned to the top, skirts that covered your knees, the ban on perfume and red lipstick. And meanwhile, Oswald always touching me. By the end it felt like I was going to explode.'

'All of that was deliberate, Sofia.'

'I'm sure it was. Hey, I just remembered something – you were in Penance at the time – Mira, that girl who made out with some celebrity Oswald had dragged to the island…'

'Alvin Johde?'

'Right. Oswald flew off the handle because Alvin went on TV and talked about how hot ViaTerra girls were. Then it came out that Mira had snogged him. The guards forced her to confess, but Oswald was never satisfied with that, he said there had to be more. In the end she had to tell him about every fucking time she had masturbated and thought about Alvin. It all got written down. One day Oswald called all the staff together. Mira had to stand in a corner, like a kid in a dunce cap. "I'm going to tell all of you everything Mira's been up to," he said, and read her entire confession out loud. With emphasis on words like "vagina" and "horny". He looked up at us now and then, with that insinuating look. The girls had to sit in front. It was awful. And still, I think all the girls sitting there got wet as he was reading. Shit, I bet that was the whole point!'

'I'm sure it was.'

'Psychologists call it Stockholm Syndrome. I don't think it

was a syndrome at all. Just a perverted nutjob who wanted to fuck with everyone.'

'But then what's the point?'

He looked interested rather than impatient.

'The point? Well, I suppose it's that guys like him have power over other people, and that they're experts at abusing it. But that doesn't mean everyone around them has to be diagnosed with something.'

'Exactly.'

And with that, she started to cry. The tears just came. She leaned over the railing, so far it felt like she would fall.

'Sofia, what's wrong?'

'I don't know, there's something about him I can't get out of my system. Something that never made sense. He was nice sometimes, Simon. For real. He told me not to kill a wasp that was flying around the office, that it was an important part of nature. He put his jacket over my shoulders one night when I was cold. Stuff like that. And when he was being nice, he was such a hell of a gentleman that it melted you. I just don't get it.'

'That's just part of the game, Sofia, that kindness. It's confusing. That's the point. People who are confused are also easily duped.'

'You're brilliant, Simon,' she said, laughing through her tears. 'Can't we just say to hell with sex, and enjoy a lifelong platonic relationship, just you and me?'

'I'm already celibate,' he reminded her.

'Yes, that's right, so you are. Shit, it's great to have you here. I really do believe he's given up the hunt for me.'

'I don't.'

'Why not?'

'I had a little brother named Daniel. Our parents were part of a religious group, God's Way. Daniel knew early on that he was gay, but when he told my parents, they refused to accept it. The devil had to be driven out of Daniel, and it broke him.'

'You never told me that!'

'No, but now I am. So Daniel decided to leave the farm. Move to Stockholm. I drove him to the station. A few hours later, he called my mobile phone and asked me not to judge him. I thought he was referring to being gay, but I had it all wrong. The police showed up later that night. Daniel had thrown himself in front of the train.'

'Jesus Christ! Why didn't you ever tell me this? It's so sad.'

'But that's not why I'm telling you. Listen. Before I left him, at the station, I saw something in Daniel's eyes. This look I'll never forget. Like a cornered animal waiting to be put out of its misery. But I rationalized it, even though that feeling stuck with me, like an uncomfortable premonition that something bad is going to happen. Sometimes I get that same feeling when I think about you and Oswald. Fuck, Sofia, I don't want to scare you! I just want you to be careful. It's actually super unlike me to go on a gut feeling like this.'

Sofia didn't say anything for a moment as she gazed at the turquoise water. San Francisco was like a mirage in the distance. A gentle breeze toyed with her hair. She tried to experience the sensation Simon was talking about, forcing herself to call up mental images of Oswald. Yet the thought of him didn't seem very dangerous. It was as if this conversation with Simon had helped her cut the last tie.

'You know, I think what you're feeling is normal,' she said. 'If something like that has happened to you, I suppose you have to live with it for the rest of your life. But I really do think Oswald has given up. That's my gut feeling.'

'Then that's that. Come on, let's walk across this bridge, so I can say I've done it.'

They continued to walk across the Golden Gate bridge in silence. When they got to the other side, Simon cleared his throat discreetly.

'Hey, I have a few visits booked for while I'm here.'

'What?'

'Well, there's this place called Common Ground in Palo Alto. They have courses in organic farming, and I'd really like to visit. It seems like it's pretty close to your place. And I'd like to go to Napa Valley and watch them prune the grapevines and prepare them for spring. And also – I know it's a few hours' drive – but I'd like to look at the citrus farms on the way to Los Angeles. There are thousands of trees there, and they're fruiting right now. We can rent a car and I promise I'll drive the whole way.'

'Simon, I thought you came here to see me.'

'I did. But that doesn't mean we can't squeeze in a few interesting field trips, does it?'

*

They had seven lovely days together. Even though they didn't have time to visit all the usual tourist attractions, Simon looked like he'd just climbed Mount Everest when Sofia took a picture of him standing in the miles and miles of orange groves. On the last night she brought him along to dinner at Melissa's place – she had become completely charmed by Simon. Melissa, too, was interested in organic farming, so they talked nonstop. Sofia watched him as he sat there gesturing and chatting eagerly with Melissa. Simon sure had changed. He had opened himself to the world. She wondered if he was aware of this and figured he must at least be able to feel the difference.

When she said goodbye to him at the airport the next day and boarded the train home, she felt hollow and heavy. It struck her that her visa would expire in three months.

For the first time, she felt like it was probably time to head home to Sweden again.

35

Today is the first day of my new life, was Anna-Maria's first thought when she opened her eyes. She had hardly slept; she had tossed and turned all night, wide awake out of sheer excitement. But it didn't matter. She felt both sexy and well-rested on this fine spring day.

Today Franz would be free.

Her fingers were already itching to check her phone. To post everywhere: Facebook, Instagram, Twitter. But it would be so much better if she waited for pictures of the two of them together. Maybe she could start by spreading a rumour. A hint that something was about to happen. She'd promised not to leak anything about their relationship, not even to her parents. It wouldn't seem right, while he was still in prison. But now there was nothing standing in her way. She wondered what her girlfriends would think. Maybe that he was dangerous. But she would just tell the truth: he could be as sweet as anything. And they would be so jealous. Because after all, wasn't he the ultimate prize?

She stood in the shower for a long time, singing despite her terrible voice. She dried her hair with a towel and met her own gaze in the mirror. Her eyes were actually sparkling.

Her phone rang just as she walked into the living room. An

unfamiliar number, but she knew who it was right away. His voice was like a gentle whisper.

'It's me. I'm free.'

She opened her mouth, but no sound came out. This fact, uttered with such feeling – she couldn't find the words to respond.

'Annie, are you there?'

'Of course, I just don't know what to say. Incredible. It's fantastic.'

'I believe the word you're looking for is "congratulations".'

'Right, I'm sorry. Congratulations! Do you want me to come pick you up?'

'No, I want to ask you a favour. If it's not too much.'

'Anything.'

'I'm going to check into Upper House Hotel in town and spend the night there. I want to stretch out in the pool and chow down on some real food after a year and a half of lard sausage – you know what I mean. Recover for a bit before I deal with the zombie club at ViaTerra. So I was thinking… oh, maybe it sounds silly…'

'Come on, tell me.'

'It would be nice to take the hog back to ViaTerra. I haven't ridden it in so long, and this nice weather is supposed to hold. Would you want to go get it? Bring it over on the ferry and meet me at the hotel? We'll stay the night and head home tomorrow.'

'You mean the Harley? Is it really okay for me to drive it?'

'How many times do I have to tell you I trust you?'

She was incredibly touched. It was a thought that had been brewing in the back of her mind, but she hadn't quite dared to let it in completely. The day he let her ride the Harley would be the day she knew he loved her. It was his favourite possession, and his trust could only mean that he valued her even more.

'Of course I'll go get the bike! When do you want me to be there?'

'As soon as possible, obviously. I want to see you. Do you think you can make the morning ferry? Then you could get the five o'clock back from Fog Island.'

'Of course. I'll be there this evening.'

'Thanks, Annie. And listen, I have a surprise.'

'What is it? Please, tell me!'

'It's not something I can describe in words. It's something you have to experience.'

A moment of confusion followed their conversation. The sexy outfit she'd so carefully laid out wouldn't work on the bike. But hadn't he intimated that they would be having sex? Why dress up? She had already set out her best underthings, but she needed a layer between them and the leather gear. She selected a clingy, low-cut dress that barely covered her ass. Running around the apartment, she tossed various objects in her purse. Time was short – she only had an hour to make it onto the morning ferry.

⋆

On the ferry ride over, she thought of his hands, and all the places on her body they would soon be touching. She could no longer hold back and fired off a quick tweet: *New life starts today. Big things happening.* It only took a few seconds for the curious responses to start arriving, but she would leave them hanging, dammit. The next tweet had to be a photo of her and Franz together.

The manor felt deserted, as always. Large portions of the lawn were dead and there were dandelions everywhere. She didn't even want to talk to any of the members – she would tell Franz that evening that they simply hadn't listened to her. She asked the guard in the booth for the key to the Harley. He seemed taken aback, but he didn't dare to argue.

She had several hours before the ferry would head back, so she made a circuit around the island on the hog, going hell for leather along the eastern side. Surely Franz wouldn't mind. Lunch was at a sleepy little café in the village that served dry sandwiches. As she ate she read all the emails from clients she'd been ignoring recently. She became so impatient for the ferry to leave that she almost destroyed a fingernail biting at it. What would Franz think? Just as the thought flew through her mind, his name popped up on her phone screen. He said he just wanted to make sure she would make the ferry. That he couldn't wait to see her. He described a shortcut to the city where you could get up to blazing speeds.

'Take that road and think of me,' he whispered.

★

There was a chill in the air when the ferry docked at the harbour, although the sun was still high in the sky. She pulled her leather jacket tight around her neck, feeling suddenly stressed. She wanted to get there before it got dark.

For the first stretch she was on her own. The brisk air nipped at her cheeks. The pale green, leafy treetops whizzed by, like a veil over everything. She couldn't remember a time she had felt so happy.

But then her thoughts clouded over. The analogy about the spider popped up out of the blue. Something was nagging at her, something he'd said. She shoved the thought aside but it returned, stronger this time. The spider that never leaves its web. Not a single little fly gets out alive – so he'd said. Yet it had happened. With both the intermediary loser and Bauman. After slowing down unconsciously, she sped back up again, annoyed. Suddenly, for an instant, it was as if she was outside her own body. She experienced a fleeting moment of freedom, as if she were emerging from a cocoon. Everything became clear, like the mist dissolving out on Fog Island. This instant, which lasted only a millisecond, was enough to distract her. Just as she landed back in the present moment and regained control over the bike, a steel cable appeared ahead of her. Shining in the sunlight low across the asphalt. For a brief, magnificent moment she was floating in the blue sky. Blue everywhere, only blue. And before she could figure out what was happening, before she even suspected, everything went black.

36

Simon would have missed the TV spot if Wilma hadn't called. Inga Hermansson had foisted the TV onto him, saying he would feel less lonely at night. But he never used it – he read the news in the paper, surfed the internet, or read books instead. Inga's worry about Simon's lack of company was sometimes tiresome. She didn't understand that he actually liked the solitude. She even brought him magazines about men's fashion and that sort of crap. As if he would dress up in fancy clothes and go hit on girls on the island.

But now Sofia's friend Wilma had gotten her hands on his number. He'd never met her, but Sofia talked about her sometimes. Wilma gave a perfunctory introduction. In the background he could hear voices and music – she was in a bar or restaurant.

'Thought I would tip you off. Just saw the news here at this sports bar. Sofia's and your idol has been released and the chaos has already begun. Watch the next broadcast and you'll see. I have to go now. And hey, can you send the SVT Play link to Sofia, so she can watch it online? I'll leave it up to you to decide whether she can handle it. Although it's probably inevitable.'

Simon didn't have time to respond before she hung up. He didn't even know if his brick of a TV worked, but it turned out all he had to do was press the on button and the screen lit up. Wilma had called just in time, because the next news broadcast would be on in five minutes. Simon was curious. What was Oswald up to now? As if the fact of his freedom wasn't bad enough, he would be back on this beautiful island again. Simon thought of Jacob, and was filled with gloom. What if it was too late now for Jacob to escape?

The news began with a piece on a motorcycle crash outside Gothenburg. A road surrounded by lush, green fields and birches, full of police cars, ambulances, and the hustle and bustle of rescue workers. At first Simon didn't understand what it was about, but then the voice said that an Anna-Maria Callini, defence attorney for spiritual leader Franz Oswald, had perished when the motorcycle she was riding left the road. She had been thrown off and killed instantly. Simon heard his own voice, as if through a thick fog. *Oh shit, oh shit, oh shit!* He slapped his forehead, full of rage.

But then he was abruptly yanked back to the news, because there stood Oswald, dressed in pressed trousers and a sports coat, stopping for a quick interview in what looked like a hotel lobby. There was a large group of reporters present.

'Can you comment on the fact that Anna-Maria Callini was riding your motorcycle when she died?' one asked, holding a microphone to Oswald's face.

'She was supposed to pick it up for me. That's all. A favour, nothing more.'

'Can you comment on your relationship?'

'It was strictly a business relationship,' Oswald said as a tiny wrinkle of irritation appeared on his forehead. 'Listen, boys,' he went on. 'Anna-Maria was one of the best lawyers in the country and her death is a tremendous loss, not only for me but for the entire justice system. I will be returning to ViaTerra now.

We will cease all work for a week. I ask you to leave us in peace during this time of sorrow.'

He even managed to squeeze out an actual goddamn tear, Simon thought. *This is insane.*

The voice of another reporter came from behind Oswald.

'How does it feel to know that she was riding your bike? From what I understand, that bike cost a fortune.'

Oswald's face shifted colour in a split second, from relatively pale to angry red.

'How could you even bring that up?' he snapped. 'How fucking shameless are you?'

Yes, he actually swore, but somehow it sounded proper. Simon went cold inside when he realized that this news feature would only help Oswald's image. That he had once again wriggled his way out of an unpleasant situation. Simon's heart rate had increased without his noticing, and now he could feel the sweat breaking out on his palms. All at once he knew he had to call Sofia. It didn't matter if it was four in the morning in California. But the phone rang and rang; she never picked up. Simon assumed she was sleeping.

He tried to call again when he woke up the next morning, but there was still no answer. Yet he wasn't worried – she was probably out with friends. He remembered that Wilma had asked him to send that link to the news clip, so he sat down at his computer, found the program, and sent it off, hoping fervently that she would get back to him.

When Simon got home that evening, there was still no response from Sofia. Something felt wrong. He couldn't quite put his finger on it, but that magical contact they'd always had felt broken.

That night, Simon went to bed with a heavy heart.

37

Damian Dwight leaned back in his lounge chair. He tried to relax, to take in the beautiful pool, the palm trees, the blue sky. The quiet and the calm. Yet he felt like his skin was crawling. His drink had gone warm and tasted like cat piss. The woman soaking up the rays beside him, drenched in suntan oil, annoyed him. They were only two in the pool area, and there must have been a hundred chairs, so why did she have to choose the one right next to him? On a typical day he probably would have hit on her, but this situation was far from normal. All this suspense was making him paranoid. His childhood eczema had returned, appearing on the insides of his elbows and knees. His mind was churning, as if his thoughts were competing to see which could come up with the worst imaginable scenario.

He'd woken several times during the night to check his bank account, but the numbers stared back at him unchanged. The internet was full of sordid headlines and images from the scene of the accident, and some of them made him feel sick. He hadn't expected her death to affect him. It wasn't as if she was his favourite person. But that sheet-covered body on the gurney, the overturned motorcycle – suddenly it all seemed so personal. He wasn't the sort of man who was full of warm feelings for others, so why was this single tear trickling from the corner of his eye? It wasn't so much that he regretted it, as that he felt duped. A mind-boggling sum that couldn't be spoken aloud, that had to be written down. The eyes that saw right through him, fully aware he was a little fish that wanted to swim in bigger waters. The challenge had turned him on, the suggestion that of course he too could produce something big and bold. And suddenly there he was, on a deserted country road, holding a thick roll of steel cable. The only bright spot in this whole mess was that the cops were sure it was an accident.

The woman in the lounger next to his had sat up and was smiling at him expectantly. He took what was left of his drink and dumped it into the pool, mostly to annoy her. But she only laughed. He grabbed his towel and went back to the hotel.

The receptionist at the counter looked up and smiled when she saw him coming.

'Sir, an express letter has arrived for you,' she said in shaky English.

Damian felt something cold mix with the sweat on his back. It spread up to his hairline, where it began to flutter uncomfortably. Just as he was about to open his mouth, she stood up.

'A letter. Here!' She held up a brown envelope. He took a few fumbling steps forward and accepted the letter, which seemed light, almost weightless. Yet he could feel something firm inside. He didn't dare to open it, he just wanted to get back to his room.

'Is there anything else I can help you with?' the woman asked.

'No, I'm fine. By the way, who delivered this letter?'

'A messenger. DHL.'

With the illusion that no one knew his whereabouts shattered, he felt even more paranoid. He stood still outside his room for a moment, his mind forcing him to picture the barrel of a gun aimed at him from behind the door. He stuck his card in the reader and opened the door slowly, but there was no one there. A cool breeze came in the half-open window. It was as if the room were breathing faintly in all its emptiness. His laptop was where he'd left it on the desk. All at once he became hyperaware of the envelope in his hand. His name and the hotel's address were on the front. No return address, but it was postmarked in Sweden. He squeezed it and felt the hard object inside. Once he'd slit the envelope with one finger, he found himself staring at a clothespin. No message, just a well-worn clothespin made of bleached wood. He inspected it as if it were a bomb about to detonate.

This, he thought, *is a message. It couldn't be any clearer.*

Panic squeezing his throat, he sat at the laptop and logged in. When the bank's website was unavailable he swore, but he tried again and got in. He logged into his account, and at first he thought he was seeing things – the number in front of him was so astounding that he just sat there gaping like a fool.

Only once he'd stared at the breath-taking number for a long time did he dare to let out a sigh of relief.

A whole new life took shape in his mind. But he also felt a twinge of melancholy. He would never see Sweden again. But it couldn't be helped. Really, it was a minor sacrifice. And he had no choice, after all. Franz Oswald wasn't the kind of man you wanted to defy.

He gazed out the window at the palm trees swaying in the breeze. For the first time in several days, he was able to be in the now. He found himself standing there with a sheepish smile on his face.

38

Jacob watched as the black Mercedes glided onto the property. He'd been keeping an eye on the front gate all day; he couldn't help it. He knew everything would change as soon as Oswald set foot at ViaTerra again. It had been so quiet before his arrival, the air trembling with shame and agony. The staff no longer darted back and forth across the courtyard like diligent ants. By now it was too late to make it look like everything had been fine while the boss was away. And no one wanted to be the first to run into Oswald when he returned. So all they could do was wait. And hope.

Jacob wondered what it would be like. Surely it couldn't be worse than when Madde was leading them. Was that even possible? There was something about Madde. Her anxious energy. It was never quite convincing when she said 'Franz said' or 'Franz wants this and that.' Some of those orders didn't sound like the sort of thing that would have come from Franz Oswald. But then again, she and Bosse were the only ones who'd been in contact with him. So how could Jacob be sure?

The car stopped outside the main entrance to the manor. The guards came running, both Benny and Sten, and they opened both car doors for him. Those idiots! Oswald stepped out of the driver's seat. Jacob only caught a quick glance of him in profile. He was wearing a sports coat and had his hair in a ponytail; he tossed the car key to Sten. Benny ran ahead and held open the manor house door. Oswald looked up at the banner they'd hung: *Welcome home, Sir!* it read. They'd stayed up late to paint it. It had to be perfect. Not a spot of paint outside the lines. But Oswald shook his head. Jerkily and quickly, he walked in through the main entrance. Even from his hiding spot, over fifty metres away, Jacob could feel Oswald's suppressed rage.

Jacob wondered how Oswald could be so angry straight off the bat. He'd only just returned home. A few seconds, and they had already managed to infuriate him.

Oswald slammed the door behind him. Everything grew silent and still. To Jacob, it seemed that it had never been so quiet on the property; it felt like doomsday was near. He had the sensation of having ended up in the wrong place on earth. That this was all a nightmare, and he would wake from it soon.

Jacob had felt lost for a few years now. He hadn't been born on a farm like Simon – he'd just been interested in animals for as long as he could recall. It had seemed like the right decision, to take a position on a farm after finishing agricultural school. But then, from the very start, it felt wrong. His relationship with the animals was too personal. He suffered every time the pigs had to be taken to the slaughterhouse; he couldn't bring himself to euthanize sick animals; he always thought that the livestock quarters were too cramped. And then there was the part he'd never dared to tell anyone else. He thought that the animals spoke to him telepathically. Especially the cows. And although he knew it was physically impossible, there was nothing he could do to force their wordless messages out of his head.

ViaTerra had seemed like the perfect place for him. Back in the beginning. An organization that believed in the supernatural, and kept animals. If only he had known! And now he was stuck. He had a personal connection to every single cow, to the boar and the ram. It was inconceivable that he would leave them in this chaotic, unpredictable environment. There was no guarantee that anyone would feed them each day if Jacob wasn't there.

The silence lasted for several hours, until Corinne from the household unit came running into the barn.

'The whole staff has to gather in the dining room!'

'Why are *you* telling me?'

'I'm Franz's new secretary. Now hurry, Jacob.'

'Damn, that was fast. What happened to Madde?'

Jacob desperately hoped Madde wouldn't be relegated to the barn, so he had to take care of her.

'I have no idea, but I'm sure Franz will tell us.'

Together they ran to the dining room. He cast a sidelong glance at Corinne before they walked in. She looked nervous; surely she was already sensing what awaited her. But she was Oswald's type, so thin she looked almost anorexic. And she was only seventeen – ready for Oswald to help himself – and pretty, but not tough like Sofia had been. Jacob wondered how long Corinne would be able to stand the pressure of Oswald's office.

The dining room was dead silent when they stepped inside. A few annoyed faces turned to look at them. Almost every chair was full, so they had to sit at the very front. Oswald was already there. He was leaning against the podium he used for his addresses and didn't even deign to glance their way as they slipped in and took a pair of empty seats. Jacob wondered if

Oswald even knew he existed. They'd never spoken, just the two of them. And this very fact made Jacob fear Oswald even more. It felt like if Oswald ever truly fixed his eyes on Jacob, he would be able to read his mind.

'Is everyone here?'

Oswald looked at Corinne, who nodded and gulped audibly.

Oswald wasted no time in beginning to shout. It was so loud that several of the staff flew out of their chairs like soldiers coming to attention. This was new – Oswald had always begun his lectures in a mild tone of voice before, dropping a few sarcastic comments before he really got going. But now he was bellowing.

'You are like a flock of stupid, lost geese. There is not a single bastard here I can depend upon. You just don't have a clue what I want done!'

He paused and drew a breath.

'I don't know what I'm going to do with you, because you're nothing but a burden, a goddamn leech sucking the strength right out of me.'

Jacob heard Corinne's anxious breathing beside him and saw that her knuckles went white as she squeezed the armrest. Poor thing. But in some strange way, Jacob felt that he wasn't really part of what was happening in this room. Now that he had spoken with Simon, now that he knew there was a life outside these walls.

Oswald fell silent for a moment, observing them. He shook his head. The air in the dining room was thick with shame. Then Oswald launched back into his tirade, speaking so fast that Jacob could hardly make out the words. His voice had gone down half an octave. He was no longer shouting, but his voice was sharp and full of frustration.

Wasn't it obvious that the annexes should have been ready for guests by the time he arrived home? Didn't they even know how many letters he'd received in prison? Hundreds each day, from all over the world. And everyone who wrote had one thing in common. They wanted to know more about the ViaTerra philosophy. Did they even understand the enormous interest in ViaTerra that existed out in the world? Did they know how many copies his new book had sold? No, that's what he thought. And could they get it through their heads that he didn't give a shit about polished door handles? And then there was Anna's escape. She had slipped out right under their noses. And the guards had been snoring in the booth. As usual. There were two things he'd wanted done while he was gone: get the annexes in order and shut Sofia Bauman up. One single person. Although she had more guts in her than in all the rest of them put together, he did have to admit that. Because they hadn't even been able to accomplish that one thing. So now he had only one option. He would have to handle everything on his own. Same as always. And Madde, by the way – she would have to jump from Devil's Rock morning, noon, and night, until her stupid mouth could produce a single sensible sentence.

So now all they could do was get a move on. Because there would soon be guests. In two weeks he would open the gates to them. And for their own good, everything had better be in order. And by the way, he was going to shoot that pathetic dog they'd brought in.

With that final remark, Oswald left the room with Corinne tripping at his heels. Jacob remained in his chair with a lump in his throat. He couldn't bring himself to stand even when the others began to saunter out of the dining hall. Two weeks of pure hell lay before them. He already knew he would be on hands and knees scrubbing the floors of the annexes before the night was over. He was so tired and disappointed that he was near tears. Now he was alone in the big dining hall; it was quiet in there, beyond the shouts from the courtyard. Those frantic yelps as an 'all hands on deck' mood swept over the manor. Because now the annexes must be scoured and swept until Oswald was satisfied. Jacob hoped against hope that the guards wouldn't overreact and shoot the poor dog. Sometimes Oswald made empty threats; you could never be sure. Maybe he should hide the dog in the barn until everything had calmed down. Jacob heard the door open; he turned around slowly.

Bosse was standing there.

'Jacob, we're cleaning the annexes tonight.'

Jacob just shook his head. Bosse walked over to him.

'Why are you sitting here?'

'I'm trying to figure out how I'll take care of the animals too. They need food and clean stalls and so forth. I can't just leave them to fend for themselves.'

'Well, go do it, then.'

'What?'

'Go take care of the animals. I'll cover for you. If anyone asks, I'll say you're under the weather. We don't want any epidemics now that Franz is home.'

Jacob couldn't believe his ears. He stared at Bosse. This being before him wasn't a person, he was a wreck. Red-eyed, his hair uncombed and greasy, a few days' worth of stubble, pale, greyish skin. Bosse wasn't well. There wasn't even the tiniest speck of light in his future now that Oswald was back. Bosse was in charge of the staff, and after the dressing-down that had just taken place, it was only a matter of time before Bosse would be jumping from Devil's Rock alongside Madde, morning, noon, and night.

But Jacob saw something new in Bosse's eyes. A misplaced calm. A lack of frenzy or hysteria.

All at once he understood.

It was almost the same kind of telepathic connection he had with the cows.

'I'm just going to say one thing before I go take care of the animals.'

'Okay, what is it?' Bosse asked.

'That there's a way. That's all I'm going to say. So don't ask anything more.'

'I'm interested in that concept,' Bosse replied.

This conversation seemed magical to Jacob, because they were standing there talking and each knew just what the other was thinking, and yet there was nothing to grab hold of, no words that could be used against them. Just a miraculous understanding.

'In a few weeks. There'll be a chance then.'

'Let me know.'

'Right, I'm going to go to the barn now. Thanks for covering for me.'

39

The sky was beginning to darken as she boarded the train home from the airport. The clouds were heavy with rain, but the sun peeked out now and then, its rays flickering over her face. She already missed Simon. She wanted him to be back on Fog Island so she could call and chat. Suddenly she felt homesick for Sweden. The seasons flew by so quickly here in California, like eternal spring and summer. She missed the rugged autumns and winters of home, and she missed her parents and friends so much her chest ached.

She hadn't spoken to Benjamin yet. He'd sent an email to say she should do what she wanted, that they'd unsnarl their relationship when she got home. *Unsnarl* – as if they were talking about tangled hair. As if it was something you could fix like a cup of coffee, and everything would be just fine. There had been a slightly surly undertone to that email.

Her thoughts turned to Mattias, and they must have had a little mind-meld because her phone rang and his name popped up on the screen.

'Did your friend go home?'

'Yes, I'm on the train home from the airport, why?'

'I'm standing outside your apartment.'

'What are you doing there?'

'I've been longing to see you for a week.'

'I can't let you into my apartment.'

'Why not?'

'I don't know you yet. I don't know if I can trust you.'

'Or maybe you don't trust yourself. To be alone with me, that is.'

She hung up. Mostly to hide how hot she got when he talked like that. Surely he would be able to hear it in her voice. She wondered if Mattias would try to go all the way if she let him in, or if he had some other agenda and would invite her out someplace exciting. Either option seemed tempting and thrilling, all at once.

She called him again.

'I think the call dropped. We went through a tunnel.'

'There aren't any tunnels between the airport and Palo Alto.'

'Fuck it. You can come in. But only for a little while. Then I need to go to bed – I have to work tomorrow.'

*

He was sitting outside the front door to her building. There was a bench there, beside a flowerbed and a small fountain. The very sight of him made her feel guilty about all this two-timing. About her dishonestly towards both him and Benjamin. She had to tell him, get the truth out there.

'I have a boyfriend in Sweden. It's serious.'

He rose slowly and walked over to her.

'He must be a fucking loser.'

'What? You don't know shit about him.'

'He was an idiot to let you come here alone. Whoever he is.'

'I'm not interested in starting a new relationship.'

'Hey, chill out. I'm not looking for anything serious. I like to take things as they come.'

'You can come in for half an hour, max. Then I have to go to bed. I'm beat.'

'Okay.'

She hoped there would be someone in the elevator, but it was empty. There was a sharp odour of garbage – someone had just taken out the trash. He leaned against the elevator wall and looked at her but said nothing. It took ages for the elevator to reach the fourth floor, but he held her gaze the whole time. She tried to spot something in his face, a reason to distrust him. But it was like there was a veil over his eyes and she couldn't quite see through it. Maybe it was lust. Her belly fluttered.

She walked ahead of him to the apartment door, but the lock gave her trouble until he took the key from her hand and opened it. She didn't want to admit to herself that the trouble had been her own hand, shaking, so she snapped at him that she could open it herself.

The apartment air in the apartment was stale and too warm, so she opened the balcony door. The stuffy room seemed to sigh in relief as cool air streamed in. She went back to the entryway to take off her shoes and jacket. He was standing motionless just inside the door. When he handed her the key, she hung it on its usual hook. Her hand was no longer shaking. There – she had gotten a grip on herself. Now she wouldn't do anything rash. Just a cup of coffee, and then she would send him on his way. She had to work through this, concentrate on thinking logically. What did she even know about him? He might have an STI, or he could be a serial killer. Then again, she had googled him. Everything he said seemed to be true. Education, where he came from. He didn't seem sketchy at all on his Facebook page.

Then came Ellis's voice, as it had sounded on the phone. *Surely you aren't planning to remain faithful to Benjamin forever? It's just that cult, they made you think like a goddamn nun.*

Just one tiny slip-up, she thought. *And then I'll reconcile with Benjamin. If he wants me back, that is.*

She took a few steps forward and Mattias followed. He was practically on top of her now. The silence of the apartment was like a vacuum pressing them together. He stood so close, smelling like soap and leather. She took a few more steps, trying to buy time, but he was behind her immediately. His breath on her ear. The warmth of his body was all down her back, even though he was barely brushing against her.

She gave in and leaned back against him, sinking into his body. He bent down and kissed her neck, and she felt the muscles around her spine relax. Clearing her throat, she knew she had to say something, because he was about to take over completely.

But no words came out.

His hands started at her shoulders, slid down to her waist, and were suddenly all over her. Her ass and thighs, up across her belly. She'd wanted this to happen, and yet she stiffened. He let his fingers find their way through the gap in her blouse to stroke her stomach; he undid the buttons, pushed the cups of her bra aside, and touched her breasts. He loosened her skirt, letting it puddle around her feet, and pulled down her panties. A finger ran up her inner thigh – all the way up, until it slipped inside her. When she moaned, he covered her mouth with his other hand. She tried to turn around, but he pressed back, pushing his body against hers from behind, his leather jacket on her back, the hard bulge in his jeans against her ass.

'Stand still,' he whispered. 'Perfectly still, and quiet.'

The sun found a break in the clouds and shone through the living room window. It blinded her at first, shining on her naked body. His hands were everywhere again. The trembling was back; she couldn't hold still, she needed to turn around. It felt like she would implode if she didn't move. But he stopped her before she could swing about, as if they were doing a dance with predetermined steps.

'Calm down. Close your eyes. I don't want you to see – only feel.'

She heard him undressing, quickly, impatiently.

His jacket falling to the floor, the thuds as he kicked off his shoes, the sound of his belt being undone, the zipper of his jeans.

She closed her eyes. A faint gust of wind swept through the open balcony door, raising gooseflesh all over her body. It made her impossibly excited to stand there naked before him, a person she hardly knew.

He grasped her shoulders and turned her toward the sofa, pushing her ahead of him. She was about to lie down, but suddenly there was an arm around her waist, holding her up, and his other hand fumbled for the thin runner that hung off the coffee table. Right away she understood, before he had time to blindfold her. *How bold,* she thought, *for him to do this the first time.* He swung her around, laid her on her back on the sofa, and stretched out her legs – because she was completely dependent on his eyes now. Through the thin fabric she could only make out vague contours and his form falling over her like a blanket.

Just then the sky went dark and rain began to strike the window. Wild, out of control. The tension between them and the sudden storm took her breath away. She raised her arms to touch him, make contact, but he gently moved them away.

'I just want you to feel what I do to you. No looking, no touching.'

He ran two fingers up her inner thigh again, and she gave a little cry as they slipped inside her. His hands were all over, showing up on various parts of her body when she least expected it. His tongue on her belly, on her thighs, within her. Only when he pressed into her did he tear away the blindfold.

'Look at me!' His eyes were wild. The sinewy muscles of his arms were tense; there were beads of sweat on his chest. He swore and called out her name and it sounded so strangely beautiful.

And when all the deliciousness was over, her body, which had been tense as a bowstring just a moment ago, collapsed into a mound of jelly. She tried to open her mouth to say something, but she couldn't produce a sound. She was so thoroughly worn out that she fell asleep immediately.

*

She must have slept for a long time, because the room was pitch black when she woke up. The rain was still drumming the windowpanes. The runner that had served as her blindfold was back on the coffee table, wrinkled, but neatly arranged. There was a blanket over her and the balcony door was closed. Right away she knew he had taken off – he'd left an emptiness behind. Not even his scent lingered.

She got up off the sofa and realized she was terribly thirsty. At the fridge, she drank juice straight from the carton, sweating even though it was cold in the room. There was a strange sensation in her stomach, a mixture of guilt and profound sexual excitement. It seemed strange that he'd left her like that, without a word. Just then, her phone rang.

'I didn't want to wake you. You conked right out, and you looked so cute asleep.'

'I just woke up.'

'Then you were asleep for more than three hours.'

'Damn! I guess I really was out.'

'Two months.'

'Two months what?'

'In two months I'm going home to Sweden.'

'Oh.'

'So I thought we could make the most of it. Then we'll see. I'm already thinking about everything I want to do to you.'

A thrill ran through her body and warning bells went off. His dominance. Her submission, so unlike her – she'd thought. But now she shuddered with pleasure when she thought of his hands. The ambivalence she felt was exciting in and of itself. It was like being pulled between two static poles so that sparks flew in between them.

Mattias is dangerous, she thought. *Deliciously dangerous, when it comes to sex. Probably not dangerous at all in other ways.*

'Are you still there, Sofia?'

'I have to work tomorrow.'

'What about this weekend?'

She left him hanging for a moment.

'I'm free,' she said. 'We can see each other then.'

40

A palpable silence lay over the manor. Simon remembered how soundly you slept when you'd been working without sleep for days in a row. The odour of sweat in the dorms. Sleep became so precious that you fell into bed without showering first. Sour puffs of bad breath came out with each snore.

It was cold for the end of April. A heavy spring rain had just ended; it had been replaced by a damp chill that crept under his jacket. He really hadn't wanted to go out, but on this evening he had no choice. Duty called – or adventure did, depending on how you looked at it. The lights were on in the guards' booth and he took a detour to be on the safe side. He stood still outside the gate for a while, wanting to make sure it wasn't a trap. What was about to happen was huge, incredible. But the silence held, aside from the sound of raindrops falling from the trees. Then came a faint whisper from inside the wall, gentle as rustling leaves.

They had come.

As soon as he opened the gate, he saw them. They were only a few metres from Simon's hiding place behind the oak. Simon took a step forward, and Bosse recoiled.

'Shit, it really is you!' he whispered.

Bosse was wearing only his uniform shirt, no jacket, and he

had a small backpack over one shoulder. Simon could see that his eyes were full of worry. It wasn't only the cold air making him tremble.

'Are you really sure you want to do this?' Simon asked.

'Definitely. I can't stand it any longer.'

Simon turned to Jacob.

'What's the situation here? How much time do we have?'

'Everyone was allowed some sleep after a week without. The annexes have to be ready for guests in a few days. But everyone's out cold for now. As long as you don't set off the alarm, no one will see you. Sten's in the booth, I'll go distract him. Although he's probably already snoring.'

Simon had the urge to simply pick Jacob up and haul him away. How could he stand this? Jacob seemed to read his mind.

'Soon, but tonight it's Bosse's turn.'

*

They walked through the forest until they were out of sight of the manor. Simon noticed that Bosse was limping.

'Did you hurt your foot?'

'Nah, it's nothing. Just twisted it a little.'

'What happened?'

'I tripped on the rocks before my ice bath.'

'What's an ice bath?'

'It's a new punishment for those of us who didn't behave while Franz was away. We go to the cliffs and take a dip every day. Under guard.'

'Jesus, Bosse. That's incredibly dangerous. The water is cold as hell!'

'Franz says even old folks can manage wintertime dips.'

'Yeah, but they get to have saunas afterwards, and they're allowed to sleep at night. He's gone completely off the rails, can't you see?'

'Yes, I suppose that's true.'

*

Bosse was practically paralysed for his first few days in Simon's cottage. This bundle of energy, a man who had dashed around ViaTerra like a fanatic saviour, who had worked hardest of all, the most devoted member, sat around on Simon's sofa, staring at nothing like a gaping fish. But Simon understood. There was nothing for Bosse to hold onto. He had no life beyond the walls. Simon was familiar with Bosse's background – his parents had died in a car crash when he was four, and after that he'd been shuffled around to various foster homes. He'd become a bit of a thug in his teens. Oswald had plucked him up at a lecture. Later he'd said he fell for Bosse's devoted gaze.

ViaTerra had been like a salvation for Bosse. He was almost like a personification of the cult, with his ambition and devotion to Oswald. He'd become Oswald's right-hand man. But that was before Oswald started to become annoyed by him, a fate that befell everyone sooner or later. Simon knew Bosse had had to tolerate innumerable cruel nicknames and dressing-downs, and that Oswald had struck him several times.

Simon suspected that it's always possible to free people, but that you must free them *towards* something, not just out into empty space – and for Bosse, there was no world beyond those walls.

Bosse, like Anna, spent almost all his time sleeping at first, and he ate unusually greedily. On the third day, he started talking nonstop. He said basically the same things Anna had, but he also told Simon what had happened when Oswald returned. Madeleine had been the first target, and she was followed by Bosse. The worst thing was probably how Oswald had forced them to sit still on chairs for twenty-four hours while someone watched over them and poured water on them if they dozed off. They were expected to spend the time reflecting upon the consequences of their irresponsibility.

It would have been so easy to tell Bosse that it was high time he realized that what he was describing, what had happened to him, was absolutely outrageous. But Simon knew Bosse still had doubts, and needed to come to this realization himself. It couldn't be forced upon him.

He tried to get Bosse to walk around the pension's property each day, to get some fresh air. But not even that was easy, because the search for him was in full effect. It lasted not just a few days, as for Anna, but a whole week: motorcycles driving back and forth on the road. Cries and shouts from the forest, where search parties combed in lines. Guards showing up at the pension again and again.

Inga patiently explained that she certainly wasn't harbouring any runaways. But no one came to Simon's cottage, a fact that baffled him.

*

Bosse's ability to read and write was substandard, so Simon didn't give him any books. Instead he let him use the computer and go online. On the fifth day, Bosse looked surprisingly alert when he woke up.

'Listen, it's actually insane that I tolerated all that crap. Where should I go? If they find me, it'll be even worse than it was for Sofia.'

'Speaking of which, tell me about the Sofia Bauman project.'

Bosse was startled.

'How did you know about that?'

'Doesn't matter. Just tell me.'

'It was this project where the goal was to shut Sofia up. Harass her so she would never dare to attack Franz again.'

'Did you work on it?'

'Yeah, at first. It was Benny, Sten, and me. But Franz flew off the handle when he found out some of the things we did. I mean, we did go a little overboard when we painted "slut" on her door and stuff like that. That wasn't really Franz's style. Callini came to ViaTerra and chewed us out royally, and with that voice… well, it wasn't pretty. So she sent Benny and Sten to Penance. Franz swore he would deal with me once he was free. And he did, of course, as you know.'

'But what else did you do?'

'Stuff online, mostly. From the guards' booth. There was a hacker who worked with us. And then there was that dildo we sent to her neighbour, some old lady.'

'Jesus Christ, Bosse, that's disgusting! What about the dog?'

'What? Which dog? The one Benny got?'

Simon let out a sigh of relief.

'No, a different dog. Never mind, it's not important. Listen, I think you should report this to the police.'

Bosse went pale.

'Please, no, I could never do that. It would be like turning myself in, I was in so deep. And it doesn't even matter now that Sofia's in the US, does it?'

'What? Does Oswald know she's there?'

'Yeah, Madde told him one day at assembly. She said Sofia ran off with her tail between her legs. It sounded like a victory, sort of. For ViaTerra, I mean.'

'But she hasn't heard from them at all since she moved.'

'No, but Franz hasn't forgotten her. You can be sure of that.'

'Bosse, why is he so fixated on Sofia?'

'Isn't it obvious? The way she messed up his life.'

'Yes, but it's more than that. I can just feel it.'

Bosse thought for a moment.

'Do you remember the time Sofia and Benjamin tried to run away?'

Simon did. Oswald had placed cameras in Sofia and Benjamin's room, and had discovered them discussing their escape plans.

'After that, Franz had a meeting with me. He said Sofia had to be put under extra surveillance, that she was never allowed to leave the property, and that she was an important part of his future plans. That's all I know.'

'Sure, but why would he completely drop it, just because she moved out of the country?'

'I don't know, Simon. Maybe he got tired of the cat-and-mouse game. He gets tired of everyone and everything eventually.'

Simon thought about Sofia, who had finally contacted him a few days ago. She hadn't responded to his emails, and when she finally called he understood why. She'd gotten it on with that Mattias and, for some strange reason, she was ashamed to tell Simon. It was temporary, she said. She would work everything out with Benjamin when she got home. 'It's not like I'm your dad,' Simon had replied. 'You can do whatever you want.' And yet he found he was annoyed with her.

The knowledge that Oswald was aware of Sofia's whereabouts made him paranoid. He decided to change the subject with Bosse.

'We have to talk about where you're going to go, Bosse.'

'I'll do anything. As long as they don't find me. Where can I hide? It feels like I'm taking advantage of you, but I don't have any money. Where do I start? I think I need to find a job.'

Simon observed Bosse as he sat on the sofa. The colour had started to return to his face, and there was a new glint of life in his eyes. Yes, Bosse was a good worker. No doubt about that. Simon gazed out the window, where the pension's property extended to the forest. Everything was turning green. The white points of the greenhouses pierced the pale spring sky. Simon turned back to Bosse; an idea had come to him although he hadn't been consciously trying to come up with one.

Suddenly he rose from the sofa and went to the telephone to dial his old home number, on the farm. His mother picked up and was so happy to hear Simon's voice that she started crying. Yes, they sure could use an extra set of hands now that spring was here, as long as this fellow could work hard. Didn't Simon want to come home too?

'No, I can't come,' said Simon. 'But you have to promise me something. Not a single attempt to save him – no praying, no laying on of hands, no conversations about God's Way.'

So it was decided – Bosse would travel to Småland and spend some time working on Simon's parents' farm.

41

They saw each other a few times a week. He never slept over; he vanished during the night and each time she woke up she was wrapped in a haze of heavy, aching sexual craving. Benjamin was like an excited puppy in bed, tongue and paws everywhere. Mattias was calculating and methodical. Only at the very last moment did he lose control, and the tension in the lead-up to this drove her crazy. He made her suffer and he made her ecstatic. He undressed her and redressed her, bound her and freed her; he was never rough but always dominant.

Although they did other stuff together it was mostly a sexual relationship, but that just made it even better. She began to need him like a drug. And then there was the feeling of having a secret. Delicious, hot shame.

When he suggested they travel back to Sweden together, she was surprised at first.

'That way it won't be as lonely on the plane, and also I'm going to miss you so fucking much, just so you know.'

'But you know I have to talk to Benjamin, figure everything out before…'

'Oh yeah, that old drip.'

But in the end she decided to fly back with Mattias. Her visa would expire soon, and she did miss home. She wrote to everyone to let them know when she would arrive. She'd sublet her apartment in Lund but decided to let the guy renting it stay to the end of the month; she could live with her parents in the meantime.

One week before their flight home, Mattias called.

'Listen, I found tickets for half the price, but for a day earlier. Can you leave then?'

Her mind went straight to her dwindling bank account.

'I can, but I'd have to let everyone at home know.'

'Don't. I want you to myself for a whole day in Gothenburg. In my apartment.'

'I can't, you know I have to…'

'Talk to Benjamin, blah, blah, blah… Look, just one last day. At my place. Then you can take the train home and it will be up to you if you want to see me again.'

She felt a thrill of excitement when he mentioned that apartment. It sounded like he was planning something.

'I'll pay for your ticket and deal with rebooking. What do you say?'

'Okay, fine.'

'But don't tell anyone we're coming early. I want you to myself for a whole day. Promise me.'

'We'll be totally jet-lagged.'

'I like you when you're all sleepy and submissive.'

It seemed too good to be true. She would get to sleep with him one last time and come home with an extra ten thousand kronor in hand. She decided to take a train to Lund the night after they got back. To surprise her parents. There was no way she could visit Benjamin in Gothenburg, given the situation.

*

On the last night, she sat on the balcony to think for a long time. She'd sold all her furniture and donated everything else to a thrift store. All that was left in the apartment was the bed, which the buyer would pick up the next morning, and her two big suitcases.

The spring sky deepened into a blood-red sunset. The air stood still. She thought about Melissa, who had cried when she said goodbye. Her colleagues at the library. The freedom she'd felt in Palo Alto. The lovely light and the endless green. But in the end, she knew this wasn't her real life. It struck her that she hadn't dreamt of Oswald for weeks. In fact, she hadn't even thought about him recently. It must mean he had given up – obviously that was the case. And with this realization, a weight she hadn't even been aware of lifted from her chest.

At the same time, a pang of loss hit her. The feeling was so illogical that she didn't even try to understand it. But he was the only person she'd ever known who refused to allow himself even a modicum of self-doubt. He always had a plan and never budged a millimetre from it. Sofia herself had spent the last two years feeling like a bug that had lost its sense of direction and was flying around in circles. But now her hell was over. She would go back to Sweden and everything would be normal again.

*

They flew nonstop from San Francisco to Kastrup, and from there to Landvetter outside of Gothenburg. Mattias was unusually quiet during the trip; he mostly just listened to his iPod and stared out the window, and he hardly ate a bite. For a few hours, he slept with his mouth open and his head resting against Sofia's shoulder. There was a new sort of tension between them, not just their usual sexual attraction. He almost seemed nervous, drumming his fingers on his thigh, tapping his feet against the seat ahead of him.

'What's wrong?' she finally asked.

'Huh?'

He took off his headphones.

'I was asking what's up with you. You seem a little tense.'

'Nah, it's nothing. I just don't know if I'm happy to be going back to Sweden. What if I can't let you go?'

'Oh, chill out. It's not like we're going to live that far away from each other.'

She couldn't sleep a wink on the plane. Each time she tried, she got a crick in her neck and felt cold and began to sneeze in the cool, dry air.

They took a taxi from the airport to Mattias's apartment, which was in the city centre. As Sofia stepped inside, she felt like she had entered a gap in time, as if she was no longer in one place but hadn't yet arrived at the next. The apartment was so breath-taking as to be surreal. The ceilings had to be over four metres high. Everything was white or grey, and looked freshly renovated. It was luxury Scandinavian minimalism in the extreme – nothing superfluous, but it was clear that each item had cost a fortune.

There was an antique tile stove in the living room, and it was flanked by huge bronze sculptures: a phallic symbol and a bird with outstretched wings. The few pieces of furniture included a conversation group and a stereo and TV system. On the walls hung three framed photographs that were of an erotic, almost pornographic, nature. The first depicted a squatting woman holding up her hands, which were bound with rope. Only her eyes were in focus. The next showed a man's back, and the face of a gagged woman lying beneath him. The man's hand was fisted in her hair. The third picture was a close-up of a woman's face. She wore a thick, studded leather collar; her eyes were closed and her mouth was half open.

Mattias's voice came from behind her.

'Those were taken by a renowned photographer. Dieter Rysch. Have you heard of him?'

She still wasn't quite present. The sight of the photographs had taken her breath away. It dawned on her that Mattias's predilection for domination was a lifestyle, not just an adventure they'd had together.

'No, never,' she responded, swallowing. All of a sudden she felt uncomfortable with him.

He came over and placed his hands on her shoulders. He guided her to the bedroom, which hardly contained more than an enormous bronze bed. Infinite reflections of her bounced back from the walls and ceiling, which were covered entirely by mirrors.

He stole up behind her, pressed himself to her back, and put his hands on her breasts.

'Hope you like our little place here.'

'Our? Do you live here with someone?'

'No, a good friend owns this apartment. He's almost never here, he's always travelling on business. So we share, sort of.'

'The rent must be sky-high.'

'I don't pay any rent. I help him out with some stuff instead – I mean, we're really good buddies.'

'Damn, you've got a pretty sweet deal here. Who's the guy? Anyone famous?'

'No, just a businessman. A successful one.'

'But what do the two of you *do* here?'

'Isn't it obvious? Bring girls here. Have fun. You're not jealous, are you?'

'Hardly. Just wanted to make sure I hadn't ended up in a brothel.'

He pinched her cheek.

'You're not being fair. You have to admit that this place is classy.'

She mumbled something, unsure whether she was shocked or impressed. And too tired to decide.

'Listen, can I go to bed now? I'm so fucking tired.'

'Of course, but first you need a bath, to wash off all the travel.'

'Why?'

'Come on, I'll show you.'

He led her to the bathroom, which was past the bedroom. Everything here was done in marble, and the bathtub was so high that you had to go up two steps to get in. Above the tub was a massive skylight. He ran a bath as she took off her clothes, which she placed in a neat pile on a bench just inside the door. As she sank into the water, she thought she would doze off in no time, but then she glanced up and caught sight of the sky through the window. You could see the stars so clearly. It was like taking a bath in space. She stared up at the heavens as the warmth of the bathwater spread through her body.

Her pleasure was interrupted by Mattias, who swore loudly and repeatedly out in the bedroom. He came to the door.

'My fucking computer is out of battery and I left my power

cord on the plane. Can I borrow yours? I need to send a few work emails.'

'Sure, it's on the sofa in the living room.'

It was quiet for a long time, aside from the tapping of his fingers on the keyboard. She felt like there was grit under her eyelids. Her chin dropped to her chest. The water had gone cold, so she dragged herself out of the bathtub and wrapped herself in a towel, sending up a silent prayer that he wouldn't want to have sex – she was so tired. She found him in the kitchen, where he was pouring two glasses of wine.

'Drink this – you'll sleep like a log. I'm going to sleep too, but I have to take care of a few things first. Then we'll have the whole day here together tomorrow.'

The wine was bold and spicy. She drank half the glass but found herself feeling slightly nauseated. Back in the bedroom, she crawled under the covers, feeling dizzy and weak. Just before she fell asleep, she thought it felt like she'd been there before.

*

Little by little, she woke up. Her head felt heavy and it was hard to open her eyes.

Tonight I'm going home, she thought, but her joy was immediately clouded by a violent wave of nausea. Her limbs wouldn't obey when she tried to stretch them out; her muscles weren't getting the messages sent by her brain. Her body seemed to be paralysed. She couldn't feel a thing from her neck down.

Then she heard Mattias's voice. Quiet, whispering. And then another, deeper voice.

There was someone else in the apartment.

42

Jacob had learned to gauge the mood at ViaTerra, and right now he could tell something was up. He stood at the barn door, watching the courtyard, sure that today was the day.

Oswald had sent the entire staff to the pond north of the manor house. They had been instructed to clear out brush around it because, in Oswald's words, it looked horrific. Everyone but the guard at the gate would take part. Besides, it was good for your health to spend a whole day outdoors, Oswald had said. But he wasn't fooling Jacob. Oswald cared as much about his staff's health as he did about the forest – which was to say, not at all.

Oswald's interest in the staff had cooled just a few weeks after his return. He'd shouted at them that they were completely useless and that they could just do whatever the hell they wanted, because he no longer had time for them. That was always when the staff seemed to suffer the most – when he turned his back on them. They had nothing to hold onto. All the air went out of them, and they wandered around the property like drones, disheartened and full of despair.

The trigger for Oswald's outburst had been such a minor thing. Erik, who worked in the ethics unit, had forgotten to call Oswald 'sir' during an assembly. Oswald had asked him,

'Who do you think your boss is?' When Erik's response was 'Bosse,' Oswald unleashed a tirade of insults before stalking into the manor house and slamming the door. The staff just stood there, at a loss, but then Oswald had returned.

'If you don't understand who your leader is after all these years, you might as well go home to mommy and daddy and flip burgers at McDonald's.'

'Sir, I'm sorry, I just meant who my *immediate* boss is,' Erik said.

This enraged Oswald all the more, so he threw up his hands and left them again. This time he didn't come back.

Soon Erik was digging a deep ditch by the wall. And when Bosse ran away, the staff's situation got even worse. Somehow, Bosse's escape was their fault. But Jacob didn't feel guilty in the least. His hesitation had evaporated as soon as he'd made contact with Simon. He knew that he, too, would run away one day. Hopefully he would manage to avoid Oswald's piercing looks until then, and stay out of trouble so he wouldn't be under watch around the clock.

Elvira wasn't on the property that day. She'd been sent to the mainland so her aunt could meet the babies. She seemed to have made out well: full-time nannies to care for the children, the same top-notch food as Oswald ate. Jacob had also heard that she was given a sizable sum of money each month. Rumours spread quickly through the small group, and many people were envious of her. But not Jacob. He noticed that Oswald visited the little cottage sometimes, and in those moments he had no desire to trade places with Elvira. None at all.

Jacob had wormed his way out of working by the pond with

the excuse that a cow might calve at any moment, although in fact he knew it would be at least a week. Oswald certainly didn't want to have to deal with a cow in labour, so Jacob was allowed to stay behind. He had decided to use this time to make up for his negligence of the animals – mucking stalls and putting down fresh straw, that sort of thing – but now and then he peered out the barn door.

It was at one of those moments he saw the car rolling through the main gate. A black car with tinted windows. It crept across the courtyard like a predator on the hunt and stopped in front of the manor house.

Two men got out of the car: Benny and a dark-haired guy he'd never seen before. And then Oswald came out to the front steps, harried and annoyed. He snapped at Benny, who backed up a few steps and stared down at the gravel.

The day was overcast, and a drizzle fell from the sky like a light dusting. Spring seemed to have stopped in its tracks the past few days. The island was swept in a thick, grey blanket that wouldn't lift. Oswald was already wet with rain, and he shook his head in irritation. His voice floated over to Jacob.

'For Christ's sake! Hurry up!'

The men opened the back door of the car and pulled out a tarp-wrapped object. It seemed heavy; they struggled to get a grip on it to lift it. Jacob's first thought was that it must be some new machine for Oswald's gym, which had just been expanded.

Oswald held the door as the men carried the large bundle inside. They must have been in there for ten minutes. Jacob lingered until they came back out. The strange man hopped in the car as Benny went over to the guard booth and opened the gate. The car vanished into the mist.

Jacob looked at his watch. Quarter past one. He was hungry and decided to go to the kitchen and search for something edible. He knew the staff had taken sandwiches to the forest and hoped there were some leftovers. As he crossed the courtyard he thought about what was under that sheet. Oswald was usually proud of his new gadgets and never squandered the opportunity to say that only he was allowed to use them. But this time he had sent everyone away, and that piqued Jacob's curiosity.

The lights were on in the kitchen – the staff must have left in a hurry, because there were still utensils and bits of food all over the counters. Jacob made a few sandwiches and stuffed them in his coat pocket. He was just about to turn out the lights when he realized he was thirsty, so he went to the fridge and took out a bottle of water, which he put in his other pocket. He hoped no one would notice he'd been there.

Out in the courtyard it had stopped raining; the mist was dissipating and seemed to float up into the sky. Jacob stopped at the greenhouse, which had been neglected ever since Simon left ViaTerra. A couple of withered, dried-up plants were all that was left inside. They had never found a replacement for Simon. There had been such a ruckus when Oswald realized they could no longer serve local, organic produce.

Just as Jacob was standing outside the greenhouse, he heard a scream. Half-stifled, muffled by the thick walls of the manor house – but still so loud that Jacob went stiff. One drawn-out scream, and then another, which died out and was followed by a creepy silence. It was so quiet that Jacob could hear a single bird chirping on the other side of the wall.

43

The sight of Oswald made Simon go weak at the knees. He wasn't afraid of him, but he was immediately reminded of the claustrophobia he had experienced in the cult. Besides, Oswald looked out of place standing there in his expensive clothes with the fields and greenhouses behind him. Like a fashion spread with the wrong backdrop. He was tanned, too, and Simon was disgusted to realize that he'd already made use of his tanning bed.

'Hi there, Simon, it's been awhile.'

'You can say that again.'

'Look, I don't mean to bother you. I just wanted to know if you've seen Bosse. He's out on a lark or something, and we're worried about him.'

'Bosse? No, I sure haven't.'

Oswald fixed his eyes on Simon, who stared back. Simon didn't feel guilty in the least – in fact, he got a kick out of lying to Oswald.

'Okay, then.'

Oswald glanced around Simon's cottage.

'I see you're doing well for yourself here. But things can always change.'

'How do you mean?'

'Who knows. Maybe I'll buy the pension. I've been considering investing in property here on the island. After all, you've won prizes and all that. Then you would work for me again. Like in the good old days.'

Was this bastard threatening him?

'I don't think Inga is interested in selling.'

'What if she doesn't have any choice? Shit, I'm just kidding around, Simon. Don't look so freaked out. I'm sure you understand how worried I am about Bosse. He's been a little confused recently. If he does contact you, just tell him not to worry. All he has to do is call me right away, and we'll work it all out.'

Oswald held out a business card and Simon took it automatically.

'Was there anything else?'

'No, you can get back to whatever it is you do around here,' he said, turning around to gaze out at the fields and the greenhouses. He nodded to himself.

It occurred to Simon that Oswald wasn't only there because of Bosse. He was in urgent need of a gardener. So Simon had become interesting again. The thought made him feel vaguely ill.

He watched as Oswald got back in his car and drove off, then became aware of the little card in his hand. *Well, now I've got his mobile number,* he thought. *That might come in handy someday.*

He called to Bosse, who looked seriously shaken as he came out of the bathroom. A few minutes later, they were on their way to the mainland, where Bosse would take the train to the farm in Småland.

On the ferry, Bosse was silent, hardly responding when spoken to. His face had gone eerily pale.

'There's no one from ViaTerra here,' Simon said. 'I took a tour of the ferry and checked. As soon as we're off the ferry we'll drive straight to the train station.'

'It's not that,' Bosse mumbled. 'But… hearing his voice. He actually sounded worried. Now I feel like a coward for running away. Like I'm betraying them.'

'Listen, he's not worried about you at all. He's just afraid that you won't keep quiet about all the crap that happens at ViaTerra. You know that, right?'

'Yeah, maybe. I suppose it's hard to understand, but he helped me when no one else cared. It's complicated.'

Simon sighed.

'It's up to you. Should we go back?'

'No, definitely not. It's just… I can't go back to ViaTerra, and I also can't leave. It's like there's no way out. No matter what I do, everything will go to shit.'

Bosse shook his upper body as if he were trying to get something off him. Then he turned to Simon and gave a hoarse laugh that was immediately absorbed into the fog around the boat.

'Of course I'm still going to your parents' farm, Simon. It's just, these sick thoughts keep popping up. Thanks for helping me.'

But none of this sounded like it came from the heart. Oswald's mere presence had really rattled Bosse. Simon was starting to feel anxious, but he figured that as soon as Bosse settled into his job at the farm everything would be better.

The silence in the car grew awkward. Simon turned on the radio and tried to focus on the road and the news, but just then the broadcasters started to talk about Anna-Maria Callini's death. Again. Something about how the cause of death had been determined as a broken neck. Bosse let out a moan of horror.

'Didn't Franz tell you all that Anna-Maria Callini is dead?' Simon asked.

Bosse shook his head, bewildered.

'Oh. Well, she is. She ran off the road on his motorcycle.'

They talked about it for a while, and then Bosse sank back into his ruminations.

The train station was busy, full of people moving in every direction. Simon thought perhaps Bosse would like it – the warmth of other humans. But instead he seemed to stick out, as if he didn't belong there. He kept looking around, nervously chewing on his lower lip.

The train was half an hour late.

'I'll wait,' Simon said.

'No, fuck it. I can manage on my own. I'll just sit here on a bench and think for a while. Thank you, Simon, for all you've done for me. I'll pay you back someday.'

'Don't even mention it. And do not under any circumstances let my mother save your soul.'

Bosse laughed.

'Who knows? That stuff about God's Way doesn't really sound all bad.'

'Oh, Mom promised to leave you alone. And then there's Dad – he's a little odd, but he'll protect you. He's guaranteed to get out the shotgun if any Oswald clones show up there.'

They embraced awkwardly. Bosse was so skinny that Simon could feel his ribs through his clothes. He smelled like Simon's shampoo and the synthetic fabric of his new jacket, as if he hadn't quite found his own scent yet.

Bosse held up the phone Simon had given him.

'Are you sure you want to give me this?'

'Of course, so you can call me and we can chat. But it doesn't have a monthly contract, just a pay-as-you-go card. So you'll have to add funds when it runs out.'

'What about you, though? It's your number.'

'I'll get a new one. I don't have that many friends.'

Bosse gave him a hesitant smile. It was like he couldn't tear his eyes from Simon.

'Well, talk to you later, then.'

Just as Simon was about to turn at the end of the platform, he glanced back. Bosse had stood up and was wandering along the track with his back to Simon, getting smaller and smaller until he was no more than a blurry dot in Simon's vision.

The bad feeling he had was overwhelming as he got behind the wheel, but he started the car anyway and drove out of the parking lot.

*

By the time he turned onto the road, his uneasiness had grown so strong that one hand was trembling slightly. The thought that had been chafing deep down was now so urgent that he almost lost control of the car; he had to slow down and park on the side of the road. At first he couldn't figure out what was happening to him, why he was full of an anguish so powerful it had taken over his body. Never before had he felt this way. Or had he? An image flickered through his mind. Bosse's eyes. All at once Simon knew what Bosse hadn't managed to hide under that forced smile. That look was so familiar that Simon was tossed four years back in time as his stomach turned inside out and the world around him began to spin. The look in Daniel's eyes, and Bosse's – they were identical.

He managed to collect himself enough to start the car, make a U-turn, and speed back to the station. He was hardly aware of the other cars, or the fact that he was driving too fast; he was hardly aware of himself. He only knew he had to hurry. There wasn't much time.

When he couldn't find a parking spot he left the car in a handicapped slot, threw open the door without closing it, and left his keys behind. He ran, bumping into people. Here and there someone cursed angrily, but Simon didn't hear them; he just pushed on. He stopped at the platform where Bosse's train was supposed to be, his eyes searching frantically for Bosse, but the dot had vanished. So he set off down the platform, along the tracks. He *knew*, he had never been so sure of something. The suitcases he ran into fell to the concrete with heavy thuds; he pushed people out of the way. Straining his eyes, he finally spotted a shadow by the tracks, far in the distance. The voice on the loudspeaker announced an approaching train. Bosse's train.

'No!' Simon shouted. But the shadow didn't seem to react. Simon was no longer running – he was floating, hurtling forward like an arrow, as the sound of the train grew louder. The shadow had become a body. A figure at the edge of the tracks. Its back straight, stiff as a board. Simon shouted again, louder now. He pushed off from the asphalt and dived the last little bit. Aiming for the thighs, grabbing hold of them, pulling backwards. His head struck the platform with a bang, and Bosse's body landed on top of him.

The gust of air from the train swept over them. The racket

of the wheels on the rails was so loud that it drowned out Bosse's cry of despair. They lay like that for a moment, Simon panting and Bosse howling like a child. But Simon had a firm grip around Bosse's chest and he wasn't about to let go.

Some of the people on the platform sprang into action. People ran towards them. The train squealed and whined as it slowed down. Simon rolled away from Bosse and sat up. But before he could open his mouth, he heard Bosse's piteous voice.

'He called me, that bastard. That fucker called me.'

44

What happened next made Simon stop thinking of himself as more or less a coward. By some miracle, he managed to convince the other passengers on the platform that Bosse had epilepsy, and that he'd called Simon to say he was about to have a seizure and couldn't control his body. Suspicious eyes filled instead with compassion and understanding. Simon gathered Bosse's things, took him by the arm, and led him from the station to the car. They didn't say a word, but Bosse was sobbing and hyperventilating.

The car door was open and the keys were still there. After a lengthy silence, Simon said, 'Tell me about the phone call.'

'I don't really want to die,' Bosse said instead. 'I just stood there staring at the tracks and listening to the train coming, like it was actually tugging at me, and Franz's voice was echoing in my head like thunder, my head was about to explode, and I had no choice. I had to jump.'

'But what did he say?'

'How the hell did he know I have your phone?'

'Maybe it was a lucky guess. My number's online, after all.'

'His voice sounded so kind. He said our fates are linked, that no one can replace me. That he needs me at his side.'

Simon managed to stop himself from tossing in a cynical comment, and allowed Bosse to continue.

'He said I should just stay at the station, that he would send a car to pick me up. Everything would be okay again. But I knew I couldn't. It's impossible to go back. So I took a few steps forward, and if you hadn't come…'

Bosse burst into tears again. He shrank into himself, hiding his face in his hands, his whole body shaking. Tears and snot dripped onto his trousers.

'Oh my God, Simon, I'm so sorry,' he whimpered. 'I'm sorry, I'm sorry…'

Simon was still rattled, but the train incident seemed to have given him almost superhuman clarity. His attention was on the car Oswald was supposed to send. Benny and Sten would likely show up at any moment. The last thing he wanted was to end up confronting them. He turned to Bosse and placed a hand on his shoulder.

'We're going to talk about this. I promise. But first you have to decide – we can't stay here. You might be able to get psychiatric help here in the city, maybe rest up at a hospital. Otherwise you'll have to choose between ViaTerra or the farm in Småland.'

Bosse pulled himself together. His voice was thick when he spoke.

'The farm in Småland. Please, can you take me there?'

'Okay, but this time we're going by car.'

*

Bosse began to talk after a while. Not about what had happened, but about his thoughts, about the doubt that had driven him to madness. Was ViaTerra really the earth's only salvation?

If it was, weren't Oswald's punishments and outbursts justified? How can you save a planet from destruction with the help of idiots like Bosse, who do everything wrong? When they stopped for gas and food, Simon interrupted him for the first time.

'You know, I think it takes time to figure all of that out on your own. Sofia and I had come to some conclusions before we escaped. You escaped because you didn't really have a choice. No one has the right to convince you one way or another. And you can only come to your own conclusions in peace and quiet.'

Bosse's face lit up in a smile. His eyes turned to the ethereal spring sky for a moment.

'Shit, you're right. I just have to take it one day at a time, don't I?'

'Exactly.'

*

His reunion with his parents felt forced. Simon shook hands with his father and gently pushed his mother away when her hug lasted too long. As he looked into her eyes, he realized that he was far from having forgiven her, but at the same time he could tolerate being in her presence. He accepted the offer of coffee; she had already set the table with their fanciest dishes. Bosse, who seemed completely oblivious to the tension between Simon and his parents, made polite small talk about the weather and how lovely it was on the farm. Simon wondered if he ought to tell his parents about what had happened at the train station, but decided to let it go. He was almost certain Bosse wouldn't try again. There was life in his eyes now. Just a tiny spark, but one Simon hoped would grow.

When Simon stood up to leave, his mother took him by the hand.

'We don't drive out demons anymore in God's Way.'

'Well, that's good to hear. Take care of Bosse, now. Don't let a single one of those bastards onto the farm.'

*

Back home at the pension, he headed out to work in the greenhouses. He skipped dinner and worked until dusk began to fall. By the time he got back to his cottage he was so tired that his immediate thought was to fall into bed. But then he logged onto his computer just to check his email. At the very top of his inbox he found a new message. Simon had only to read the first line to know something was wrong. Not because of the impulsivity – Sofia often made snap decisions. No, it was the lack of humour. It sounded like a robot had written this email. Sofia never would have sent him something so vapid.

Hi, Simon!

Met someone. Need to get some distance. Heading with my new friend to a secret spot in Europe. I'll write again when I know more. XOXO, Sofia

XOXO? New friend? Every word of the message sounded fake. Even the *Hi, Simon!* part. Sofia never bothered with polite greetings.

When he considered the implications, his insides went cold. He took his mobile phone from the coffee table and dialled her number, but only got her voicemail and couldn't bring himself to leave a message. He called twice more but there was no answer; he searched through his inbox and found the one where she told him when she'd be coming home. Her plane was supposed to land at Landvetter today. So why had the email been written the night before? Had she emailed him from the plane? The last thing she'd told him on the phone was how much she missed everyone at home. Could you get so close, only to change your mind at the last second?

It was eleven o'clock, too late to call, but he had no choice. After several rings, Benjamin's sleepy voice answered. Simon told him about the email, and for a long time it was silent on the other end.

'Are you there, Benjamin?'

'I didn't get any email from her. Hold on a sec, I'm just going to check. No, shit, here it is!' he read out loud. '"Need some distance. Don't feel ready to see you yet. Heading south with a friend for a while. I'll be in touch soon. XOXO, Sofia."' What the hell?' Benjamin squawked when he was done reading.

'Sorry to wake you up like this,' Simon said.

Benjamin didn't respond.

A faint voice in the background: 'Who is it?'

There was a rustling sound as Benjamin put his hand over the receiver, but Simon could still hear him.

'It's nothing. I'll tell you later.'

Benjamin's voice was stronger when he returned, as if he were awake now.

'What is this shit? Who's the friend, do you know?'

'He's not the one I'm worried about. I don't think Sofia wrote the email. I got one too, and it doesn't sound like her at all.'

'But it's from her fucking email account, so obviously it's her, right? This isn't the first time she's gotten a stupid idea into her head.'

'Benjamin. Listen. It's not her. I just know it.'

'So what do we do? What do you think is going on?'

'Someone hacked her email. I don't know where she is. We should call her parents.'

'Don't! Her mom will flip out. She's worried enough as it is. Have you tried her phone?'

'Several times. No answer, just voicemail. Something isn't right, I'm sure of it. Can you call her parents? Just to chat. Maybe they've heard from her.'

'Sure. I'll call you tomorrow after I talk to them.'

Simon had a lump in his throat all morning. He'd hoped that hard work would dampen his worry, but he couldn't concentrate. He loaded a wheelbarrow full of dirt but ran over a rock, causing the wheelbarrow to tip over. He kicked the pile of dirt and swore.

Benjamin called later that morning.

'I talked to Sofia's mom. They got an email too. It said she would be away for a few weeks. Her mom was worried because Sofia hadn't called to talk. They almost never email each other. But she said Sofia's off work for another month. I didn't say anything about our suspicions, didn't want to worry her. But listen, that email doesn't sound at all like Sofia. What should we do?'

Simon thought about it, and in the ensuing silence he heard some muffled sobs. It dawned on him that Benjamin was crying.

'What's wrong? Are you sad?'

'Goddamn fucking shit! She's like a slippery eel that just slips right through your fingers. And now I'm worried sick. Fuck, I miss her.'

'Hey, we're going to fix this. But it's got ViaTerra written all over it. And it's not like we can go to the police just because we think an email sounds fishy, is it?'

'No, but if we don't hear from her again soon, we'll have to.'

'Then let's respond to the emails. You say you don't believe it's her. I'll pretend I buy her story.'

'Simon, do you think someone has hurt her?'

'No, not exactly, but Oswald is free and I just don't like the way this looks.'

45

The scream began as a tickle on the roof of her mouth, rose from her lungs, crashed out of her throat like a wave, and reached a crescendo so loud it deafened her. And then she screamed again. The sound was sharp, like shards of glass in her heart. Even when she stopped screaming, an inward, droning cry made her want to crawl out of her skin. The knowledge that he was there, that this was real, and worse than the most horrifying nightmare she'd ever had, gave her a violent kick of adrenaline that drove her out of her mind. A light came on, blinding her; she had to screw her eyes shut. For a brief instant she was looking at everything from above – her body curled up on a bed, his form in front of her, the way he sat down on a chair. But almost immediately she was drawn back into her brain, a thousand shattered thoughts.

Her first impulse was to scream again. Get up and punch him in the face. Bellow that he would never get away with this. But she couldn't get her body to move.

She forced herself to take control of her brain, to stifle the panic; she took back control of her body and gave life to her muscles until she managed to turn her head away. She stared at the spiders' webs hanging from the wall behind the bed.

'Sofia, you've been awfully naughty,' came his voice. 'I hope you have something to say in your own defence.'

She closed her eyes and refused to speak.

'You must answer when addressed. I suppose it's best we lay out some rules for this little hovel.'

Suddenly she knew where she was. The mouldy smell and the draught – familiar impressions from the cellar of the manor house. She felt the bed sag as he sat down beside her. His thigh against her side. His cold hand closing around her wrist. He was so close now that the scent of his aftershave made her want to throw up.

He cupped her face in his hand and turned her head towards him. She squeezed her eyes shut like a disobedient child refusing to comply.

'Look at me!'

She squeezed harder. Her body began to shake; her heart was pounding on her ribs. She had to regain control, but her whole nervous system seemed to be running on autopilot.

'I want you to listen closely now, Sofia, because what I'm about to say is vital, whether you believe it or not. You are completely at my mercy. Perhaps you think someone will miss you, but that's not the case. Mattias is travelling around Europe with a girl who is an exact copy of you. He's using your email account to send plucky little messages to your family and friends now and then. Pictures of the Eiffel Tower and so forth. There is not a single bastard in the whole wide world who will miss you. If you want to get out of here, you will have to submit. You and I have a couple of things to work out.'

She opened her eyes but cast her eyes upward to stare at the ceiling. She did not want to allow him into her field of vision, to admit to herself that he was real.

His hand wandered up her arm, stopped at her shoulder,

slid under her shirt, and grabbed her breast. He squeezed hard. The pain was unbearable. She opened her mouth but refused to scream. Slowly he let go. Her breast throbbed. His hands appeared around her throat like claws and suddenly there was no air. She grabbed the bedstead, trying to yank herself backwards, get away from him, but he leaned forward and pressed harder. A rattling sound came from her throat. Just then, he loosened his grip just enough that she could gasp for breath. But no more. She thought she was going to pass out and tried to twist away from him, but it was like she was caught in a vice. Tears sprang to her eyes. Her lungs were almost out of air. An explosion of light blinded her, but at the same instant he allowed her to draw another breath.

'First you will tell me about when we first met,' he said. 'How horny it made you when I touched you. All your dirty fantasies about me. How wet you got when I pressed my hard cock against your back in the office. Do you remember that? And don't think I don't know. Mattias told me all about it. It's all you think about, sex, isn't it?'

'You perverted bastard!'

She wanted to spit in his face, but the hand dug into her throat. In the weak light, his eyes were black as a coal mine.

'Then you will submit, Sofia. Fully and completely. You will let me extinguish that brazen spark in your eyes with a good old leather strap. Just like all the other women I've ever wanted. And then, perhaps, we can discuss your conditions here. Because you will soon come to realize that this is where you belong. Maybe we'll even work together again. Wouldn't that be fun? Although you'll have to work your way back up in the hierarchy again, of course. Start with the scut work until you beg and plead for me to take you back. And don't bother screaming when the staff get back. No one will come down here.'

'Then just strangle me,' she rasped. 'Get it over with.'

He laughed and let go of her neck. 'Oh sweetie, you've always lived life in too big a hurry. This is going to be an important lesson for you, you'll see.'

'You will never get away with this, I'm going to fucking kill you...' Her voice broke as a rattle came from her lungs.

'Go ahead and try,' he said. 'It could be amusing.'

The bed creaked as he stood up. His steps echoed across the floor. There was a long moment of silence, but then his voice returned.

'Now you've got something to think about. There's food on the table over here.'

He turned out the light again.

The last thing she heard was a key turning in a lock.

She fell into a fit of coughing that made her gasp for breath. She filled her lungs with air, trying to breathe normally again. Her heart was pounding in her chest and thundering in her ears. For a long time, she lay on her back, still. Looking around the tiny room and running her fingers across the stiff, brand-new sheets and the knobbly blanket. She found it strange that she wasn't paralysed with fear. But her brain was frantically searching for solutions.

Even in all her misery, she felt a faint sense of relief. He wouldn't kill her right away. She had time. And if she could make use of this temporary clarity of mind, she would find a way to get out of there.

She sat up, realized she was barefoot, and put her feet on

the cold concrete floor. Her legs held her as she stood up. She took in the room – it had served as a quarantine zone for those in the cult who got sick. The bunk beds had been crammed in so tight that they blocked out the light from the ceiling. It had smelled horrific, like sweaty feet and rotten herbs. But now the room was empty aside from the bed, a wardrobe, and a small table with a plastic-wrapped sandwich on top.

She walked over and opened the wardrobe. Hangers with dresses on them. Small. Her size. A drawer of underthings, all silk and lace. A pair of ballerina flats.

The bathroom on the other side of the room was clean, freshly scrubbed. A pair of towels, soap, shampoo, and a toothbrush. Beyond the bathroom was a small closet full of cleaning supplies and yard implements, but that was it. The door out was massive – and locked.

Something smelled sour. She sniffed her armpit and felt ill at the whiff of sweat. She went into the bathroom and found that there was no lock but decided to risk it. She pulled off her T-shirt and panties and tossed them in a pile on the floor. Turned on the shower and shivered until the water got warm. Then she turned it up as hot as she could stand and sank to the floor of the stall, still freezing despite the heat. Afterwards she wrapped herself in a towel and went back out to the room, wolfed down the sandwich, and drank a bottle of mineral water.

Have to make it through this.

The light of the setting sun stole through the cellar window. She sat on the bed and tried to stave off the panic that crept over her as darkness engulfed the room. Soon she walked over to the door and turned on the lights.

The staff's voices were audible from out in the courtyard.

She wanted to peer out, but the window was too high. She cried for help a few times, until her shouts unleashed another coughing fit.

Then it was quiet outside once more. She didn't know what time it was; she'd taken off her watch back at Mattias's, before her bath. *Mattias. How the hell could I have been so stupid?* The shame was so painful that she let out a whimper. It wasn't as much the fact that she'd been so gullible, as that she hadn't had even the slightest suspicion. Surely she should have noticed? But she hadn't. And that could only mean that she was a dense, worthless loser. She thought of the emails he'd wanted to send from her computer, and felt so powerless and miserable that she wrapped her arms around her body and howled as she rocked herself.

Scenes from her life on the outside kept coming back to her. Each time she even got close to a memory of Benjamin, she felt a stab in the heart. Although she recalled every detail of his face, the crow's feet around his eyes, his always half-open mouth, the way his freckles clustered, she couldn't remember how all those details fit together. She couldn't picture his face.

She lay there sleepless for a long time; although she was exhausted, she was wound up with fear. Her terror ripped and tore at her. The room seemed to shrink and blood began to thunder in her ears. Loneliness brooded in the corner of the cave-like space. Whispering to her, mocking her. She was sure she wouldn't survive the night there, and tried to picture how it would all end.

He's going to kill me. This is where I will die.

46

A new email arrived from Sofia; it said she was in Paris. A picture of the Eiffel tower was attached, and it showed a far-off figure whose face wasn't clear. It could have been Sofia – or not.

Who gets on a plane to Paris when they just spent ten hours on another flight that same day? Simon wondered. *And how daft do they think I am?* As if Sofia would head straight for the Eiffel Tower the minute she got to Paris. And then have someone take a picture where you couldn't even see her face. As if selfies were suddenly not a thing!

This had come from someone who didn't know Sofia. And that certainty made Simon feel sick. Worse than he'd felt since leaving ViaTerra.

It was night-time; he'd just finished eating and was sitting in his easy chair. He had avoided his computer all day, until now. Just to have some space to think. But really, there wasn't much to think about. The feeling of distaste in his stomach got worse. Oswald had got his claws into Sofia. That was the only explanation, but it was such an unpleasant one that he frantically tried to come up with other reasons. Reasons that didn't really exist.

His phone rang and Benjamin's name popped up.

'I got it too,' Simon said.

'What should we do? It's not her, is it?'

'Is that other girl with you today?'

'No, why? Shit, Simon, she's just a way to pass the time. To get back at Sofia, kind of.'

'Crappy for the girl, and totally irresponsible. That's you in a nutshell.'

'Lay off me! What are we going to do?'

'I think you should go to the police.'

'Oh yeah? What am I supposed to say?'

'Tell them about the emails and tell the truth. That you don't think they came from Sofia.'

'Maybe. But we don't need to get her parents involved yet, do we?'

'If you don't want to, okay.'

'Do you think Oswald's behind this, Simon? Do you think he's capable of hurting her?'

'He's capable of anything,' Simon said, but when he heard Benjamin draw a sharp breath, he added, 'Don't worry. It's probably not that bad.'

Day after tomorrow, he thought after he hung up, *I'm going to see Jacob. Maybe he will have seen or heard something. Until then, I have to stop worrying.*

His phone dinged. It was a text from Anna.

Thanks, Simon! it said, with a dozen hearts, thumbs up, and smileys.

47

Oswald called the staff to a meeting when they got back from the pond. They had been milling around the courtyard shivering in the early spring evening, hungry and tired, but this couldn't wait. Jacob slipped in and found a seat in the back row. His head was full of troublesome thoughts. Who had been screaming? What was that mysterious delivery about? Maybe Oswald would explain everything. And hopefully he wasn't angry. Jacob had gotten the barn in order, but there was no room for further disasters.

Oswald's lecture didn't start out so well. He gripped the podium and didn't say anything for a long time, which typically meant he was collecting himself and trying to hold back an outburst of rage. The room was quiet aside from a few scattered coughs. His voice thrummed with irritation when he finally began to speak.

'It's truly unforgivable that you made such a mess of everything while I was gone. Today I actually thought about firing the entire staff, sending you back to the mainland, and finding new workers. I'm serious. I'm at a loss for words, here.'

The staff squirmed in their chairs. Shame spread throughout the room. Jacob snorted inwardly – no one had ever been allowed to leave ViaTerra voluntarily. But most people were tormented by the idea when Oswald threatened it. Then again, Jacob wondered how many secretly hoped he would make the decision for them. End their suffering in one fell swoop.

'There was an inspector here today while you were away,' Oswald went on. 'I thought there was an odd smell in the cellar, and sure enough, it's gone mouldy. You let the rain come in last fall, no one did a thing about it, true to form. So now it's crawling with mould. Nice, huh?'

Jacob couldn't help but picture the whole staff scrubbing the cellar. But now he wondered if the object under the sheet could have been some sort of mould-destroying apparatus.

'It's too late for you to do anything about it,' Oswald continued. 'And besides, I don't trust you. A company will come and take care of it. Until then, the cellar is off limits. No one is to go down there. Or even go near it. Understood?'

Jacob felt himself relax. They wouldn't have to work in the cellar. That meant time to care for the animals. Time to sleep. Maybe only a few nights, until the next disaster happened, but still. At ViaTerra, time was more precious than gold.

Oswald shook his head and shrugged in resignation.

'And do you know what the worst part is? The way you stare at me. Like a bunch of goddamn vacant zombies.'

He turned to the blackboard that hung behind the podium, picked up a piece of chalk, and drew a smiley face without the smile. A circle with two eyes and a straight line for a mouth.

'This is how you look. Like blank, expressionless lumps of dough. So today we are adding a new word to ViaTerra's vocabulary. Doughface. And yes, it will count as a transgression to respond to me with doughface. And the water at Devil's Rock is pretty fucking cold right now.'

Jacob frantically tried to rouse the muscles of his face to life, but it was all wrong – now he was smiling, and surely that didn't fit the situation. Instead he tried to bring some fervour to his eyes, but now he was certain he must look insane. Luckily Oswald wasn't looking in his direction. He just shook his head and sighed.

'No food for you tonight. I can't stand the thought of you all sitting around the dining hall and laughing. In fact, I can't stand the thought of you being on my property at all.'

So they would be sent to bed without their supper, like disobedient children.

But Jacob had made an extra sandwich in the kitchen earlier that day, to be on the safe side. And he could always get milk from the cows.

He stayed put as the staff rambled out. Typically, everyone stuck around when Oswald was in a rage, but after Bosse's escape no one had taken charge of the staff. Besides, everyone was tired and cold and no one had the energy to order anyone else around.

Jacob was last to leave the dining room. He didn't rush as he walked across the courtyard; he soaked in the chilly air. He felt that it was time to leave. *The day after tomorrow I'll see Simon,* he thought. *And we'll make a plan. I'll go to an animal-rights organization when I get out. Get them to rescue the animals.*

He imagined what it would be like to be free. To be able to call his parents and tell them that this hell was over, that he was no longer a cult member whose only contact with them was found in cryptic, meaningless letters.

Just as he turned the corner around the manor house, he noticed that there was a light on in the cellar.

And then he saw something that made his skin crawl.

48

A ray of sun found its way through the window and tickled her face, waking her up. At first the warmth felt nice, but it was only a stray beam that had snuck into her prison, only to disappear soon after. A deep disgust rose in her stomach as the puzzle-pieces of yesterday fell into place. The fleeting pleasure burst like a bubble.

She screwed her eyes shut in an attempt to keep reality out. Pretended that she had only fallen asleep on the plane and was having a nightmare. Soon she would land at Landvetter. Tell Mattias she had changed her mind and take the train straight to Lund. She simply couldn't be back at ViaTerra. People didn't kidnap their enemies, not here in Sweden. But then again, Oswald wasn't a normal person.

The ray of sun had found the floor, and dust danced up into the light. It was quiet outside, aside from a bleating sheep. She thought of Benjamin. Her longing for him ran through her body like a shock. Each time she tried to quell any thoughts of him they just came back, like when you can't help but pick at a scab. What if she never saw him again? Her anguish was a melting ice cube in her stomach; it spread through her body like poison. She stared straight ahead. Breathing slowly. Managed to gather enough strength to sit up in bed.

Get it together, Sofia. For God's sake, get it together.

Today I will escape, she thought. *I did it once, so I can do it again.* She found it odd that she'd managed to get any sleep, but it must have been the drugs. Her body had been so weak, but today it was stronger. When she stood up her legs felt steadier, although she was a little dizzy.

There was a tray on the table by the door. So he had been there. Cold eggs and soggy toast. The butter had melted and hardened again. The first bite made her feel like throwing up, but she needed the energy to run if she was going to escape.

Once she'd used the toilet, washed up, and brushed her teeth, she decided to put on a dress. It was that or run through the forest wrapped in a towel. At the wardrobe she glanced through the short, tight dresses and chose the only one that went past her knees. The fabric was thin, but there was no helping it. She put on the ballerina flats.

There were two ways out of the cellar. Through the door, which was locked, or through the window. It was so high up that she would need to stand on something to reach it, but it looked like she could squeeze through. She went over to the cleaning closet and took out the ladder she'd noticed when she first peeked in. She hauled it to the wall and set it up. Trembling with anticipation, she climbed to the top. The courtyard came into view beyond the glass. It must have been early morning – the sun was still rising. It wasn't as lovely as she recalled: the water in the big pond was nothing but brown goo. The lawn hadn't been mowed. The flowerbed under the cellar window was an overgrown tangle of weeds and flowers, with bees bouncing from blossom to blossom. But the very sight of the open landscape made her heart skip a beat. Freedom was so close. If only she could get the window open.

She wiggled the latch and got it loose, but she could only open the window a tiny bit before it caught on something outside. The tree-like scent of damp spring earth struck her. She shoved at the window, but it wouldn't give way.

'It's locked from the outside,' came a voice behind her, causing her to jump and nearly lose her grip. She didn't have time to turn around before he was there, grabbing her by the hair. He yanked and she fell backward, but he caught her by the armpits with an iron grip. The ladder fell over with a crash. He dragged her onto the floor and let go of her so fast her head struck the floor. The blow was so hard her vision went black. When she opened her eyes again he was looming over her. The sun shone through the window, outlining his silhouette with a fiery aura. Her forehead was pounding and her ears were buzzing. For an instant she thought she might faint, but then he bent down and pulled her to her feet. His eyes were burning with rage, a wrath that exploded from his pupils.

He boxed her ear, a move so fast and so hard that her ears rang. A shove sent her backwards and she landed on the bed. Her brain couldn't keep up with what was happening; she tried to get up, tried to protect herself as his body fell on top of hers. But he was strong, much stronger than her, and he locked her hands above her head. Her legs flailed and she tried to kick him, but she missed; she spat at him but he turned away and looked down at her with his face full of scorn.

He slapped her cheek hard, saying nothing, just breathing heavily through his nose. It was clear that her resistance was turning him on. She could feel him getting more and more excited the more she struggled. He turned her onto her stomach and lay on top of her as he used something soft to tie her hands to the bedstead, tightening it so hard that her wrists burned. She was caught under the weight of him and could hardly breathe, but she whimpered, aware that she needed to scream, and managed the start of a roar. But then he shoved her head into the pillow until she was gasping for air. He took her by the hair and pulled her face back up again.

'Stop, stop!' she shrieked.

'Scream as much as you want. No one will come down here.'

He yanked at her dress. The fabric ripped loudly. She tried to kick him but he got to his knees between her legs, pulled her up, and shoved her thighs apart. She couldn't move. She was stuck, and suddenly ashamed of her naked body. Then came a burning pain as he spanked her buttocks. He struck her hard, senselessly. The fury streaming from him now was of a type she had never before experienced. Pent-up hate that he projected at her body in quick, violent blows. But worst of all, worse than the pain, was his silence. Not a word, not even a moan. Only his breathing, heavy and rasping. When he was done hitting her, he pushed her forward, causing her head to strike the headboard. For a moment he was still. She thought he might stop. But then she heard him unzip his pants. She considered begging and pleading but knew it wouldn't help. He wrapped an arm around her stomach and pulled her ass into the air. She squeezed all her muscles, trying to keep him out. The pain was so sudden that she screamed. It burned like fire. Her hands squeezed at the sheets convulsively. It seemed like he would rip her to shreds, that something had ruptured inside her. But he kept thrusting into her, harder and faster. His breathing came in sharp bursts. She might have been a blow-up toy. Or dead. Her screams died back into a long, drawn-out whimper. The pain was a constant wave tearing at her body. He kept going for a long time. Whether it was ten minutes or half an hour, she would never know – all her strength had drained away and she hung like a lifeless doll, waiting for him to be done. The pain had become part of her and was drowned out by a recurring thought.

I don't want to die like this.

Once he had come, he grabbed her waist and pressed her into the bed. He collapsed on top of her, heavy as a boulder. She couldn't breathe and began to struggle; it felt like she would suffocate until he rolled off of her. She could hear him zipping up. He hadn't undressed, only pulled down his trousers.

Later, a peculiar thought would pop into her mind and hang around. He hadn't even taken off his clothes. Because it wasn't about sex, only about humiliating her in the worst imaginable way. He had only gotten hard because of her fear. She would understand that he, with his heart black as coal, was incapable of enjoying sex – he only got off on the violence. A moment of clarity would come to her; it would explain why he had constantly bothered her in the office but had never gone all the way, why he rejected all the girls who hit on him. Because the only thing he wanted to do was torture and degrade women. But that insight came later. At the moment when he was finished with her, there was only one thought in her head: that she didn't want to die.

He untied her hands and turned her onto her back. For a long time he gazed at her, sneering. The bed bounced as he climbed off. She lay there motionless and silent. Her body was throbbing with shame, and it seemed to her there was no coming back from this. Everything was ruined and would never be the same again.

'We're done here, but it's not over between us. It's only just begun, you see,' he said.

'You sick bastard,' she managed. She steeled herself for a blow to the head, but he just laughed and threw up his hands like it was all a game.

'To be honest, it doesn't help that you talk to me like that. If you want a tip, that is. It will only prolong your suffering.'

His steps echoed against the floor. She turned her head away to hide the fact that her eyes were swimming with tears. But he didn't turn around. The key turned in the lock and everything went quiet. She curled up in the foetal position and cried. Her sobs were thick and hiccoughing; her nose began to run, mixing with the tears to form a disgusting mess. She cried until it hurt to breathe, then rolled over and sat up, whimpering – there seemed to be ripping and tearing between her legs. Sharp, pulsating waves of pain. Her legs almost couldn't hold her as she stood up, and she felt a stabbing pain inside. Shuffling to the bathroom, she looked in the mirror. An angry bruise on her forehead. The semen trickled out of her as she sat on the toilet, and then came a few drops of blood. Her stomach turned. She knelt in front of the toilet and tried to throw up, but all that came out was something thick and slimy. She rested her forehead against the cool seat for a moment.

Strange thoughts came to her. Everything had gone wrong. This wasn't what was supposed to happen. When she'd worked with Oswald in his office, she'd always imagined that she would kick and claw at him if he attacked her; she would fight back like a wildcat. She'd even kept a little pocketknife in her skirt pocket, a silly little way to defend herself if things got out of control. But now it turned out he was too strong and violent and he had rattled her completely. It had been a piece of cake for him, and she was ashamed of that.

She lay down on the cold bathroom floor and cried, then dragged herself back to the bed and pulled the covers over her head. She fell asleep almost immediately, even though it was the middle of the day.

When she awoke, it was dark. The sky outside was black and the moon shimmered between the ragged, passing clouds. She flung herself back and forth in the bed, screaming. But nothing happened. No one came.

She fell asleep again, and must have slept the whole night – the room was bright when she woke up. How long could a person sleep, really? She realized she was empty; no more feelings. All that was left was a vague sort of weight somewhere inside. *I have to pull myself together,* she thought. But there was nothing to hold onto. Her head was pounding, her crotch ached, and her buttocks burned.

What should I do? Please help me, God!

A glance at the table told her there was no food on it. So she was going to starve on top of everything. She was thirsty, but didn't have the energy to drag herself across the room. She turned her head to face the window and felt sleepy again and dozed off.

Some time later she became aware that he was back again. She hadn't heard him arrive, but there he was, sitting on the bed. She pretended to be asleep, breathing evenly and slowly. The hair on the back of her neck stood up, awaiting his touch, which she knew would come. His cold fingers ran down her back, stroking her tenderly, almost lovingly. It was so awful and out of place that she shivered and began to tremble. She quashed the impulse to pull away. His cold lips brushed her cheek, which only made everything worse. Because he was absolutely unpredictable.

'I know you're awake,' he said. 'But I'm going to go now. I'll leave you some reading material.'

She waited until she heard the key turn in the lock.

Then she slowly turned over to face the room.

On the table by the door was a book.

49

The book was leather-bound and looked like a diary. She opened it to find that the text on the first page was ornate, written in ink: *A Family History, recorded by Sigrid Kristina Augusta von Bärensten*. The fact that she was holding *that* book in her hands was so incredible that, for a brief moment, she forgot about the hopeless situation she was in. She'd searched for this family history for over a year while she was working at ViaTerra. Even after her escape, she'd fantasized about getting her hands on it. And here it was, right in her lap, not even looking particularly remarkable. But the question was, why had Oswald given it to her? Why did he want her to read it?

There was food on the table too, and not just any old grub. A large platter of thinly-sliced chicken, bread, cheeses, and grapes. A bottle of sparkling water and a bottle of wine. Next to the platter was a vase holding a red rose. She wondered what the hell this was all about. Some sort of atonement? There was a sinking feeling in her stomach; it was better when he was cruel all the time, easier to understand than his peculiar whims. But when she picked up the note that lay next to the vase, she was once again certain that he was rotten to the core. *Thanks for a lovely evening,* it said.

She threw the vase at the wall and it smashed into a thousand pieces. The rose fluttered to the floor and lost all its petals. She sank into the chair, pulling her legs up and hugging them, rocking herself and forcing back tears. She managed to quell her despair and decided to eat after all. She drank all of the water but left the wine, then went to the cleaning closet for a brush and dustpan to clean up the shards of glass. She picked up the family history, sat on the bed, and began to read.

A Family History
Recorded by
Sigrid Kristina Augusta von Bärensten

This is a brief account of my humble life.

There are rumours spread and stories told of the manor house on Fog Island, so perhaps it is time that people learn the truth of what happened there. In some respects, I am forever caught in the night the manor burned. Memories of the fire echo through my dreams and daydreams. The heat, the smell of the smoke, the shrieks of the animals, the flames licking at the sky, and the billowing smoke that spread over the island. But I cannot yet bring myself to write about that.

And this is meant to be a history. So I will begin at the beginning. When we first came to this Godforsaken island.

My name is Sigrid Kristina Augusta von Bärensten, daughter of Artur and Amelia von Bärensten. I am writing down this chronicle, our story, with the hope that it will bring insight into why the von Bärensten family has been so befallen by tragedy.

Father was a wealthy businessman from Gothenburg. He was a bear of a man, with raven hair, an aquiline nose, and a strong jaw. His eyes were like an augur – it sometimes hurt when he looked at one. Mother was delicate, blonde, and pale. She looked like a fairy alongside Father's towering frame.

I was born on 8 March 1920, just two months before my father had the manor house built here on west Fog Island. Certainly no one could understand why he wanted to live here, in particular. It was a desolate, barren landscape. There was not much of a village here back in those days. And the fog swept in from the sea, settling over the island like a thick blanket during the winter.

Yet it was here on Fog Island that his manor must be, and the day we first set foot on the island was captured for eternity in a photograph which I have pasted in here. There is Father with shovel in hand, Mother with me on her knee, and my brother Oskar standing beside us. He was six years old when the photograph was taken. It was the same day the yet-unbuilt manor received its name. Her name was to be Vindsätra Manor and Estate.

Each time I look at this photograph I curse the fate that brought us here.

★

The first few years are blurry in my mind. My first true memory is a scream. Mother's scream, coming from the attic.

'Why does Mother scream at night?' I asked my nurse, Emma.

'I suppose she has nightmares. Just like you do, sometimes.'

'But the screams come from the attic.'

'No, you're just imagining things. No one is allowed into the attic, you know that. Your father keeps important papers there, that no one must touch.'

'But they *do* come from the attic.'

My curiosity grew and made me brave.

It was storming that night. Bolts of lightning and roaring thunder, one after the next. I was frightened and I needed the bathroom and then came the screams, in the space between a flash of lightning and a boom of thunder. The stairs were cold beneath my feet. I held onto the railing, pulling myself up step by step, gasping when I saw that the attic door was open. I heard the scream again, but this time it was muffled, like a moan.

There was something white stretched out across a bench in the attic. *It's a pig,* I thought. I had seen a slaughtered pig on a farm. That's what it had looked like, all splayed out and bound at the legs. *It's the pig that screams at night,* I reasoned, and just then my father turned and spotted me. His eyes were wild and angry. In a trice he scooped me up in his arms and carried me down the stairs. I thought he seemed sweaty and strange, but I was glad he was holding me – he so seldom did. He brusquely lay me in my bed, in my room.

This was the only time he ever tucked me in. When I tried to speak, he put his hand over my mouth.

'You were dreaming,' he whispered. 'It was only a dream.'

As he left the room, I realized he was naked.

The last thing I heard was a key turning in the lock.

*

'There's a pig that screams in the attic,' I said to Oskar as we ate supper.

Only this, and Father was on top of me. It all happened so fast. I didn't have time to swallow; I didn't even have time to think a single thought. The blow was so hard that my chair flew backwards and I landed on the floor with a thud.

I began to cry, and then Oskar began to sob, but no one did a thing.

'Get up,' came Father's voice from across the table. 'I am tired of your lies and inventions. Go to your room immediately.'

I waited for Mother to come pick me up. But nothing happened.

I took hold of the edge of the table and pulled myself up; I noticed that I had food on my chin and chest, and I was still crying, but my howling had settled into quiet tears.

Mother sat staring down at her plate. Her fork quaked in her hand. But otherwise she didn't move.

Oskar had fallen silent. Father was trembling with rage. I slowly walked out of the dining room, dragging my feet after me, but not in a provocative way.

Never again did I mention the pig. When it screamed at night, I held my ears, and when that didn't help, I sang to myself in the dark. My door was always locked now. Father said I sleepwalked, that it was dangerous. Mother agreed.

I saw the bruises on her arms. The red marks on her neck. How she almost staggered when she walked, sometimes. It was as if all of that had been invisible before.

But I didn't say anything.

Mother is sick, I thought. *That's why she looks this way.*

Once Father began to strike us, he didn't stop. All it took was an expression, a moment of awkwardness, and he would throw himself at Oskar and me. But mostly me. We simply had to stay away from him. And it got worse.

Sometimes Emma asked permission to take us out around the island. There was a small pond in the forest where we liked to go. When the weather was good, she let us play there.

I was five or six years old when it happened. My uncle Markus, Father's brother, and his wife aunt Ofelia were visiting. I didn't like Uncle Markus; he had rough hands that lifted me high in the air and spun me around until I felt ill. Aunt Ofelia was sickly and weak.

On that day I was sitting on the swing and spinning around and around and around until I got dizzy, and then I spotted them. Mother, Father, and Uncle Markus on their way out of the gate. I sneaked after them, keeping my distance. I got distracted, because I saw a squirrel in a tree, but then I heard voices from the pond. I peered through the leaves and saw them.

Mother was floating on the surface, naked, her body gleaming like mother-of-pearl against the dark water. Father was standing behind her, holding her arms. Uncle Markus stood between her spread legs. Mother was screaming and whimpering. Father shoved her head under the water.

I forgot that I wasn't supposed to be there. I thought Mother would drown, so I cried out, losing my footing and sliding down the slope to the shore. I stood up and tried to run away, but Uncle Markus was there to grab me. He was naked and wet; the water streamed off him and onto my clothing. He sat on a rock and laid me over his knee, pulled down my underpants, and spanked me so hard it stung.

Out in the pond, Father castigated Mother.

'What is that damn brat doing here? Isn't anyone looking after her?'

He turned around and saw me struggling and yelling. And my unruliness triggered something inside him; he came up and yanked me from Uncle Markus's grasp. He carried me to the water and dunked me beneath the surface. It was black and cold, and all I could see were the bubbles that came from my attempts to scream *I'm sorry.* But his hands held me down so hard. They took my hair and pulled me up so I could gasp for breath. They shoved me down again.

When I was above the surface, in that brief moment, I heard Mother's voice: 'Artur, you'll kill her!'

But he didn't, not that day.

Mother was sent home with me. Wet and miserable, we walked through the forest.

She didn't say a word, all the way home. That was the worst part.

*

The captain popped up like a jack-in-the-box once Father disappeared. His name was Broman, and he was nice to me and Oskar: he gave us presents from foreign lands, followed us to the cliffs and let us play by the sea, spoke to Mother in a calm voice, so we wouldn't hear. But I *did* see and hear. How he brushed his fingers over Mother's bruises and said, 'This cannot continue, Amelia.'

'The captain is our secret,' Mother said to Oskar and me. 'He's only a dream, do you understand? Like the pig in the attic, Sigrid. If Father hears about Captain Broman, he will be terribly angry.'

And of course, none of us wanted that.

This roller-coaster lasted for a year. Heaven when the captain came to the island. Hell when Father returned and spread his wrath over us.

But then came the fire and put a stop to it all. I'll save that for last, because everyone got it all wrong: the police, the doctors, the firefighters, and the newspapers. I am the only living soul who knows what happened that night, and I have made an oath to myself that I will tell the story before I die. And I don't have much time now, because the cancer is spreading through my body like a drop of ink through water.

The servants put out the fire and saved the manor house, but the barns were destroyed. Smoke blanketed the island. Oskar and I were put in the servants' quarters and were not allowed out under any circumstances. Emma held me, whispering to me like I was a baby, saying that Mother and Father had gone to Heaven, that everything would be fine. Oskar stood in a corner, crying.

'Oh, what a horrible tragedy,' Emma whimpered.

'But Mother's not dead,' I said stubbornly. 'I saw her. She's coming back.'

'No, my little darling, she isn't.'

'Yes, she is.'

'No, sweetheart.'

Then I covered my ears and shrieked, 'Stop! Stop!' until she was quiet.

That was the same night Oskar fell ill. The colour of his face shifted until he was a pale green. His body shook with a high fever. His lungs whistled and his breaths were raspy; I couldn't get any sleep. I lay there shivering with a lump in my throat, until I padded out of bed and gazed out at the courtyard.

The darkness was heavy over Vindsätra. The charred wreckage of the outbuildings pointed scornfully at the sky. The moon vanished behind a cloud and a cold gust of wind came through the gap at the window, bringing the odour of smoke. As I stood there, I could have sworn I felt her breath against my cheek.

A faint whisper in my ear, barely audible.

Sigrid, I'm coming back. I'll come back to you.

*

They arrived with pomp and circumstance. Uncle Markus and Aunt Ofelia. Eager to take over Vindsätra, less excited at the prospect of taking on Oskar and me. But there were nurses, of course.

At first, it was all like a dream. Uncle Markus made considerable changes as the new lord of the manor. Parties were held on the property at weekends. The mood at Vindsätra was suddenly carefree and lively.

I was sent to school in the village and allowed to roam free on the island. I could even travel to the mainland if I was accompanied by a nurse. Oskar, who now had double pneumonia, was never allowed these freedoms, but for me it was like the start of a marvellous new life.

Some changes didn't make sense to me. Why were the new servant girls so young? Why did Emma disappear, only to be replaced by my new nurse Hilda, who was only sixteen? Why was she always so nervous and giggly when Uncle Markus was nearby? Sometimes I ran into her in the middle of the night, wearing only a shift. She often smelled unfamiliar, as if a little cloud of the men's tobacco smoke had sneaked into her long hair.

*

When Oskar died of pneumonia I was only eleven years old. It was as if his soul left the earth, while his emptiness lingered inside me. He withered away, until at last he was no more.

Aunt Ofelia told me, her voice authoritative, that Oskar had departed the earth and gone to God's kingdom, where he was playing harp with the other angels. I thought this was ridiculous, because Oskar had never been musical *or* angelic.

Uncle Markus's views on the matter were entirely different; he laid them out one evening during our supper.

'It's always been the case that the weak and feeble are weeded out of the von Bärensten line. That's the law of nature. Although it's certainly peculiar that we lost Artur. I suppose God does have His exceptions.'

He glanced at me and laughed when he found that I was choking on my soup.

'Don't look so frightened, Sigrid! There's nothing wrong with you. You're going to be one of those wildcats. Hard to tame.'

And that was the end of any conversation with me about Oskar's death. We never spoke of him after the funeral. Whenever I tried to bring him up, Aunt Ofelia cut me off.

'We will not disturb those who are at rest in the kingdom of God.'

Something inside me burst when Oskar died. A wound of loneliness that refused to heal. Some stubborn part of me refused even to accept that Mother was dead. After all, she had promised to take care of me.

One night I went to the sea to seek peace. The sun had just slipped below the horizon, but its glow lingered over the heath. I climbed down to Devil's Rock and stood at the very edge, letting the wind stroke my face. I could taste salt on my lips. Then I called for her, out loud, but my cry was carried off on the wind.

On the way home I was roused from my thoughts by a cracking sound in the forest, twigs breaking under someone's feet. I stopped. Sensed her presence. The back of my neck went stiff as if it had iced over. In that moment, I knew I must not turn around. What I would see would scare the daylights out of me.

I walked all the way back to Vindsätra as if I were wearing blinders.

I knew I wasn't ready to stare death in the eye.

*

I have always believed that there is a transitory point in each girl's life when she changes from child to woman. The way she moves, the way her entire being becomes more pliable, softer. For me, this point came during the summer I turned fourteen.

I wandered around the island in long, flowing skirts and straw hats – sometimes the wind carried these across the meadows. I realized that something had happened to me, but I didn't know what it was. I had grown forgetful and dreamy. It seemed that the colours of the world were sweeter.

Uncle Markus wasted no time in noticing this. He was like a bloodhound on a hot trail. I recall the exact moment he saw and felt it. We were sitting at the dining room table. I dropped a spoon and bent down to pick it up. When I sat up again, his eyes were on the neckline of my blouse. Then our eyes met. His gaze was so raw that I had to turn away. But when I looked back, his eyes were still on me. The tension was so unbearable that I dropped my spoon again, but it landed on my plate this time.

My aunt saw what was happening. Her throat went blotchy and red, as it always did when she was nervous. She cleared her throat, and he looked away from me. At that moment, I realized something between us had changed.

That very evening, he came to my room. I was almost asleep. He came over and sat on the edge of the bed.

'Pull down the covers, Sigrid,' he said.

'Why?'

'Sigrid, I'm going to tell you something and I want you to listen closely. From now on, you will do everything I ask of you. Otherwise, Sigrid, I will destroy your life. I will claim that you are feeble-minded and confused like your mother. And soon enough, you will be in an asylum. I promise you that.'

I pulled down the covers, because I had always had respect for him and now I was terrified. He pulled up my nightdress and scrutinized my body. His hand slid over my belly, under the top of the nightdress, and cupped my breast. Then down into my undergarments where he slowly inserted a finger into my very innermost part. It was tremendously painful. I recoiled. An image of my mother flickered through my mind. Mother, not a pig – I knew it now.

He pulled my nightdress back over my legs, stood up, and left the room.

He didn't come back that night.

I lay in my bed, my eyes closed, trying to shut out what had just happened. The tears wouldn't come, because my throat had constricted and everything was caught below it. Then the bed sagged ever so slightly. A cool hand on my forehead. I squeezed my eyes shut, but I could feel her presence in every cell of my body. The faint scent of her lilac perfume. A cold gust of air swept through the room. I slowly opened my eyes and saw her shadow vanish in the dark. I didn't dare fall asleep, because I was suddenly afraid of the dark. The hours dragged on. When morning dawned, foggy and overcast, I was finally able to fall asleep and I allowed the rush of the sea to rock my anxious mind to peace.

*

Uncle Markus was a man with precise routines. He woke at six and had his coffee and breakfast while reading the newspaper. Then he spent the morning riding around the property and inspecting the farm. In the afternoon he sat in his office, dealing with the affairs of the manor. Once a week he travelled to the mainland on business. Dinner was taken at seven with my aunt and me, and then he withdrew to the billiard room with cognac and a cigar. At ten on the dot he went to his bedroom.

He came to my room one night a week. Always on a Friday.

And he was punctual – quarter past ten. I couldn't bring myself to look at him, so I pretended to be asleep. It was easier that way. I lay there like a passive doll. My breathing even and rhythmic. My eyes squeezed shut. If I was asleep, that meant nothing had actually happened. I didn't want him there. I tried to keep out the steps, shuffling so heavily on the stairs as he approached. But I also wanted to be free.

I can get through this, I thought. *I have to get through this, so I can live my life. If I close my eyes and think of the forest and the sea, it will be over quickly. If this is all he wants, I can manage.* And when he panted, all out of breath, I thought of the way the attic sounded when the wind was in the trees, or of the breakers' soothing sound as they struck the rocks.

⋆

He came to my room on the day I turned fifteen. His steps sounded different. More decisive than shuffling. The difference was so palpable that my heart grew heavy. His acrid smell spread through the room like a rotten gust of wind.

'Put on your robe and come with me.'

He waited for me. I was plunged into a state that is hard to describe. There was no oxygen, and yet I breathed. Each muscle of my body was stiff, and yet I moved. In this state, half outside my own body, I followed him up the stairs to the attic. I stepped over the threshold and gave a sob, like an animal being smothered.

The attic was a kingdom, ruled by the master of the house. A sacristy, so holy that as children, the very thought of going there paralysed us with fear. The stories told about the attic were gruesome. It was said that God would punish anyone who stepped over the threshold uninvited in the most excruciating ways. Because this place, which rested on top of the manor house like a cupola, had been created for the strongest and boldest men so that they could escape life's usual drudgeries.

I had, of course, caught a glimpse of the attic one time: Mother, tied down with rope. Now its details took form. I screwed my eyes closed in an attempt to escape reality. The canopy bed – the room's centrepiece – and the ropes and whips. Sweat broke out on my nape, trickling down my back and sending one last, degrading drop between my buttocks. A rough hand covered my mouth before a scream could escape my lips.

'You will obey,' he said. 'Just do as I tell you and everything will be fine.'

I could hardly stand on my two legs when he was finished. Everything was spinning and my body was burning. He told me I would get used to it, then carried me down the stairs and laid me in bed.

Only once he had closed the door did I notice that everything was different. The house was breathing, panting and moaning sorrowfully, its walls creaking and its windows rattling faintly. There was something abnormal about the ticking of the wall clock; it seemed strained and frantic. I turned to face the room, my fear swelling. A shadow behind the wardrobe expanded and reached onto the rug. Out of the darkness was born a silhouette, and there she was, standing before me. I cried her name but she shushed me, whispering that she would come to comfort me whenever he violated me. I screwed up my eyes. If it was true that she wanted to help me, why was I so afraid? Suddenly I felt tired and was swallowed in endless darkness.

*

It turned out that Uncle Markus's fixation on details and manic sense of order were what saved me from complete degradation. There couldn't be any marks. I had to wash myself afterwards, comb my hair and put it up. He never spilled any seed in me. Everything was methodical and planned, even though he was rough and hurt me.

Each Friday night, at ten on the dot, I was to be in the attic. I cried myself to sleep afterwards each time. Sometimes Mother sat beside me to comfort me. I realized now that in some incredible way she had survived the fire and had hidden here at Vindsätra to take care of me. She didn't exist, and yet she was there. And I knew one thing for certain: I would never dare to speak to anyone about her, so transitory was her presence and so invaluable was the comfort she brought me.

I stopped eating and became thin, because I thought Uncle Markus wouldn't want me that way. But he forced me to eat, spoonful by spoonful, while Aunt Ofelia stood watch. I locked my door one Friday, but he went to fetch the master key and boxed my ears. I bit my nails, but then he had Aunt Ofelia soak my fingers in vinegar.

My body became a claustrophobic prison with no way out. I constantly carried a heavy stone in my belly. He forbade me to visit the mainland and sent a chaperone when I walked around the island. He made Hilda accompany me to school.

But who could I talk to? No one on the island would have dared to question Count von Bärensten.

The most astounding part was that no one could see in my eyes what was wrong. Life went on as if nothing happened up in the attic.

One night, when I returned to my room, Mother wasn't there. No matter how much I cried out for her, the room remained empty and lonely. I knew she had left and that I was perfectly alone in the world. That was when I realized I had to escape.

*

The main gate was always locked, but there was a smaller gate behind the annexes that led into the forest. My plan was to sneak out in the morning, head through the forest to the harbour, and take the ferry to the mainland.

And then what? I wasn't sure. The city was an unknown realm. Maybe I could find a farm somewhere that needed an extra pair of hands.

The fog was thick that day, and the air was damp and heavy. I had packed a few necessities in a backpack and dressed in long pants, an autumn jacket, and heavy boots. The guard didn't notice me sneaking through the gate. I began to walk in the direction of the harbour. At least, I thought I did. After an hour it became clear that I had gone astray. There was no sun to guide me, and the landscape seemed to repeat itself. The fog thickened until I could hardly see the trees.

Exhausted and close to tears, I sat down and tried to think. Then I heard the hounds barking – worked up, eager, as dogs sound when they're on the hunt. I knew it was him – no one else hunted so early in the autumn. I launched myself from the rocks and set off, stumbling over roots and stones, scratching myself on twigs, but rushing on. Yet the dogs grew closer.

And then I realized who their quarry was.

The dog darted out of the forest in attack position. I threw myself down into the moss and lay perfectly still. I heard its growl; I heard hooves coming closer – I closed my eyes and prayed to God, sincerely begging Him to save me from what was about to happen.

He brought the horse so close to me that its hooves were right next to my body, then dismounted and pulled me to my feet.

And then he hit me. My face first, until it sounded like there were church bells in my ears and I fell backwards into the moss. Then my body, which he pounded with his fists, straddling me.

And last of all, he kicked. Until one blow hit my head and everything went black.

*

When I first woke up, I had no idea where I was. But I recalled everything that had happened. A brutal headache pounded at my temples. I couldn't make my eyes focus. My aunt's blurry face hovered over me.

'Thank God you're awake, Sigrid. Something terrible has happened.'

'I know what happened, I...'

'Shh, don't exert yourself. A man attacked you in the forest. A real brute. Uncle found you just in time. But the man got away. Oh, it's just awful. You should thank God that your uncle was out hunting. Otherwise that man might have killed you.'

'But that's not what happened.'

'We know exactly what happened. And he had torn your clothing off. What wretchedness!'

'But Aunt Ofelia, listen—'

'Your uncle believes it was a hired man from one of the farms. He's there now. You must rest, you mustn't get up.'

'But it wasn't like that.'

'Oh yes, little Sigrid, it was. The doctor was here. He said you might be a bit confused, because that brute hit you in the head. But you'll recover. Oh, little Sigrid.'

The red blotches spread over her neck like hives. All at once I realized she knew what had really happened. And exactly what occurred up in the attic.

I turned onto my side, fluttered my eyelashes, and pretended to fall asleep.

My aunt padded out of the room.

I was bedridden for several weeks, saying that I didn't feel well. I refused to get up. No one spoke of the fact that I had attempted to escape. The clouds floated past outside my window. Days became nights. The moon shrank and grew again. My wounds healed but I couldn't bring myself to get out of bed.

One day he came into my room. I turned my face away.

'You will be travelling to Switzerland,' he said. 'For a long visit.'

*

I was sent to a boarding school where nuns watched me like hawks. They were always getting after me with urgent tirades about God's mercy and forcing me to go to confession. Yet I didn't dare to reveal the secret that burdened me so. It was my certainty that my uncle was giving money to the school to buy the nuns' favour.

It was out of the question that I should come home on holidays. My uncle always found some reason to postpone my visit. I was just as relieved each time.

I took my baccalaureate exams the same year as World War Two broke out, in 1939. On that day, proud but weighed down by an uncertain future, I made a decision. Everyone was talking about the war by then, even at the school. I decided to try to forget what had happened in the attic. Because everything was going to change. The world was at war, people were dying, and life would never be the same.

*

The fog lay thick over the sound on the day I came home. The ferry heaved against the swells and I knew we were close, but the island was hidden behind a curtain. As it majestically appeared, the shapes of the firs, the boats, the spires on the roof of the manor house, I imagined that this was the start of a brand-new life.

But the air was vibrating with frustration when I arrived home at Vindsätra. Uncle Markus had a new plan, and it couldn't wait. Almost immediately he called me into his office.

'We must start thinking about finding a suitable husband for you, Sigrid,' he said, eyeing me up and down.

I knew I had changed. There wasn't much to do at boarding school besides study and eat, so I had filled out.

He put a finger under my chin and lifted my head until I had to look him in the eye.

'You're looking pretty. A little less food from now on, perhaps.'

I wondered how he could think about this while a war was raging in the world.

'And you're not a virgin, of course,' he said, raising his eyebrows. 'But a charitable man will look past that.'

I recoiled.

'Sigrid! Why do you take everything so seriously? I have a few prospective suitors. You take care of your appearance, and I'll take care of the rest.'

In that moment, I saw all my dreams for the future go up in smoke. I'd dreamed of getting a job. I wanted to travel and see the world. All of this turned to nothing in an instant.

'That will be all. Now go rest up. You've had a long journey.'

I felt a blush spread from my neck to my face.

'Uncle. I would prefer to find my future husband myself, if it's all the same to you.'

He began to laugh.

'I see, and how will you do that? Sigrid, you have no contacts whatsoever. I'm only going to introduce you to some viable candidates.'

I didn't know how to respond. So I didn't say anything. As usual.

My room had been aired out and smelled of soap. I sat on the bed and looked around, trying to tell if she had been there, but the room seemed empty.

*

I was given a respite from marriage for several years.

Uncle Markus was called to the capital on matters involving the war, affairs that increased our wealth by enormous sums. He stayed for a long time and life began to feel tolerable again.

But then my uncle came home for Christmas one year. It was snowing that day, so heavily that we had to use a horse and carriage to fetch him at the harbour. When he stepped off the ferry, I spotted a man at his side. A long, gangly figure with the collar of his coat turned up around his neck. Orange hair stuck out under his hat and his nose was red from the cold. He aimed a bewildered smile at me and put out a gloved hand. The snowflakes swirled down and stuck in his pale eyelashes.

'This is Gustaf Stjernkvist,' my uncle said. 'He is my accountant and will be staying with us for a while.'

That I would wed Gustaf was carved in stone from the start. He followed me around the manor like a shadow, courting me insistently. There was something feeble and spineless about Gustaf, something I couldn't put my finger on and wouldn't understand until much later. And by then it was too late.

*

At Easter of 1944, my uncle returned to Vindsätra for good. He immediately called me to his office.

'Gustaf has asked for your hand, Sigrid. I intend to announce the engagement as soon as possible.'

'What if I don't want to marry him?'

'Then there are other things we can do. Everything is just

the same up in the attic. You and I had a good time, Sigrid, but now I want you to marry Gustaf.'

My jaw dropped.

'Sigrid, can't you take a joke? There now, go say yes to Gustaf.'

'He didn't even propose to me!'

'He will.'

We married at Whitsuntide in 1945, when the golden rain was blooming. It was two weeks after the end of the war. Everyone was so happy that we were pulled along in their wake.

But our marital problems began almost immediately.

*

While Uncle Markus's sexual urges were excessive and sadistic, Gustaf Stjernkvist's were substandard, to say the least. It was especially embarrassing for us on the wedding night. He just stroked me awkwardly for a while, then turned onto his side and fell asleep.

When this had gone on for a week, I gathered my courage and asked him what was wrong. Gustaf mumbled that there was nothing wrong with me, but that this lack of interest in women's bodies seemed to be something he had been born with.

Dismayed, I asked why he'd married me at all. He responded that it seemed like a practical solution, and that he was fond of me.

We made several attempts to consummate the marriage, but it was clumsy and a failure each time. Hanging over us was the threat that our family line would be erased. We had to have a child.

Uncle Markus soon got wind of what was going on. Gustaf was called to his office and stayed there for a long time. I waited outside the door, anxious. Listening to my uncle's angry voice and Gustaf's gentle one. When Gustaf came out, his face bright red, my uncle asked me to come in.

'Gustaf is going to the mainland to visit a doctor in the city,' he said. 'You already know what it's about.'

I nodded, demoralized.

'Don't look so glum, Sigrid, I'm only trying to help. And for your part, you must find out what your husband wants and give it to him.'

I don't know what got into me just then – something burst. The injustice – that I had to stand before him like a disobedient child and be scolded for something that was out of my hands. I turned on my heel, walked out of the office, and slammed the door.

*

Gustaf travelled to the mainland the next day. My uncle didn't say a word to me all day. The silence stung, and there was a sense that something more, something worse, was coming. After dinner I got word that Gustaf had missed the ferry and would not return until the next morning.

I fell asleep late that night and had nervous dreams. I woke to find myself freezing and thought I must have kicked off my covers. But then I sensed something else in the room and sat up in bed. His hands came from behind, throttling me.

'You have been naughty, and now you must be punished,' he hissed in my ear. He shoved me onto my stomach, tied me to the bed by my wrists, and began to beat me. Not wildly, like when I had run away, but methodically. He beat me black and blue until I passed out from the pain.

By the time I came to, he had left the room.

I dragged myself to the toilet and vomited until my stomach was empty. Then, out of the blue, I felt her cool hand on my forehead. Maybe I imagined it. But I didn't want to know. All that mattered was that she was back.

When Gustaf returned from the doctor the next day, I told him everything Uncle Markus had done to me. From the very first time until what had happened the night before. But Gustaf turned his back on me.

'What's wrong?' I asked in horror. 'Aren't you going to help me?'

'There's nothing I can do,' he said. 'If I cross your uncle I will never again be able to get a job and I will live in poverty for the rest of my life. He would destroy my reputation as an accountant. You'll have to make sure not to upset him again.'

'But Gustaf, surely you can't just let him do this to me?'

'You bear a certain amount of responsibility yourself, Sigrid. You provoke him. Let's focus on having a child. That's what he really wants, after all.'

And yes indeed, Gustaf managed to make it happen once or twice, but when Uncle Markus asked him how many times he'd spilled his seed in me everything went to hell. Suddenly Gustaf had to visit the doctor once a week. And Uncle Markus resumed his visits to our bedroom.

He was too strong. I didn't have the energy to fight back. I didn't have the energy for anything at all. I just lay there like a dead fish and let him have his way.

Forgive me for not standing my ground. Forgive my fear

and weakness. I so fervently hope that I can be forgiven before I die. The consequences of my silence were so disastrous.

Six months later, when it became clear that I was expecting, the terrible secret began to consume me. Because Uncle Markus had long since stopped caring where he spilled his seed.

50

The door flew open and banged against the wall. Sofia was so startled she almost dropped her book. Oswald stood in the doorway with a sheaf of papers in one hand, dressed in gym clothes, sweat dripping from his forehead. He looked unusually smug; his eyes were truly burning.

'The new theses!' he cried in triumph, holding up the papers. There was nothing about him that hinted at what had happened the day before. Here he stood, her rapist, speaking to her as if they were the best of friends. She wondered if he was so insane that she might be able to convince him to let her go.

Then she saw that he was disgustingly big and hard under his running tights and quickly turned away. Did his own religious nonsense turn him on, or was he planning to assault her again?

As he closed and locked the door, she hurried to set the family history on the bedspread.

'Did you read it?' he asked.

'No, I was just about to start,' she lied. She didn't want him to quiz her about its contents. Not until she was done reading.

He placed the stack of papers neatly on the table by the door. Then he came over and sat on the bed.

'I was finishing up my spinning session when it struck me

that you have to read the theses. Then you'll understand how serious your betrayal is.'

'Let me go!' The words just slipped from her mouth. 'You've punished me, so let me go.'

'Oh sweetie, what you call "punishment" was no one-night stand. You mean more to me than that, don't you understand?'

'You are horrid. You cannot keep me here any longer.'

His eyes narrowed. He grabbed her by the hair and pulled her face close. She tried to twist away, but he only pulled harder, until she cried out.

'Acceptance,' he said. 'That's what these new theses are about. The thin line between life and death. Accepting the role life has given you. In your case, it's all about placing your life in my hands. Do you remember Lily?'

'Who?'

'She was my girlfriend here on the island when I was young. We played with ropes and whips and so forth. One night she started to struggle. It didn't end well. For her, that is. Don't make the same mistake as Lily.'

'Jesus Christ, you monster! As if that scares me.'

'But it does, Sofia. If it doesn't now, it will when there's a leather strap around your neck. I can promise you that.'

He pulled her closer, his cold lips brushing her forehead.

'Oh, darling. There's so much life in you. Far too much for your own good.'

He went to the table and picked up the stack of papers. As he sat back down beside her, he set them in front of her.

'These are the notes I made in prison. The new theses. It was while I was working on these that I succeeded in reaching what we might call the core of life. I tried out a few of the exercises on the inmates there at Skogome. You better believe they were psyched up after that. There's an overview – I'd like you to read that first.'

She looked down at the stack, which must have been a decimetre thick, and hoped he wouldn't make her read out loud. On the topmost sheet was a note written in red pen, scribbled down in large, sprawling letters. *Fucking illiterate.* Sofia looked up at him, baffled.

'Oh, don't mind that,' he said. 'My new secretary was supposed to type up my notes, and she's not as efficient as you were. As you can see. In any case, you can read all that later. This is what I wanted to show you.'

He browsed for a moment, then pulled a sheet from the bottom of the pile. He smoothed it out and placed it on her lap. She read it silently to herself.

A fact all the great thinkers have overlooked.
The thin line between life and death.
True strength and power are located on this very line.
Jesus and his sheeple preach love and understanding.
The Buddhists try to obliterate desire.
The existentialists: Death is final; the flame can never be rekindled.
Religious oddballs: Resurrection! Reincarnation!
Life OR death.
Black OR white.
All of humanity is fumbling blindly.
Only I can distinguish that line.
The border between the two sides.
THERE lies all the power you will ever come across.
Between them.

There, and nowhere else.

She looked up at him, fighting the urge to laugh, frantically trying to look serious. He gazed at her expectantly as she desperately fumbled for something good – and above all, deep – to say. Something to buy her more time. Time to find a way to escape. She'd survived any number of his idiotic riddles and little tests in the past. All she had to do was come up with something he hadn't thought of himself. 'The line doesn't exist. You can't see it, only feel it. That's the point,' she forced herself to say.

His gaze became introspective. Then he began to nod slowly, running his hand over his stubble. There was that smile – the one his eyes hinted at although it never quite reached his lips.

'That's right, Sofia. Exactly! You understand. I'll be damned – you get it. Not bad. Maybe now you know why you're here and not out there with all the average meatball-eaters. Well done!'

He rose hastily and patted her on the head.

'Now I have to go shower. Read the family history. We can talk about it when you're done. After that, you can read my notes. I'll leave them here.'

He took the stack of papers and left it on the table by the door. He lingered a moment before leaving the room with both hands making victory signs.

51

She rested her head in her hands and let out a long breath. Suddenly she began to laugh, shrill and hysterical. Her built-up tension began to dissipate: she couldn't stop thinking about his absurd twaddle, and soon enough she was cracking up until she was bent double, tears running down her face. But it wasn't a pleasant, freeing laugh. Just something she had to get out. At last she pulled herself together and began to focus. She picked up the family history and resumed reading.

This was meant to be a history of my family, but it has turned into a confession. What is the use of that? After all, it's too late.

But there were happier times. When Henrik was born, I was filled with the conviction that everything would be okay. He was a wonderful child. Healthy and cheerful, almost four kilos at birth, and he slept through the night so well, crying only when he was hungry or tired.

I felt so fortunate that I almost forgot my suspicions about his paternity. As determined as I was to hold onto this wonderful thing that had happened to me, that I turned a blind eye to other events. New maids were hired. The sounds that came from the attic couldn't be shut out. But I convinced myself that perhaps this was better for them than poverty.

But then something happened that triggered a domino effect of incidents that would end in yet another tragedy at the manor. My uncle had decided that Henrik should learn to play the piano. We had a grand piano, and despite Henrik's tender age, my uncle thought he had a certain talent. So he hired a piano teacher, William Lilja, a stylish man with hair much longer than what was considered appropriate for the day.

From the moment William arrived at Vindsätra, Gustaf was transformed. To think I didn't understand! Those profound gazes between him and William; the way they grazed past each other so cautiously. And Gustaf's sudden enthusiasm about Henrik's playing, although he did no more than plink away.

One evening in January, a snowstorm blew in over the island. William had to spend the night at the manor. I woke to shouting voices and discovered I was alone in the bed. Henrik had been wakened and was whimpering in the nursery. I picked him up and carried him towards the racket; by now I could tell that my uncle was the one shouting. I opened the door to the bedroom. What I saw nearly caused me to drop Henrik.

Gustaf was lying naked on the floor, blood flowing from his nose. My uncle was standing over him, his hands in fists. In the bed lay a terrified William, the covers drawn up to his chin. When my uncle turned around, his eyes were wild with fury.

'This is what your twisted husband is up to!' he roared. 'Take him away, before I kill the pervert.'

I tried to talk to Gustaf back in our bedroom, tried to ask how long this had been going on. But he only turned his back on me and cried himself to sleep.

I thought of William, who was a prisoner of our dark house,

of the storm, until dawn, when he would be sent home with his career as a pianist in shatters.

We were awoken early the next morning by a sharp, impatient rap at the door. In stormed my uncle, in full riding gear.

'Get up and get dressed!' he shouted at Gustaf. 'I'm going to make a man out of you.'

And Gustaf, full of terror but hoping to placate my uncle, went with him on the hunt that day. It had stopped snowing, but the morning was cold and raw.

Only an hour later, I heard my uncle calling from the entrance hall. Henrik and I were upstairs, and we ran down right away. Henrik rushed over to Uncle Markus but was brushed aside.

'Send the boy away, Sigrid. I need to speak with you and Ofelia.' My aunt had dragged herself out of bed and was also there in the entryway.

As I took Henrik to the nursery, my thoughts became chaos. Why had my uncle returned alone? Why was he so shaken?

'There has been an accident,' he said when I was back. 'It's Gustaf.'

I screamed and fell to my knees.

'He was cleaning the barrel, somehow a shot was fired, I don't understand how that idiot…'

Uncle Markus hauled me off the floor and embraced me. Rocked me. Only once did he hold me like that.

'I want to see him,' I said.

'No, that's not possible. Believe me, Sigrid, it would be too much. The shot went through his head. I'll call the police now – you two stay here with Henrik.'

I have always believed that God the Father is the only

supernatural being in this world. But there's something more. The unspoken, the invisible, that which is not concrete but can still be suspended in the air. And in that instant I felt it. It poked at me, nudged at me, until it was clearer than the burbling water of a brook in springtime.

So obvious it was, that lie.

*

Now, in hindsight, I wonder if I should have let it go. After all, I couldn't get Gustaf back. Everyone was in agreement that it had been an accident, including the police and the medical examiner. But I was so sure they were wrong. I knew Gustaf and his cowardice. It was unthinkable that he would have cleaned a rifle without making sure it was unloaded. This heedless behaviour was so contrary to his nature that I couldn't let it go.

The day after the funeral I stood in the doorway of my uncle's office, waiting for him to glance at me.

'Uncle, I don't understand how Gustaf could have died. He was always so careful…'

'What are you suggesting?'

'I only want to inquire about how it happened.'

'We're done talking about this. If you know better than the entire legal system, then you should contact them.'

He had that look on his face. Each time that look appeared, it was very bad news for me. But nothing happened that day.

I woke in the middle of the night to his breath in my ear. To his hand grabbing the back of my neck. He tied my hands to the bedstead with rope. Tore off my nightgown. Began to beat me, so hard I knew he had lost control.

I'm going to die, I thought. *This is the end of my life.*

But I didn't die that night. Beat me black and blue – that he did. I was so sore afterwards that I could hardly move, and I was sick with shame. But I survived. And she came to me that night. To comfort me.

*

Now, I'm sure you are wondering how on earth I could stand all of this, and why I didn't ask anyone for help. Couldn't I have taken Henrik and run away? Surely any life would have been better than this.

That question is not easy to answer. If I ran away, I would be sentencing Henrik to a life of poverty. My uncle had inexhaustible resources with which he could hunt us down. And after all, the last time I'd tried to escape, it hadn't gone so well. I had no other living relatives, no close friends, and no job training. Every part of my life was contained within the manor walls.

I was convinced I was in a trap and would never be able to get out. So I chose the simplest way: I became completely submissive. So compliant and humble that I never provoked Uncle Markus. As long as I remained quiet, took care of Henrik, and cast my eyes downward, he left me alone. And this was a miracle in my miserable life.

I'm doing this for Henrik, I thought. *So he can grow up and take over the manor one day, and spread light and warmth here. This is my lot in life, and I have to make the best of it.*

Perhaps another woman will someday read this. Perhaps she will be in a similar situation. So I want to say it's important to be shrewd. I could have gone out on the property to pick some poisonous plant and then mixed it in his liqueur. Perhaps I could have tucked a burr under his horse's saddle. And now I'm sure you're saying 'Oh no, that would be dreadful!' But life isn't always pleasant. And when you don't speak up, there are consequences.

Now I'm thinking about Henrik. Wondering how he turned out the way he did. Whether it was his upbringing, or if it was already there inside him. Or if it was a fatal combination of the two – like pouring magnesium into water.

*

Henrik was six years old when I realized something was wrong.

It started with the anthill. A piercing, naked scream came from the forest near the annexes. I rushed over and found him brandishing a shovel. He was standing in the middle of the anthill, stabbing the shovel into it as he bellowed. I ran over and lifted him away, trying to calm him. His whole body was covered in angry ants, which I brushed off. When he was quiet, I tried to talk to him.

'Ants aren't dangerous if you leave them alone.'

'I'm not afraid of them, I just want to kill them.'

Two days later, he poured petrol over the anthill and set it aflame.

The strange behaviour continued. First with insects – he would pull off their legs and wings or burn them to death by focusing sunbeams through a magnifying glass. Then he turned to torturing small animals on the farm. At last I got my uncle's permission to take Henrik to a child psychologist. The doctor first spoke with Henrik, who appeared to give sensible answers to his questions. Thereafter the doctor listened to me as I told him about everything Henrik had done.

'What could it be? Is he sick?'

'He's so young,' the doctor said, looking at Henrik, who was pressing his nose to the aquarium in the waiting room and making terrible faces at the fish. 'It might go away on its own.'

'But what is this – what is wrong with him?'

'If he were an adult I would say mild psychopathic narcissism, but it may be a phase of development that he'll grow out of.'

'Can something like this be hereditary?' I asked, full of dread.

'Perhaps, but it's often a combination of heredity and environment. We'll let it rest there for a while. Come back if he doesn't improve.'

And it did go away. As quickly as these ideas had begun, they vanished.

I felt great relief.

Thank God, he won't turn out like them.

★

Henrik often brought playmates to the manor. This made me happy, because children spread warmth and cheer to the otherwise empty, gloomy house. My uncle had no objections. Anything to keep Henrik happy, and – above all – normal.

The first incident occurred when Henrik was ten years old. A boy and a girl had come for a visit. When they'd had enough of running around the great rooms, they retreated to Henrik's room.

It was the silence that bothered me first. My uncle was on

the mainland for the day, and my aunt was resting as usual. It was so quiet in the manor that the rhythmic ticking of the Mora clock echoed off the walls. At first I supposed the children were immersed in some quiet game. But then I grew anxious, padded up the stairs, and put an ear to the door of the nursery.

I could only hear a faint murmur inside. I cracked the door and peered in, but all I could see was a pair of feet so I threw the door wide open.

The girl was naked on the floor. Both arms were extended above her head and her hands were tied to a bureau. The boy was holding her feet; her legs were spread, and there between them sat Henrik with a long, blunt object in his hand.

I kept calm to avoid scaring the girl.

I made Henrik untie the rope and helped the girl back on with her clothes. I took the object, which I could now see was a screwdriver, from Henrik's hand. None of the children said anything. At last I asked the girl why she had let the boys do this to her, and she responded that Henrik had promised her money. And he had plenty of it, because my uncle passed him bills regularly.

I thought of the girl's parents, about whether I should talk to them, but she seemed relatively unaffected and I decided nothing serious had really happened.

When the children left, I tried to speak to Henrik but he only stared at me.

That night, as I was going to bed, I immediately felt that someone had been in the room. There was a vague sense of danger about. At first everything looked perfectly normal, spic and span thanks to the servants. But then I saw the object on the bed, neatly placed on the pillow. A noose made of thick rope, neatly displayed on the pillow. I screamed and everyone came running – Henrik, my uncle, a few maids. I went to Henrik and shook him, because it had to be the same rope he'd used to tie up the poor little girl. But Henrik pulled away from my grip and flatly denied it. And, as usual, my uncle took his side.

'You've always been a bit forgetful, Sigrid.'

It wasn't until I was lying in bed that it occurred to me she might have been there. Everything was so unnaturally still in my room. The window was open. The sea whispered quietly as it was stroked by the wind. And I could have sworn I heard her whisper from far off in the sound.

★

For the next few years, Henrik acted perfectly normal. This seemed to be his pattern – he would make trouble, and then nothing would happen for some time.

It was during this period that Aunt Ofelia suddenly died of a heart attack at the age of fifty-two. Uncle Markus was fifty-five then, virile and in good health, a man in the prime of life. Now we three were the only ones at the manor. And the servants of course – we had plenty of them.

I grew more and more restless. But then, in one of Uncle Markus's better moments, he suggested I should get involved with charity work in the village. This brought back some of my spark and I created the Sigrid von Bärensten Fund, which still grants stipends to help girls of little means with their schooling.

But back to Henrik. It was his fifteenth birthday. He wanted to have a party at the manor, with his friends, and Uncle Markus really went all out. I had seldom seen such pomp and circumstance on the property.

The girl was perhaps fourteen or fifteen. She was impossible not to notice. She wore knee-length white boots and a clingy patterned dress – even though low necklines were out of fashion in the sixties, her dress did show off a bit of her chest.

And she was dazzlingly beautiful besides.

Henrik's eyes were on her like glue, and my uncle noticed. I heard them whispering as I walked by.

'Do you want her?' Uncle Markus asked Henrik. 'You can have whatever you like – it's your birthday. Ask her to sleep over.'

And somehow, remarkably, they convinced her to stay.

Uncle Markus had long since stopped caring what anyone heard from the attic. He often left the door open when he had the maids up there at night. So I didn't suspect anything when I heard a scream after the party had ended. But then there was another scream, louder this time – as if from someone in distress.

I hurried up the stairs to the attic. The girl was half-lying on an easy chair. My uncle held her down as Henrik stood between her legs. They had torn off her clothes, which were scattered across the floor.

I didn't want to see any more. I didn't go in. Dear God, forgive me, but what could I have done?

I waited until the howling stopped and I heard steps on the staircase.

I waited outside the door to my uncle's office.

'Uncle, what have you done to that poor girl?'

'Nothing she didn't want to have done. She'll be back. Her family is poor. We have much to offer her.'

'Henrik must absolutely not… Lord Jesus, she's underage.'

The blow came so suddenly that I lost my footing and had to grab at the wall.

'Go ask her! Go! She's sleeping in one of the guest rooms. Go, I said!'

I didn't go to see her. I already knew what she would say. I didn't want to know how they'd bribed her. So I kept my mouth shut. Again. I went up to my room, unsure how much longer I could live with myself. I felt so miserable and alone that I wanted to die.

But by the next time it happened, I had gathered my courage. My conscience was nudging me. The feelings of guilt were growing. The girls were so young.

They had left the door to the attic open that night. I was down in the sunroom working on my embroidery. That damn embroidery I didn't even care about. But it kept my hands busy and calmed my nerves.

I had seen the girl sweep through the great rooms on her way up to the attic. High-heeled boots. A clingy knit dress. Black eyeliner and red lips that hid her tender age.

The screams began half an hour later.

'I don't want to!' she cried.

I put down my embroidery and went upstairs to the attic. Her screams had died down into a despairing whimper. She stood with her head against the wall, naked. Her hands were bound high above her head with rope. Henrik had a whip in his hand and Uncle Markus was in the corner.

I was filled with thick, oozing shame.

I padded downstairs to my room and took out my camera, which, ironically enough, had been a Christmas present from Uncle Markus. Then I sneaked back upstairs and stopped outside the door.

They didn't notice me. Henrik was pressing up against the

girl's back; he had entered her from behind. She was silent now, letting him do what he wanted. My son turned around and looked at Uncle Markus with a triumph in his eyes.

I took a picture.

They didn't notice I was there. I took another.

*

Right away, I could see in the police officer's eyes that something wasn't right. He looked nervous and apologetic.

'Well, Mrs von Bärensten, we have developed the film you brought in, but there are certain issues.'

I listened, my heart sinking.

'Your uncle isn't visible in the image, only a shadow that could be anyone. Your son and the girl are there, but I've made some inquiries and the girl says everything was consensual. That she and Henrik were playing in the attic and your uncle wasn't there at all. I'm sorry, but I can't do much with this. Surely you don't want me to apprehend your son – he's only fifteen. Perhaps you must simply keep a tighter rein on him.'

He handed me the pictures I had taken. You couldn't see Uncle Markus, only Henrik and the girl in the shameful pose I had captured so well.

'But what goes on up there – it cannot continue,' I tried. 'You have to take me seriously.'

The officer placed his hand over mine.

'There, there, Mrs Bärensten. Boys are curious creatures. I'm sure he'll grow out of this behaviour soon. But by all means, if you would like to file a report...'

'What would you do with it if I did?'

'I suppose we would have to talk to your uncle. See what he has to say.' The officer stood up hastily. 'If you want my opinion, I think you should stop playing detective and set the boy straight instead.'

In that instant, a cold hand squeezed my heart. I was totally alone.

But then, once again, everything seemed to get better. Henrik was sent to boarding school in France. Uncle Markus had business in the capital city and only came home on weekends. For several years, the manor was quiet and peaceful. I volunteered and worked on my trust. I thought the worst was over. Mother had vanished and I hoped she had finally found peace.

Then Emelie and Karin came to the manor, and everything changed. They couldn't have been more dissimilar.

Karin blew into our lives like a breath of fresh air. She filled every room with her energy, bringing new life into everything that had been dead. Emelie was more like an object, a pattern on wallpaper. She came from a rich family and had been selected by Uncle Markus to marry Henrik; she was quiet and withdrawn.

Karin was our housemaid. Her thick, dark hair fell to her waist. She was round with lovely eyes and a carefree laugh that seemed out of place in the dark rooms.

Uncle Markus was over seventy by now, but the glances he cast after Karin proved that he was in no way limited by his age. But Henrik was the one who fell head over heels. His eyes devoured her; he followed her everywhere. Karin rejected his advances, polite but firm. And there I was again, an onlooker, watching this game of cat-and-mouse which I just knew would end in disaster.

It took several years to happen.

Henrik prowled around Karin like she was a cat in heat.

But somehow, remarkably, she managed to keep him in check. Until one ill-fated day.

I had been on the mainland and returned home late that afternoon. It was winter and darkness had already fallen. The door to Uncle Markus's bedroom was closed and I knew he was having a rest. His age had finally caught up with him and he looked tired sometimes, much to my unspoken joy.

The silence that met me when I walked into the house was broken almost immediately by a piercing shriek from the kitchen. And another. Even louder. By the time I got there, it was too late. Henrik had Karin on the floor, in a chokehold, going at her like a steamroller. As I came through the door, he let out a muffled groan and rolled off her.

I was ten or fifteen minutes too late. If only I had increased my pace a little, jogged back from the ferry! Henrik turned around and spotted me. He sat up. Karin was screaming in frustration. I just stood there as if I had dropped from the sky. I had the urge to gather Karin into my arms, but she got up and glared at me furiously. She reached for a cast iron frying pan and threw it; it barely missed Henrik's head as he ducked. She ran out of the kitchen as Henrik remained on the floor. He looked at me with a sheepish grin.

'Shit, Ma, we were just having some fun.'

At that moment it was as if Uncle Markus were sitting there staring at me. The trajectory of life was an infinity symbol and we had returned to the point where all the evil began.

★

It was six months before we saw Karin again. Uncle Markus was the one who first got wind of what had happened. Karin was pregnant and the child was Henrik's.

Despite months of diligent begging and fawning, Karin stubbornly refused to have anything to do with us. But Uncle Markus was like a bulldog. The child *would* grow up at the manor. I have no idea what finally convinced her to change her tune.

One night she was just there, big as a house, with a suitcase in either hand. Her anger was a thundercloud around her.

It was out of the question for Henrik to marry Karin. She came from a poor family. But Uncle Markus would have that child, the greedy old pig. So Henrik married Emelie. She was, and remained, a shadow in our lives.

On the night Fredrik was born, a snowstorm ravaged the island. It was absolutely impossible for the ferry to cross the sound, so the village doctor came to us to deliver the baby.

I held Fredrik in my arms that night. He was wrapped in a blanket. Huge dark eyes gazed at me without fear, wise but unfathomable. I wondered who he was, and whether one day he might flat-out change the world.

The next morning, Uncle Markus didn't come to breakfast. This was unthinkable, so I went straight to his room. I found him dead as a doornail in his bed, his eyes staring at the ceiling. A heart attack, the doctor said, but whatever it was it hadn't come a day too soon.

Karin lived in the annexes with her son, but she refused to work for us – she took a job in the village café. I took care of Fredrik each morning. Henrik watched him in the afternoons. They clashed from the start. Fredrik was by turns angry, insolent, and rambunctious. No one but Karin could handle him. Emelie had begun to study on the mainland and wanted nothing to do with Fredrik. So it came to be that Henrik was often alone with the boy.

It happened when Fredrik was three. Karin was at work and I was in the village. A storm was heading for the island, so we both returned home early that day. The house was empty; it felt eerily deserted when we came in. Karin called out for Fredrik, but there was no response.

'They must be out on the grounds somewhere,' I said. But Karin was anxious. 'It's almost dark. What would they be doing out there?'

'Maybe checking on the animals? Let's wait a bit.'

There was a thud and Henrik appeared on the stairs that led down to the cellar. When he spotted us all the colour drained from his face, but he didn't have time to say anything – Karin shoved him aside and hurtled down the stairs. I followed her.

The first thing I saw when Karin opened the door was Fredrik's eyes, blinking like an owl's in the light that streamed in. He was tied to a chair in the middle of the room. Naked. His arms bound behind him, his legs tied to those of the chair. A clothespin was clamped on his little penis.

'The boy has to learn discipline, dammit,' came Henrik's voice from behind us.

It took no more than thirty seconds. Karin loosened the ropes and swept Fredrik into her arms. She shoved past us, up the stairs, and dashed out with Fredrik held close. I could see a bruise on his back. I had the curious thought that it was odd we had never noticed anything.

This was the last time Karin set foot in the manor.

*

Now I suppose I will have to write about the fire. Everyone got it all wrong. They thought my mother took her own life, crushed by the captain's death when his ship went down. They thought my father committed suicide when he realized Mother was dead. None of this is true.

I know because I was there. I was only a small child, but my memory of that night is the clearest of all the memories in my senile brain.

My brother Oskar woke me up. He shook my arm so hard I sat up in bed with a start. Someone was shouting downstairs – it was Mother, calling for help. The shot came as we were going down the stairs, and it was so loud we froze. Mother cried out again, screaming our names.

Father was on the dining room floor with a hole in his forehead. His empty eyes stared at the ceiling. A dark stain was beneath his head, spreading across the expensive, speckled rug. A figure was standing behind him. At first I didn't know who it was. Her face was so badly beaten it looked like an open wound. Her clothes were torn and blood ran down her bare chest. She was holding a large can. She caught sight of us.

'Run to the annexes! Go!' she cried.

We took off. Out the door and across the courtyard.

It all happened at once. The flames flickered in the house and Mother's figure dashed across the yard. She stopped and called out to us.

'I'll come back to you.'

Someone saw her on Devil's Rock before she jumped. At least, that's what they said.

All that was left of Father once the servants had put out the fire was charred remains. The police labelled it a suicide. After all, the pistol was right there beside him and the room stank of paraffin.

Only Oskar and I saw Mother that night. We were the only ones who heard what she said. We made a secret pact, as only children can do. We had seen and heard nothing. And we were determined to take our secret to the grave.

Now I wonder what would have happened if I had done to Uncle Markus what Mother did to Father, just shot the bastard and burned the place down. Whether my life would have turned out a different way.

*

She came back to me here at the nursing home. It was almost too good to be true. I was sitting and gazing out of the window, as usual. The delightful scents of summer were blowing in on the breeze. The grove of birches was green. It was around Midsummer when she came. The sound of her rustling skirts behind me. Her breath in my ear. Her hands stroking my old, brittle hair. I thought it was strange that she seemed so young. Here I had been so determined to drive out old ghosts, but there she was beside me again.

The spell was broken when the door opened and an aide came in.

'Sigrid,' she said. 'Listen to this. People have seen the ghost of the countess out at Devil's Rock. Wearing a cape and everything. Where do folks get such outlandish ideas? Wasn't she your mother?'

I attempted a smile, but my blood had frozen to ice.

*

Just a few days after the tragic incident in the cellar, a police officer was stamping his feet on our doorstep. I had already shouted at Henrik until I was hoarse. For the first time ever, I had shouted at him. But what good would it do?

The police investigation went nowhere and Henrik and Emilie soon moved to France. I moved into an apartment in the village.

I haven't spoken to Karin since that day. We have run into each other in the village a few times, but she only gives me a chilly nod. She moved away from the island and didn't return until Henrik was gone for good. But now she lives here again, with Fredrik, in their little cottage in the woods. She holds her head high, that Karin, despite everything that has happened.

For many years, neither Henrik nor I could stand the thought of selling Vindsätra. Anyway, we had more money than we needed. But then, a few years ago, a doctor came by and put down an offer. Wanted to turn the place into a convalescent home. It felt like liberation when I handed over the key.

Now we're rid of this misery, I thought. I expected it would help me forget.

But it didn't. Because now here I sit at this godforsaken, dreary nursing home, writing as death breathes down the back of my neck, and I still can't forgive myself for everything that happened.

I cannot find any meaning in the sad little life I have lived.

I can feel her presence now; I can see her sitting in the chair across from me. I want to ask her about the meaning of life, but then I realize that she, too, has grown old, because she has no teeth; her face is wrinkled and her eyes are so sunken in their sockets. And when I reach out my hand to touch her, she fades away. Her mouth and eyes become black holes and her body dissolves into a fine dust that falls over me and this book.

And here I sit, all alone in the world.

They say life is short, but that's not true. Life is neither long nor short. It is nothing but a bloody game of Russian Roulette – you can only wait and see. Sometimes what happened to me just happens.

But then I look out of the window and see Fredrik.

He can't see me from where he's standing in the path. He's talking to a girl who looks like a fairy. The doctor's daughter, I think. Maybe they're on their way to the beach, because he's wearing shorts and she's in a sundress. He's so pretty, Fredrik is. That dark hair gleams like copper in the sunshine. That sinewy, tanned body. He's so sure of himself; you can tell. He takes after Karin, thank God.

So now I pin all my hopes on Fredrik. I'll send this book to Karin and ask that one day, when he's grown, she give it to him. Perhaps he can take over the fading torch that was once our family, and make it burn strong again.

And then my life will not have been in vain.

Recorded and signed on this day by
Sigrid Kristina Augusta von Bärensten

52

Simon was on his way to ViaTerra to meet Jacob. The brisk evening chill worked its way under his clothing. A thin mist, typical of Fog Island, blanketed the landscape.

Another email had arrived from Sofia's account. A picture of Paris, with a cathedral in the background. After some googling, he had understood that it was the Sacré-Cœur. *View from our hotel* was all it said. He wondered how many hotels had a view of this particular landmark. Whether they could be traced somehow. But it seemed ridiculous, because after all he knew she wasn't really there. And now Simon wondered where this would all lead. Whether it would end with an email that reported Sofia had vanished. Or, even worse, that there had been an accident. That she had thrown herself into the Seine and couldn't be rescued. His thoughts were running away with him – he couldn't stop them.

He hoped it would be dark before he got to the manor. It was easier to sneak in undetected that way.

★

The last rays of the sun were lighting up the sentry box when he arrived, making it glow in the twilight. Two guards were inside; he could see their shadows. The sound of a motorcycle came from within the walls. Extra surveillance. So something was up. Now he assumed that Jacob wouldn't show, but still he snuck around to the back of the property, opened the gate, and slipped in.

He could no longer hear the motorcycle. No Jacob. He waited for a while and was just about to leave when there was a rustling sound behind him, and there stood Jacob.

'I've made up my mind,' he said straightaway. 'In a week, I'm going to escape. There are some things I need to take care of before then, but I'm not going to chicken out this time.'

Simon's heart gave a leap.

'Awesome! You won't regret it. Why are there so many guards around today?'

Jacob glanced anxiously towards the courtyard.

'I don't actually know.'

'I've got the feeling Oswald is up to something fishy,' Simon continued.

Jacob, who was otherwise a good and attentive listener, sometimes zoned out and stared off at nothing – and he was doing so now.

'Did you hear me?'

'Sure, I was just so surprised, because I have the very same feeling. That something's up.'

'Well, have you noticed anything?'

'Yes – I mean, it's something about mould.'

'What?'

'In the cellar. No one is allowed down there anymore. Or even in the vicinity.'

At that moment they heard the motorcycle again, and it

seemed to be heading in their direction. There was no time for Simon to interrogate Jacob. He had the eerie feeling that they were about to be discovered, that they would be like deer in the headlights.

'Find out what's in the cellar,' he whispered. 'See you tomorrow morning at six.'

He hurried through the gate. The motorcycle was practically on top of them. He heard Jacob lie down on the ground, the rustle of last year's leaves crunching beneath him, and he hoped they wouldn't find him. He dashed through the woods for a while before daring to return to the road. He felt shaken. It couldn't be a coincidence, what Jacob had told him, and he shuddered to think what it might mean.

*

Jacob heard the motorcycle getting closer and pressed himself to the ground. He tried to think of a plausible explanation for being there. He could say he was looking for a sheep that had run off. But why would anyone lie on the ground to do that?

The motorcycle stopped. Then came the sound of the kickstand flipping down and the static hiss of the walkie-talkie – like cackling geese.

'What's going on over there?'

'There's no one here. You must have been seeing things.'

'Then forget it. We've been called to a meeting.'

'Oh, shit. I'll be right there.'

Jacob took a roundabout path back to the barn. At the door he ran into an angry Corinne.

'Where have you been? I've been looking everywhere for you.'

'I was out checking on the pastures to see if we can let the animals out.'

'How the hell can you tell in the dark?'

'It took a little longer than I expected. What do you want?'

'Assembly after dinner in the dining hall. Franz wants to talk to the whole staff,' she said, marching away, still angry. Jacob would have liked to sneak over to the cellar window, but assembly meant that the courtyard would soon be full of staff members. He would have to postpone his spying. He hoped this wouldn't turn into one of those times they all had to work through the night.

A bunch of staff came out of the annexes, heading for the dining hall. Jacob joined them. Lina from the kitchen spotted him and gave him a friendly smile.

'Hi, Jacob, do you know what this is all about?'

'No, but I'm sure it's a sequel to the mould story.'

Lina didn't respond, just rolled her eyes. Jacob had always thought she was cute. He wondered if she, too, had had enough. If perhaps she was ready to get out.

As they passed the cellar window, Jacob noticed a light on down there.

*

Oswald was already stationed in the dining hall. They quickly sat down in the back row. Oswald looked annoyed, but not insanely angry as he sometimes did.

'We're going to deal with the mould day after tomorrow,'

he said. 'A company will be coming to fix it, and I want you all out of the way. You will finish the work around the pond that you never completed. At eight you will gather here and march out to the woods. And none of you is to go anywhere near the cellar until then. It's bad enough I've had to be down there, inhaling that crap. If I have to remind you about what needs doing, it's getting everything ready for guests. Everything still looks like shit.'

Corinne stood beside him, nodding after each sentence. She was already looking wan and tired.

Erik raised his hand. *How does he have the guts?* Jacob wondered. Erik was still in disgrace, still digging his ditch, which was starting to resemble a moat.

'Sir, I'm sorry for bringing this up, but I thought I heard sounds from the cellar. Some sort of howling, like an animal.'

Oswald's dark eyes looked down at Erik, full of an indifference that verged on disdain. But then something unexpected happened. Oswald began to laugh. It started as a soft chuckle, but it grew into a shrill guffaw that prompted the entire staff to join in. Jacob's arms broke out in gooseflesh.

'It's probably that evil old countess haunting the place,' Oswald said at last, which unleashed another round of laughter among the staff.

Oswald silenced them with a raised hand.

'Seriously, though, Erik, it's not out of the question that some animal got caught down there, the way you've all been neglecting this place. The entire cellar will be inspected the day after tomorrow, and then we'll find out what kind of crap is down there. Or maybe you heard the babies, over at Elvira's. Who knows. Any more questions?'

It was dead silent.

'Okay then, you know what to do.'

*

Jacob was on tenterhooks all night. The minutes crawled by, and he kept gazing towards the manor to see if it was the right time to sneak over to the cellar window. But there always seemed to be someone around, so he decided to wait until everyone had gone to bed. At last he heard the muffled voices of the staff as they walked across the grounds to the dorms. Soon – once the windows of the manor went dark – he would gather his courage.

The lights were still on at Elvira's when he set off, but the rest of the manor was dark and still. Jacob wondered if Oswald was with Elvira. What would he say if Oswald caught him sneaking around at night? There would be no believable lie. It simply could not happen. The sentry box was illuminated, and he saw two guards there. One was leaning back in his chair – asleep, probably – while the other was on the phone. Everything seemed quiet and calm. A sense of desertedness, emptiness, seemed to emanate from the courtyard, so he set off for the house. Just as he passed Elvira's place, a dark shape appeared before him. His heart leapt into his throat and he stopped short. But then the moon peered out from behind a cloud, shedding a faint light on the yard, and he saw it was Elvira.

'Jesus Christ, you scared me almost to death,' he whispered.

Elvira was standing right in front of him. Her skin was ghostly pale in the moonlight, and her eyes were wide open. At first he thought she was frightened too, but then he realized her cheeks were stained with tears.

'What's wrong?' he asked.

'Nothing. I saw you coming. I just wanted… Fuck, it's so lonely in my cottage. I have no one to talk to but Franz.' Her tears were flowing now. There was no sound, no sobbing or sniffling, only a river of tears. 'I feel so abandoned, Jacob. I don't know if I can stand it much longer.'

He placed a hand on her arm, felt the thin fabric, and realized she was standing there in nothing but her nightgown.

'I'd be happy to come in and chat for a while sometime, if you want me to.'

'Franz would never allow it. But can't you tell me what's going on at ViaTerra? Quick, before the guards see us? I have no idea what you're all up to.'

'Oh, pretty much the same old stuff. Right now it's all about the mould smell in the cellar. Franz is furious, as you may have noticed.'

Elvira's face took on an expression of mild surprise.

'Weird. I was in the cellar a few weeks ago. Franz asked me to clean it. It was a real pigsty down there. But I didn't notice any mould.'

Jacob's heart beat faster.

Elvira shook her head. 'Nope, I don't think the cellar's ever been in better shape. It's so claustrophobic in the cottage, so it was nice to have something to do. I scrubbed the bathroom like crazy, but when I was about to start on the walls Franz told me to stop and go back to the babies.' She grabbed Jacob's hand. 'I have to go, so no one sees us. Maybe you can drop by sometime when Franz is gone. Like, sneak in. And look, you're not going to mention that I was outside, are you?'

'Of course not. Take care of yourself, now.'

She vanished as quickly as she'd appeared. Jacob hurried to the manor house, walking along the walls until his foot struck the cellar window. There was a bang and at first he was afraid he'd broken the pane, but when he bent down he saw it was undamaged. There was a padlock on the window.

He crouched down and shaded his eyes so he could see in.

Someone was lying on a bed down there, their face turned away. The thin body seemed familiar somehow, but it was the hair that Jacob recognized. It was spread around her face like a dark sea, full of rippling waves.

Jacob only knew one person with hair like that.

53

As she finished reading, the room vanished around her. She lost herself in the text and didn't notice that darkness was falling until she had to strain her eyes to make out the elaborate cursive. She underwent a metamorphosis and became Sigrid von Bärensten. Suffering alongside her. Becoming furious with her at times. She so fervently wanted everything to turn out okay. She reached the last chapter, when Sigrid gazed out the window to see Fredrik, Franz, or whoever the fuck he was.

All at once she knew why Oswald had given her the book. And there was something more. The final page was dotted with what looked like grey soot. She wondered if the old lady had been so muddled that she had dirtied the book herself, or whether it was in fact the final trace of Amelia von Bärensten on that page. The woman they said haunted the island.

She sat motionless for several minutes, staring straight ahead, returning to herself and her breath and the situation she was in, in an entirely new way. Like a small section of a long string of miserable events that could only end in tragedy. She thought of the little boy with a clothespin on his penis and felt a pang of empathy, but quickly returned to her conviction that Oswald had always been evil, that his soul was an inky black lump through and through. He probably thought the family history would plunge her into a state of permanent hopelessness.

Something Sigrid had written had etched itself into Sofia's memory. She flicked back through and found the text.

Perhaps another woman will someday read this. Perhaps she will be in a similar situation. So I want to say it's important to be shrewd. I could have gone out on the property to pick some poisonous plant and then mixed it in his liqueur. Perhaps I could have tucked a burr under his horse's saddle. And now I'm sure you're saying 'Oh no, that would be dreadful!' But life isn't always pleasant. And when you don't speak up, there are consequences.

She ran her finger across the words. She wished she could underline them, but she didn't have a pen. Instead she dog-eared the page. The idea that shrewdness was vital – and here she had been anything but shrewd. For the first time since she'd been brought back to ViaTerra, she felt herself smile. She knew what Oswald got off on: her sassy attitude. In the office, all it had taken was for her to get really upset and he had pressed himself against her back, his erection the size of a baseball bat. Yet she kept battling him. And that was not being shrewd. Not at all.

Suddenly she became aware that he was standing in the doorway and watching her.

'She was my grandmother,' he said. 'A real ninny. And I suppose now you're thinking I spend all my time wringing my hands about what my pathetic dad did to me. But I don't. He got what he deserved. That goddamn idiot crawled over to the window when I burned down the house. Then he transformed into a charred corpse before my very eyes. The only thing I regret is not chopping his dick off with a bolt cutter.'

He approached the bed. She tried to suppress a stream of

unpleasant images, to look unmoved although what she wanted most of all was to put the book aside and throw up.

'Do you understand what this book is proof of?' he asked.

'How much you and your forefathers hate women?'

'Don't take everything so personally. I don't *only* hate women. All of humanity is full of brainless morons. Don't you understand why I gave you the book?'

'No, not really.'

'Then you're dumber than I thought. You can't comfort people and save the world from destruction at the same time. Most people are so stupid and pathetic that they deserve to drown in their own blood. Lucky they have me as a lifeline. That's what I've come to talk to you about.'

'I see. Well, that sounds interesting.' She bit her tongue at the cynical undertone.

'It's not interesting at all. It's simply what's necessary for you to understand what I'm thinking. What I really want is for you to decide what role you're going to play in this story. Because I'm going to pick it up where that old bitch left off. It's going to be a masterpiece of strength, power, and rehabilitation. And now you get to decide your own fate. Within reason. Won't that be fun?'

'I doubt it.'

'Chill out, Sofia. People like you have to make everything so damn complicated. Do you know what ViaTerra stands for?'

'Yes, it's Latin, it means "the way of the earth".'

'True, but really it's just a cheap Spanish wine. It sounds good, though, doesn't it? You have to give people what they want. That makes them more receptive to what's important. The rest is all just trivia.'

'So you saw a bottle of wine and thought, *that sounds like a good name for a cult!* Seriously?'

'Something along those lines. Seems there's no limit to your sarcasm today. Did the old bitch's sob story put you in a bad mood? ViaTerra is not a cult. What do I have to say to get that through to that bird-brain of yours?'

There was that deep, quiet, hoarse voice. The one that warned of an outburst hovering just below the surface. She knew the tone all too well; she felt a passing flutter in her stomach. If she pressed the wrong button, he would explode.

He was all geared up for this confrontation. But now she had to stop sassing back. Because today she was going to be shrewd.

Oswald sat down on the edge of the bed. He was wearing jeans and a white shirt, and he smelled like he had just showered. His hair was still damp. He took her hand and stroked the back of it with his thumb. She buried the urge to pull away and stared down at the knobbly blanket.

'I'm about to tell you why you got what you deserved yesterday. Listen carefully.'

He leaned over her, gripping both of her wrists and holding them down on the bed.

I could kick him in the nuts right now, she thought. *Just pull my leg back really fast and give him a hell of a kick.* But she knew that was a stupid idea; it would only lead to her being raped again.

'Haven't you figured out what ViaTerra is all about? The theses and all.'

'Yes, I have.'

'Okay, but I'm going to tell you anyway. I am the founder of ViaTerra. ViaTerra is the only hope for humanity. I sat behind lock and key for a year and a half. For no reason whatsoever.

Because of your big mouth. Did you really think you would get away with it? Don't you understand why you have to be punished?'

He pulled her arms over her head until she was all stretched out on the bed before him.

'Answer me!'

'Sure, I get it. The theses are important. For humanity.'

'I don't know what's worse, your backtalk or your stupidity. They're not *important* – they are life itself.'

'I understand.'

She forced herself to relax and lie motionless beneath him.

'You will answer properly when I speak to you. You can go back to your boring, pointless, average-Swede life, but it won't change a damn thing. Because you think of me constantly, don't you?'

'Maybe.'

'What the hell kind of answer is that?'

He shook her until the base of the bed creaked. His eyes were wild. She had to do something, say something, because he was at the breaking point. But if she tried to come up with something quickly it would be all wrong, and how could any words check the crazy look in his eyes? All at once, she knew what she had to do.

'I can tell you.'

His eyes lit up with a spark of interest, but there was something awfully creepy about his crooked smile.

'Tell me what?'

He was distracted enough to loosen his grip on her arms slightly.

'About when we first met. You wanted to know, right?'

'You think about it all the time, huh? Fuck, you get wet when you think about it, don't you?'

He let go of her arms and sat up in bed. All ears now.

'You can start with the first time. At the lecture,' he said.

So he did remember.

'You popped up behind me. Really close. You gave me that card with your number, but at first you wouldn't let go when I tried to take it from you.'

'How did you feel?'

'I guess you turned me on.'

'Describe how you felt.'

So she told him, selecting various memories at random. Filling in extra details here and there. It was easier than she'd expected. She had to use events that had really happened because his memory was so sharp, but she could certainly exaggerate her feelings. And as she spoke, she saw the rage in his eyes ebb away. She emptied her last reserves of false prudishness.

'It really wasn't okay for me to feel like that,' she managed to say.

'You can say that again. When all is said and done, you're nothing but a little slut. Now we both know why you flipped out and escaped. Well done, Sofia. A step forward today.'

He patted her knee and yawned loudly. Already bored with her docility.

I'll be goddamned, she thought. *A tiny dose of flattery and he's already satisfied.*

'Tomorrow you and I will have the whole place to ourselves,' he said as he stood up. 'The zombie club is going on a hike, well out of earshot. Because this time I want to hear you scream. Really loudly.'

She mumbled something inaudible, but deep inside her something whispered: *He's going to kill me next time.*

'And afterwards we can sit here in your cosy little corner and have a nice glass of wine, romantic as hell,' he said, heading for the door.

As soon as he locked it behind him, she took out the family history and read it again from cover to cover. She thought of Sigrid von Bärensten's last words and how everything had gone so wrong. Would it be possible to set it right again? Amelia, the countess, had tried. But wasn't it always the case that as soon as you got rid of one devil, a worse one took his place?

A fresh kind of fear enveloped her: what if he strangled her with a leather belt? She could already feel the air rushing out of her lungs, the start of a panic. But the worst part was thinking of his face above her own as he choked her, the power he would have over her then. The thought was so painful that she couldn't stand it. She tossed and turned in the bed, biting her lip until she tasted blood, screaming and beating her fists against the dull surface of the mattress. Then she made up her mind to fight back, to resist with all her strength. What was left of it. She had to find some weapon she could use to defend herself. Why hadn't she thought of that?

She got out of bed, turned on the light, and went to the little closet. Although she searched high and low, the closest she thing she could find to a weapon was a screwdriver from the half-empty toolbox. So complacent of him to leave the closet open. It was like it hadn't even occurred to him that she would try to attack him. Sofia went back to the bed and put the screwdriver under the pillow. Again and again she pictured herself thrusting it into his eye, and each time she shuddered.

But at last she managed to fall asleep, drifting into a dense, ravenous darkness.

★

She woke with a start to find his hands on her body. Disoriented and still half asleep, she tried to turn her back on him, but his hand encircled her throat. Roughly holding her in place. She bent her head back and felt the shaft of the screwdriver through the pillow. She tried to free an arm, but he was sitting on one and the other was caught under the blanket. She had no strength. The air was draining from her lungs. His other hand slipped between her legs. One finger pressed inside. She was still so sore that she screamed, but his grip on her throat tightened.

'I just want to remind you that I'm still angry. You can tell me whatever you like, but I'm not going to forgive you yet. Tomorrow we'll see what you're made of.'

He removed his finger and let go of her neck.

Suddenly he stood up and was gone.

She couldn't fall back asleep. She was restless, trembling uncontrollably and covered in a cold sweat. For the first time she wondered if it might be preferable to die.

54

It was early morning. The sun was rising, but the manor was still in darkness. Simon thought it was a good time to stop by. There was a guard in the booth and a light on in the kitchen, but otherwise the property was deserted.

Jacob was waiting for him inside the gate. Simon could sense his eagerness right away.

'I saw her, Jesus Christ, I saw her!'

'Shh, Jacob, you're shouting! Who did you see?' Simon asked.

But Jacob seemed incapable of lowering his voice.

'Sofia. She's in the cellar. She's on a bed down there!' he cried.

'What the fuck?'

Simon realized that he, too, had raised his voice. His ears began to buzz. *I knew it, I knew it!*

'At first I was going to call the cops, but obviously I don't have a phone, and then I thought I should talk to you first. Could she be there of her own free will?'

'No, definitely not.' Simon felt dizzy; there was a bitter taste in his mouth. *Got to get Sofia out of there right away. But how?* 'No, don't call the police. Oswald will hide her, or… shit, I don't even want to think about what he'll do to her if the police show up. Look, I have to come up with a solution and talk to Benjamin. Are you coming with me?'

Jacob shook his head.

'I have to let the animals out to pasture today. If I'm going to leave, they'll be better off outdoors. They can survive for a long time out here. But the whole staff is going out to clear land in the woods tomorrow. Only Oswald and a guard are staying behind. Elvira and the babies are going to the mainland. I can escape then.'

'Make sure you are able to stay behind when the others leave. We're going to need you here. Take my phone so we can talk. I'll get another one somehow.'

Jacob stared at the phone Simon had placed in his hand.

'I mean, you can't just call any old time. If someone were to hear...' he said.

Simon took the phone back.

'I'll put it on silent. Just keep it in your trouser pocket and you'll feel when it vibrates. We have to get Sofia out tonight somehow.'

'That'll be tough. He's got two guards at night. And the cameras are on – they're always aimed at the front of the manor house.'

Simon thought for a moment, but each idea ended in some impossible problem.

'I need some time to think... Let's do this: you stay here and let out the animals and find out if the cellar window is big enough for us to pull Sofia out. Then we could get her when the staff are gone tomorrow. I'll call you when I've figured something out. When's the best time?'

'Right after evening assembly. I'm always alone in the barn then.'

'Here, take my key for the gate,' Simon said. 'In case you need to get out before then. And then you can open it for us when we get here.'

Jacob stared at the key, then squeezed it as if it were the key to the mystery of how the universe had begun.

Simon jogged all the way home to the pension. He found Inga and asked if he could borrow her phone to make a call because he'd lost his own in the fields.

'Of course, Simon. Keep it for the day. Hardly anyone ever calls me anyway.'

Simon hurried into the cottage and dialled Benjamin's number. He got the voicemail three times before a sleepy Benjamin answered.

'Hop in the car and start driving. You have to get the nine-thirty ferry. I found Sofia.'

*

Benjamin showed up at Simon's cottage panting and sweaty. It seemed he had run all the way from the ferry. Simon was already at the computer, working on a plan. He told Benjamin about his encounter with Jacob. When he was done, Benjamin sank onto the sofa and slapped his forehead again and again.

'This is insane! We have to go to the police, Simon. We can't handle this on our own.'

'Yes we can. We have to. Oswald knows the police on the island and won't let any officers through that gate until he's hidden Sofia somehow or another. We can't take that risk. I have a plan, and I want to run it by you. It feels like I'm overlooking something.'

Benjamin's forehead creased in despair. He looked overwhelmed. He hadn't been on the island in over two years, and now here he was in Simon's cottage, thoroughly nonplussed. But Simon continued his monologue.

'If we just run up to the manor and try to get Sofia out, whatever guard is left will be there in under a minute. And then there will be a row. We could probably get past him, but he or Oswald would call the police and say we're trespassing. It would be chaos, and I don't want to take any risks. We need to get a head start somehow.'

Benjamin nodded eagerly.

'What if I go to the booth and distract the guard? I can argue with him for a while as you and Jacob get Sofia out. Benny did contact me once. I can say I have information about Sofia.'

He paused for a moment to think. It was a good plan, but it wasn't watertight. The guard had a motorcycle. He could catch up with them. And Oswald had contacts. Simon mentally reviewed his favourite action films and – bullseye.

'I've got a better idea. We'll set off a smoke bomb or a fire bomb in the cellar once we've got Sofia out. Or something that makes a hell of a bang, to attract the attention of the guard. You don't think the guard would come after us if there's a fire at the manor house, do you? He and Oswald will be the only ones there. Jacob said Oswald was sending the whole staff into the forest first thing tomorrow morning.'

'Shit, wouldn't that be arson?'

'Nah, it would only be a bang. Maybe a tiny fire in the cellar. They'll put it out. There are sprinklers everywhere. I'll argue with the guard and give you time to get Sofia out, and then I'll come around and set off the bomb before we escape.

So you don't have to suffer the guilt for the rest of your life,' Simon said dryly.

Benjamin stared at Simon and shook his head.

'Simon, you've really changed since we last saw each other. I like this plan. Just think of how disappointed Oswald will be when Sofia vanishes right under his nose. But won't the security cameras be on the whole time? How do we know they won't catch us that way?'

'Jacob has sneaked into the guards' booth a few times. He sent me an email from their computer. Around three in the morning, the guards go to the kitchen for a sandwich. They leave the booth unmanned in the meantime. Jacob can go in and turn off the cameras so they won't be recording. It will freeze the image.'

'How do you know all that?'

'I helped out with the electrical stuff once in a while when I was there. And listen, we can make sure Edwin Björk will attest that you haven't set foot on the island. He always knows everyone who's on the ferry.'

'What about Jacob?'

'We'll say Jacob escaped to the Björks' just like Sofia did. And that he's been hiding there since early this morning. Björk and his wife Elsa will say so.'

'Have you talked to Björk?'

'Yeah, before you got here. It gets even better: he has a small motorboat, and he'll be waiting for us so he can take us across the sound with Sofia.'

Benjamin's eyes were full of doubt.

'Shouldn't we just go to the police?'

'It's not that simple. There are pictures and emails to prove that Sofia isn't here. We can't take the risk that Oswald will try to hide her.'

'But the police know what they're doing.'

'Sure they do. Here on Fog Island? Don't be so naïve, Benjamin. You always believe the best of everyone. Do you even know whether that Östling character is still chief of police? Don't forget, he was super tight with Oswald. I'm not taking any risks – we have to get Sofia out. Then we can go to the police.'

Benjamin's gaze turned inward.

'Shit, just think of her, down there, all alone. She must be fucking terrified.'

'Exactly. And that's why we need a fool-proof plan. Don't you see that?'

'Of course. I just want to get Sofia out.'

Simon sat down at the computer and surfed for a bit, mumbling to himself.

'What are you doing?'

'I think I found the solution. We don't have time to go to the mainland for supplies, but we can make a small bomb by ourselves, a Molotov cocktail. Listen to this: "A glass bottle filled with flammable liquid, usually petrol or alcohol, which is touched off by an ignition device, often of make-shift construction, such as a rag stuffed into the neck of the bottle. The flame spreads quickly. Makes the sound of an explosion."'

'Jesus, Simon, that sounds lethal. We don't want to set the whole manor on fire, do we? I mean, arson… you can get years in prison for that.'

'You know what, Benjamin? I don't care. That bastard has ruined so many lives. I don't give a shit if his nasty manor burns down, as long as we get Sofia out. There won't be anyone there but Oswald and a guard. As long as they don't run straight into the flames and commit suicide, no one will die. Can you think of a better way?'

Benjamin shook his head.

'This is nuts. You don't have a crush on Sofia or something, do you? You seem even more desperate than I am.'

'I don't like her like that, Benjamin. I would go insane if I spent more than a week with Sofia. She's way too impulsive, too messy. We're just friends. Really good friends. Anything else?'

'No, it was just a thought.'

'Great, then let's get to planning. First I have to talk to Jacob – he needs to stay until tomorrow and freeze the security images during the night, and let Sofia know we're coming. And open the gate for us.'

Simon fished Inga's phone from his pocket.

'Jacob has a phone?'

'Yeah, for the moment he does. Smart, right?'

Benjamin scratched his head and wondered what had gotten into Simon.

He decided he would never again underestimate someone who seemed a little slow and liked to poke around in the dirt.

55

Jacob shared a dorm with five other men. The room couldn't have been much larger than twenty square metres, so there wasn't a lot of space between the beds. At first Jacob had enjoyed sharing a room – the camaraderie, having someone to talk to after the long workdays. But that was before all the punishment, discord, and forced sleeplessness. These days the place looked more like a room in a ghetto, and the odour of unwashed bodies was often intolerable.

Jon, who slept in the next bed, was so close that Jacob would only have to reach out a hand to touch him. The bed creaked mercilessly. So Jacob had to lie perfectly still.

He squeezed the phone tight, listening to the heavy breathing and occasional snores of the others. It was midnight. He had to stay awake for three hours. At three o'clock, the guards would go to the kitchen for their sandwiches. Then he would freeze the security images and warn Sofia. If only she was still in the cellar.

He was worried that Simon would decide to call. He hadn't dared to turn off the phone – he didn't know how to start it up again.

Jon flipped onto his stomach and let out a long sigh that smelled of the kale and beans they'd had for dinner. Jacob turned to face the wall. His eyelids were drooping; his body was crying out for sleep.

Just then he heard steps from the hallway. Quick, heavy, purposeful. Exhausted staff members dragged themselves to their dorms for the night; Jacob had learned to recognize their shuffling steps. This was different. Still, he jumped when a knock came at the door, which soon flew open. There was Benny, shouting that they had to gather for assembly in the dining room right away.

Dazed faces squinted in the light. But, like firefighters or soldiers, they were used to this. It was an exercise they had mastered: bouncing out of bed, throwing on their clothes, urging their bodies to be fully awake within minutes. No one speculated on who had called the meeting – there was only one person who did so in the middle of the night. Instead, each person ransacked their conscience. Jacob hoped no one would notice that he had been fully dressed under the covers. But the others were too busy stumbling around, grabbing their clothes, and looking for their shoes in the mess.

He lingered for a moment after the others had left the room, pretending to have trouble with his shoelaces. His cheeks were hot and his heart was pounding. That goddamn phone – he couldn't let go of it, but it would seal his fate if there was a body search. He had no idea what was going on, but he had an unpleasant hunch that whatever it was it somehow involved him. He hoped the meeting would be short. If everything went well, there was still time. If everything went to hell, he would have to try to sneak to the barn and call Simon – unless the meeting ended with him under orders to dig the ditch with Erik, under guard.

*

Oswald wasn't standing by the lectern; instead he was in the middle of the room with his arms crossed over his chest. His face was a mask, impossible to read. As Jacob walked by, he thought he felt Oswald's gaze on him. He shuddered and tried to look unconcerned and, above all, innocent.

The staff seemed unsure what was expected of them; they stood around in small clusters, waiting for directions.

Lina popped up beside Jacob and tugged gently at his shirt-sleeve.

He looked down at her and smiled but didn't dare say anything.

'Line up along the wall!' Oswald said. 'Facing me. Can you manage that?'

A moment of chaos ensued. They pushed and shoved, crashing into each other and stumbling over one another's feet until they were in a long line against the wall.

Oswald glanced around, a resigned look on his face.

'What a team,' he said dryly. 'I'm impressed.'

These rapid shifts between sarcasm and suppressed rage were the worst. You never knew when he would explode or who would be the target. This would be the worst moment to annoy him.

Jacob had ended up far down the line, just a few people from the end.

'Fine,' Oswald sighed. 'This will have to do. Here's the deal. In this room is an imbecilic whackjob who thinks he can defy me. The guards have seen someone sneaking around the property in the middle of the night, near the cellar. As I'm sure you understand, I am a little tired of being disobeyed. Perhaps this person would like to reveal himself?'

Total silence. Not a sound. Most people cast their eyes downward. Jacob vanished into a state of shock, no longer aware of his surroundings, but was dragged back to the room by the sound of his heart pounding. His first thought was that it was all over. But then he felt the others' fear, the terror that spread through the dining room, and he realized he was far from the only one harbouring a secret.

'Okay then. I guess you'll each have to look me in the eye, one by one,' Oswald said. 'It won't take long, I assure you. I can expose guilty people in the blink of an eye. Furthermore, guilt has a smell – and the odour of burning is strong in here at the moment.'

He walked up to the first person and stared intently at them, lingering for a moment before moving on. Slow but determined. There was something about the way he moved: he was graceful and resolute, but he had an impenetrable aura that made you feel small and insignificant. It struck Jacob that the impeccability Oswald projected might be just a shell that hid his true demons. The thought helped him relax a little; he stopped squeezing the phone so hard. He, too, could put up a façade. He must not look guilty when Oswald reached him.

He noticed that Anders, who was standing next to him, was already breathing too fast, nervously.

Oswald stopped in the middle of the row and shook his head.

'Well. If this isn't quite the doughface parade. Why do I put up with you all?'

He moved on. So close. Jacob was flooded with thoughts. *What if they find the phone? And trace it to Simon? What will happen to Sofia? Oh my god, what will I do?*

He was dragged back to the present moment by Anders's voice, which sounded unusually squeaky.

'It was me, sir!'

Oswald stopped.

'I'm sorry, sir! I was working late. I thought I saw Elvira in the courtyard in only her nightgown. I went to check on her. I wasn't going to the cellar, I swear, I was just passing by, I…' The words caught in his throat.

By now Oswald was in front of Anders, leaning over him. His face was twisted with rage; his eyes flashed. It was as if electricity was streaming off him. Anders stared at him in fear, completely paralysed.

Jacob smelled the sharp odour of urine first, and when he turned his head he saw the dark stain spreading down Anders's trouser leg. Oswald, who had noticed it too, was flummoxed.

All of a sudden, his face went back to normal. He took a step back and began to crack up. No one dared to join in. His laughter echoed through the room, so chilling that Jacob got gooseflesh.

'Look at this bastard! He pissed himself like a dog. He *looks* like a fucking dog. All that's missing is his tail.'

The staff began to laugh too. It was hesitant at first, but then it grew and exploded, all mixed up with relief and Schadenfreude. The tense atmosphere became a little less oppressive now that they could take comfort at the expense of a fellow staff member.

Anders was trembling uncontrollably, and Jacob thought for a moment he might faint, but he just reeled backwards and sunk his chin to his chest in a pose of absolute submission. Jacob had never seen Anders so shattered.

Oswald turned to Corinne.

'He will be sleeping in the doghouse with that fleabag of a mutt tonight. And he has to salute the dog each time he runs into it. Maybe that will get him to listen to me. At least the fucking dog comes when you call it.'

With no further ado, Oswald turned to look at Jacob. His eyes were vacant. But then something glimmered deep down in his pupils. Recognition, or maybe suspicion. His eyes narrowed, his mouth opened – all while Jacob fought to keep his gaze steady. For some strange reason, his scalp was sweating. He tried to calm his wild pulse. He could feel his scrotum retracting. A frightening thought gnawed in the back of his mind. *What if he can see straight into my brain?* But Jacob decided he was not about to give Oswald that sort of access.

Then Oswald closed his mouth again. He turned to the staff. 'You can go now. Make sure Anders bunks down with the dog. We need more peer pressure around here.'

Oswald stayed put while the staff hurried off. A group had already gathered around the doghouse by the time Jacob walked outside. He saw Anders's back, how he knelt on the ground to crawl into the tiny house. Anders – the toughest, the loudest, the one who always picked on everyone else, who had testified against his own daughter – now completely destroyed.

A chilly wind from the northwest whipped across the manor. You could hear the sea crashing in the bay. It must be freezing in the doghouse. Jacob pictured Elvira's look of despair and realized he didn't feel sorry for Anders. He only hoped he would be nice to the dog.

Back in the dorms, he had trouble calming down and felt doubt creeping in for the first time. What he was about to do was so reckless and dangerous after tonight's intermezzo that he wondered if it would only make everything worse and put Sofia in a more serious bind than she was already in. Once again, the others were asleep. Their grunts, snores, and odours, and the merciless darkness, brought out his courage again. Not a chance he was going to tolerate this for another day. Even another second was unbearable.

He stroked the back of the phone with his thumb and steeled himself.

56

Although it was still dark, a blackbird was warbling outside the cellar window. Then came a gentle knock on the pane. She sat up in bed. Something was scraping against the window, like a branch brushing it in the breeze.

She turned on the light and saw a person's shadow outside. She ran over to the closet to get the ladder, which she dragged to the wall. She propped it open and climbed up. A face was pressed to the window – a face she didn't recognize at first. But then she saw it was Jacob, the guy who cared for the animals. She became dizzy with joy, almost lost her balance, and had to grab the windowsill to keep from tipping backwards. The window opened just a little before the padlock stopped it. Jacob put a finger to his lips. She could see his face clearly now.

'I have to be quick,' he whispered. 'Simon knows you're here. We're going to come get you tomorrow, when the staff are out in the forest.'

'Jacob, you have to hurry. He's going to kill me next time.'

'We'll come, I promise. Can you fit through the window if we pull you out?'

'Yes, I'm sure I can. Can't you take me with you now?'

'No, we have to break the padlock. And the guards…' Jacob gave a start and turned around. 'Shit, I think they're on their way back to the booth from the kitchen. Be ready – early tomorrow morning.'

His face disappeared. She wanted to break the glass, grab at him, make him pull her out. But he was gone. She climbed down and folded the ladder, then dragged it back to the closet in case Oswald came by. Then she sat down on the bed, her head spinning – waves of relief, but between them, the fear that something would go wrong.

She tried to fall asleep, but it was impossible. Her heart was fluttering like a frightened bird trying to escape from her ribcage.

To battle her growing unease, she began to pace. *Out, out, have to get out.* The refrain was on repeat in her brain. She wondered what time it was. It was still dark. When would the staff leave?

She lay down on the bed again, thinking about what she would do when she got out. *If* she got out. It stung to think of Mattias. When she recalled how she had misjudged him, she felt like she was suffocating. Why hadn't she seen through his smarmy propositions? He had followed her all the way to San Francisco and then spent three months diligently watching her. Just to bring her here. Oswald would never let her go. If she didn't manage to escape, she would die in this musty underground cell. All at once, she was overwhelmed with exhaustion.

As quick as blowing out a candle, she dropped off.

★

She was roused from sleep by someone jostling her back and forth; she found herself dazed, her body leaden with fatigue.

She had slept so soundly that it hurt to open her eyes. He was towering over her, shaking her whole upper body. The ceiling light was blinding, but she could see his eyes. Clouded with fury.

'Sit up!'

He let go of her and paced back and forth while she sat up, still half asleep. Morning hadn't come yet; she must not have slept for more than an hour. And now she wondered what on earth was going on. He came back to the bed and stood with his arms crossed, observing her for a moment – calm on the surface, but with that insane look and those faint twitches from the muscles of his face. His pants and shirt looked wrinkled – he couldn't have gone to bed.

'Who was here?' he asked.

She put on an expression of bewilderment.

'No one has been here.'

'Don't lie to me, Sofia. I already know Anders was sneaking around the property in the middle of the night. Now I want to know if he talked to you.'

He was furious, his voice so loud he was almost shouting. His face had turned red. Sofia wondered if he had mixed up Anders and Jacob; he wasn't usually too particular about what names he called the staff.

'Why would Anders talk to me? I don't understand what's going on.'

'No? Well, you will soon. Might I remind you that Anders is Elvira's father, and after all, you and she were so tight. I've already had a chat with her but of course she's flatly denying everything. And you know Elvira. She transforms into a sobbing martyr as soon as you so much as poke her. So now you and I are going to get to the bottom of this.'

'There's nothing to get to the bottom of. I didn't talk to them.'

'We'll find out soon. It's all about trust and obedience. If we're going to be able to work together, you must be completely loyal. I thought we had made some progress, and now this.'

'But you're the only one I've talked to, I swear.'

'We're done discussing this. Get up, we're going to take a little walk.'

She gasped for breath and realized two things simultaneously: he was going to move her, and she wouldn't be there when Simon and Benjamin arrived. The whole plan had gone to hell.

She rose on trembling legs. She had to pull herself together and keep from crying. All she was wearing was the old T-shirt she'd had when she arrived, and her underwear. She'd washed the shirt in the sink and hung it to dry in the bathroom. It was still a little damp. She felt silly and pitiful, standing there with her bare feet on the cold concrete floor as he eyed her thoroughly. She felt the sudden urge to attack him, grab the screwdriver from under the pillow, but she knew how strong he was. Better to play along until he calmed down.

He walked around to stand behind her and pulled her arms behind her back. He used something that felt like rope to bind her wrists and hustled her over to the door. In the midst of her misery, she felt relieved that she would get to leave the horrible cellar room.

The stairs that led out of the cellar had no lighting. It was total darkness, and all she could hear was his heavy breathing as he led her up the steps.

She was blinded by the bright light in the great hall. Although she had been nearly certain he would take her to the attic, he pulled her toward the main entrance instead.

'Now, don't get any ideas,' he said. 'Benny's the guard on duty and he already knows you're here. The rest have crashed after a royal dressing-down, so no one will see or hear you.'

Ice-cold air hit her as he opened the door. The weather had turned, and a fresh breeze sighed above them. The sky was turning indigo; daybreak was close. She hesitated, but he took her arm and dragged her down the front stairs.

'Go to the little gate in the wall,' he said. 'And make it fucking quick.'

She moved across the courtyard as if in a trance. The only thing that felt real was the hard gravel beneath her feet. Not even the cold could touch her, because her whole being was suffused with fear – where was he taking her? She floated forward like a ghost. His claw-like fingers squeezed her arm.

'Where are we going?' she asked.

'We're going to test your loyalty,' he said, letting out a hoarse laugh.

All at once, she knew where they were headed.

*

The wind picked up as they reached the heath. The ground poked and sliced at her feet. She had begun to shake with the cold, and tears stung under her eyelids. The moon was almost full, and it illuminated the heath in a deep purple tone. The sea, black and thundering, came into view. White foam hissed atop the waves, which rolled in one on top of the next. A tiny streak of light glowed on the horizon, but otherwise the sky was dark. Devil's Rock extended out over the water, majestic and bare and merciless. He guided her to it, tugging at her arm, forcing her to walk faster.

I'm as good as dead, she thought. *Have to do something, have to react.* She threw herself to her knees, pulling him down with her. She tried to get up and run but it wasn't easy with her hands tied behind her, and he was quick to lift her right up again.

'Stop making trouble, otherwise this will end badly,' he said.

'Please, have mercy on me!' she cried in desperation.

'I'm not a merciful man! Don't you know that by now?'

Then she began to cry for help, bellowing until she thought her lungs would burst, but the sound was swallowed up by the roaring wind.

They had reached Devil's Rock. He led her to the very edge and stood behind her with a firm grip on her shoulders.

Down below, the sea crashed against the rocks. An eddy under the cliff tossed water in all directions; it splashed up on them. She couldn't take her eyes from it. A swirling mass of seaweed flew up at them. The water was flowing in through all the cracks between the rocks. The salt spray hitting her skin made her feel like the water was having a taste of her, getting ready to swallow her whole.

The incredible power of the water pulled her down. She was so cold her teeth were chattering and her body was shaking. She could feel her heart pounding under the thin fabric of her T-shirt. The storm had made the edge of the cliff slippery and slimy. She almost lost her footing, but he steadied her. At first she thought he would shove her into the sea, but he held her tight.

'The sea is greedy, Sofia,' he hissed into her ear. 'And the current is strong tonight. Now: say the words. The words you say before you jump.'

She let out a shrill scream, shaking uncontrollably.

'Never!'

'If you do, maybe I'll untie your hands before you jump. Say it! That, or admit that you talked to Anders and Elvira.'

'I didn't talk to them.'

'Then say it!'

The little chant was still imprinted in her brain. The strange plea for the sea to cleanse you of sin.

She began to cry and the tears were washed away by the saltwater spray.

'May I leave my betrayal in the depths and rise to the surface pure and full of devotion,' she mumbled.

'Louder. Shout it! Shout it out to the sea.'

She screamed the words, bellowing like the old foghorn. She pressed against him, trying to make him back away from the edge. But he put his arms around her, holding her firmly, and pushed back. Then, suddenly, he let go and put one arm behind her knees and the other at her back. In an instant he had scooped her up. He took a few steps forward until he was standing at the very edge of the cliff. He held her over the sea. The weightlessness made her dizzy and she had the insane feeling that he might have already let her go. She felt herself floating in the air and then falling helplessly. But then he took a few steps back again and she realized she was still in his arms.

'Did you talk to anyone?' He had to shout to be heard over the sea and the wind.

'No, I swear, no!'

'You're a witch, you'll float.'

'Please, I'll do anything!'

He took another few steps back and staggered as a sudden gust of wind caught him. For a second she thought he would drop her, but he recovered his balance, turned around, and walked back to the slope in front of the rocks. He set her down on the ground so she was facing him. He grabbed her by the hair and pulled her face close.

'Now you know how thin the line between life and death is. The only question is, who has the power? From now on you will obey me. Spread your legs when I want you to. You will kiss my feet and call me sir, like everyone else does. Do you promise you will?'

She nodded frantically.

'Great. We can go home now, and you can sleep on this little lesson.'

He was quiet on the way back, nudging her in irritation whenever he thought she was moving too slowly. The fear that he would change his mind made tears trickle down her face. She had stepped on something sharp and her heel was throbbing with pain – it felt like the skin was broken. But she didn't dare speak up about it. She could no longer feel the cold; her body was numb and felt stiff as a board. But she dragged herself on.

Once they were through the gate, he stopped and pulled her body close so her back was against his stomach. He was rock-hard, still excited after the incident by the sea.

'You're beautiful, Sofia, you know that?' he whispered. 'Not as tight as a fourteen-year-old, but still beautiful. And while we're on the subject, you have a delightful ass.'

She dug her fingernails into her palms hard, to quash the impulse to turn around and spit in his face.

He loosened one arm and at first she thought he was going to pull off her underwear, but then she realized he had broken a twig off a tree. He turned around and stuck it in the lock, fiddling with it for a moment.

'Keep all the bastards out,' he mumbled.

Daylight gleamed on the gravel outside. Dew had settled; it had cooled her sore heel as they crossed the lawn, but she could no longer feel her other foot. Her fingertips were numb too. Something strange was sticking out of the doghouse – a pair of feet? She turned away, convinced she was so shaken that she was hallucinating. She just wanted to get inside the house, back to her little prison. Never had she wanted something so much. There was still time, if only he went to bed now.

Dear God, make him go to bed.

He untied her hands when they got to the cellar room. The light was still on and the warm air hit her. For an instant the world became calm again, gentle and quiet. She almost broke down with relief.

'Now the two of us will get a few hours of sleep,' he said, his voice soft. 'Hope you're looking forward to tomorrow as much as I am.'

'No…' she bit her tongue. 'I'm sorry, I meant yes.'

'Yes, what?'

'Yes, sir.'

57

The sky was overcast right above the manor, where leaden grey clouds were piling up, forebodingly heavy. All was quiet; Simon could tell the staff had left the property, but the light was on in the sentry box. He stopped and dialled his own number. Jacob answered almost immediately, his voice soft and mumbling. As if he didn't know how to answer a cell phone.

'Are you there?' Simon asked.

'I'm on my way. Are you going to distract the guard?'

'Yes, but you have to let Benjamin in. He's coming through the forest. Once you've got Sofia, I'll join you. Leave the gate open.'

Jacob mumbled again, breathing heavily into the phone. He was tense, just like Simon. All the colour had drained from Benjamin's face on the way over. He'd tried to chicken out as soon as he saw the manor ahead of them. But Simon had trudged onward and chided Benjamin to pull himself together.

Benny was in the booth and looked surprised when he caught sight of Simon.

'What are you doing here?'

'So, I have some information about Sofia. In case you're interested.'

Benny seemed more confused than curious.

'Okay, what is it?'

Just then, Simon felt the phone vibrating in his trouser pocket and took it out. His own name showed up on the screen of Inga Hermansson's phone.

'Excuse me, I have to take this,' he said, walking to a grove of trees beyond earshot of Benny.

'The gate,' came Jacob's frantic voice. 'There's something in the lock, I can't get it out. There's no time, oh shit, I don't know what to do.'

He heard Benjamin's voice in the background, a string of curse words, and then:

'Fuck, I have to hurry!'

Simon thought of Sofia down in the cellar. The staff sent away and how Oswald must have planned this. Just like everything else he ever did. Maybe he was already down there with her. They might be too late.

'Run to the greenhouse and get a ladder,' he instructed Jacob. 'There's a birch trunk Benjamin can lean against the wall and climb up. But you'll have to help him down on the inside so he doesn't set off the alarm.'

Simon glanced in Benny's direction, but he seemed deeply absorbed in the magazine he was reading. The urgency of the situation gave Simon an idea. He knew it was insane, but he had to try. He took the little card with Oswald's number from his trouser pocket and dialled it, his fingers stiff. He sneaked another look at Benny, who was still reading. Oswald answered with an annoyed, snappish 'Hello.' Simon imitated a Stockholm accent as best he could.

'Am I speaking with Franz Oswald von Bärensten?'

'Yes, who is this?' Oswald sounded tired. As if he had just woken up.

'This is Peter Ljungman from *GQ*. As you may know, we run an article about Sweden's best-dressed man in our July issue, and it so happens we're considering you.'

'How did you get my private number?'

'I have to admit it was difficult, but we thought you might be interested.'

Oswald's voice transformed, becoming supple and ingratiating.

'Well, I must say I'm honoured, but what would the practical considerations be?'

From the corner of his eyes, Simon saw Benjamin jumping over the wall, and then Jacob and Benjamin rushing across the courtyard toward the manor house. The alarm hadn't been triggered. Everything was quiet as the grave, and Benny was still reading as he absentmindedly picked his nose.

'Well, we'll have to do an interview,' Simon went on, but he was cut off by a click from the phone. He would never know what had happened in that moment. Perhaps Oswald was at the window and saw Benjamin and Jacob. Perhaps he could tell there was something off about the call. In any case, he had hung up on Simon. And now there was no time to waste.

Simon began to run. He dashed through the woods to the far side of the wall, the bottle and lighter jangling in his pocket. Fir branches and twigs whipped at his face. His eyes tried to find the birch; he found it leaning against the wall and grabbed a branch to haul himself up. He stood atop the wall, swaying for a moment, but managing to avoid the alarmed barbed wire. He got a foothold on the ladder on the other side and climbed down. Benjamin and Jacob were crouching by the cellar window, pounding away at the padlock. He ran up to them, squeezing the bottle in his coat pocket.

Now they could hear Sofia's voice down there, shouting at them to hurry. Screaming and whimpering in turns.

The padlock came away from the wood with a sharp crack.

58

She couldn't let herself fall asleep, but it wasn't hard – she was on full alert. She sat upright in bed, waiting, wondering if she had ever been so awake. So unnaturally focused, with a buzzing undertone of fear that something might go wrong. At last she knew from the cold light that it was early morning. Voices drifted over from the courtyard. She was curious, but she didn't want to get out the ladder yet. Instead she pulled over the chair that stood by the door. She gazed up and could see part of the courtyard. Someone was standing there, talking to the guard. A woman with a huge baby carriage. It was Elvira, and yet it wasn't. She was dressed in a shapeless coat, her hair was up in a messy bun, and her face was so white it seemed to glow against the pale sky. From this strange angle, she looked like a middle-aged lady. The guard said something that sounded like 'drive you to the ferry,' and then they vanished from Sofia's field of vision.

Sofia recalled Elvira as she had been before: bound and determined to keep fighting. Strikingly beautiful. She remembered the Elvira who had lain on Sofia's sofa with her big belly, laughing at how they were putting the squeeze on Oswald with their blog. There had been so much life in her back then. Now she looked dead. But behind her cheerfulness, Elvira had always carried a veil of sadness. Fifteen years old, a future in shambles, with no redress in sight.

My life isn't the only one he's ruined, she thought. *This isn't just about me. And he might be here any moment. To sabotage everything.*

It had gotten so quiet outside. She gazed up out the window and saw only the deserted lawn. She was increasingly doubtful that they would be able to pull her through the window. A cold chill went down her spine. What if she got stuck up there, her body halfway in heaven, halfway in hell?

She climbed off the chair. A decision was forming in her mind. An incredible plan, still taking root, and so reckless that she tried to shut it out. But it kept sneaking back in and growing.

She pulled the chair over to the door, which seemed thick and heavy, as if it led to a crypt. It would take a lot of strength to kick it in. She shoved the chair under the handle, then went to the closet and dragged the ladder over to the wall. All her movements were jerky, and she was breathing so strangely. The ladder didn't want to open. *Goddamn piece of shit ladder!* She kicked at it furiously until it gave way, pretending it was Oswald she was kicking, and experiencing a certain amount of satisfaction. But that feeling was overshadowed by another thought, darker and more dangerous.

Something in the closet had etched its way into her memory. And sure enough, there they stood. Two cans of petrol, the type you'd use for a lawnmower. Shoved into a corner, covered in a thick layer of dust. She picked them up and set them in the middle of the room. The sight made her heart leap. She felt that she was experiencing an instant personality change. Her anxiousness was gone; it had been replaced by a sort of callous distance. She was only partially inhabiting her own body; she could see herself from the outside as she moved around the room.

Her movements were methodical. Her body was like an avatar in a computer game, responding to various commands and performing different tasks. It ate a dry sandwich, which expanded in her mouth, but she stubbornly chewed and chewed, washing it down with water. It put on her dress and pulled the T-shirt over that. It put on her ballerina flats.

All while the petrol cans stood waiting.

The thought struck her light a bolt of lightning as she sat there. Matches! She hurried to the closet to look for some. Digging around, scattering things here and there, swearing to herself. But then she found a lighter in the bottom of a bucket. She clicked it and a tiny flame appeared. She stuck the lighter in one side of her bra, then crumpled up a piece of paper that was on a shelf and stuck that in the other side.

Now she could hear the buzz of the staff gathering in the courtyard. A shrill, commanding voice. Roll call.

Soon. Soon Benjamin and Simon would come.

Please, please, for fuck's sake hurry up.

She took the family history from beside the bed and stashed it in her clothing. Her bra and the tight dress held it to her body.

She could hear the staff moving across the courtyard; it sounded like they were marching.

The petrol cans. She lifted one in each hand, feeling their heft. She wondered how much surface the liquid would cover. What she was about to do was absolutely insane, she thought, but she felt strangely calm.

Then she opened the first can and inhaled the vapours, which were so strong that it gave her a kick. She began to spread the petrol on the floor, slowly and carefully. She opened the second can and splashed its contents onto the walls, as high as she could. The room smelled worse than a service station now, and she wondered if the smell could make you faint. She sent up a silent prayer that they would come soon.

Time stood almost still. She sat down on the bed. There was nothing more to do, just wait. And she was no good at waiting.

There was a thud from the stairs, from inside the house. She went stiff, but then it was quiet again. Then came another noise, outside the cellar window this time. Pounding, like a hammer. Another thud, inside the house. These two sounds were like an outer and inner force, pulling her apart.

She hurried to the ladder, squeezing the book against her chest, making sure it was secure. A face appeared in the window. They had come. They had really come! She realized that the sound had come from the padlock, which they had broken away. And now there was a sharp, impatient rap at the windowpane. Her body began to tremble uncontrollably. Her hands were sweaty and almost slipped off the steps of the ladder. She was on her way up when she heard the doorknob turning behind her. She froze out of sheer reflex. Impatient rattling at the handle, banging at the door, and Oswald's voice, roaring.

'Sofia! For Christ's sake, open up! I'll kick down the door!'

The chair under the doorknob creaked, as if at any moment it would give way and fall to pieces.

'Open up, you fucking slut!'

She grabbed hold, pulled herself up, and all of a sudden she was face to face with the windowpane. She fumbled with the latch and as soon as it was loose the window flew open. Her own voice was bawling: '*For God's sake, hurry up! Help me!*' She couldn't see their faces, only their hands reaching down, and her arms were pulled upwards, like the branches of a tree reaching for the sun.

She felt herself hoisted up and out the window. Her belly scraped against the windowsill, but she didn't feel any pain. Only her hearing was painfully sharp: Oswald was kicking the door and the racket was like a sledgehammer on metal. His voice cursing, lengthy harangues; he had completely flipped out. She screeched when her feet hit the ground, shouting up at the sky. Benjamin's face was right next to hers. It felt like a dream as he tugged her close. Simon was beside him.

'Hold on, there's something I have to do,' she managed to say as she stuck her hand under her dress and fumbled for the lighter in her bra. But Benjamin held her tighter. He was pressing her firmly to his chest, locking her arms in place. He shouted at Simon.

'Shit, light it up! The fucking guard is coming!'

The sound of a motorcycle starting. Simon pulled a bottle from his coat pocket. As if in a fog, she watched him light the rag sticking out of it. She didn't understand what it was until the bottle was flying through the window.

'Run, run!' she screamed. 'I poured petrol…' Her voice sounded weird, like a stranger's.

The crash of the bottle breaking. They had already turned their backs on the manor and were pelting away when the explosion came. A loud sparking and crackling that grew to an inferno of pops and the sound of growing flames.

They sprinted to the wall and the ladder leaning against it.

Jacob's voice came from alongside her: 'I have to open the gates for the animals. I'll catch up.'

Angry shouts came from behind them. But they didn't turn around.

They climbed up the ladder. Benjamin first, then Simon, who reached down and pulled her up until she was standing atop the wall. The alarm was blaring. She jumped down and landed hard on the ground. Benjamin grabbed her hand and yanked her along.

They dashed along the forest paths. A gentle rain was falling from the grey sky, dampening their faces. Her body was so exhausted after her time in the cellar, but she forced it to move. Pushing her muscles. Her heart was racing and her lungs burned. The pain in her heel had returned, and it shot a jolt through her every time she took a step. She stumbled over a root but got up and pressed on.

Benjamin took her arm and pulled her along. Simon showed up on her right side to take her other arm. They were almost carrying her now. A clearing came into sight, and then the vast sea, spreading out before them like a frothing grey blanket. Simon picked her up and carried her down the rocky slope.

A motorboat showed up out of nowhere, moored just next to the rocks. Simon helped her aboard, and when he let go of her she felt intensely dizzy. It was like all the blood had drained from her head, sucked down into her legs.

She sank to the deck but felt Benjamin's hands pulling her up and into his arms. He rocked her like a baby.

Jacob had caught up to them.

'It's fine, they're not coming after us. They're trying to put out the fire.'

She hadn't turned around yet.

It wasn't until the boat had set sail that she saw the smoke billowing from the manor house. Great flames licked at the sky. The wind carried the ash toward them across the dull grey sky.

59

Another explosion from the direction of the manor. They were heading across the sound in the little motorboat. Edwin Björk was going fast. The prow whipped up the water, which flew up in sheets and spattered over them. Again and again the boat bounced on the waves, and they all nearly lost their footing.

'Simon, what did you put in that bottle? That place is fucking burning down!' Benjamin cried.

Simon scratched his head, puzzled.

'It was me,' Sofia said. 'I poured petrol in the cellar. Everywhere. On the floor and the walls.'

She was still clinging to Benjamin, refusing to let go.

Simon shot her an odd look and Jacob stared, his mouth agape. All that was visible of Edwin Björk, in the wheelhouse, was the back of his neck.

'What the fuck?' Benjamin said. 'Are you out of your mind?'

'No, I'm not.' Her eyes burned with tears of anger. 'He beat me and raped me. That bastard was going to strangle me while he forced me into sex today. What the hell did you think he was doing with me in that cellar, playing Monopoly?'

She hadn't quite boarded the boat. In some strange way, she was floating in the air. It still felt like tentacles from the cellar were trying to pull her back, but they were pried away one by one as they put distance between the boat and the island.

Benjamin held her away from him. He sniffled, close to tears.

'Oh, fuck. Shit, shit. I didn't know,' he said.

They embraced again, mostly to avoid seeing each other cry. She pressed her face to his shirt and inhaled the scent of his sweat. Felt his heart pounding in his chest. Only when the heavy sky opened and they were drenched with raindrops that washed away their tears did she dare to let go and look at him again.

There should have been something strange between them – jealousy, some sort of scar, or at least an uncomfortable feeling of distance after the time they'd spent apart. But all she saw in front of her was Benjamin as he'd always been: big, calm, and safe. Drops of water clung to his eyelashes and a trickle found its way to the corner of his mouth.

'That bastard is going to pay for this,' he said. 'We are sure as shit going to put him away.'

'I don't want sympathy,' she mumbled. 'I don't want to talk about it yet. He was about to kick down the door when you arrived, just so you know.'

'What if we killed him?' Jacob wondered in horror.

'We didn't. Those walls are made of stone. The floor above is wood. The fire will spread upwards,' Sofia said.

They heard Edwin Björk calling from the wheelhouse.

'That's true, what she said about how the manor was built. But I still hope he kicks the bucket.'

Simon and Jacob were sitting down now. Simon began to chuckle.

'Jesus, Simon. Stop laughing like that, it's creepy,' Benjamin said. 'He could pin everything on us. The guard saw us, after all.'

'No, he can't,' Simon said.

'Why not?'

'We were never there. Sofia has a watertight alibi – Oswald made sure of that. Jacob ran away this morning and hid at Edwin's. Elsa has been with him all day. Benjamin wasn't on the ferry this morning, as Edwin knows. And I'm just a damn farmer who spends all his time poking around in the dirt. Inga Hermansson can attest to that.'

'There is someone who knows I was there,' Sofia said. 'That pig Mattias, who I met in San Francisco. He's got control of my email.'

'He could confess to everything,' Benjamin said.

'He won't,' said Simon. 'Surely you don't think he's going to admit to kidnapping Sofia and hacking her computer and all that. People like Mattias are just pawns in this game. He's in a delicate position right now. He may be an idiotic Oswald clone, but he's not *that* stupid. We'll contact him when we get where we're going. He's going to be really useful.'

Benjamin gave a hoarse laugh.

'Simon, you're amazing! But Sofia, you have to report Oswald for rape,' he said.

Sofia made a face. The very thought of standing in a courtroom again, face to face with Oswald's snide smile, was so deeply repulsive that her knees felt weak.

'No way am I doing that. He already raped Elvira, who was fourteen at the time, and all he got for that was the chance to rest up for eighteen months while he wrote his awful book. This will be better, with the whole fucking thing burning to the ground.'

They heard sirens and could spot flashing blue lights on the last bits of the island that were still visible. Sofia pressed the family history to her belly. It seemed like a miracle that she hadn't dropped it during her escape. Part of her was still back in the cellar, her heart pounding; another part was full of an inner peace.

The sea stretched out before them. The rain had stopped. The damp air seemed to be breathing, stroking the heat away from her cheeks. The wind whispered in her hair, in the voice of Sigrid von Bärensten: *That bastard is going to get what he deserves.*

A plan began to take shape in her mind, a scenario that brought a tiny taste of triumph, although she couldn't quite shake the feeling that Oswald would wriggle out of this again, as usual. But then she had a mind-boggling thought. The pieces fell into place. The doors opened wide. She felt herself break into a smile.

Of *course* it was that simple.

They had almost reached the harbour by now. She had to remind herself again and again that this was all real. The hard deck of the boat, Benjamin's warm embrace, the dark sky above them. There was a lot left to do. She thought of how she would recover her email account and put the screws on Mattias; of how it would feel to see her parents again; of where she would get her hands on some clothes; of the fact that she really was starving.

And then she wondered how on earth it would be possible to be separated from Simon, who was sitting there looking at her so tenderly. A warm, loving feeling spread through her. Simon began to chuckle.

'Damn, this was really fun!'

The fire was a ball of red against the sky on the other side of the sound. Like an early sunset.

It's almost too bad that that beautiful old manor house is burning, she thought.

'But of course, I wasn't there,' she mumbled quietly to herself.

Epilogue

Detective Superintendent Titus Berg pulls down the blinds in the interrogation room, adjusting them meticulously and thoughtfully. It's not even sunny out. He just wants to show Oswald that this interrogation will proceed at Berg's pace and on his terms.

In the autumn of his life, Berg has grown a little cranky and gruff. But that only makes him better suited to questioning suspects. And he's going to crack the nut that is Oswald. About time.

Oswald has been irritable and impatient since he stepped into this room. He's practically steaming. *Greed,* Berg thinks. *Look what it's done to him. Strange that people can never seem to have enough money.*

Now Oswald is sitting before Berg and glaring. The fact that one of his eyebrows is almost completely burned away lends a touch of the amusing to his otherwise symmetrical face. His entire presence screams *bully.*

'Isn't it about time for us to get started?' he asks, annoyed.

'You know, I was about to ask you the same thing. Isn't it about time you tell us what really happened out on West Fog Island? We know that fire was set on purpose. Only you and the guard were there. The guard corroborates your story, but there's just one problem.'

'Which is?'

'That it's all one big lie.'

'But I told you: there was a group of people who came to set fire to the manor. Benjamin and Simon, and Jacob who worked in the barn, and that slut Sofia Bauman.'

'Now, now. Let's not be so careless with our language,' Berg says dryly. 'A religious man like you…'

'I'm not a goddamn priest. Could you just listen to me?' His voice is shaking. He's about to lose control.

Berg fixes his eyes on Oswald, who stubbornly stares back.

'You know as well as I do that all those people have watertight alibis. Sofia Bauman was in Copenhagen, on her way back to Lund from Paris. Surely you aren't suggesting that she stretched out a very long arm and set fire to your place from down there?'

'But she was at the manor! I told you to talk to Mattias Wilander, but obviously you haven't.'

'Yes, we have. We talked to him and Sofia Bauman together, actually. An attractive couple, although it seems they're going to break up. In any case, they've been living it up in Paris for a week, and they got home a whole day after the fire. We even verified this with the staff from the hotel they stayed at.'

'That's not true!' Oswald interrupts. 'Mattias works for me. There's been some sort of misunderstanding. For fuck's sake, he lives in my apartment in the city.'

'Oh yes, we know. But it seems you've got another defector on your hands. He said he can't deal with all your bullying anymore. That everything changed when he met Sofia Bauman.'

Oswald's eyes dart furiously around the room.

'Sofia Bauman is a criminal. She tricked him, don't you see this is a conspiracy?'

Berg shakes his head.

'Could you stop bringing up Sofia Bauman? I must say, you seem a bit fixated on her.'

It's in this instant Berg sees a transformation in Oswald, or maybe it's only a feeling. A crack appears in his obstinate façade. Something has cracked, almost imperceptibly, but it makes the air between them quiver. Berg has experienced this feeling during other interrogations. He has seen the fear deep down in the target's eyes when he realizes he has been caught in his own trap. Is it only an illusion, or has Oswald really gone pale beneath his fake tan? He's probably at the breaking point. Just where Berg wants him.

'Know what I think?' Berg asks.

'No, how the fuck could I know that?' He's shouting now. Tiny bubbles of spit have gathered in the corners of his mouth. A vein at his temple is pulsating.

'I think you have a grudge against those people because they defected from your cult. I've spoken with them. The whole bunch. Really nice folks. It's unusual to find such straightforward and honest young people these days. Lucky for them that they left while they still had a chance.'

Oswald leans across the desk. For an instant, Berg thinks he's about to fly off his chair and punch him.

Berg stands up. He doesn't want to end up in a fight with Oswald. Not yet, anyway. He fingers the folder in front of him. The one from the insurance company.

'How much insurance have you got on that place on the island, again?'

'You know that already.'

'It's a hell of a lot of money, isn't it? But what I don't get is why you took the risk. You've already got more than you need. Why do people like you have to be so goddamn greedy? Naturally, the insurance company is keenly interested in the outcome of this investigation.'

Oswald stands up so hastily that his chair tips over and hits the floor with a bang.

'Fuck you!' he screams. He turns around and stalks out of the office, slamming the door behind him.

Berg sighs. Oswald won't be going anywhere. There are two guards outside the room.

As Berg listens to the agitated voices outside, he considers the life ahead of him. This is going to be a great end to his career. It's almost a miracle that this case popped up right before his retirement. The media will drool all over the trial. And one thing's for certain: this time, Oswald isn't getting off so easy.

The door opens and the guards lead in a sullen Oswald and force him into the chair.

This is going to be good, Berg thinks. *Really, really good.*

About the characters and events

All people and events in this book are fictional. Franz Oswald, West Fog Island, and ViaTerra are products of my imagination. At the same time, of course, I have been inspired by real-life incidents from the twenty-five years I spent as a member of a cult, and from my time as a defector.

I have taken certain liberties in my descriptions of the University Library in Lund and the Skogome prison facility. The staff who appear in the books are also fictional.

I hope my story can bring a deeper understanding of how a defector's life may look. Cults and religious sects are not the only groups from which a person might need to flee. The cult mentality, when one person seizes power over a group or an individual, is found in many places in society, from abusive relationships to bullying situations to dictatorships.

It takes time to heal wounds after such a life. But it's possible, and it's never too late to create a new life for yourself and find freedom.

Thanks!

Thank you to everyone who has given me help, support, and encouragement as I was writing this book and its predecessor *Fog Island.*

My wonderful parents, and my son John and his family in the United States.

My husband Dan, whom I tortured through every page, several times.

Ann-Catrin Sköld Pilback, my mentor, language police, and friend who believes in these books as much as I do. Sometimes more.

The test readers for this book, Johan Zillén and Britta Larsson.

Jonas Ornstein, who has encouraged me from the start and helped me be brave enough to take risks.

Ulla McLean at Skogome Prison, who showed me around and patiently answered all my questions.

Eva Sköld, who gave me better insight into the Swedish justice system.

All my friends who work to help survivors of the injustices of cults: Anna Lindman, Håkan Järvå, Noomi Andemark, and everyone else. And a special thanks to all the defectors in the United States, my former colleagues who have had to deal with endless harassment but have never allowed themselves to be silenced.

All the readers who have contacted me with comments, questions, and cheers of support.

Other authors who have given me pointers and support: Jenny Rogneby, Emelie Schepp, Elisabeth Akteus Rex, Caroline Eriksson, Tove Alsterdal, Rebecka Aldén, and many more.

Maria Enberg and Edith Enberg at Enberg Literary Agency for all their encouragement and help.

Thanks to my first publisher, Frida Rosesund, who worked so hard on this manuscript.

And a big thanks to everyone at my new publishing house, Forum: Karin Linge Nord and Lisa Jonasdotter Nilsson, you are magical!

And thank you Johanna Rydergren for your superb editorial work.

And thank you to HarperCollins and to my fantastic publisher Kate Mills, and copyeditor Jamie Groves. And last, but not least, to my translator Rachel Willson-Broyles for doing a splendid job as usual.

ONE PLACE. MANY STORIES

Bold, innovative and
empowering publishing.

FOLLOW US ON:

@HQStories